PRAISE FOR RICHARD B. SCHWARTZ

Proof of Purchase

It's like this guy is just channeling Raymond Chandler on every page. . . . The ending . . . would make Mike Hammer proud.
— Jochem Steen, *Sons of Spade*

In this engaging hard-boiled mystery, one of three in Schwartz's Jack Grant series (Frozen Stare; The Last Voice You Hear), the seasoned California PI looks into the disappearance of an ex-girlfriend at the request of the woman's husband. When her mutilated body turns up in the woods, Grant makes it his mission to track down her murderer. With the assistance of Lt. Diana Craig, an attractive fast-riser in the San Bernardino police department, Grant follows leads that point to his client, as well as to a consortium of underworld bosses who are branching out into a mega-real estate project. The pair find time, between car chases and gun battles, to begin a relationship. . . . Fans of Robert Parker will enjoy encountering Grant . . . .
— *Publishers Weekly*

The Last Voice You Hear

It's not often that an author's second book is as good as the first, and even less frequent are the instances when an author . . . top[s] it with an extraordinary second . . . deliver[ing] a walloping good tale as well. Richard B. Schwartz has done just that. In *The Last Voice You Hear*, Mr. Schwartz places himself on par with our finest contemporary murder-mystery writers. This is a book you won't want to miss. . . .
— Alan Paul Curtis in *Who Dunnit*

The author . . . writes vividly, putting the reader right into the scene. Schwartz explores the meaning of right and wrong, crime and justice.
— Mary Helen Becker in *Mystery News*

The story rockets along . . . a fast-moving, well-told story with a surprising conclusion that blurs the line between crime and justice.
— Joseph Scarpato, Jr. in *Mystery Scene*

Jack Grant, the Vietnam vet and Pasadena-based PI who debuted in Frozen Stare (1989), returns in this engrossing sequel by Schwartz, author of several scholarly studies of Samuel Johnson. Schwartz knows his London, but surprisingly he evokes California with equal ease, mainly with vividly etched strokes. An apparently maniacal killer is on the loose in London, someone strong and very practiced at impalement. So far, so nasty. But when a victim is dispatched in similar fashion in Disneyland, of all places, Jack Grant is called in. He discovers the killer's identity, but there's a problem: there's a method to the killer's madness. Moreover, Grant has an ethical problem of his own: he's plagued by his conscience, since he understands and even sympathizes with the murderer's cause. The cinematic climax takes place high above the floor of the California desert, and Schwartz squeezes every last drop of suspense from his setting. . . . The result is a high-tension thriller awash in sanguinary detail. Paper towels, anyone?
— *Publishers Weekly*

Frozen Stare

I welcome Richard Schwartz to the club. It's been a long time since I've seen two more engaging characters entering the series scene.
— Sandra Scoppettone

Grant and White play nicely off each other and the switch-on-a-switch works well.
— *Kirkus Reviews*

This tale, in the California private eye tradition, has a rousing finish and is an enjoyable read.
— *Publishers Weekly*

A new author devoted to the hard-boiled tradition. . . . Schwartz has the hard-boiled formula down pat. . . . Schwartz does not break any rules in Frozen Stare. . . . He writes crisply. The narrative moves at a slam-bang pace as bodies pile up. . . . As a dedicated student of the hard-boiled school of detective fiction [Schwartz] has learned his lessons well.
— *The Washington Post Book World*

Gives a whole new meaning to the phrase 'cold-blooded murder'. . . . This is a quick read with plenty of action. Schwartz's first novel is a winner!
— *Sarasota, FL Herald Tribune*

This is a delightful tale, full of amusing touches, and the relationship between Grant and his good cop friend, black Frank White, is a joy. I hope that Schwartz can keep this standard up for a long time to come.
— *The Armchair Detective*

Nice and Noir: Contemporary American Crime Fiction

Opinionated but always fascinating, shrewd and smart, but always readable. . . .
— *The Thrilling Detective*

BOOKS BY RICHARD B. SCHWARTZ

FICTION

The Jack Grant Novels

Frozen Stare
The Last Voice You Hear
Proof of Purchase

The Tom Deaton Novels

Into the Dark
The Survivor's Song

CRITICISM

Samuel Johnson and the New Science
Samuel Johnson and the Problem of Evil
Boswell's Johnson: A Preface to the Life
Daily Life in Johnson's London
After the Death of Literature
Nice and Noir: Contemporary American Crime Fiction
The Wounds that Heal: Heroism and Human Development
(with Judith A. Schwartz)
ed. The Plays of Arthur Murphy, 4 vols.
ed. Theory and Tradition in Eighteenth-Century Studies

MEMOIRS

The Biggest City in America: A Fifties Boyhood in Ohio
Accidental Soldier: A Reserve Officer at West Point in the Vietnam Era
Postwar Higher Education in America: Just Yesterday

EBOOK

Is a College Education Still Worth the Price? A Dean's Sobering Perspective

A TOM DEATON NOVEL

THE SURVIVOR'S SONG

RICHARD B. SCHWARTZ

For Judith, for always standing up

Justice . . . limps along, but it gets there all the same.

Gabriel García Márquez

I

ON THE BEACH

ONE

It began with screams, the screams of a child walking carelessly in the sand, his eyes dazzled by the gold-white glare of the late-morning sun. The screams shook his body and plunged it into a dance of shock and horror, his right foot entangled in twists of kelp and skeletal remains, a bony right hand entwining his ankle as if it were desperate and demanding his attention.

Ben Morgan, 5, his parents Jim and Marcy sitting on a blanket above the tideline, some forty-five yards away, close enough to see his movements, too distant to see their cause. Jim ran toward him, kicking loose sand behind him, dropping his magazine.

Ben had been calling out, "*Watch me, mom! Watch me!*" his mother offering smiles and gestures of recognition. Then the screams became indistinct, vague and feral, elongated vowels and choked breaths. His father cleared his foot of the bones and Japanese kelp, lifted him to his chest and hurried Ben to his mother. Marcy wrapped the blanket around him, comforted him with shoulder pats and reassured him that he was now completely safe.

Neither Jim nor Ben had paid much attention to the hand. Ben was too young to identify the 27 carpal, metacarpal and digital bones and had no awareness of the sesamoid bones, the ossified nodes embedded in the tendons. He didn't notice how fresh they all were, how whole, how perfect. All that he knew was that something terrible had touched and grasped him and all that his father knew was that he had to extricate his son and return him to safety.

Marcy rubbed his back as Ben cried, "*I want to go home! I want to go home!*" "So do I," she said to Jim, who stood before them, catching his breath and suppressing his feelings of confusion and loss. They had fled the Buffalo winter, flying on miles, securing the perfect hotel deal, beating the higher rates of the Christmas rush, trading ice for sand and lead-gray skies for blue. Now his son was screaming, his body convulsing, his wife frightened and angry.

He took his cell from their beach bag, called 911 and waited on the sand for the arrival of the police from Laguna Beach, shuffling from foot to foot, trying to stifle the nausea and waves of acid that rose in his throat.

Officer Todd Boylan responded to the call in twelve minutes, verifying that the remains were human and thanking Mr. Morgan for his timely and conscientious efforts.

"You said that your son discovered the remains, Mr. Morgan?" he asked.

"In so many words, yes, Officer. He was walking along the tideline and they washed up around his feet."

"Is he all right?"

"He was pretty shaken up. My wife took him back to our room."

"Is there anything we can do to help make him more comfortable?"

"Thanks, but I think he'll be OK, Officer."

"After he's calmed down some, you might tell him that the remains of the person he found . . . well . . . they'd been lost . . . and now the person can be returned to his home and put in a proper resting place."

"Good idea. I'll tell him that, Officer."

"He's probably feeling that he wants to get as far away as possible from what happened, but the person he found was probably pretty far away from where he'd prefer to be, so things will be set right for him now."

"Right."

"And after he's had a chance to rest and get over what happened ... "

"Yes?"

"The power of ice cream should not be underestimated. We've got the best on the south coast."

"Thanks for your help, Officer Boylan. I appreciate it."

"Not a problem. We'll be in touch. By the way . . . not that you want to linger over the point, but did you notice the size of those bones?"

"They're big, aren't they?"

"Yes, they are. Look at that femur."

"I don't know how to estimate height, using a bone like that," Jim Morgan said. "I own a paint and wallcovering store."

"I'd say we're talking 6'4" to 6'6" or so," Boylan said. "The femur is the longest and strongest bone in the body, Mr. Morgan."

"The thigh bone, right?"

"Yes. That's what it is. Somehow it doesn't look very strong now, does it? Not with all of the slime on it. At least there are no bite marks."

"Does this sort of thing happen very often around here?" Morgan asked.

"In the movies all the time, especially when there are sharks involved. And there *are* sharks out there, Mr. Morgan, but actually . . . no, it doesn't happen all that often. We get bodies, of course, but generally they're fresher than this one. They decompose, fill up with gas and just float in. This one's been out there awhile."

Boylan nearly said, "I wonder what happened to his feet," but kept the thought to himself. Morgan's face was still ashen and his thoughts were elsewhere.

TWO

Lieutenant Bill Brighton was the second person to arrive on the scene. He was carrying a small aluminum case containing photographic equipment and other tools.

"How are you, Todd?"

"Good, Lieutenant."

"Has the M.E. been called?"

"Yes, Sir. Dr. Barnes is in surgery—just finishing up, they said. He'll be here as soon as he can."

"You talked to the person who found the remains?"

"Yes, Sir. A man named Morgan, from Buffalo, New York. Actually his five-year-old son found them . . . or was found *by them*. He was walking along the tideline, playing in the sand and the bones suddenly washed up and lodged around his feet."

"Wonderful," Brighton said. "Probably scared him half to death."

"I'm sure it wasn't a very pleasant experience for him."

"How's he doing now?"

"OK, I think. His mother wrapped him in a towel and hurried him back to their hotel. Both she and her husband are with him now."

"Kids like skeletons when they're in movies or classrooms, but this is a little too real for someone that age."

"I figured I'd check back with them in an hour or two, see how they're doing."

"Good idea," Brighton said. "If I can help in any way, just let me know."

"Will do," Boylan said.

"Now let's have a look at what the boy found."

Boylan had covered the remains with a sheet of white cloth and anchored the corners with some rocks and driftwood. "I didn't want to upset other people on the beach," he said. "They're edgy enough with a uniformed officer standing around."

Boylan pulled back the sheet and Brighton began taking pictures. He also measured the leg bones with an aluminum tape measure. "This was a tall man," he said.

"I estimated somewhere in the neighborhood of 6'5", Boylan said. "Just a wild guess, but I've seen a lot of leg bones and very few this size."

"Works for me," Brighton said, "though your estimate may be a little conservative."

"How long do you think he was out there?" Boylan asked.

"Hard to say. The M.E.'ll have a better sense of that. I suspect it's been awhile, considering the absence of any flesh. I wonder what happened to the feet and the lower jaw."

"I was wondering that too," Boylan said.

"The jaw bone's the largest and strongest bone in the face," Brighton said, "but it's attached to the temporal bone of the skull with a disc of cartilage. My sister-in-law has problems with the TMJ, the temporomandibular joint."

"You sound like an expert, Lieutenant."

"No, not really. I just hear her talking about it all the time. When she opens her mouth you can hear her jaw pop and click. It's nasty, because it's one of those things that you have to move all the time. When you chew . . . when you talk . . . she said that statistically you move it something like every three seconds. I like her and all, but I can't stand to hear the noises when she pops it. Looking at the remains of this guy . . . it makes me queasy. I don't know whether to feel good about him or feel sorry for him. At least his jaw isn't popping, but on the other hand it's not *there* to pop. I don't know which is worse. Not that it makes any difference to him now, but there had to have been a time when it did."

"Bones are weird," Boylan said. "The wife and I were in Philadelphia once, visiting one of her old roommates and her family. We had some time free and we were walking around Rittenhouse Square. The cement slabs of the pavement had heaved a little; she tripped, and fell forward. She was able to break her fall a little bit, but her face came down on the cement pretty hard and it turned out that she suffered a hairline fracture of her nose. We went into a hospital emergency room to get the cuts and scrapes cleaned up and the ER doc had a set of X-rays taken. That's how they found the break.

"It wasn't a big deal. She was all right. They patched her up and we went out to dinner that night. Aside from people looking at me as if I was a wife-beater she was OK. It was really weird though . . . seeing the X-rays. You could see her skull, of course. Now that's no big surprise. If we didn't have a skeleton underneath our skin we wouldn't be able to stand up or hold our head up or anything. You gotta have that. On the other hand . . . it's weird to see your wife's *skull*. She was only 24. I didn't expect to see her skull that soon . . . not that I ever expected to see it for that matter, but certainly not that soon. It gives you, I don't know, a different *perspective* on things."

"I know what you mean," Brighton said. As he put his measuring tape back in his aluminum case his cell phone twitched in his pocket.

"Brighton," he said.

"Leonard Barnes, Bill. I just got out of surgery. The desk sergeant said you were on the case."

"I'm not sure about the case, Dr. Barnes, but I'm on the scene with Officer Todd Boylan," Brighton said.

"I was told that the skeletal remains washed up on the beach; is that correct?"

"Yes."

"Then there's no reason for me to study them *in situ*. Could you ask someone to bring them in to the lab?"

"I'll bring them in myself."

"I'll get washed up, change my clothes and meet you there," Barnes said.

THREE

Barnes was holding his coffee cup as if it contained a rare form of plasma. "Hi, Bill," he said. "Did you want some of this?"

"How old is it, Doc?" Brighton asked.

"Not very. I dropped a scalpel in it and it didn't float."

"Sure," Brighton said, picking up the urn and helping himself.

"I've had a great morning so far," Barnes said. "Seriously. I resected a bowel and removed a gall bladder. Both in good time and without any incident. I just didn't have enough coffee before I started. Are those the remains?"

"Yes," Brighton said, pulling back the sheet covering the examining table.

"Whoa, big boy," Barnes said. He measured the femur and tibia. "I'd say he was somewhere in the neighborhood of 6'6"; I can do some other measurements—with the hands, for example—but 6'6" is a good working number."

"What else can you tell me?" Brighton asked.

"This'll be very crude until I have the chance for a full examination," Barnes said, "but I can give you some initial impressions."

"Great, shoot," Brighton said.

"The remains are male, not just from the height, but from the pelvic structure and the shape of the skull. Caucasian, though that's getting trickier day by day, but I'd still say Caucasian. From the asymmetry in the upper limbs he was probably right handed. That's usually a safe guess anyway, but there's enough physical evidence here to suggest that that's the case. He wasn't young at the time of death and not decrepit either. I'd say sixtyish. That's a ballpark number, not a precise one."

"How long do you think he was in the water, Dr. Barnes?"

"That's tougher, Bill. I'll need help on it. However, we *should* be able to say whether or not the cause of death was drowning."

"Really?"

"Yes. We'll check acid extracts from the femoral bone marrow for the presence of diatoms."

"Diatoms?"

"Algae."

"But the time of death will be harder … ?"

"Hard for me at least; I've got a colleague at UCSD—a forensic anthropologist. She's been doing some new work with taphonomy in marine settings. It's basically the study of how organisms decay over time. Only in this case we've got saltwater and the predatory inhabitants of saltwater as additional factors. I don't know how precise they can get in their estimates, but I'll give her a call and we'll give it a shot."

"Thanks, I appreciate that," Brighton said.

"My job," Barnes said. "Plus you've got me interested. I wonder what happened to his feet."

"I was going to ask you," Brighton said.

"All I can give you is the first paragraph in the textbook," Barnes said. "The ankle joint is supported by three groups of ligaments. It fractures when it's forced beyond its normal range of motion or when it's struck directly. The list of obvious possible traumas would include collisions, blows, twists, and falls."

"I don't think any of those would feel very good," Brighton said, "particularly if they were extreme enough to separate the feet from the legs."

"No, it's not something you'd voluntarily want to have done to you," Barnes said, as he took a deep sip of his coffee.

"What percent of the male population is that tall?" Brighton asked.

"I'll ask the anthropologist," Barnes said. "That's a tougher question than it first seems. Americans have been getting taller; we don't know when this individual died, so we don't know his height versus that of his peer group. We even vary in height at different times of the day. Height varies across cultures, in part because of the differences in nutrition. I can't give you a clear answer. I'd say this, though. Think about your daily experience. The average white male you encounter is around 5'9" or 5'10". This individual—assuming he's a U.S. white male who died fairly recently—is out of the ordinary. Not in the NBA, but certainly in the general population. If you're thinking about the number of missing persons you're still trying to find and identify, this person will represent a small proportion of the total."

"Right," Brighton said.

"But it might be much easier than that, depending on your records."

"Why is that, Dr. Barnes?"

"Because you've got the majority of the upper teeth intact. And at first blush they look pretty good. Well, actually, they look pretty bad, but that's because they haven't been anywhere near *Crest* or *Colgate* in awhile. They do, however, look as if they had reasonably good dental care. There are crowns over one of the molars and one of the bicuspids."

"That's very helpful. What else do you see, Doctor?"

"A missing lower jaw, of course. Whether that's a bit of evidence or purely accidental, I don't know. There is no obvious evidence of gunshots or blunt force trauma, but the feet and lower jaw are missing for a reason."

"It's tough with no flesh or organs."

"Right," Barnes said, "but if it can be determined that he did not die of drowning, that would be very interesting."

"Yes, it would," Brighton said.

"I'll get back to you as soon as possible on this," Barnes said.

FOUR

"Hi, Chief," Bill Brighton said, looking at the caller i.d. on his cell.

"Hi, Bill," Chris Dietrich answered. "Is this a good time to talk?"

"Sure."

"I've got a second or two and thought I'd call. What do you hear from the M.E.?"

"Not a whole lot yet, but there are some initial facts."

"Yes?"

"The decedent was around 6'6" and close to sixty at the time of death. It's a he, not a she, right handed in all probability, with the top row of teeth intact. They include two crowns, quality work according to Dr. Barnes. He also thinks he may be able to determine if the man died from drowning or not."

"How would he do that?"

"He checks the bone marrow for the presence of algae."

"Interesting. How long does he think the dead man's been in the water?"

"He doesn't know yet. He's going to talk to some professor at UCSD. The flesh is all gone but there are no bite or nibble marks on any of the bones."

"Anything else?"

"The lower jaw is missing and so are the feet."

"Cleanly?"

"Yes. There aren't any chop marks or hack marks or anything like that."

"Unlikely that a boating accident wouldn't leave at least some evidence."

"Right. At first I thought that he might have gotten his feet caught in the propeller of a boat, but there aren't any rough marks on the leg bones and the separations are symmetrical."

"The M.E. may have some ideas after he thinks about it some more."

"Right."

"In the meantime, I'll ask someone to start doing some runs through the Missing Persons files."

"Thanks, Chief."

"Did the M.E. say anything about race?"

"He said Caucasian, but that it's getting more and more difficult to be certain of that."

"I was thinking it might have been someone from a foreign commercial vessel. Just because he's floated up on our beach doesn't mean he was actually from someplace nearby."

"Right. In the case of an accident or something that they didn't want investigated, they could have simply tossed the person overboard."

"Right. I guess there's always the chance of modern-day piracy also. Somebody's got a nice big Hatteras . . . somebody else wants to separate him from it … "

"And from his feet too, Chief?"

"Make it harder to swim and guarantee a quick bleed out."

"I hope there's a simpler explanation," Brighton said. "I've got enough nightmares already."

"I know what you mean, Bill," Dietrich said. "I'll call you after we've had a look at the files."

After he clicked off, Dietrich picked up his fork, moved the fettucine on his plate around, put the fork back down, and drank the remains of his scotch.

"What's the matter?" his date asked, returning from the ladies room. "Don't you like your dinner?"

"It's fine," Dietrich said. "I've just lost my appetite for a moment."

"You haven't tried your wine," she said.

"Well, I hadn't finished my scotch yet, so I figured I should do that first."

"I understand. Do you want to get something else to eat instead of the fettucine?"

"Thanks, but no. I think I'll get another scotch though."

"Suit yourself," she said. "Not much sustenance in it."

"Think of it as medicine," Dietrich said.

"It's actually a depressant," she said.

"I know, but sometimes it's what you need."

"Are you upset with me in some way?"

"No, of course not; I just talked to one of my lieutenants. We found some human remains. Not very appetizing stuff."

"You don't mind if I finish my dinner, do you?"

"Of course not. Enjoy it."

"I will," she said. "The last man I dated was a chef. He was always second-guessing what was going on in the kitchen and telling me all the details."

"So that was worse?"

"Oh, always. I was on a perpetual diet with him."

Dietrich smiled. When the waiter approached he ordered a second scotch.

"Make it a double," his date said. "Save yourself another trip."

"Is your pasta all right?" the waiter asked.

"Yes, it's fine," Dietrich said. "I was just overcome with thirst."

The waiter smiled and left.

"Maybe I'll get some dessert in a little while," Dietrich said, as his cell phone twitched.

FIVE

"What's the newest read?" Tom Deaton asked his father, a one-time O.C. fisherman and the retired harbor master of Newport Beach.

"Mild heart attack," Wayne Deaton answered. "It's not like it's a good thing, but it could be much worse. They may do a little tinkering."

"Tinkering?"

"A bypass," his father said. "They're still thinking about it. It's no big deal. These days . . . it's like having your adenoids out. Besides, Saddleback Memorial is a good place. You've logged some time there."

"Yes, it's a good place," Tom said, "but I'd rather see you around the harbor than there, on your back."

"It's all that lasagna and sausage catching up to me," Wayne said. "I'll be OK. Besides, I loved that lasagna and sausage; it was worth it."

"Mom made the best," Tom said.

"Yes, every Sunday," Wayne said. "Sometimes on Wednesdays too. Wednesdays were usually homemade soup, but sometimes she'd surprise me."

Tom didn't say how much he missed her; both of them already knew. "When will they decide on whether or not to do the surgery?" he asked.

"They said tomorrow. The internist and the cardiologist want to talk to the surgeon. Besides, there's a related story … "

"What's that?" Tom asked.

"There's this nurse in the cardiologist's office . . . she's always lecturing me . . . she's talking about cholesterol levels and blood pressure and diabetes and other stuff . . . she tells me that bypass surgery is *very* serious and that it could have been prevented."

"She sounds like a real ray of sunshine," Tom said.

"Yes, right. Anyway, she says to me, 'Have you ever seen *All that Jazz*?' As a matter of fact I haven't, I said, but I've seen *One Flew Over the Cuckoo's Nest*."

"What did she say to that?"

"She said that sarcasm is not attractive, particularly in the elderly."

"But she still loves you."

"I'm afraid she might," Wayne said, smiling.

"*All that Jazz* has a scene in it involving open heart surgery. It's pretty gory."

"I know, I saw it."

"I thought you said you hadn't seen it."

"I told the nurse that. I was needling her."

"Turnabout's fair play, I guess," Tom said.

"But it's not attractive," Wayne said. "That's OK. I'm trying to let her down easy."

SIX

Tom drove back to the family cottage in Laguna Hills. His father had offered it to him after his wife died and he began living full time on his boat in Newport Beach. Modest in its time, it would be unaffordable now. Tom still felt his mother's presence there, but his father said he felt closer to her on the boat. Named for her--the *Katharine Elisabeth*--she had had two good years of weekends there.

Tom checked his landline answering machine for messages--two wrong numbers, an alumni association solicitation for the UCI annual fund, and a call from the LBPD Chief: "Tom, Chris Dietrich. I figured you were probably visiting your dad, so I stayed off of the cell. Give me a call when you get back. Call me on my cell; I'll be up until at least 11:00."

He called him right away.

"Chief, it's Tom Deaton."

"Thanks for calling back, Tom. How's your dad? You said he had a spell."

"Feisty as always . . . he's been fighting and flirting with one of their nurses. The down side is that they've diagnosed a mild heart attack. They'll probably do a bypass."

"Sorry to hear that, but I'm sure he'll be fine. Sometimes it takes a wakeup call to get you to change your habits. Routine surgery could probably add another twenty years to his life."

"That's what I told him. Better to have a single setback and recover than to go down for the full count. What can I do for you, Chief?"

"Nothing tonight, Tom. I just wanted to touch base with you now because I'll be out of the office for the next two days. I want you to take over the John Doe case that Bill Brighton started on."

"The guy on the beach?"

"Yes."

"Will this cause any problems for Bill, Chief?"

"No, no. He's got his hands full already. This is probably a long shot anyway."

"Should I take that as a compliment, Chief?"

"You know what Lon Williams always says, 'You're the St. Jude of the Department.'"

"The patron saint of hopeless cases, right?"

"Yes," Dietrich said. "It's a compliment. I gave you the Bennett case because I knew that you were recovering from surgery and needed to get back to the work. Then you broke it and closed it."

"I had a lot of help."

"We always get help," Dietrich said. "We don't always close cases."

"I heard that the upper dental work was intact; Bill thought that might be enough to identify him."

"Right. That's true. He did think that. So far, however, we haven't found anything. Hell, the ocean is the ocean. The guy could have floated in from anywhere. We've checked dental records for San Diego, Orange, and L.A. counties and haven't hit yet. The height should have helped. How many 6'6" guys over 55 who have had good dental care wash up on our beaches?"

"I don't know, Chief, but I imagine it's a small number."

"I need somebody with some imagination on this, Tom. That's no reflection on Bill. He's a well-rounded investigator, but maybe somebody who sees nooks and crannies and angles might be better on this one."

"I'll see what I can do, Chief. Is Hector available to help?"

"If you need him, sure. Somehow I think of Hector Campo as more of a street cop, not somebody who can work files the way you can."

"What I'm thinking, Chief, is that this guy turned up without any lower jaw and without any feet. There may be a perfectly good explanation for that. It may even turn out that he's been in the water for fifty years. But … "

"Yes?"

"But this was a big man. If somebody helped separate him from his feet he's probably not the kind of person you'd invite to afternoon tea."

"More like an alley fighter in the south Bronx."

"Right. That's why I'd like to have Hector nearby."

Tom's father still talked of 'morning nautical twilight' rather than 'first light'. Whatever you called it, the glimmer was faint, in part because of the foliage, in part because of the cloud cover. Tom tied his tie and slipped on his jacket, filled his insulated mug with fresh, hot coffee to take off the morning chill, and got in his unmarked.

He wanted to get an early start on the John Doe. After talking to the Chief last night he had called Officer Todd Boylan to see how the Morgans were doing.

"They're going home today," he said. "They're still a little shaken up. The boy seems to be handling it better than his mother and father. Maybe he's in some kind of shock."

"It's not something that happens every day," Tom said, "especially when you're on vacation."

"Right," Boylan said. "My old man used to talk about industrial accidents all the time. He worked in City of Industry, supervising this room full of lathe operators. Every now and then he'd see body parts coming down the belts along with the made-to-order steel. This one guy took off a thumb and was asked to demonstrate how he had done it so that the safety officers could warn everybody else. 'Sure,' he said, and then suddenly he added, 'Damn, there goes the other one.'"

"I appreciate your checking back with them, Todd," Tom said. "I'm sure they appreciated it."

"Not a problem," Boylan said. "They seemed like nice people. I guess it was much better to be the ones to find the remains than to be the guy whose remains they found."

"I agree, Todd."

"What do you make of the missing feet, Detective?"

"No idea yet, Todd."

"If I was some kind of predator … "

"Yes?"

"It's not what I would have eaten first."

"No, me either, Todd," Tom said, smiling to himself initially and then trying to push the image from his mind.

SEVEN

The dental files were a dead end. Most good dental records include information on general health, including the patient's prescription medications. Height and weight are not taken as regularly as they are in the internist's office, but they're recorded early and then checked, if only perfunctorily. "Any changes in your general health?" "Yes, I lost ninety-five pounds, Doc." "Oh, OK, let me check that incisor."

Tom did a computer run for all missing dental patients over 6'4" and 50 years of age. The individuals kicked out did not have dental histories that matched that of the John Doe. None were even close. Tom went back fifteen years, then twenty, then thirty. Nothing.

"Wait a minute … " he said to himself. Before he could act on his intuition his cell phone rang.

"Tom Deaton," he answered.

"Tom, this is Sarah."

"Hi," Tom said.

"How are you?"

"I'm fine. How are you, Sarah?"

"I'm fine too. I read about your solving the Bennett case."

"Yes, we had some luck on that."

"I heard that you were hurt in the process."

"Yes, but nothing too serious. I'm fine now. I just needed some bed rest and a little time to heal. That's all finished now."

"Well, I just wanted to check in with you and see how you were doing."

"We should have some coffee or lunch sometime," Tom said.

"Yes. That would be nice," she said.

"I'll call you," Tom said.

"OK. Bye," she answered.

She sounded noncommittal at best. He wondered why she had bothered to call at all. They had broken up nearly a year and a half ago. There was no formal announcement or negotiated understanding. They had simply drifted apart. She was dating a lawyer from Oceanside for awhile, though she claimed there was nothing involved but friendship. When Tom was admitted to the hospital for surgery several months later she had come to visit him. The visits were more good-Samaritan than conjugal.

She had been unable to reach him and had called his father, who told her he was in Saddleback Memorial. Wayne liked Sarah. He was always pushing her cause with Tom, though Tom doubted the level of her seriousness. "It's some form of guilt," he told his father. "Not deep *guilt* guilt, but she probably feels bad that we broke up just before I got sick. Her coming around . . . her checking on me . . . it's something she does out of a sense of obligation. That's all."

"I think you should give it another chance," Wayne would say. "Go out to dinner with her once in awhile . . . that doesn't cost you anything . . . just see what happens."

"When I reach out she pulls back," Tom would answer. "I don't want to make her feel uncomfortable."

"Do you still have feelings for her?"

"I don't know. When we stopped dating I suppressed any feelings that I might have still had. I figured it was better to just move on."

"Well . . . you know what I think," Wayne would say. "I'd give it another chance."

That wasn't something he would concern himself with at the moment. The remains of a human being had presented themselves on a local beach and it was his job to reunite them with whoever was missing a loved one or identify whoever it was who was ultimately responsible for their being there and who was hoping never to be found.

Now where was I, he thought. Of course. We've been spinning out slasher- and horror-movie scenarios, thinking of the grisly ways in which feet could be separated from legs, and overlooked the most obvious explanation for their absence.

He googled for statistics on diabetics—over 35,000,000 currently afflicted in the U.S., with nearly 100,000 related amputations per year. Some lose toes, some feet, some legs. Those who have lost one foot have increased odds of losing a second.

The age was right and so were the clean separations. He went back to the missing persons records and changed the variables for his computer search. It was not improbable that the individual—assuming he *was* a diabetic—had been sedentary and obese as well. He kept the parameters conservative, however, casting the net as widely as possible: over 6'4", over 50, diabetic.

The computer spat out a long list of possibles. When he narrowed the search to include individuals who had had amputations the numbers fell precipitously. There may be tens of thousands of diabetic amputees, but none of that age and height, who had lost both feet and were residing anywhere near Laguna Beach. The sole exception was a man who had lost some fingers and had been last seen in the desert north of Palm Springs.

He took out the *diabetic* variable and looked for simple amputees. Again—nothing within the appropriate statistical range. There were a lot of missing persons and some missing amputees but none that fit the profile in question. He then checked for height alone and found several possibles within that age range, but each had existing dental records and none of their upper jaws matched John Doe's.

He took a deep drink of his coffee and decided to take a different tack.

EIGHT

To fall into the missing persons lists requires the filing of a missing persons report, he said to himself. What if no one knew that the person was missing? What if the person or persons who knew that the man on the beach was missing wanted him to remain undiscovered?

There were multiple homicide files—closed cases, open cases, open cases under active investigation and 'miscellaneous' cases. The latter included suspected homicides in which the body had been found and those in which the body was missing but foul play was suspected. He did a run through the miscellaneous file data base and found a series of individuals within the conservative height and age parameters. Most had dental records which excluded them from consideration. Some were Alzheimer's patients who had a history of walking away from their home locations and had disappeared and never been found. The reason that they were included in the file was that they could have been robbed and beaten and then died. The likelihood that they would have been taken out to sea, however, was remote in the extreme. Similarly, the likelihood that they would carry any significant sums of money was limited. Most walked away in their bathrobes and slippers. They weren't driving in Porsches and sporting gold-and-diamond-encrusted Rolexes.

One case caught his eye. The man was the owner of a series of *Jiffy Lube* franchises who also owned a 60' motor yacht. He was 6'5" and 62 years of age at the time of his disappearance. His shops were in the San Gabriel Valley but his boat was moored in Santa Barbara. It had not been disturbed at the time of his disappearance and was inherited by his son, who lived in Virginia and was there during, and a month's prior to, the time of his father's disappearance. The dental records were very dated and it was entirely possible that the man had required crowns later in his life, but no evidence of that fact. Similarly, the teeth were crooked, but with adults undergoing orthodonture with increasing frequency, there was the possibility that the later configuration of his mouth might have matched John Doe's, but, again, no hard evidence of that fact.

Tom could check with orthodontists, but the case remained a long shot at best. The harbor master in Santa Barbara signed an affidavit to the effect that the man had not been seen on or near his boat for at least three weeks prior to his disappearance. His home was in San Marino, nearly 60 miles from Laguna Beach.

"If I'm thinking of disposing of a body in San Marino," Tom thought to himself, "I'm going to the desert or the mountains. Unless I'm seen in the process the likelihood that the body will ever be found is next to nil. If I toss it into the water, even with weights, the possibility that it will be found could be higher."

The man's file included his medical records. There was no record of any amputations and no record of diabetes. The son testified that his father was in excellent health. He watched his diet, exercised religiously, and prided himself on his physical condition.

A second case also drew Tom's attention. The man was 75 years of age at the time of his disappearance and 6'8". He had played forward for the Lakers when they were in Minneapolis rather than in Los Angeles and had later moved to Palm Desert. He was farther away than the *Jiffy Lube* man—120 miles from Laguna Beach. His dental records in Minnesota were listed as 'unrecoverable' and there was nothing in California. There was no record of his having owned a boat and no recollection on the part of anyone who knew him of his having a friend or friends with boats. He did have a pilot's license, but had not flown in the fifteen years prior to his disappearance.

His financial records were in order at the time of his disappearance, with no records of major withdrawals. He was diabetic, but there were no records of amputations. His HMO employed a nurse practitioner with responsibility for monitoring the plan's diabetics. Her records showed that he had responded well to three separate medications and that his blood sugar levels were always within the desired parameters.

Two weeks after his disappearance his car had been found along the Pines to Palms highway, in the 60+ mile stretch from Banning to Palm Desert. The man was an avid walker and the local police surmised that he had parked his car and walked into a wilderness area, suffered some mishap, and died. His body was then dismembered by animal predators and was now, like his Minnesota dental records, unrecoverable.

That was certainly plausible. And even if the man had been the victim of foul play it was highly unlikely that his body would have been transported from the Palm Springs/Banning/San Jacinto Mountains area to the Pacific.

"I suppose this is significant progress," Tom said aloud. "I'm certainly doing an excellent job of *eliminating* possibilities."

He picked up his cell phone and called the M.E.'s office. "I'm sorry," his receptionist said, "but Dr. Barnes is in surgery this morning. Can I ask him to give you a call?"

"This is Detective Tom Deaton at the Laguna Beach PD; he has my cell number. I'd appreciate it if you'd ask him to give me a call. It has to do with the remains of the John Doe that washed up on the beach here. Chief Dietrich has asked me to take over the case from Lieutenant Brighton. I was wondering if he had an update for us."

"Just a second," the receptionist said. There was a long pause; she came back on the line two minutes later. "I talked to his nurse," she said. "She told me that he's been trying to make contact with a forensic anthropologist at UCSD. So far he hasn't been able to link up with her."

"Thanks," Tom said. "Just give him the message that I called and that I'd appreciate any update he might have. If there's nothing new he doesn't need to call me."

"Will do, Detective. Good luck."

"Thanks," Tom said. He clicked off and added, "It's starting to look as if I'll need it."

NINE

One of his doctors had told Tom to get out of the office for lunch. "You need the break," he said. "Get out in the sunshine and fresh air. That's very important."

He followed the advice for awhile but then began to regret the lost time. Nearly half of the period was spent in traffic and that was more like work than like a break or mini-vacation. He tried the places within walking distance of the Department but grew tired of their menus. Eventually he ate at his desk, enjoying the extra time it afforded him. It also gave him the chance to catch up on some non-professional reading. Sometimes he surfed the web, following up on items that had aroused his curiosity. He finished off his sandwich and fruit in fifteen minutes and then had another forty-five to spend as he chose. Besides, as a senior detective he had a desk by a window, so he could open it and get fresh air along with the sunshine. He told himself that he could tell the doctor that he always followed his advice (more or less).

Today he had added a package of walnuts to his usual lunch and as he was finishing the last handful his cell phone rang. He looked at the number of the incoming call: it was the number of the M.E.

"Detective Deaton," he answered.

"Tom, it's Leonard Barnes."

"Thanks for calling back right away," Tom said.

"I wanted to touch base with you. I was finally able to reach my anthropologist colleague. She was on the east coast for a couple days for a professional meeting. She's coming up this afternoon. Want to join us and have a look at what's left of your John Doe?"

"Absolutely," Tom said. "What time?"

"Two thirty."

"I'll be there," Tom said and clicked off.

After finishing his lunch and puttering some more with the electronic files, Tom drove up into the Hills, to Saddleback Memorial. The medical facility leased space to the city for the use of its Medical Examiner. Leonard Barnes was an Irvine surgeon, on retainer to Laguna Beach. He enjoyed the break from his surgical practice and enjoyed working with the LBPD. He was of medium height and weight, with blue eyes and sandy brown hair. The latter was curly and worn tight against his scalp, matching the thin brown mustache which he had added recently. His eyes were lined and pouchy, but sharp in color. He seldom blinked. His hands and wrists were toned and muscular. He had a voice that could have served him as a radio announcer and he spoke in 'sometimes-wrong-but-never-in-doubt' tones.

The Medical Examiner's suite included two examining tables and a mini-morgue. When Tom arrived Barnes was examining the skeletal remains that had interrupted the Morgans' weekend. Barnes greeted him, said "Just a sec," and washed his hands with strong soap before shaking his hand. "It's always good to be careful," he said, "especially when you haven't been using gloves. How are you Tom?"

"I'm good, thanks," Tom said. "How are you?"

"Fine," Barnes answered. "Took out a diseased thyroid this morning, the great majority of it anyway. We'll get the rest with the radioactive cocktail. Repaired a hernia; don't do that very often. Been busy with this case?"

"Yes, trying to identify our friend there," Tom said.

"Any luck?"

"Not yet. He's pretty elusive, at least as far as our records are concerned."

"Maybe Sally can be of help." Barnes looked at his watch—one of his few affectations--a blue, James Bond Seamaster Omega. "She should be here any moment."

She actually arrived at 2:47. "I'm sorry," she said. "There's no rush hour in San Diego anymore. The traffic's *always* terrible."

"Thanks for coming," Barnes said. "Sally Cornell . . . Detective Tom Deaton."

"Professor ... " Tom said.

"Call me Sally," she said. "What have we got here, Len?"

"Male skeletal remains. Came in with some kelp on Laguna Beach. Upset some New York tourists. Not the sort of thing that the Chamber of Commerce would approve."

"Let me have a look," she said, putting down her purse and snapping on some rubber gloves from the cardboard dispenser on the side table.

"Tall," she said. "Very tall. Six-five or six, I'd say, at first blush. Older. Not aged, but not middle aged either. Sixty maybe, somewhere around there. I wonder what happened to his feet. That's very odd. Wait, let me rephrase that. The really odd thing is that so many of the remains are intact. Why not the lower jaw and the feet too?

"Most of the time the remains are disarticulated, in part because they often turn up as the result of some dredging process. Before they settle in the sand they go up and down with the body gases, first floating and then eventually sinking."

"Can you tell how long the remains have been in the water?" Tom asked.

"That's the sixty-four dollar question," she answered. "The problem is the number of possible parameters. You can tell a lot about the remains, but what you can observe has to be placed in context. That's where it gets tricky. Let me give you a brief laundry list. The condition of the remains can depend on water temperatures, access to water surfaces, access to scavengers, the season in which the decedent went into the water, the dispersal forces at work, the biodiversity of the area, the weather, the geology of the sea floor, the water chemistry . . . In some cases you need a marine biologist's help. For example, you could estimate how long a particular scavenger had been attached to the remains by the amount of growth it had undergone, but you'd first have to know the average size of that particular scavenger in those particular waters.

"You've got to know your scavenger and his or her appetites. For example, crabs like eyes and facial flesh. They'll go for soft internal organs. You might start with a first-order scavenger like sharks and rays. Once the integrity of the human body surface is lost, the next group comes in. And it doesn't take them very long. We're not talking piranhas around here, but other fish can make pretty short work of carrion.

"The problem *here* is that the majority of the remains are intact. Obviously there haven't been any big crunch-bites from a large predator. I don't even see any small bite marks. The feet weren't chewed off. The separation lines are too clean and precise.

"You've got a couple gastropods attached to the right femur, but they're very small. They could have been feeding on the kelp; you did say that there was kelp entangled with the bones . . . If I had to guess I'd say that the body spent very little time in the water, in part because of the absence of major disarticulation and the general absence of evidence of predation."

"Weeks?" Tom asked.

"Possibly. Possibly a few months, but not years. Possibly a few days. The fact that there's no flesh suggests a longer period, but who knows where this big fellow's been in the meantime. Any likely candidates in your Missing Persons files?"

"No," Tom said. "None."

"Let me take a closer look," she said. "We've got intact dental work on the upper jaw. We can also check the marrow and see if that tells us anything."

"We really appreciate this," Tom said.

"For me, this is fun," Sally said. "I'll call you as soon as I learn something."

TEN

As soon as Tom returned to the office he checked in with Chris Dietrich. He was at a meeting in Sacramento, but would return the next day. Tom briefed him on the meeting with Barnes and Sally Cornell and told him that he'd let him know as soon as they learned anything new.

"Thanks, Tom," Chris said. "I'm surprised that she thought that the body had only been in the water a short time. I mean, it makes sense, since so much of the skeleton is intact, but I've got to believe that we would have received a report on a missing person who had disappeared that recently."

"Right, Chief," Tom said. "And like I said earlier, I checked with Departments up and down the coast—not just with regard to the information on the shared data base, but I asked everybody I talked to about any rumors they might have heard, suspicions they might have had . . . you know . . . unofficial stuff that they might have been aware of. No one knew anything, nothing fitting these parameters, at least. There are always people missing, of course, but this case has enough details to catch peoples' attention. At least *I* think it does. So far we've got nothing."

"I understand," Dietrich said. "Keep plugging away and let me know when the anthropologist checks back with you. Did she seem as if she knew what she was talking about?"

"Yes. She was very good. You go into a meeting like that expecting some kind of silver-bullet solution, but the ocean's a complicated place and the number of things that might have happened there makes for a long list. She appreciated that and explained it all well. She said that she loves to do this kind of work. I think she'll give it her best shot."

"A quickie solution would always be nice," Dietrich said. "Unfortunately they're few and far between. Maybe she'll come up with something when she looks more closely at the dental work. It sounds as if it was quality work, probably American. That would eliminate most foreign sailors . . . if they hadn't already been eliminated by the issue of height."

"Right. If you figure that some commercial captain wanted to hide the fact that somebody went into the water it would have to do with something involving the law. Proper procedures weren't being followed; proper authorizations hadn't been secured. There's nothing in the official record to suggest that we've had any recent problems like that. Or possibly we're dealing with smugglers, drug runners, something patently criminal. In any of those cases it's less likely that the person would have been older and even less likely that he would have had quality dental work done."

"I agree," Dietrich said. "At least we're eliminating possibilities . . . or in some cases narrowing them."

"That's what I've been telling myself, Chief."

"OK, Tom, I better get back to my meeting. We're about to start a working dinner. Should be fun—keep our minds off of what we're eating at least."

Tom clicked off and did a run through the electronic files of the *Times*, the *Register*, and the *Union-Tribune*, checking to see if there had been any competitions or other marine events along the coast that might have resulted in an accident of some sort. He then called his father to touch base and seek advice.

"Good to hear your voice, son," Wayne Deaton said. "They're doing the surgery tomorrow and some tests today. I didn't expect to be here until later in the week; I would have given you a headsup. I was just about to feast on my consommé and lemon jello. How are you?"

"I'm fine, Dad; I'll come see you later this evening. I'm working this John Doe case … "

"The guy who washed up on Laguna Beach."

"Right. Have you heard any talk, anything at all, related to the case? I just checked the major newspapers along the coast. There haven't been any recent reports of problems or events. Everything seems quiet, at least officially so."

"I haven't heard of anything," Wayne said. "There was a large sailboat that went down a couple of months ago, but the owner and his guests were all picked up. There was a guy in a motor yacht whose license was suspended because he nearly ran into an elderly couple in a smaller vessel. He was full of beer and basically suffering from too much weekend. Nobody was hurt, fortunately."

"How about commercial activity?"

"Nothing beyond the routine traffic. There was a big dustup over a Chinese ship that was refusing to let Homeland Security check some of its cargo, but that was about a year ago. The problem was resolved and there were no reports of anyone going overboard in the process. Not many leads, huh?"

"No, not yet. The Medical Examiner has called in a forensic anthropologist. She's studying the remains now. She seems very competent, but so far she's basically confirmed most of what we already knew and begun to convince us that it's going to be very hard to give clearcut responses to our most important questions."

"It's much easier if everything's reversed and you know the decedent," Wayne said. "If you can identify the remains and know exactly when the person was lost, you can learn all kinds of things from the condition of the remains, but basically you're just developing a huge data base that might be helpful in the future. It's like . . . here we have the skull and rib cage of John Jones, who drowned on April 18, one mile east of Catalina. Looking at the remains, we learn x, y, and z. When we find similar remains in the future we've got a potentially comparable case to help us in our investigation. At this point, however, the baseline information is thin and scattered. Too much water. Too many predators and scavengers. Too many different patterns of movement and temperature … "

"That's pretty much what the anthropologist said," Tom added. "We're not giving up. It's just a high hill that we've got to climb."

"I understand," Wayne said. "Call me whenever you think I can be of help. Hell, call me anyway."

"Will do, Dad," Tom said, and clicked off. It was nearly time for dinner, but he wasn't hungry yet. He checked meteorological records over the past six months and harbor records in the principal ports along the southern California coast. Somehow, activity—activity of any kind—seemed preferable to waiting for the phone to ring.

His dad was in good spirits, telling him that the surgery would be a walk in the park. After visiting him he decided to sleep on his own boat, the *Better Days*. Listening to the water in the Dana Point Harbor marina, he was hoping for some kind of inspiration. He didn't expect to learn anything, but he had exhausted all of the other available possibilities. He put his cell phone on the shelf above his foldout bed, waiting for a call that was unlikely to come any time soon. He hated to wait, hated it intensely.

ELEVEN

Tom defrosted the single bagel he had in the galley freezer, split it in half and put it into the toaster. He filled a glass with some grapefruit juice, drank it, and then rinsed it out, while his coffee brewed. There was no news of any note on the radio. The weather forecast was predictably good. Scattered high clouds, bright sun, 70 degrees near the coast, 75 inland.

When he finished his bagel and coffee he washed up, showered, and got dressed. When he came out of the shower his cell phone beeped. He had not heard it ring when he was in the shower; it was now signaling him that he had a recorded message. He dried his hands, face, and hair and picked up the phone.

The message was brief. "Detective Deaton . . . Sally Cornell. Len's meeting me at the M.E.'s lab at noon. I think you'll want to join us."

He looked at the clock: 7:05. Academics gave more advance notice than police officers. Tom finished drying off, found a fresh shirt and fresh set of socks and underwear and got dressed. His father's surgery was later than expected—scheduled for 10:00 and expected to last five to six hours. He saw him at 8:00, reassured him, and arranged for updates from the nursing staff. His father told him to stop worrying. "I'll be good as new," he said. "Go solve your case."

He ran into Bill Brighton in the station hallway later that morning and brought him up to date on the case. Bill thanked him and wished him luck. He also saw Lieutenant Lon Williams, who had been on the periphery of the case, and told him of recent developments. He looked at his watch: 11:00. He decided to leave. If he was early he could get some coffee while he waited. He didn't want to be late.

Sally Cornell was wearing jeans and a designer tee shirt. Her hair was pulled back and she was wearing a lab apron. Her eyes were lined and a little puffy.

"Long night?" he asked.

"Yes," she said, "but I think it was productive. I already talked to Len last night on one issue. There were no diatoms in the femoral bone marrow. Your John Doe didn't drown."

'That's interesting."

"Very interesting, particularly in light of other developments."

Before he could ask another question the door opened and the Medical Examiner entered. It was 11:50. Len Barnes was as curious as Tom. He was also carrying a bag that was damp along the bottom.

"I'm afraid I spilled some of the upscale coffee," he said. "I also figured this group for *black*; hope I was right."

"Works for me," Sally said. "Thanks."

"That's fine," Tom said. "Thanks."

"Well, what do we have?" the M.E. asked.

"An interesting one," Sally said. "Like I said earlier, there were no diatoms. He didn't drown. That doesn't necessarily mean that he was murdered, but I think that's where the smart money will be."

"How long was he in the water?" Tom asked. "Any idea?"

"I'd say well over forty years," she answered.

"Really? In that condition?" Barnes said.

"The dental work is the key," she said. "First, you have to accept some of my assumptions."

They waited for her to continue.

"I assume that kids get cavities and fillings and adults crack their teeth and get their old fillings replaced. Most candidates for crowns are in their middle years or beyond. And most fillings eventually need to be replaced. Sometimes the same tooth is refilled several times."

"Right," Barnes said.

Tom nodded in agreement.

"The material used is continuously improved, but doesn't always change that much," she said. "The Chinese used silver amalgam to fill teeth in the 7th century. Different formulas were used over the years. The gamma-2-phase amalgam formula was standardized in 1895. It consisted of equal parts of liquid mercury and an alloy powder containing silver, tin, copper, zinc and mercury. Around 1970 the ingredients changed. The new formula results in what some people call 'high-copper amalgam'. The alloy powder is *30%* copper rather than the *6%* of gamma-2-phase. The new formula is cheaper to manufacture, has greater mechanical strength and better resistance to corrosion. John Doe's fillings are 'low copper' rather than 'high copper'. That means he didn't have any fillings after 1970."

"What about the crowns?" Tom asked.

"The adhesive dates from the same time as the fillings. I know what you're thinking—maybe he had dental work done in some backwater that was decades out of synch with modern practices. Not likely. The crown work is too professional. This is state-of-the-art work, but for 1950 or 1960. The crowns are all porcelain; that wasn't popular or common until around 1950. Prior to that you'd see gold or porcelain over gold."

"But if he was in the water for that long the remains would not have been largely intact," Barnes said. "There would have been evidence of predation also."

"Consider this," Sally said. "There was also no detectible smell of decomp. Believe me, I got up close and personal with him and the only thing I could smell was salt water. There are cases of remains that have been in the water for as long as eighteen months and the smell of decomposition is still detectible."

"That would confirm the belief that he's been dead for decades," Tom said, "but what about the absence of predation? Are you thinking that he was in some form of container?"

"That's exactly what I'm thinking," she said.

"And the container came open recently, releasing the skeletal remains," Tom said.

"Yes, or (a longer shot) the body was stored and recently released."

"A container would have had to have been water tight," Barnes added.

"Yes, or largely so," she said.

Tom started to ask another question, but she interrupted him. "You're wondering about the feet, right?"

"Yes, I was."

"The standard external dimension of a casket is 7'. That's in the U.S. In some parts of the world they're much smaller, with an internal dimension of, for example, 6'1". If you need a longer model you have to pay more. In the U.S. the problem is more with girth than height. We're getting wider as well as taller. An oversized casket is—in the industry—called a 'B-52'. With the lining materials and shoes, John Doe would have been a tight fit. That's if he was in a contemporary casket."

"But it's quite possible that the feet were removed so that he could be wedged into whatever container had been prepared for him," Tom said.

"Yes. Do you want me to answer your next question."

Tom smiled. "Go ahead. You're doing great so far."

"The circular saw was invented in the 18th century. The hand-held version, with replaceable blades, was available in the 1920's. With the right blade you could get a nice, smooth cut. Precision work; no rough edges; no problem."

TWELVE

Tom caught Chris Dietrich on his cell. "I just got back from meeting with the M.E. and the anthropologist," Tom said. "She was working mostly from the dental work and the lack of decomp smell. The bottom line is that she thinks he's been dead for at least forty years. In all likelihood the body was in some kind of container which recently came open. Hence the fact that there are no significant predators' marks and little or no evidence of long-term scavengers. She speculates that his feet were removed with a Skilsaw so that the body would fit in the container that had been prepared."

"Ouch," Dietrich said.

"Yes. There were also no signs of algae in the femoral bone marrow, so he didn't drown. Maybe he bled to death when they took off his feet."

"No evidence of gunshots or blunt force trauma."

"No, none, Chief."

"Whoever went to that much trouble didn't want the body to be found. Ever."

"I agree," Tom said.

"Wonder why they didn't just dig a hole in the desert."

"I thought about that, Chief," Tom said. "The only thing I could figure was that with the constant growth in population and the constant expansion of living space, they figured that a wilderness area could eventually be visited and a desert area could eventually be developed. Most of it was all desert anyway. They *really* didn't want to take any chances of the body being found."

"That could make it easier to identify him," Dietrich said. "When people take those kind of pains, the target may have been high-profile."

"I'm about to start checking," Tom said. "This time with a completely different time frame."

"My flight's being called," Dietrich said. "I'll be in the office in a couple of hours. We can touch base then, Tom. I appreciate the update. Good work."

"Thanks, Chief," Tom said, and clicked off.

Tom checked on his dad, was assured that everything was fine, and began doing archival searches through newspaper files. The problem was that there was no marine connection now. The decedent could have been killed anywhere and for any reason. His body was disposed of at sea, but that didn't mean that his life was in any way connected with it. He could forget sailors and yachtsmen, at least for the moment. It was also less likely that the man's height would be flagged in newspaper stories ('The *very* tall John Jones disappeared today … ´) and thus it would be less susceptible to identification by search engines. Assuming that the anthropologist was right, they had made great progress in bracketing the likely time of death, but the available data bases were unlikely to highlight the remaining salient facts ('The *very* tall John Jones who disappeared today also happened to have nice dental work, including some lovely porcelain crowns … ´).

He needed anecdotal information, since all that he had was anecdotal evidence. There was one person who could provide it.

His dad was groggy in recovery, but smiling and anxious to talk. Tom got good reports from the surgeon and an optimistic prognosis. "This was textbook, Tom; he'll be fine. Give him an hour or two to sleep." His dad was awake when he returned from the hospital cafeteria.

"You need somebody from the old days who always had his ear to the ground."

"Exactly, Dad."

"I know just the person, only it's a she not a he. What are you doing next week?"

"What do you mean?"

"I plan to sit up tomorrow and walk in about three days."

"You want to introduce me."

"Of course. Trust me, it'll help."

"I'll talk to the surgeon and the cardiologist; I'm not going to rush anything."

"They'll need the bed," Wayne said. "Routine operation these days; stop worrying. I'll call my friend. Well . . . soon. Maybe tomorrow I'll call. Tomorrow or the day after . . . I should probably catch a little sleep first."

"I'll talk to the docs," Tom said. His dad smiled, turned his head, and fell asleep.

As it turned out Tom needed the extra time. Since there was now no rush on the case and no statute of limitations on homicides Chris asked Tom and Hector to work with Bill Brighton on a drug case—fentanyl was coming across the southern border in unprecedented quantities and giving the local dealers an embarrassment of riches. With full trunks and expanding markets the distribution procedures became sloppy around the edges and the police took instant advantage of the unanticipated opportunity. The cells were filled with new occupants and the hallways with expensive lawyers. "This is more like crowd control than surgical strikes," Bill said. It actually took two weeks to sort out the challenges. When Tom rallied with his dad he looked as if he had been able to make good use of the additional rest. He joked that he was pale but rested and ready.

The *Canyon Vista* retirement community consisted of freestanding 'villas' around central recreational and medical facilities. Smaller residences started at $950,000, with additional fees for all available services. The beauty parlor appointments were booked three and a half weeks in advance and the shih-tzu walkers were doing a brisk business.

"Tom, I'd like you to meet Madeline Terry," Wayne said. "Mrs. Terry is an old friend."

"Your dad looked after me after Kenneth died," she said. "He also looked after our boat. He made sure that we only paid twice the market rate for fuel and repairs, not four times that much."

"It was all John Wayne's fault," Tom's father said. "He made Newport Beach fashionable and the prices skyrocketed."

"Duke Wayne was a very nice man," Mrs. Terry said. "He was a gentleman. An old-school gentleman. You can rent his boat now, if you can afford it. It's actually a converted minesweeper—136 feet and three decks. You probably knew that; your dad certainly does. Kenneth and I used to see him all the time. Duke, that is. Wayne Deaton too, of course."

"My father tells me that you are one of the most knowledgeable people in the county," Tom said.

"I don't know about that," she said, "but I'm older than dirt and I've been here most of my life."

"I work for the Laguna Beach Police Department," Tom said.

"Yes, your father mentioned that," she said, before giving him a chance to continue. "You're working on a case and you'd like my help."

"Yes, ma'am, I most certainly would."

"Would you like some tea?"

"Iced tea?"

"They can put ice in it," she said, signaling a woman wearing a business suit, with a name tag.

"What would you like Mrs. Terry?"

"Iced tea for the men and Darjeeling for me. We'll order lunch in a few minutes."

"Certainly," the woman said, and left.

"Normally I'd have a little white wine," she said, "but if you're going to put me to work I'd better stay alert."

"You're very kind to meet with us," Tom said.

"Nonsense. I've always got time for handsome young men."

A uniformed waitress brought the tea and a basket of brioche with a square of Irish butter. "Thank you, Mary," Mrs. Terry said. "Now, Detective, fire away."

"We've just recovered the skeletal remains of a man on the beach in Laguna … " Mrs. Terry didn't blink; she took a nibble of bread and a sip of tea and let Tom continue.

"We believe that he died at least forty years ago. Perhaps longer. He was probably reasonably well-to-do, since he had state-of-the-art dental work. He was right-handed in all probability and he was exceptionally tall."

"How tall?" she asked.

"Approximately 6'6"."

"How old was he at the time of his death, Detective?"

"Approximately 60, ma'am."

"And he died around forty years ago?"

"Yes, ma'am."

"And were there any chunks of cement clinging to his feet?"

"No, ma'am; why do you ask that?"

"Because I think I may know who it is you're talking about, Detective Deaton. I'm surprised that *his* body was *ever* recovered."

THIRTEEN

"We used to see him at the clubs. I don't mean bars, I mean Club clubs—dining clubs, yacht clubs, country clubs. Kenneth called him an *aspirant*. That was a polite word. Kenneth was always kinder than some people deserved. I thought he was a pretender. My granddaughter would call him a *wannabe*. He had money, that's true, but he wasn't . . . he wasn't . . . Detective Deaton, you'll have to bear with me on this. I don't want to sound pretentious or arrogant . . . "

"That's quite all right, Mrs. Terry. You're being very helpful. Just use your own words."

"Thank you. I would say that he wasn't . . . *civilized*, though he worked very hard at appearing so. He was always running on about art and chamber music and the latest recital he had attended, but there was no real *polish*. It was all recently acquired. He knew which wines to order and which clothes to wear, but when you got close to him, very close, you could always . . . well, you could . . . you could always smell a hint of the gutter.

"It wasn't a matter of old money versus new. It wasn't a matter of which schools he had attended (someone told me he had attended Princeton [or was it Yale?]); our best friends were mostly high school graduates and veterans, but they had come by their success through application and tenacity."

"How had he acquired his wealth, Mrs. Terry?"

"He was a criminal, Detective Deaton. Didn't I say that?"

"A criminal?"

"Yes, a gangster."

"He was part of organized crime, then."

"Oh yes, he was very *organized*."

"What was his name, Mrs. Terry?"

"His name was Gray Sullivan. Actually his name was Michael Sullivan. *Gray* was his nickname. They called him that because he was, literally, so gray. He had gray hair, gray eyebrows, gray suits . . . He had gray eyes and even gray skin. As vicious as he was he was also dull. He was dull in his demeanor, dull in his thoughts and dull in his speech. Somebody once commented on the *banality* of evil. That's the best description of Gray Sullivan that I can offer. He was evil and he was banal. Kenneth used to say that a whole room grew dull whenever he entered it. His presence was like a virus, a dullness virus.

"In most cases you could simply avoid a person like that. The problem was that he was very powerful. He was powerful because the man for whom he worked was very weak."

"And Sullivan did his dirty work?" Tom asked.

"He dreamed up a lot of it without any help," she said. "The word *ruthless* was often used to describe him. He had absolutely no sympathy for anyone who was hurt by his actions. His own goals and desires were always paramount. He presented himself as the loyal assistant, the underling, but he was well aware of his actual position and he always knew how to exploit it. You have a very difficult task facing you, Detective Deaton."

"Why is that, Mrs. Terry?"

"Because the number of possible suspects with which you will have to deal will be so long. No one who met that man could have liked him and each and every one of them had reason to wish him dead."

"Yourself excluded, of course."

"We never had anything to do with him. We saw him as some sort of insect or rodent that had escaped from behind the floorboards. He tried to intimidate Kenneth once. He proposed what he described as a legitimate business venture. Kenneth passed. Immediately. Gray told him that he 'might want to reconsider that decision'. Kenneth said something to him that I couldn't hear, walked into the other room, made a two-minute phone call, and returned. A few minutes later one of the waiters approached Gray and told him that there was a phone call for him. He left to take it and when he returned his skin nearly looked white, which was no mean accomplishment, considering its general tone. He never bothered Kenneth again."

"Who did your husband call, Mrs. Terry?"

"He called New York."

"I see," Tom said.

"Kenneth was not in the habit of consorting with scum like Gray Sullivan, but he still knew how to deal with them."

She picked up her teacup and took a long sip. "So there you have it," she said. "Of course, it could be someone else, but someone of that height . . . and that age . . . from that time . . . someone who disappeared and turned up under very strange circumstances . . . I'd bet that he's your man."

"I don't know how I can thank you, Mrs. Terry," Tom answered. "You've been very, very helpful."

"Just come back and visit me some time," she said. "And bring your father. He's a good man. Solid. *Standup*, Kenneth would have said."

"I will," Tom answered. He and his father rose. Wayne kissed her hand and said, "Always a pleasure." She put her hand around his neck, pulled his face closer to her's and whispered something in his ear.

When they got back in Tom's car and pulled out of the visitors' lot Tom asked his father what she had said to him.

"You mean when she whispered?"

"Yes."

"She said I could come alone also."

"You've still got it, Dad."

"If only I knew what to do with it … " Wayne answered.

Tom smiled. "Thanks for your help on this."

"Forget it," he said. "*Your* problem now is whether or not you want to bring whoever killed that guy to justice. It sounds as if he might have been rendering a public service."

FOURTEEN

Tom dropped off his dad and drove straight to the station. Chris was shuffling papers while talking on the phone but waved his hand, directing Tom to sit down. He completed his call and asked Tom about his dad.

"Pale, rested and ready," Tom said, as Chris smiled.

"Great," Chris said. "He'll outlive us all."

"I hope so," Tom said. "I may have an i.d. on our John Doe."

"Really? That was fast."

"Michael Sullivan. Ring a bell?"

"Faintly. The Michael Sullivan I've heard about was from a long time ago."

"You would have been in pre-school. Probably heard about him years later."

"Gray Sullivan?"

"That's him."

"He was the underboss for Victor Brienza."

"Right again," Tom said.

"As best I can remember he just disappeared."

"Right. We still have to do some more tests and make a few calls but it looks as if *that* Michael Sullivan is back."

"So Len's anthropologist's estimate of the time of death was too conservative."

"Right. He disappeared in the late 50's. He's been floating around in his casket or capsule or whatever for a long time."

"And she said that he didn't drown, but she didn't come up with any other likely cause of death."

"No," Tom answered.

"Victor Brienza disappeared also," Dietrich said. "Maybe he'll float up on the beach next."

"They all disappeared," Tom said. "The boss, underboss, consigliere and each of the capos."

"Brienza was replaced by a man named Orsini."

"He's long gone as well," Tom said.

"And there are no other survivors from those days?"

"I'm still working on that, Chief. So far I haven't found any."

"How did you i.d. him?" Dietrich asked.

"A friend of my father's. Actually a client. He used to look after her and her husband's motor yacht. A woman named Terry."

"Madeline Terry?"

"Right. Do you know her?"

"I know *of* her. Her husband was Kenneth Terry. At least that was the name he went by here."

"What was his real name, Chief?"

"For all I know it was Terry, but there was a rumor that he was a relative of Johnny Torrio."

"Capone's mentor."

"Right. This is old-time crime. Torrio was shot by Bugs Moran, but lived. Big Al nearly returned the favor on St. Valentine's Day. They hated each other. Johnny lived a long time though and eventually died of a heart attack in a barber's chair."

"My father never mentioned that possible connection."

"Too much of a gentleman," Dietrich said. "If the rumor was true—and remember, it was nothing more than a rumor—Kenneth Terry was a straight arrow citizen and public benefactor. He was also very protective of his privacy. His businesses were all squeaky clean. He and his wife donated a couple of parks to local communities and they were strong supporters of the arts. If Terry *did* have mob connections he had severed them long before he rose to prominence in Orange County."

"His wife said that her husband was threatened by Gray Sullivan once and that her husband braced him and then promptly called New York."

"His father may have lived in New York," Chris said. "Retired then, of course. He retired young. I'm sure he could have still dropped a dime or two and put the fear of God into someone like Gray Sullivan."

"Mrs. Terry said he was called to the phone shortly after her husband made his call and that he came back looking whiter than a klansman's Sunday best."

"Interesting," Chris said. "The West Coast mob was always a second-rate affair. The people in New York, Chicago, and Detroit called them the Mickey Mouse Mafia. They were mostly talking about the people in L.A.; the Orange County offshoots were smaller by several orders of magnitude."

"Our very own mob," Tom said.

"For awhile at least," Chris said. "Then they disappeared."

"And now, suddenly, they're gracing our shores again."

"I'd like to know more," Dietrich said. "You close one case and you may be on the way to closing them all."

"Just what I was thinking."

"We need a survivor who might know more."

"Exactly," Tom said.

FIFTEEN

As soon as he left Dietrich's office Tom called his dad. He had a lot of questions.

"I understand, Tom," Wayne said. "I don't want you to think I was holding out on you. The bottom line is that Ken Terry was not related to Johnny Torrio. That was a myth. Ken's people were from eastern Europe, not Italy. Their pre-Ellis Island name began with a T-e-r and then ended in a long series of unpronounceable consonants."

"So how did the Torrio rumor start, Dad?"

"I don't know, Tom. All I know is that it wasn't true."

"But you heard what his widow said about her husband calling New York."

"Yes, but all the big businessmen at the time would know that the local mob was controlled by the east and Midwest. If they had a problem, that's who they would call. They might have to put up some cash to make their problem go away, but that wouldn't have been any problem for Ken Terry."

"Think about the way that she said it happened, Dad. It was like . . . a two minute call and suddenly the problem was solved. The mob wasn't advertising in the Yellow Pages. How did her husband know who to call and why did she say 'New York'? She didn't say that he called someone back East who could help him with his problem. She said, 'He called New York.' If it happened just the way she said it happened it doesn't sound as if they were calling for the first time."

"I understand, Tom. I just don't have an explanation for it. Maybe . . . "

"Maybe his wife had the mob relations," Tom said.

There was a long pause before Wayne responded. "You might be right."

"But you don't *know* whether I am or not."

"No, I don't, Son. I'm not being coy with you. I really don't know."

"You've got to admit, it's an interesting possibility."

"Yes, but are you thinking that she may have had something to do with Sullivan's death?"

"No. I'm just saying that she may know more than she's saying."

"That's *always* possible. Anyway, how can I help you?"

"I'm looking for a family survivor," Tom said, "somebody who was related to Sullivan or his boss or better still, somebody from the family that replaced his. Somebody from *those days* who could shed some light on the case or a relative who could put us in touch with somebody who could help. Maybe an old foot soldier of some sort."

"So the Department is going to investigate this."

"Yes, we are."

"If you find one thread and pull it there's no telling what might be attached."

"Exactly our thinking," Tom said.

"I've got an idea," Wayne said. "I'll take her some flowers, tell her that she was very helpful. I'll sign the card with both of our names. She'll thank one or both of us. That can open the door for a follow-up question. Nobody knows the O.C. cave dwellers and survivors the way she does. She may also have some special knowledge of those with mob connections. Either way you slice it, she's your best source for potentially useful information."

"Sounds like a plan. Thanks, Dad. I appreciate it."

"No problem," Wayne said. "I'll get some of those stargazer lilies. They smell great. People will comment on them—it'll make her feel good."

Wayne called late the next morning. "I just talked to Madeline Terry," he said.

"That was quick," Tom said.

"Right. I picked up the flowers late yesterday and dropped them off at the front desk of her place last night. I didn't want to barge in on her or look too pushy. I also didn't want to raise any suspicions."

"What did she say when she called?"

"She said, 'Aren't you the thoughtful one?'"

"She called you rather than me. Like I said, Dad, you've still got it."

"I'm not sure that I want it. Anyway . . . she said it was a lovely thought and that she appreciated it very much. She said it was totally unnecessary, since she enjoyed talking to us and hopes to do so again. Soon."

"Did you pop the question?"

"Eventually. We made some small talk and then she said that we shouldn't hesitate to call on her whenever we have any questions about the old days."

"Or about the new days?" Tom said.

"She didn't say that, but she knows a lot about them as well," Wayne said. "Anyway, I said that you had a question, but that I couldn't remember it. Then I hemmed and hawed awhile and finally said, 'Oh yes, now I remember. Tom was wondering if there was anybody still around from those days who would know the principals or someone related to them.'"

"Good. You'd make an excellent detective, Dad. You're very devious."

"Thanks . . . I think."

"And what did she say?"

"She said that the granddaughter of one of the Orsini brothers lives in San Clemente. She's married to a doctor there."

"Did she give you a name?"

"Susan Wilson."

"But she didn't have an address," Tom said, teasing him.

"She had a neighborhood."

"Seriously?"

"Yes. She lives in a canyon, right by the Pacific Golf and Country Club. Do you want to know her husband's handicap?"

"Did she know it?"

"No. She just said he won a tournament there last year."

"Dad … "

"Yes?"

"You've earned a rest. Take it. And thanks again."

"I'm pacing myself," Wayne said. "Don't worry. "I take catnaps. I promised the doctor … "

"Thanks again."

"You're welcome. Now it's time for the slippers and afghan … "

"Good. Go for it."

"I'm already nodding off."

SIXTEEN

Two days later Tom was at Susan Wilson's door; she asked him to join her in the kitchen. "How did you find me?" she asked. She was wearing white painter's pants, a spattered tee shirt and paper painter's hat and washing the remains of the blue latex paint from her roller in the kitchen sink. She had strawberry blonde hair, bright blue eyes and a body that was the result of steady exercise, good nutrition and solid genes. Tom wondered if she was concerned about her nails as she worked them into the roller, loosening clots and moistening dried edges.

"If this isn't a good time … " Tom offered.

"It's as good as any," she said. "I wanted to take a break anyway. How do you think the dining room looks?"

"It looks very nice," Tom said. "You don't usually see classic colors like that in southern California homes."

"I'm old fashioned," she said. "Unfortunately the slate blue doesn't cover very well. You'd think that it would, but it doesn't. I'll need at least three coats. It'll really highlight the chair rail and white cabinetry when it's finished."

"Colonial Williamsburg comes to San Clemente."

"Right. Something like that. Now, what brings *you* to San Clemente, Detective Deaton?"

"I'm looking for a relative of the Orsini brothers," he said.

"Which Orsini brothers?"

"Dominic and Giancarlo."

"And why do you want to talk to one of their relatives, Detective Deaton?"

"I'm working on a case, Ms. Wilson. I need information."

"Call me Susan. I don't feel old enough to be a Ms. or Mrs. yet."

"OK, Susan. Aren't you a direct-descent relative?"

"Giancarlo Orsini is my grandfather, Detective Deaton."

Is, Tom thought, not *was*.

"Tell me more about your case."

"I assume you know about your grandfather and uncle's work," Tom said.

"Yes, I do," she said. "That has nothing to do with us. My father is a retired military officer and businessman. He never followed my grandfather's line of work. My husband is a doctor; I do some freelance work."

"I understand," Tom said. "I'm not trying to point fingers or disrupt any lives. I simply want to clear a case."

"What kind of case, Detective?"

"It appears to be a homicide . . . from many years ago."

"There's no statute of limitations on homicide, Detective. Everyone who watches television shows knows that."

"I understand, but it's highly unlikely that whoever was responsible for the decedent's death is still alive. If I could get testimony concerning the person or persons responsible I could clear the case. I don't anticipate making any arrests, Susan. I'd be happy to just close the file."

"Who's the victim?"

"Michael Sullivan. Some called him 'Gray'."

"And this was in . . . what . . . the 1950's or so?"

"Yes. He disappeared then."

"Way before my time," she answered.

"You said that your grandfather is still alive?"

"Yes. I haven't seen him in some time. He's very old and becoming frail."

"And does he live in Orange County?"

"Oh no, he lives in Sicily. He's lived there for decades."

"He was Dominic Orsini's consigliere."

"He was my great uncle's *lawyer*, Detective Deaton."

"Either way, it's very unlikely that he was involved in Gray Sullivan's death. I'm not implying that your uncle was either, but—classically—the consigliere remained separate from direct involvement in the family's . . . *activities*."

"This could prove to be very embarrassing for our family, Detective Deaton. I very much doubt that my grandfather would be willing to speak with you."

"How many other direct descendants are there, Susan?"

"As far as I know, there's no one but me."

"And as you said, you and your father have severed any ties with organized criminal activity."

"That's true, but ... "

"Susan," Tom said. "This isn't quite ancient history, even for southern California, but it's so distant in time that it shouldn't taint you in any way. Besides, it could be very interesting. Everyone knows that those days are past—not the days of organized crime—but of that kind of organized crime, with those structures and rules and expectations. It's the stuff of story books."

"Are you saying that you would be functioning more as a historian than as a policeman, Detective Deaton?"

"No, not exactly, but I *am* interested in the story as well as in clearing the case. I'd like to meet your grandfather."

"And what kind of promises would you be willing to make?" she asked.

"I'm not sure I know what you mean," Tom answered.

"I don't want my grandfather harassed."

"Of course not. How is his health?"

"His health is delicate, but his mind is strong."

"He doesn't have to talk to me if he doesn't want to," Tom said. "And he doesn't have to answer all of my questions. We have protections against self-incrimination, as you know. It may be that he could sketch in some background that would enable me to have a better understanding of the case. He might be able to help me and still maintain his personal detachment from the case."

"I take it that you know the meaning of the word *omertà*, Detective Deaton."

"Yes, but like I said, your grandfather would not be compelled to answer all of my questions."

"If you could leave me a card I could make some enquiries and get back to you, Detective Deaton."

"I would appreciate that very much," Tom said.

"No promises."

"I understand."

Tom called Chris Dietrich on his cell phone the moment he got back in his car. He explained Susan Wilson's relationship with the Orsini brothers and summarized the gist of his conversation with her.

"So she's the little suburban housewife sprucing up her dining room, but also talking about Mafia vows of silence."

"Yes," Tom said.

"The acorn doesn't fall too far from the tree, I guess," Dietrich said. "Do you think she knows things that she's not telling us?"

"I'd bet on that in a heartbeat."

"So the old boy's still alive."

"Yes, living in Sicily."

"Keeping a low profile or keeping his hand in the game?"

"Maybe a little of both."

"Come on in and let's talk."

"I'm on my way, Chief."

SEVENTEEN

"**B**efore you go I would want to be sure that it's worth the trip," Dietrich said. "I mean . . . what's in it for him? If he *doesn't* know anything, the trip isn't worth your time. Assume the most likely scenario: he *does* know things, but he won't want to reveal them. Hell, he's sworn an oath not to. If he *is* willing to reveal things to you it will be for a specific reason, a self-interested reason. You'd have to be very suspicious of everything he says."

"Of course. But what have we got now, Chief?"

"We've got squat. Even if we get something—very little maybe, but something—it's more than what we've got now."

"Maybe he's been itching to tell his side. Now that everybody else is gone, he can," Tom said. "Being consigliere is a very tough job. He offers advice. If he's right the don can take the credit. If he's wrong he can get the blame. He's not a street guy; he's a guy in a suit. That means that the street guys are likely to be suspicious of him. I guess the best way to put it is that he's a staff guy, not a line guy. The boss, the underboss and the capos all have line responsibilities. He's like a warrant officer. That can be a very political job. But there's a big difference between Washington politics and mob politics. In Washington a decision is made and everybody whose advice was not taken runs to the *Post* or the *Times* with their sob story. Off the record, of course, or on 'deep background', but they tell their story nonetheless. They get it off *their* chest, regardless of the consequences. They get some vindication or at least stitch their ego back up. In the mob you can't do that. You shoot your mouth off and you catch a .22 in your brainpan . . . if you're lucky."

"So this is his chance to clear the air."

"Maybe. Maybe he's an old guy who nobody visits anymore. My mother used to say that we have to say a given number of words every day, just to feel whole. That's why you don't want to be seated on a plane next to somebody who lives alone. Maybe he's been saving up his words and looking for the opportunity to share them with somebody."

"Possibly," Dietrich said. "He might also want to frame somebody or settle some old score."

"Maybe," Tom said. "Hard to know until I ask him and see what he says."

"And the granddaughter is going to contact him and see if he's willing."

"That's the plan."

"What's in it for her? She's probably very comfortable painting her walls in designer colors and sipping her Mai Tais by the pool. Why would she want a story to come out that would associate her with the mob, especially after her father worked so hard to distance himself from it?"

"Good question. She'd want old man Orsini to make the decision though. She wouldn't hide the fact from him that some detective is reopening a case and wants to talk to him about it. That has to be his call. Of course, if she thought it was a bad idea she'd tell him that, but she wouldn't want him to hear about the investigation through back channels. She said he was at her wedding. That's a big deal for him to come over here for a single occasion, especially at his age. They're probably close."

"Right, she wouldn't decide unilaterally. How old is she, late twenties, early thirties?"

"Yes."

"She was probably married seven to ten years ago. He would have been pushing 80. Getting all the way over here and then all the way back . . . that was a commitment."

"Right."

"And the age thing may work in our favor as far as she's concerned. This all happened a million years ago in California time."

"That's what I told her, Chief—not quite ancient history, but a long time ago. This is the stuff of legend and lore, not recent family history. The biggest part of the story could be the fact that the old boy's still alive."

"Right. And Hollywood loves these guys. It's not like New York. In New York they're a drag on the economy. In Hollywood they're a business opportunity. The Black Hand . . . the Mustache Petes . . . they're long gone. Now it's the Goodfellas and Tony and Carmella . . . This isn't *crime* in L.A.; it's *romance.* Scriptwriters would be lining up to make pitches. You can see the opening scene . . . a guy in a suit that some Italian tailor spent months making. A table in the shade under a clear blue sky. A couple of glasses of limoncello. A grove of olive trees. 'Tell me, Don Giancarlo. Tell me about the old days … '"

"And there's a fedora that matches the suit," Tom said. "And a haircut that would cost you $250 here. And a prop. Maybe a cigarette. Maybe a walking stick with a silver handle. Something he fondles when he talks. Something that grabs your attention while you're hanging on his every word."

"Hell, I want to go there and hear him myself," Dietrich said.

"Maybe the granddaughter wants to hear the story too," Tom said. "If they *have* distanced themselves from the old family business but grandpa has still been close to her, this is a way for her to learn more about him, get to know him up close and personal."

"We're probably being too optimistic," Dietrich said.

"Right, Chief, but like you said, we don't have squat now. Where's the harm in trying to learn more?"

"When is she supposed to get back to you?"

"No fixed time. As soon as she can. In the meantime I've got something I've got to do."

"OK, when she calls . . . if it looks promising . . . go for it."

EIGHTEEN

The meeting with Madeline Terry was still gnawing at him, and as soon as he finished his meeting with Chris Dietrich Tom hit the files and the newspaper archives. Kenneth Terry had gotten his start in O.C. real estate. With money borrowed from his parents he bought two run-down homes, remodeled them and flipped them. From there he bought a small orange grove in Anaheim and developed it—some private homes, some rentals, a little commercial space. He was five years too early. If he had held the land until Walt built Disneyland he would have been richer than Midas rather than simply off to a running start.

He still made a bundle. A generation later when the original Rancho was broken up he bought huge tracts in Mission Viejo and built houses that sold for a modest $36,000 each. Now a two-bedroom, two-bath house there runs you a little over $500K. Terry was smart enough to hold some of his property in reserve and develop it later, as prices escalated. That brought him his second fortune.

The third came in Irvine, as this and other sections of Orange County morphed from the outskirts of L.A. into independent entities with exploding populations and deep-pocket buyers. The old $165K refuges for red-eyed commuters were transformed into cool mil retreats for the O.C. well-to-do.

Prior to his death Kenneth Terry was building condos in San Clemente--tidy little 10-mil properties with blue-water and blue-sky views and all the comforts of home (if you're a Maharaja in Rajasthan). If he had been in New York there might have been some mob smell around the edges of his operations, but in the O.C. he was strictly Mr. Clean. The fact that his work took him throughout the county and involved him in a succession of relationships with those who aspired to share the wealth or were at least willing to grease the skids in return for some modest but legal consideration, made it eminently plausible that his wife would in fact know everyone and everything that mattered in the area. Their social life had a direct bearing on his business success. He was like the church usher trying to hype his insurance business or the local undertaker advertising in the parish bulletin, except that Kenneth Terry's hand-held calculators required room for many more zeroes.

Madeline Terry was Terry née Constable—a distant relative of the English painter. She had graduated from Vassar in the days when that meant silver spoons and big money rather than a long list of AP courses and top SAT scores.

Tom checked on her husband, wondering how the Torrio rumors had started. Maybe it was the nagging suspicion that all big money was tainted in some big way, even the money made by a guy from the Bronx who had barely made it through high school and fled the snow and slush for sun and sand before the experience of the war had made that a significant trend.

Madeline and Kenneth had met on neutral territory, at a wedding at the old *Wentworth* Hotel in Pasadena, before it became the *Sheraton* or the *Ritz-Carlton* or, now, the Langham Huntington. Sixteen months later they celebrated their own wedding—once the Constable family had been assured that young Mr. Terry could look after their eldest daughter in a suitable fashion.

They had had two daughters, one the wife of a Dartmouth professor living in relative but genteel poverty and the other the wife of a Park Avenue neurosurgeon whose name ended in the words 'the fourth'.

Kenneth had been eight years older than Madeline. It was the law of averages, not some crippling disease, that had sent him to his eternal reward nearly a decade ago. Madeline continued their philanthropic work and tended his memory in what appeared to be attentive and loving fashion. She made grand entrances from time to time, but increasingly the exits came earlier and earlier as she watched her own health and paced herself for the long distance run. Hospitalizations were reported from time to time, but without any significant details.

Tom wanted it all to be true, even if it meant that there was no silver-bullet solution for his case at hand. She seemed like a nice person and he liked her. Besides, she liked his father and that gave them something in common.

Later that evening he had a thrown-together dinner of leftovers and read himself to sleep. At 6:00 he rose, shaved, showered and left for work. He had checked twice to make sure that his cell was turned on and he had checked three times to make sure that there were no lost messages. At 7:15 he turned on his computer and checked his email. He had given the address to Susan Wilson (whose husband also checked out as legit—an ear/nose/throat specialist with an M.D. from UCLA and bachelor's from Stanford). The first line of text that was illuminated announced that he had fifteen new messages.

NINETEEN

Most of the messages concerned bureaucratic give-and-take. Reports were ready (or not). Calls had been received (or not). Forms had been processed (or not). The evidence room had located the requested materials (or not). There were a few items of a more personal nature. Hector Campo had forwarded a *Register* story on gangs in the city of Orange. As a plainclothes police officer and former gang member himself, Hector took a special interest in their activities. Tom's father had forwarded some political cartoons and a puff piece about the Newport Beach marinas. There was nothing from Susan Wilson. Tom hit the *Check Mail* icon. Still nothing from Susan Wilson. He started to move the cursor toward the icon a second time, stopped, reminded himself about the need to avoid compulsive behavior, and went back to his archival searches.

He continued to look for information on the Orsini brothers. There was an obituary notice for Dominic that included a funeral crowd shot. The atmosphere was upscale and subdued: no flowered horseshoe sprays with wishes of **Good Luck**, just roses, lilies, birds-of-paradise and black suits, black dresses, and black veils. The individuals in the picture were not identified. The interment was in the family mausoleum at the Catholic cemetery in San Juan Capistrano and it was by invitation only. The grainy photograph was taken with a lens slightly less powerful than that of the principal telescope on Mt. Wilson.

Tom tried to find a joint photograph of the Orsinis, as well as a single shot of the surviving brother, Giancarlo, but so far he had been unsuccessful. He tried every search engine, each standard internet site and passworded law enforcement site. Giancarlo Orsini was nowhere to be found, neither in the files of the state of California, nor in those of the Federal Government or Interpol. He had never been arrested. There was no DNA, no fingerprints, no photographs, no nothing.

There wasn't much else on his brother Dominic. He had been indicted on a charge of interstate theft in the 1950's, but was later acquitted. There was suspicion, innuendo, rumor, and miscellaneous gossip but precious little evidence and nothing ever approaching a successful conviction. The single, repeating photograph of Dominic Orsini was in the uniform of an Army buck sergeant. He had served in the Third Army as a tank driver.

The Mafia had helped the U.S. Army during the invasion of Sicily and after; Tom wondered if Dominic or Giancarlo had ever put in a good word or placed some calls. Dominic looked serious enough, though both his head and his garrison cap were cocked to the side, in the style of the day. The photographer's lighting gleamed on his cheek and forehead, though the eyes were dark. He looked like a man who could take orders as well as give them.

The reported cause of death was cancer of the chest cavity. There was no protracted hospitalization. The disease had spread throughout his system in a matter of weeks and though it was discovered early it was found to be inoperable during exploratory surgery. Tom thought of his own recent bout with a grade I astrocytoma. Far better to develop a tumor in the 21st century than in the 20th.

Most of the stories about the Orsinis consisted of speculation concerning their rise to power after the unexplained disappearance of the heads of the Brienza family. One imaginative reporter had written at length about Victor Brienza's affection for the limelight and his sudden disappearance from it. He talked about the famous magician's illusion, **Metamorphosis**, using the stages of the illusion as a metaphor for Orsini's replacement of Brienza. In that trick the magician is chained, cuffed, bagged and locked in a trunk. His assistant stands atop the trunk and pulls up a large drape to conceal herself. At the instant in which her head is covered there is a rustling of the cloth and the head of the magician suddenly appears, replacing hers. The magician then drops the drape and proceeds to open the trunk, remove the bag, unlock the lock at the bag's apex, and reveal the assistant who is cuffed and chained inside.

In the reporter's version Victor Brienza disappears and Dominic Orsini suddenly appears in his place. When the trunk is opened and the bag is unlocked at the top the bag is empty and Brienza has vanished. "Along with the rest of the Brienza family," the reporter added.

It was clear that both the press and the general public expected Victor to turn up with a bullet in his head or his tongue pulled through his slashed throat, but that was never to be. Victor Brienza simply vanished into the mist. The reporter—a man named Brandon—returned to the story from time to time, but eventually seems to have lost interest.

Giancarlo never figured in Brandon's reportage, except for an occasional brief mention. He truly *had* remained in the shadows or on the sidelines, choosing to offer his counsel to his brother in the most discreet fashion possible. Tom sorted through the archive of Marshall Brandon's stories, thinking that one or more might have been titled in such a way as to elude his search engine keywords. He found a single additional reference to Victor Brienza. It concerned the disappearance of a teenage boy from what was then just beginning to be called Little Saigon. Brandon reported that the young man had vanished like Victor Brienza, but hoped that the young man—unlike Brienza—would eventually be found.

Tom went down the hallway in search of a cup of fresh, strong black coffee, but he heard his phone ring when he was twenty feet away from his desk. He hurried back, picked up the receiver, and said "Deaton."

"Detective Deaton?" the voice said.

"Yes, speaking," he answered.

"This is Susan Wilson calling. We need to talk."

"I'm at your disposal, Susan," he said.

"Can you come down this afternoon around 3:00?"

"Yes. I look forward to seeing you. I hope we can move forward on our project."

"I'm afraid it's a little more complicated than that," she said.

TWENTY

"The dining room looks very nice," Tom said.

"Thanks," she answered. "It looks fine from a distance, but if you look closely you can see some white flecks peeking through. I think it'll need one last coat."

Tom smiled, anxious to move beyond the small talk.

"Anyway," she said, "we have other things to talk about. I'm going to have some iced tea. Would you like some?"

"Yes," he said. "That would be very nice."

"Sugar or lemon?"

"Artificial sweetener if you have it."

She nodded and walked to the kitchen, leaving him in the reception area beyond the dining room. She was dressed more formally today: a wool skirt, flowered silk blouse, and pearls that looked more like Mikimoto's than J. C. Penney's. When she returned with the tea he noticed the size of her oval-cut engagement ring diamond—no less than a full 2 carats.

She sat down on the love seat opposite his and rearranged the pillows to provide her more back support. "I should be too young to need these," she said, "but I've been spending too much time on that ladder."

"It's still the best way to insure that the job is done right," he said.

She smiled, took a sip of her tea, and asked him if his tea was to his taste. "It's fine," he said.

"Anyway," she said, "I spoke with my uncle. He seemed surprised to hear from me. It was late in the afternoon there and he was probably ready to take his nap. I told him who you were and that you wanted to speak with him and I assured him that you would be willing to discuss the parameters of the conversation. I didn't use the word *negotiate*, but that was the implication. He said that he would need to think about that, but that the subject could be addressed after you arrived. I'm sorry. It may prove to be a wasted trip if he's not prepared to meet your expectations."

"That's all right," Tom said. "I'd rather discuss such things with him face to face."

"That's what he said too," she responded. "I think it's a male thing. He wants to be able to see your eyes when he talks to you. He said something about taking your measure. He used an Italian expression; I wasn't familiar with it. He had to translate it for me."

"How soon would he be willing to talk?"

"That's an issue; he actually wants to speak with you immediately."

"Immediately?"

"He's scheduled to visit with a friend of his in Messina. They meet every year at the other man's villa there. My uncle said that they get together and talk about the old days. He used an Italian expression. This time I understood him. I think they also do some business together. The man is an exporter and my uncle advises him on legal affairs. My uncle has a little time in between. He said that if he agrees to speak with you it could take several days. He'd like you to come the day after tomorrow."

"Assuming I could make the connections I'd leave tomorrow and arrive at the city of my connecting flight the following morning. I could then be in Sicily by midday or early afternoon—assuming, again, that there's space available."

"You might need to take a slightly circuitous route," she said, "but there are plenty of flights to Europe. The connections with Sicily are trickier at the last minute. Of course, there are trains and ferries … "

"If it cuts into our discussion time I'd still like to try to do it as soon as possible," Tom said. "Even if I can't get there until the following day … "

"He's actually made a hotel reservation for you. Taormina is filled with tourists and the nice places fill up fast. I have the information written down; I'll give it to you."

"Thanks," Tom said.

"I hope your cell phone works internationally."

"I think I can add that service; I'll contact them before I leave."

"He said that you could contact him through the hotel. The manager there will know how to reach him. Otherwise he'll meet you in two days, at 3:00, at the theatre."

"The theatre?"

"The ancient theatre. It was built by the Greeks and expanded by the Romans. That's the usual interpretation, at any rate. It's quite striking. You can see Mt. Etna and the Bay of Naxos in the distance."

"And the Greeks performed tragedies there?"

"And comedies," she added, smiling.

He was on his cell to Chris Dietrich as soon as he got back in his car.

"Day after tomorrow?" Dietrich said. "That's pretty tight."

"At his age I don't want to waste a day. He's got a trip to Messina planned. If I don't see him now it could be two weeks or more before I'm able to connect with him."

"I'll ask Julie to see what she can get for you," Chris said.

"I'll be there in a few minutes, Chief," Tom said.

"It won't take long to check availability," Chris answered.

"The choice was via Rome or Milan," Julie said. Her last name was Li--the Chief's executive assistant.

"I booked you out of LAX to Milan, with a stop in New York. From Milan you fly to Catania. You can then get a car to take you to Taormina. It's just a little ways north. Forty-five kilometers or so."

"Thanks," Tom said. "I really appreciate it."

"How about your cell phone?"

"I've got to talk to my provider," Tom said, "to get it to work there … "

"I'll call them," Julie said. "Give me your phone."

"You're a godsend," Tom said.

"Next time you have to take me with you," she said. "Meanwhile, you'd better start packing."

II

TAORMINA

TWENTY-ONE

Lots of fluids but no alcohol. Loose fitting clothes, shoes with laces to accommodate the swelling. That's what Tom's doctor always prescribed for long plane flights. With the time difference between L.A. and New York, Tom had to leave LAX in the early morning and connect with Alitalia in New York in order to arrive in Milan just before 8:00 the next morning, secure his luggage, clear customs and immigration and then find the gate for his flight to the eastern coast of Sicily. When the flight attendants began pushing drinks he would pass, choosing water, a light meal, and a tablet of melatonin instead. I'll be glad later, he told himself, no matter how inviting that martini and red wine may have looked at the time.

He hadn't really paid much attention to the information which Susan had passed along to him. He had handed the large post-it note to Julie, so that she'd know where he'd be staying. Now when he reviewed Julie's typed itinerary he saw that he was staying at the San Domenico Palace Hotel and that they would provide car service for him from Catania. Chalk one up for the consigliere. When he looked at the travel book on Italy and Sicily that he had picked up in LAX he saw that the San Domenico Palace was actually an updated 15th century Dominican convent. The good news was that it was beautifully sited, overlooking the bay. The bad news was that it was at the opposite end of town from the Greek theatre. He counted streets and estimated that the walk would take him about 20-30 minutes, depending on the number of tourists and tour groups that were blocking his path.

He checked the room rates for the San Domenico Palace. Five stars. Hundreds of euros. At least he got breakfast. He could plead that it was his informant's choice and that the staff at the hotel were the communications link with that informant. He really didn't have any choice and neither did the taxpayers on whose behalf he was traveling. Besides, the consigliere might be more moved to tell the truth on the grounds of a former convent. Pretty to think so, at least.

The flights all left and landed on time and were otherwise uneventful, though each of the airports was crowded with customers and there were scattered thunderstorms west of New York. The car for the San Domenico was actually a small van, though the driver was nowhere in sight. Tom stood next to it with his luggage and was eventually approached by a short man carrying a cardboard cup of coffee, who nodded to him, said "San Domenico?" and then took his bags, positioning them neatly in the back of the van. "Would you like a coffee before we leave?" the man asked, in halting but grammatical English.

"No, thank you," Tom responded, wondering whether he would have sounded foolish saying "*Grazie.*"

His hotel room was small but very nicely appointed, with a balcony and view of the Bay of Naxos. He checked his watch: 2:30; he had a minute or two to spare. He had shaved on the New York to Milan flight and looked reasonably presentable. He washed his face and hands, combed his hair and locked his room door. The corridors were wide and still very monastic, with many religious icons and decorations. This provided a sense of peace, something that he welcomed, but something that he realized could provide a false sense of security.

He walked to the Piazza IX Aprile, with the churches dedicated to San Giorgio and San Giuseppe and then made his way through the heart of the city's shops and cafés. He could feel the Greek, Roman, and Moorish influences which had marked the city over the centuries, turned right and walked toward the theatre. Checking his watch (2:56) he hurried past the shops and street vendors. Tour groups were entering and leaving the theatre when he entered. They wore numbers on paper discs attached to their shirts and blouses, designed to remind them of their particular group and their particular bus.

The theatre still functioned. He noticed a sign that indicated that James Taylor was scheduled to perform there the following week. He surveyed the theatre. In Roman times it was said to accommodate nearly 5,000 people. When he walked to the center and turned toward the stage area he saw the bay to his left and Mt. Etna in the distance. There was smoke issuing from it under the bright sun against the blue sky, but as he looked across the open seats there was no sign of Giancarlo Orsini.

He sat in the very center of the theatre, apart from the tourists, so that he would be easily recognized. He was also a perfect target there, but though the thought crossed his mind briefly he did not feel threatened or ill at ease. Nor did he feel particularly jet-lagged or tired, perhaps because of the stunning view and warm sun.

At five minutes after three a young woman approached him. She was well dressed and wore fashionable shoes and jewelry. "Mr. Deaton?" she said.

"Yes," Tom answered.

"Welcome to Taormina."

"Thank you," Tom said.

"My name is Gina Abruzzi. Signore Orsini asked me to meet you here. I apologize for being late."

"No problem," Tom said.

"And how were your flights?"

"Very nice. Very smooth."

"You come to Taormina on a very beautiful day."

"Yes. I believe that most days are beautiful here."

"They are. That is why so many people visit us. Would you like a coffee or an apéritif?"

"That would be very nice," Tom said, "but is Mister Orsini waiting for us?"

"Oh no. He sends his regrets that he was detained. He would like to have dinner with you this evening in your hotel."

"I look forward to that," Tom said.

"Come with me," she said. "I know a good place where we can sit and relax for a few minutes."

"While they search my hotel room?" he thought to himself, then decided instead to enjoy the day and a few minutes of the young woman's company.

TWENTY-TWO

"This is a pleasant place," she said, indicating a small café at the southwest corner of the Piazza IX Aprile. The waiter was clearing the last available table and gestured to them to take it.

"In the shade," Gina said. "I'm always grateful for that."

The waiter approached them again and stood between them, waiting to take their orders.

"Limoncello," Gina said.

"Espresso," Tom said.

"A double?" the waiter asked.

"Yes," Tom said, "thanks."

"They're used to dealing with Americans," Tom said to Gina.

"Oh yes. They all speak English, French, and German, and sometimes a little Japanese. In each city and town in the Mediterranean there is a street such as this—lined with shops and restaurants. Everyone who works there speaks many languages. They have to."

"How long have you been working for Mr. Orsini?" Tom asked.

"Oh, I do not work for Signore Orsini. I am doing this as a favor. He is retired, as you must know. He has a secretary who takes calls for him and prepares correspondence and occasional legal documents. I work at the hotel."

"At the San Domenico Palace."

"Yes. I know that you will be comfortable there. You are dining this evening in the Principe Cerami restaurant. That is our finest dining facility. It is named for the nobleman who discovered that he had actually inherited the convent. There was an old will that was discovered. He converted it into a hotel, the finest in Taormina. We believe so at least and are still very grateful to him."

"I'm looking forward to meeting Mr. Orsini and to dining in your restaurant. What would you recommend that I order?"

"That depends on how adventurous you are. Everything is good. Some things are more exotic than others. Signore Orsini will probably begin with the sea bass tartare. I like the millefeuilles of tuna, but the black pork loin is also nice. For first course he will have the macaroni with lobster. I recommend it. There will also be ravioli, risotto and tagliolini. For main course the lamb cutlet with foie gras is exceptional, but I would inquire about the fish that is featured that day. That is what Signore Orsini is likely to have. The guinea fowl is fine and there is always turbot."

"And then a nap?"

"Perhaps," she said. "You will not go away hungry. Remember to save room for the chocolate creation. It varies from day to day but it is never to be missed. There will also be wine, of course. We have an extensive cellar. Signore Orsini prefers local wines. He is something of an expert on them."

"He must have a strong constitution."

"I don't understand … "

"He must be in good physical condition for a man of his age."

"Oh yes, he is very vigorous. His health is sometimes delicate, but he does very well. Do you know his nickname?"

"No, I don't."

"He is called the *superstite*. The survivor. Sometimes it is shortened and he is called the *super*."

"That's a good thing to be."

"Yes, though it can be lonely."

"I'm sure he has many friends."

"He does. We have a saying that translates as something like 'friends are the family you choose.'"

"We have the same expression," Tom said.

"In that case Signore Orsini still has a very large family."

Tom had at least fifty questions churning in the back of his head, none of which he could comfortably ask. The Mafia was a fact of life—a significant fact of life—in Sicily, even today, but he could not ask her about it, at least not yet. She had not broached any of the subjects with him in which she was likely to be interested either. Perhaps she had learned to keep such questions to herself or, perhaps, she already knew most of their answers. She knew the consigliere well enough to be able to anticipate his dining selections. Perhaps in his family of friends she was a surrogate niece or daughter, perhaps his eyes and ears in the San Domenico Palace, or both.

"How is your espresso?" she asked.

"Excellent. I'm sure your limoncello is as well."

"Yes. The secret is in the vodka. You must use 100 proof, not just some well-known brand. The greater the alcohol content the less flavor from the vodka itself. It is also more effective in preventing freezing. And of course you must have Italian lemons. Thick-skinned ones. They are easier to zest. And you must avoid the white pith; it will spoil the taste entirely. The recipes are very simple, but the execution must be precise."

"And worth it."

"We certainly think so," she said. "It is very refreshing. Sitting here in the shade, but feeling the warmth of the sun, looking out at the bay, sipping limoncello . . . it is all very nice."

"What time am I to meet Mr. Orsini for dinner?"

"Eight o'clock. I hope that is not too late for you."

"That's fine. And will I be seeing you again?"

"I'm sure that we will see each other around the hotel. If you need anything and have any problem in securing it, call me."

"And your office is … ?"

"I am the hotel manager."

"I see. I'm very grateful that you would take the time to meet me."

"For Signore Orsini I would do anything."

He turned those last words over in his head as they walked back to the hotel. Her relationship with him appeared to have been built on a foundation stronger than money and certainly stronger than simple courtesy. Fear? Love? When they returned to the hotel she shook his hand and said, "Remember, Mr. Deaton, if there is any way in which I can be of help to you, you should feel free to call."

"I will do that," he said. "Thank you again."

Someone *had* been in his room—replacing the fresh flowers and adding a bowl of fresh fruit and a bucket with iced mineral water. The attached card read, "With the compliments of the Manager." Her signature—*__Gina Abruzzi__*—was printed under her title. Tom checked several other items in the room but they had all been left undisturbed.

He then got out his blazer, wool slacks, and a fresh white shirt, set the alarm on the nightstand clock, and took a nap. When he awoke the light had shifted noticeably, though the sun had not yet set. He shaved, showered, dressed, and went downstairs to the restaurant.

Six minutes later he saw him.

TWENTY-THREE

He was very tall and very sure-footed, particularly in light of the fact that he was wearing a stiff wool suit and heavy leather shoes. The wool was dark blue with chalk stripes. His shirt was noticeably starched. The only soft items in his wardrobe were his red silk tie and red pocket square. He was dressed . . . well . . . like a lawyer, but more a Washington lawyer cum diplomat than a buttoned-down solicitor or histrionic barrister. He actually reminded Tom of the Dean Acheson school of demeanor and couture: vaguely English, strictly formal, and, at first blush, slightly affected.

His moustache was neatly trimmed and his hair had been meticulously cut. There was still some black amid the gray and no wisps or bedhead kinks. It was probably the result of a razor-cut. If his health *was* delicate he showed no signs of it. He looked as if he could stand for two or three hours if he needed to, working the crowd at an athlete's pace.

"Detective Deaton," he said, "so nice to meet you."

"How do you do, Signore. I've been anxious to meet you as well."

"Please call me Giancarlo . . . and may I call you Tom?"

"Certainly."

"We can talk better if we dispense with formalities, don't you agree?"

"Absolutely."

"Susan speaks very highly of you. She has made some enquiries and she tells me that you are a person of skill and a person of integrity."

"That's very kind of her."

"This situation of ours . . . it is very odd or, at the least, *uncommon.* Don't you agree?"

" I do. Considering our positions. It is also uncommon in that the events that I would like to discuss with you are in the distant past. The remote past."

"Which is farther, *distant* or *remote*?" Orsini asked.

"Good question. I'm not sure. I *can* say that my interest in talking to you is historical as well as professional."

Before Orsini could respond the waiter brought a bottle of wine to the table, showed him the label, and waited for his nod. He then removed the cork with a flourish and poured enough for him to taste. The consigliere nodded again and the waiter filled each of their glasses 1/3 full. Orsini smiled and turned the bottle toward Tom so that he could read the label. The wine was from Corleone.

"My idea of a jest," Orsini said, smiling impishly. "It's also very good wine. Made from Nero d'Avola. This winery also makes Cabernet Sauvignon, but the Nero d'Avola is more authentically Sicilian. This is actually a *riserva*. I think you'll enjoy it. Very grapey, but with a great deal of depth and balance."

"I gather that the *Godfather* was actually filmed near us here."

"Yes, in several locations," Orsini said. "Not in Corleone, however. Too modern for Coppola's purposes."

"It's a great movie," Tom said, "a great *American* movie. I'm not sure how authentic the Sicilian sequences are."

"That's a very skillful way to ask me a question," Orsini said, smiling again.

"The chance of a lifetime for me," Tom said.

"How is the wine?"

"It's excellent."

"Let's order and then talk some more," Orsini said.

He ordered just as Gina predicted he would, except that he ordered the lamb after enquiring concerning the fish of the day. Tom ordered the lamb as well, commenting that he knew that Giancarlo was an expert on the hotel's menu.

"It is rare for me to pass on the fish," he said, "but I'm enjoying this wine so much that I want more of it and I know that it will pair well with the lamb. Now," he said, "with regard to our friends the Corleones . . . you know, of course, that I am a lawyer and as a lawyer it is important for me to maintain both the tenets of the law and the confidentiality of the communications that I have had with my clients."

"Particularly your brother," Tom said.

"Yes, my brother Dominic, but I advised others as well."

"I understand. And I would not ask you to violate lawyer/client privilege."

"You must uphold the law as well, Tom," he said, smiling.

"Yes, of course. Nor would I expect you to incriminate someone who is still alive."

"And you realize that none of my associates *are* still alive."

"That is my working assumption, but you would know better than I."

"Of course. Let me say something and you correct me if I am wrong."

"Of course … "

"You would like me to talk about my experiences with you in ways in which I would be comfortable, in the hope that some of what I might tell you could enable you to close outstanding cases without sending anyone living to prison."

"Precisely. That's exactly what I would like you to do. And, as I said earlier, I believe that your experiences and those of your associates would—in and of themselves—be interesting and informative and give me (and my superior) a greater appreciation of the nature of those times and the individuals whose actions helped to shape them."

"You are playing the *diavolo*, Tom."

"I am?"

"Yes. You are tempting me. You sense that this is a story that I would *like* to tell and you are doing all in your power to ease the way."

"Yes, but I think the story would be . . . *heavenly*—in some senses of the word."

"The devil has always been an able rhetorician, Tom."

"But if I am playing the devil your role is that of the saint, Giancarlo."

"Perhaps, but in stories such as these the devil is usually the most interesting character. I am not sure that my ego could remain intact. After all . . . being upstaged by the devil ... "

"Your role would still be interesting, however. You know the old joke about the lawyer having a nicer home in heaven than any of the popes."

"Because there are so many popes there and so few lawyers ... "

"Yes," Tom said, both of them smiling now.

After completing their main courses they passed on the chocolate creation but had black coffee with anisette. "That was excellent," Tom said, "truly exceptional."

"And we can do it again . . . several times even," Orsini said.

"I'd like that," Tom responded.

"You know that I am not a young man. I guard my time very jealously. Before I would agree to an extended conversation with a man—any man—I would want to be assured that the conversation would be interesting. You have removed any doubts that I might have had on that score."

"Thank you," Tom said.

"I will tell you this at the outset," Orsini said, "if there is some issue that I cannot speak about directly I will tell you so. And if there are issues about which there have been rumors but no certainties, I will tell you that also."

"Perfect," Tom said. "When can we begin?"

"Tomorrow. Have a nice sleep and also be sure to have a swim. Gina will tell you when and where we are to meet. I will have to check my schedule in the meantime and see what can be arranged."

"Until then ... " Tom said, shaking his hand and thinking that an uncertain time and unknown place would insure that any attempts at eavesdropping would be forestalled. He also thought that a swim sounded like an excellent idea.

TWENTY-FOUR

The pool sat at the base of the hotel compound, above the bay. Surrounded by flowering vegetation and ringed with olive trees and scattered palms, it offered drinks from the bar and food from the Anciovi restaurant. Tom was swimming on his back and side so that he could see Mt. Etna from multiple angles. He had had a light breakfast of rolls and butter, fresh fruit, and black coffee. While he permitted himself five or ten minutes of simple pleasure in the presence of the physical beauty surrounding him, his thoughts quickly turned to Signore Orsini and the course of their impending conversations.

He had left a note for Gina, telling her that he would be at the pool if she had any messages for him from the consigliere. Except for a German woman reading a Günther Grasse novel and a hotel attendant stacking towels and arranging chaise longues, he had the pool to himself. He drifted for a few minutes, then went into a more systematic exercise routine, doing laps in a steady, deliberate crawl. Eventually he reached the end of the pool, flipped over, pushed off, and floated on his back, looking up at the pure blue sky. The moment was broken by a sudden loud splash that sprayed his face with chlorine-laced droplets.

He turned and did a sidestroke as Gina swam toward him. "Good morning," she said. "Did you sleep well?"

"Yes, very well, thank you," he said. He couldn't see the dimensions of her swimsuit but it was clear that there was very little of it.

"This is very refreshing, is it not?"

"It's wonderful," he said. "And it's sited so beautifully."

"Yes, this was not part of the monastery. Too much luxury. Too much joy for the body."

"The Dominicans are more intellectual."

"Yes," she said, treading water slowly. The top of her bikini was more of a belt than a halter. It barely covered her nipples. He wondered if part of her role was to provide distraction as well as information. If so, she was expert at both.

"Would you like a coffee?" she asked. "I'm going to have one."

"Yes, that would be very nice," he said. She swam to the side. As she pulled herself out of the water the bottom of her bikini came into view. It was barely able to cover the essentials. Either it was perfectly elasticized or it had been glued to her body. Before she wrapped herself in a beach towel she patted her hair as dry as she could, ran a comb through it, and spoke to the pool attendant, who then left immediately.

Tom gave her a few minutes to get settled before he joined her. There was a small table between their chaises. Tom thought it best to utilize it as a symbolic form of separation between them.

"Have you been here long?" she asked.

"About thirty minutes," he said.

"I got your note. I haven't heard from Signore Orsini yet. I decided to begin my day here. I must go on duty in a few minutes, but it is always good to check the full operation directly."

"Better to work here then, than in a factory," he said.

"Yes, I have been very lucky," she said. "I started my career at a small hotel in Pisa. Then I was assistant manager at a property in Sienna. I love the hill towns. I applied for a position in San Gimignano, at the Relais Santa Chiara, a very nice property also though not quite like this one. They hired someone else and I was very disappointed, but then I was offered a senior position here and was promoted to manager when my predecessor retired, so all was for the best."

Tom was trying to make the image of an ambitious hotelier fit with the image of a near-naked water nymph. Perhaps he was simply too conservative, too American. The pages of his college novels were filled with stories of Englishmen and Americans exposed to the lushness of Italy for the first time and barely able to recover from the experience. Then again, perhaps it was all a distraction. If so, it was certainly a successful one.

"How was your dinner last evening?" she asked.

"Excellent."

"You had the lamb?"

"Yes. You checked?"

"No, I was guessing. The fish was in a white sauce and Signore Orsini prefers red wine."

"You're right."

She smiled and nodded. "Well," she said, finishing the last of her coffee, "I should put on my suit and attend to my work. I will let you know as soon as I hear from the Signore."

"I'd like to take a little walk through the city," Tom said. "I'll be back in time for lunch if he wants to meet then."

"I doubt that he'll be available until this evening," she said. "I'll leave the message on your phone. You can call the hotel at any time and access your messages there."

"Thanks," he said. "Once again, you've been very helpful."

She smiled, her nod more of a modest bow, that conflicted oddly with her physical presence when she turned and walked away, her towel clinging in interesting and revealing ways.

It would still be night in Laguna, but after he dressed and left the hotel Tom called Chris Dietrich's office line and left a message, updating him on his safe arrival and his first meeting with the consigliere. "He's very intelligent," Tom said, "and very polished. He's agreed to talk to me. I don't know yet how much I'll learn. I doubt that he'll let anything slip by mistake. He's too clever for that. He'll tell me what he wants me to know but that may still be of some use. By the way, it would be better if you didn't call me at the hotel. The manager is very close to the consigliere and she could intercept anything you might say. Leave any messages on my cell. Thanks, Chief. I'll be back in touch regularly."

As he returned his phone to its black case and passed the Palazzo dei Duchi di Santo Stefano he thought he saw someone out of the corner of his eye, someone trying to keep pace with him but still look otherwise engaged. Then he thought of Santo Stefano and the endless pictures of the first martyr, being stoned to death.

TWENTY-FIVE

"You see, I am like an African griot," Orsini said. "I cannot tell any part of the story without telling the entire story and I must begin at the beginning … "

They were sitting at a large table in a quiet corner of one of the newer restaurants on the Corso Umberto, *La Baronessa*. Tom was eating their signature dish, sformatino, a layered pie with ricotta and aubergine, Orsini the millefoglie: swordfish layered paper-thin. They had switched from the local wine to a Gaja Barolo and were half-way through the second bottle.

"We called the old Don *The Mountain*. His name was Carlo Monte. To his face people said 'Don Carlo'. Everyone seemed to have three names: the legal name—surname and given name—the more familiar name, though still a title of respect, and the private name, which could be a term connoting love and respect or a term connoting . . . their opposites.

"He was a big man, in every sense of the term. Well over six feet in height and nearly three hundred pounds in weight. He would say 'nearly twenty stone'; it was not an affectation; he had been educated in England."

"That would be very rare at that time," Tom said.

"Yes, but he was a favorite of the Jesuits. He had been a student at Regis High School, in New York. All of these people began in New York. They sent him to Stonyhurst College for a year and then arranged for him to study at Oxford. They had their own house there and let him live with their seminarians. Later people teased him, saying that if he had stayed there he could have been an *Oxford* don. He studied literature and language. I was only a boy at the time, but I could see how special he was.

"His father was a good man, a leader of a small group, but the stress of the position weighed on him and he sometimes turned to drink. He retired early. He was not harmed in any way. He simply moved back from California to New York and lived out his days on an estate on Long Island. Don Carlo replaced him and the family businesses prospered in every conceivable way. The population of Orange County was very small in those days and there had been very little development. Just before the second world war there were only 130,000 people there, twenty years earlier less than half that many. The area had been part of Los Angeles, but it formed its own county when it felt that it was receiving less than its fair share of resources from the north. This was in the late 1880's. I'm sure you are aware of all this, for you have spent your life there."

"Yes," Tom said, "but I didn't see it change from an agricultural community in the way that you probably did."

Orsini nodded in agreement. "The war was extremely important. Two air bases were built—the Los Alamitos Naval Air Station and the Army Air Base in Santa Ana. In 1943 the El Toro Marine Base opened."

"And that brought business opportunities . . . of all kinds," Tom said.

"Yes. This is awkward, of course, but as you no doubt realize, the Monte family would see some of their activities in very different terms than strictly legalistic ones."

"Could you pursue that a little further ... " Tom asked.

"Of course. Many of the business enterprises which the family conducted were classified as illegal, but there are *legal* issues and *moral* ones. During prohibition it was suddenly illegal to make and sell wine, but not altar wine. It is not immoral to drink wine, if one does so in moderation, but it is sometimes illegal to do so. Prostitution is illegal, but not in Nevada. Gambling is illegal, but not in Nevada and not on the property of Native Americans. Lotteries are illegal if conducted on the streets, but not if they are controlled by the states. It would be illegal for you to smoke a Cuban cigar in Laguna Beach, but not in London or Rome. For that matter it would be illegal for you to smoke a cigarette in certain parts of Laguna Beach, but not in others.

"Several years ago I had some osteoarthritis in my foot and was taking naproxen to relieve it. I neglected to bring enough with me to London and tried to buy some over the counter. I was informed that that was a very strong drug and, as such, was carefully controlled in the United Kingdom. In America *Aleve* is now available everywhere. A few years prior to that I had a persistent rash that was controlled very effectively by a small dab of cortisone cream. In America any concentration greater than one half of one percent was sold only in prescription form. In England twice that concentration was readily available over the counter.

"I am not arguing for moral or cultural relativism," Orsini said. "I abhor relativism. What I am saying is that we humans have needs and desires; some are necessities, some are luxuries, and some of them are sources of pride while others may be sources of shame. Nonetheless, those needs and desires are accommodated by business enterprises. In some places and times they are legal. In some places and times they are not. However, those needs and desires persist and they are, inevitably, satisfied. That is what Don Carlo would have said if you had asked him about his businesses and he would have quickly added that he was aware that he could be casting these issues in the light most favorable to himself. 'I understand logic—its use and misuse,' he would say. 'Remember, I was educated by the Jesuit fathers, the pope's shock troops.'

"At any rate, the arrival of the troops did bring opportunities for Don Carlo. The families of Los Angeles were not known for their . . . shall we say, *effectiveness*, and they were closely watched by the organizations in the East and Midwest. Las Vegas, for example, was a great prize and it in particular was carefully guarded. Activities in Orange County were, in effect, subsidiaries of a subsidiary, but just as the County sought its independence from the north and the north's control, Don Carlo sought his own independence. It was a delicate line that he walked, but he was able to do so because of his efficiency and his personal integrity. I would not say that individuals from beyond our region did not seek to control him, but I would say that they realized how special he was and that economic realities sometimes trump the desire for control."

"Until the economic realities change," Tom said.

"Precisely," Orsini responded. "A percentage of something is *something*; a percentage of nothing is *nothing*. A percentage of something large is attractive. When it shrinks its beauty fades."

"Fundamentally, this is business," Tom said.

"Yes," Orsini said, "and when we talk of *business*—regular commercial enterprises--I would quickly point out that Don Carlo's arguments with regard to human needs and desires and practices also . . . apply."

"There is just as much *blood* spilled, but some of it is less *liquid*," Tom responded. "No, let me rephrase that. There are different kinds of actions, some more . . . *vivid* . . . than others, though they may be equal in their results. We need blood to carry oxygen to our hearts and brains, but we also need food and clothing and shelter. We must have a source of *livelihood*. If a man has a limb broken by a street soldier . . . that is more . . . *dramatic* than if a business competitor forces him to lose his livelihood or his reputation, but the results could be very similar, in some cases the latter being more severe."

"This is why I talk to you, Tom," Orsini said. "You understand these things. I am a lawyer. What do lawyers do? The lawyer for a man such as Don Carlo might find ways for him to operate within the law or to defend himself when he is accused of violating the law. He might represent him before people of influence, people whose decisions could go in any direction. What do other lawyers do? They suck the life's blood from clients in endless litigation. They destroy good people with frivolous lawsuits. They are evil characters out of Dickens, but *evil* nonetheless.

Which would you rather deal with? Which does the greatest harm to a society? It is a relative question, of course."

"But still, a good and fair question," Tom said.

"And when you say that," Orsini said, "I know that to some degree, perhaps to some considerable degree, you believe it. You believe it in your heart. You want to please me and you want me to talk with you; that is your job. But you are not a hypocrite, Tom. I would know that if you were. That is why I talk to you."

Tom took a drink of his wine and finished his sformatino. "However this goes . . . " he said.

"Yes?"

"You must continue to pick the restaurants and offer advice with regard to what we eat and drink there."

Orsini smiled. "This is heaven, is it not?" He then signaled the waiter and ordered coffee. "Dolce tonight?" he asked Tom. "The zuppa inglese here is very, very nice."

"How about limoncello instead?"

"You see, you have needs and desires," Orsini said.

"I do, indeed."

"Trust me, these people here . . . they know just how to satisfy them."

The limoncello was kept in a large jug with a noticeable crack at the lip. The waiter left the full bottle on the table, with two small crystal glasses. "You see . . . authentic," Orsini said.

"That *is* a good sign," Tom said. "It is homemade."

"Oh yes. You wait. It will be exquisite in its simplicity," he said.

"So tell me, Giancarlo, what happened to the Don?"

"Ah, that is very sad."

TWENTY-SIX

"He was not perfect. You should not have the impression that he was a saint or that he never did anything wrong. There were certainly times when he upset us. For one thing, he had a very bad temper. He kept it under control most of the time, but there were moments in which he exhibited it and those who were unfortunate enough to be in his presence at the time talked of those moments for years. He could also swear like a dock worker, though never in the company of women or children. He could also be disorganized, waiting to finish things until the very last moment. I have to say, however, that many of his faults were the obverse side of his virtues. His approach to life was passionate and robust. He had an enthusiasm for things that was simply remarkable. He always seemed happy, always engaged, at the end of his seat, with his hands in the air and his eyes flashing. Most of all—and this is very important--he was never *small*. Not in his actions. Not in his words. And never in his generosity. His anger usually grew out of his impatience and his frustration. It was not meanness of spirit but . . . disappointment that he was not surrounded by . . . *fullness*. Does that make any sense to you?"

"Yes. He was the sort of person who packed several lifetimes into one and cherished every moment."

"Precisely. And any moment that was lost or wasted was a terrible thing to him. So many of us . . . we assume that life will have its dull points, that the day will chiefly consist of drudgery and trivia, but that, if we are lucky, there will be a bright moment or two. Don Carlo was just the opposite. He assumed that life was an unending feast or holiday and that the intrusion of anything less, anything that reduced life's joys—in any way and to any degree—was not just unacceptable, but absolutely intolerable."

"But you were very young at the time," Tom said. "You must have heard others say this."

"Yes, they all said it, but I was old enough to see these things in him. If you entered a room and he was not yet there you could feel the incompleteness. It was like a table without wine or a morning without the smell of coffee. And his eyes! When he looked at you it was as if his eyes were spotlights and you were at the center of the universe. And when you looked at him you could see all of the joy and all of the intelligence and all of the wisdom in the man. As I told you, he was a big man, a very big man, but he always seemed to be in motion. Even when he was reading a book he seemed to be moving. He was gripping the cover, staring at the words in each chapter, squeezing the corner of each page, pulling the beauty and the meaning from it as if they were trapped there and needed to be freed . . .

"When he died there was a private viewing of his body. Just for the family. I was allowed to attend. We each went into the room by ourselves. It was as if we would each have one last meeting with him.

"I will never forget it. It still haunts me. You know, of course, that when you die it is very difficult to counter the effects of gravity. The sides of your mouth fall. Even if it is just a little, it is noticeable. You see it around the eyes and in the cheekbones. It is as if the soul has escaped and the skin has shrunk and fallen as it left. One expects it. Even as a young man I expected it, for I had seen others in death.

"I walked into the room and he was lying on a cushioned table. I have never in my life seen anyone so *still*. For me he had always been in motion. He was more *alive* than anyone I had ever seen, including my own parents and my brother and sister. His hands were folded across his stomach and his fingers were absolutely motionless. His eyes were closed. His lips were closed. Everything about him had changed. I cannot say that it was as if he was totally transformed, for it was clearly Don Carlo's body. And he did not appear to be in pain. And there *had been* pain. It was inoperable cancer, after all (very much like my brother's). You hear these clichés about death, but this was very different. No one has ever been so still to me, because no one had ever been so real and so alive."

"And you were how old, Giancarlo?"

"I was little more than a child—in my early teens."

"And this was not just the loss of a great friend. It was the loss of an . . . organization or institution."

"It was the loss of everything, Tom. Don Carlo's successor was to be his brother Gino. He was younger, by eleven years even, but he was sick as well. Don Carlo had cancer of the liver at a time when transplants were not even contemplated and his brother Gino had cancer of the lungs. We were more aware of Gino's illness than Don Carlo's, since he was hospitalized for weeks in Los Angeles. We had already prepared ourselves for his death and then we lost Don Carlo as well."

"And there was no other successor?"

"There *was*, but he was not immediately available. He was not a blood relative, but he was a close friend. A trusted friend. A man who commanded respect and even affection. His name was Vincente Mastrapaolo. I had not met him, but I heard my father speak of him. He had been part of Don Carlo's family but he was then in New York and he simply could not be spared. Everyone wanted Vincente but he could not be in two places at once; New York wanted him and at that time everyone in California sought New York's blessing and avoided its disapproval.

"Vincente wanted to come but he simply could not. 'Perhaps in a year,' he said. 'I will do all that I can to make it sooner.' That is what he said but everyone knew that he would not be permitted to leave. If Vincente Mastrapaolo had become the Don it would have still been very different. Don Carlo was irreplaceable, but Vincente would have maintained the independence which Don Carlo had achieved and he would have led the family successfully. These are very realistic people, Tom. You understand that. They take your measure very quickly. They knew that the old Don was dead and that their lives would never be the same, but they believed that their lives would still be good, because Vincente understood the family and he understood the . . . life. He knew what was expected of a Don and he would be capable of *doing* what was expected."

"So this situation was extremely rare," Tom said. "Normally if there was no natural successor there would be immediate conflict among those aspiring to take his place."

"But there was no such conflict, Tom, only a great sense of loss. The situation *was* unprecedented. It was like a political vacancy—a presidency, even--with no available candidates. Don Carlo had one great *fault*, or so it might be termed in retrospect. He was so successful and so beloved that no one considered the possibility that he could ever be lost. Least of all, Don Carlo. He was only 64 at the time and his brother Gino was only 53. He had not made any plans for his own succession because Gino was there and he was the picture of health and vigor until just before the end. I would not criticize Don Carlo. He was so beautiful, so full of life. How could he turn himself into a bureaucrat? There were ranks, of course, but the family operated on a sense of collective will and expectation. Everything was going so well that no one faced the fact that it could all end."

"And it *did* end."

"It was systematically destroyed, Tom. It fell apart piece by piece and stone by stone."

"Are you saying that individuals wanted to see it destroyed?"

"There may have been some of that, but it principally died because of the vanity and incompetence of the man who followed Don Carlo."

"Victor Brienza," Tom said.

"*You* speak his name," Giancarlo said. "I would prefer not to. When I do I feel as if I need to clean my teeth and tongue afterwards. I will tell you that story tomorrow. My heart is full with thoughts of Don Carlo and I do not want to discuss that man now."

TWENTY-SEVEN

He had planned to meet Giancarlo for lunch, but Gina informed him that there had been a change of plans and that would not be possible. Tom wondered if the consigliere was manipulating him. Later that afternoon he called Chris Dietrich and told him of their conversations.

"It sounds as if he's opening up to you," Chris said.

"Yes, but it's hard to say whether it's simple openness or part of some larger design. He's very intelligent, Chief. He weighs every word before he speaks. When he expresses emotion he does so with great honesty and plausibility, but I always have the feeling that I'm in the presence of a polished actor. He *could* have been an actor, really. He has the flare and the persona. Half the time I expect to see him wearing a cape or carrying a walking stick."

"Maybe it's a status thing. He has to project that role to command respect."

"If so, it's working. Everyone who comes in contact with him nearly falls at his feet and I don't have the sense that they're doing so out of fear. There seems to be real love and admiration … "

"He hasn't talked about Sullivan yet … "

"No. He's just getting to Sullivan's boss, the person who replaced Carlo Monte as head of the family."

"Brienza."

"Yes."

"Tell me what he says."

"I will, Chief," Tom said and clicked off.

Dinner that evening was to be at *A'Zammara* on the Via Fratelli Bandiera—a rustic place with unpretentious, hearty food. Tom had meatballs wrapped in lemon leaves; Giancarlo had veal involtini. The wine was from the slopes of the volcano. "Much of Sicily is relatively barren," Giancarlo said, "but the soil around Etna is very rich and produces great fruit. I think you will enjoy this dry red wine."

"It's excellent," Tom said. "I trust your business went well today."

"Oh yes," Giancarlo said. "It was an appointment with my physician. I had neglected to note it, but my assistant reminded me. I am fine . . . all things considered."

"We were talking about Don Carlo and about his successor."

"Yes. Hyperion to a satyr. That's what Hamlet says. Don Carlo might be compared with Hyperion, but Victor Brienza was no satyr. The satyr is very sexual, you know. Victor Brienza was in love only with himself. They called him *the Model* because he was always staring at himself in the mirror. Some even called him *Marcel,* because of his hair. He had little waves in it, like the black men with brilliantine. Do you know what I mean?"

"Yes. Did he actually put that on his hair?"

"There were rumors to that effect. I know that he combed it constantly and when it grew thin above his forehead he positioned it very carefully. It was silver and blond, though, not black. He looked as if he was made up for a play. He was very . . . fastidious. That would be a polite way of describing him. He also had delicate health and drank chalky substances before each meal. He was really much more like an old woman than like a man. He weighed himself constantly and when the results were not to his liking he would order his underlings to remove his scale and get him a new one. He had a special suit that he wore to important meetings and he had his assistants help him with all of the accessories that accompanied it."

"It sounds as if he enjoyed the role."

"That is *exactly* what it was to him, Tom. It was not a duty or a responsibility. It was a *role*. And he *loved* it. He would find reasons to play it. He increased the number of family business meetings and he was always anxious to attend a wedding or baptism or funeral. Wherever he went he wanted to be the focus of everyone's attention. If it was a baptism and he was not asked to serve as the child's godfather he was very disappointed, even angry. There are more pictures of this man than of a modern film star. His vanity was endless and that is the proper word, not *pride*, not *self-esteem*, not *confidence*. It was never anything but simple vanity. You see, his parents had been wealthy … "

"In the same business?" Tom asked.

"No. They were importers. Very successful. They would have birthday parties for him in New York ballrooms. It is the sort of thing that a small person never gets over. He comes to believe that he is as important to everyone as he believed himself to be to his parents. When others do not treat him in that fashion he wonders why. He combs his hair a second time; he changes his clothing; he alters his smile. If he is still unsuccessful he replaces those who stand around him with individuals who will stare at him with greater attention. One now sees stories of spoiled celebrities—fodder for the tabloid press. If he were here now he would seek to take their place. He was only comfortable when the lights were shining on him, but there was a great irony there, for when the lights *were* on him he showed himself for precisely what he was: a complete and utter fool.

"For example, he was unable to speak without notes. I am not talking about long and complex speeches, Tom. I am talking about simple greetings: *Good evening. I am so happy you could join us for this dinner in which we honor our friends, Giancarlo and Tom. Please be seated. Buon Appetito!* As God is my judge, Tom, he could not say those few words without a set of cards to prompt him. He held them in his hands nervously, shuffling them and making a fool of himself. Don Carlo spoke in paragraphs. He spoke like a poet. Giuseppe di Lampedusa met him once and said to him that he could have written *Il Gattapardo*. 'It would have been better,' he said, 'if you had done so.' Brienza could barely write his name without assistance. He would ask his underlings to draft simple correspondence for him. And, remarkably, it somehow served to feed his vanity. The worse he appeared the more acclaim he sought."

"He was in Signore *Monte's* shadow."

"Yes, Tom, that metaphor was not overlooked. The comparisons were so obvious and they were always to Brienza's disadvantage. I will tell you how small a man he was. As a birthday present for his brother, Gino Monte commissioned an oil portrait. It was very handsome. It did not have all of the power and personality that Don Carlo projected in person, but it came close. They hung it in the building that the family used for meetings. When Brienza succeeded Don Carlo he had it removed. He said that it was being repaired, but I know that he had it destroyed."

"Tell me, Giancarlo," Tom said, "how could such a man be selected to serve in that important capacity?"

"How do such things ever happen, Tom? Politics. Politics pure and simple. The man had no worth, but he had the proper connections and people believed that they could manipulate him. And they were right. They *did* manipulate him. What they failed to realize was that in manipulating him they were destroying all that Don Carlo had built. And they did not care, because they were so selfish, but, eventually, they *did* come to care … "

"When they began to disappear?"

Giancarlo smiled. "I will come to that. And I will tell you what I know. But first we must have something sweet, something that will remove the taste of Brienza from our mouths. You must taste some Malvasia. It comes from Lipari and it is very rare. We call it *drinkable gold*."

TWENTY-EIGHT

"I repeat my wish, Giancarlo, you must be my wine consultant forever."

The consigliere smiled. "It *is* lovely, isn't it? Now, where was I? Ah yes, the selection of Victor Brienza as Don. As I told you, the family wanted Vincente Mastrapaolo, but that was not to be. Victor had worked too hard to secure the position. He had dedicated all of his energies to the task. He had planned for months. I will give him that much credit. He *campaigned* for it with all of his heart. He had talked to the heads of all of the families in New York and Kansas City and Detroit. He had promised to never set foot in Las Vegas and he had promised to wash the feet of the people in Los Angeles. He compared himself to a doctor who would first *do no harm*."

"But that would be immediately perceived as a sign of weakness," Tom interjected.

"Of course. And it endeared him to all of them. He would open his businesses to them and all that they would need to do was hold their wallets open as he dropped the money in. Plus, he was Sicilian. I would quickly add that he was Sicilian by blood but not by culture; he was raised in New York. Still, it makes a great difference. Think of it this way. If Notre Dame appointed a Jew as its president it would be an admission that there were no Catholics in the world competent to serve. The heads of the other families believed that they had to have a Sicilian because it was essential that the don—even the don of a small, remote family--*understand* the tradition in which he was working. Had they been challenged, that is the explanation that they would have given, and they would have argued that understanding the tradition would trump Brienza's palpable shortcomings with regard to competence and experience. The problem with Victor Brienza is that he did *not* understand the tradition; he was a fool who understood *nothing*. He had never been a street soldier; he had never been a captain, a counselor, or what the tabloids like to call an underboss. He had been in charge of investments for one of the New York families."

"A money launderer?"

"Let us just say that he handled *investments*," Giancarlo said. "He had a small staff—all green-eyeshade men. This was like being a small shopkeeper in a company town. There were no significant management responsibilities and no significant challenges. The entities which directly handled the investments were chosen—and managed—by others. Victor Brienza was little more than a bookkeeper, but he worked hard at being a pleasant bookkeeper. He bowed and scraped and satisfied the right people. They were *comfortable* with him; they *knew* him. But there was nothing else there; he was an empty suit of clothes. I know that I have my biases but you must believe me--I am not exaggerating when I say that he was a complete nonentity … "

"But that was the point," Tom said. "He was *their* nonentity and they could count on him to do their bidding. He owed his position to them and his position was very important to him."

"More important than anything, as I suggested earlier. The situation is quite understandable and one can see how he was appointed. I should not say *appointed*; he was forced on Don Carlo's family, but then they were made to believe that there was really no other person suitable, so it was presented to them as something natural and reasonable."

"But ultimately this would be doomed to failure," Tom said, "because the other families would be gaining access to a shrinking operation. If he was truly incompetent the pie would get smaller and smaller. Better to have a much smaller share of an operation that was certain to grow geometrically."

"The depth of their error was incalculable, Tom. No, I take that back; it was quite calculable. In Orange County in 1950, there were 200,000 people. By 1987, there were 2,000,000. This was the opportunity of a lifetime. And the details of the operations there could never really be controlled from Detroit or Kansas City or even Los Angeles. They had to be watched and nourished and enhanced, particularly in a time of growth. Even if you had someone there who could be manipulated, it was still essential that that person be highly competent."

"So why didn't they remove him?" Tom asked.

"Because he was their man. To admit his failure was to admit their own failure. I have talked to the people from those times. 'Every day,' they would say, 'we expected to see him removed. It is how we survived. It was unthinkable to us that he could be allowed to continue. He was a complete fool. But then . . . after ten years . . . we realized that he was not going to be removed.' Instead the others systematically inserted themselves into the operation."

"They micro-managed him."

"Yes. They tried to. They went so far as to control his personal staff. They controlled his disbursal of funds among his captains. And he *tolerated* it. But then, of course *he* would. Tell me, Tom, have you ever seen the film, *The Hill?*"

"The Sean Connery film. With the sergeant who kept running men up and down the artificial hill."

"Exactly, and Connery's character confronts him. Do you remember what he said to him?"

"Something to the effect that he would do anything to be able to wear a uniform."

"Yes. He said he was the sort who would become a *dustman* if he could then wear a uniform."

"A garbage collector."

"Yes. *That* was Victor Brienza. He would do anything, *anything* that would enable him to act as if he were a don."

"The pity is that he actually *was*."

"Yes, officially, but whenever anyone looked at him they would say to themselves that he would never have been hired to serve at the *lowest levels* of the organization. And yet, he was at the *top*. I will tell you a story, Tom, and it is a story that you must promise not to repeat."

"Yes … "

"When a person's relationship with this organization is to be *formalized* … "

"Yes?"

"There is a ritual that that individual undergoes. It is quite moving and sometimes very dramatic. It always proceeds in the same manner. First he cuts his finger. Then he spills his blood onto a sacred image. This would usually be a representation of some saint. The image is placed in the initiate's hand and it is set on fire. The initiate must withstand the pain, passing the image from hand to hand until it is consumed. At the same time he must swear 'may my flesh burn like this saint if I ever fail to keep my oath', that is—his oath to keep faith with the principles of the organization."

"Yes?"

"When Victor Brienza took this oath he was practically in tears--not from emotion at the importance of the oath, but from the pain of the burning statue. He nearly choked on the words. And you must realize, Tom, that this is a point of honor for those being so initiated. They are surrounded by those with whom they will stand. All eyes are on them. It is a test, a test that no man would want to fail. They made jokes about Victor Brienza. They said that the statue must have been that of a virgin, because he himself was a complete virgin with regard to the work of the organization. They said that he juggled like a master and cried like a baby. There were even rumors that he had obtained some dental anesthetic and had his hands injected with it to reduce the pain."

"Really?"

"Yes, Tom, really."

"That's quite a story, Giancarlo."

"Yes, Tom. It also has the virtue of being true."

"He seems so utterly different from the impressions that most have of this . . . *organization*."

"He *was*, Tom. The Sicilian adjective is *mafiusu*; it comes from the Arabic word, *mahjas*. It suggests many things. Those who belong to this organization focus on the associations that that word has with *pride*, with *honor*, and with *social responsibility*. One of its principal purposes, after all, was to protect the weak from the powerful. There are other connotations, however, suggesting the propensity to boast or to brag. I would say it is fair to associate the word with *bravado* or with the tendency to *swagger*. There are many, many connotations, Tom, but none of them could possibly be associated with someone like Victor Brienza. It would be comparable to the difference between a Welsh coal miner and a male hair stylist. I am not saying that he was homosexual. That would be unfair to those people. He was in love with himself, as I told you earlier."

"As you said, Giancarlo, he was a man of vanity, not a man of pride. There is a great difference between the two."

"Precisely. And I acknowledge that pride is one of the seven deadly sins, Tom. But of which would you choose to be accused?"

Tom took a drink of his wine.

"We must have more of that," Giancarlo said, and signaled to the waiter. "If am to tell you of Brienza's man Sullivan, I must have more to drink. I have had to exhibit bravery in my time, Tom, but speaking of these two together in the same evening tests even me." He smiled as he finished the few drops remaining in his glass.

"You see," he said, "I am telling you more than you thought that I would."

"Yes," Tom said, "and every word is fascinating, but in its way very sad."

"What I am giving you, Tom, is what the lawyers would call a *case study*. The sins, the failings, the stupidity . . . the courage . . . these could appear in any organization. *That* is why I wished to talk to you, not to explain the problems that could beset our organization, but to explain the problems that could beset any organization that required virtue and strength and instead received foolishness and vanity. I feel it deeply, of course, but my personal feelings are less important than the *lessons* which this experience has taught me."

TWENTY-NINE

"Gray Sullivan worked for Owney Madden in the thirties ... "

"In the Irish mob . . . in Hell's Kitchen," Tom said.

"Yes. They were sometimes called the *Westies*. Madden was an interesting fellow. Like Gotti later he was known for his expensive suits. His principal operations involved bootleg liquor, nightclubs, taxicabs, and laundries. He even had an interest in the Cotton Club and a piece of Primo Carnera, the boxer and, later, wrestler. Luciano made him the representative of the Irish organization in New York.

"Sullivan actually worked directly for Eddie McGrath, who was Madden's principal bootlegger. He succeeded Madden in the forties and fifties before retiring to Florida. He was particularly known for his ties with politicians and unions. That's where Sullivan came in. He had gone to school at Brown and had a law degree from Yale. He brought class and connections to the organization and enabled McGrath to make inroads in groups that would normally be closed to him.

"What they all liked about Sullivan—in addition to his surname, of course--was that he was a person with no scruples whatsoever. When it came to his own success or survival the man was absolutely ruthless, particularly with regard to the powerless. If he was confronted by one of his equals or superiors such as Cockeye Dunn or Squint Sheridan he would pull back into his shell and let them have their way, even if he had to undergo some humiliation in the process. He would say things like, 'I'm just an advisor. Mr. McGrath is in charge.' However, whenever he had the chance to exercise authority over underlings or control the weak and defenseless he stepped on them as if they were insects."

"So he was a coward *and* a bully," Tom said.

"Yes, as such men so often are. And he seemed to particularly enjoy the bullying, though publicly he always deferred to McGrath and, earlier, Madden. He was, quintessentially, the man behind the scenes, but he had some limited line responsibilities and when he exercised them he did so with violence and a noticeable meanness of spirit."

"How did he get from New York to California?" Tom asked.

"It was very simple," Giancarlo said. "The people in New York quickly realized that Victor Brienza was an ineffectual fool and they forced Sullivan on him. I couldn't read their minds, of course, but I always assumed that they believed that Sullivan would prop up Brienza and run the operations behind the scenes while he primped in front of the mirror and went out to dinner with his entourage. As an Irishman his position was very awkward and that would *force* him behind the scenes, even if he aspired to a more prominent role. They also counted on the fact that he would be an earner no matter what the cost. If he had to crush people or eliminate them he would always be up to the task. In fact, that is exactly how Brienza used him. Sullivan even described himself as 'the Don's son-of-a-bitch.' Some people even called him 'Sonny' as a result."

"An Irishman in a Sicilian organization . . . I suppose stranger things have happened," Tom said.

"As a counselor it would be odd, but not impossible," Giancarlo said. "The striking thing in this case was that Brienza went so far as to make him underboss. *No one* understood that. Particularly when he made Billy Mush consigliere, but that's another story. I'll get to him later.

"An Irish underboss was simply incomprehensible. This made him the heir apparent and that was something that no one in the organization could understand. It also put him at risk, of course."

"But from what you've said he was probably a survivor … " Tom said.

"Yes, he was," Giancarlo said. "For awhile."

"So he was actually controlling the family."

"Not so much the family as the operations," Giancarlo said. "He allowed Brienza to play the role of Don and deferred to him whenever anyone else was in their presence. It was an interesting balancing act, because the Model had actually asked Sullivan to run meetings for him. *In his presence.* I'm not talking about when Brienza was unavailable. He was *there*, Tom. The family would assemble. Brienza would sit at the head or center of the table and then turn to Sullivan and ask him to conduct the meeting."

"That's incredible," Tom said.

"The pretense was that Brienza wanted to give his full attention to the substance of the meeting and not be distracted by procedural details, but that was, of course, preposterous … "

"These were not formal sessions with minutes and memoranda or Robert's Rules of Order," Tom said.

"No, not hardly," Giancarlo said, smiling. "More like the meetings with President Lincoln when he responded to the unanimous nays by striking the table and saying 'the ayes have it'."

Tom smiled. "You would know far better than I would, Giancarlo, but my assumption would be that the purpose of these meetings would be to . . . exercise leadership . . . not indulge in democratic experiments or sing *Kumbaya*."

Now Giancarlo smiled more broadly. "There would be discussion," he said. "And reports. The family had multiple enterprises and different individuals had responsibility for those enterprises. Don Carlo or, later, my brother Dominic would inquire about the success of those enterprises and about impediments to success and the ways in which those impediments could be addressed, but it was imperative that the Don be in charge, because he held the final decision and his views were paramount."

"But under the other organization—with Brienza sitting silently and Sullivan conducting the business … "

"Yes?"

"There would be impasses," Tom said. "Unless the answers were obvious and Brienza could simply nod his head, he would be forced to consult with Sullivan and he would not want to do that in front of his captains."

"Precisely," Giancarlo said. "After an awkward silence these matters would be deferred."

"And that would result in more and more things being done behind the scenes, which, in turn, would create suspicion and paranoia."

"Yes, so it would seem to me," Giancarlo said. "Mind you, I did not attend these meetings, though I heard from individuals who in turn had heard from individuals who were there."

"Carryovers from Don Carlo's family."

"Yes."

"Their presence must have been awkward," Tom said. "After working with a person of great competence they must have been nonplussed at what they saw and heard."

"Indeed," Giancarlo said. "That is why they did not last long … "

THIRTY

"Some simply retired. They kissed the Model's ring, bowed three times, and departed. Many moved back to New York, a few to Florida. Some were forced out . . . with varying degrees of urgency."

"The fact that they had been associated with Don Carlo would have been a considerable liability," Tom said.

"Yes. Brienza was a fool, but he was intelligent enough to realize that people were constantly making comparisons between his ineptitude and Don Carlo's success. The bottom lines spoke for themselves. He also knew that each time he spoke and stumbled and slurred his way through simple speeches those who were forced to listen to him heard Don Carlo's words in their heads and were appalled by Brienza's incoherence."

"The only real solution was to remove all of them and substitute wholly new people, people who had no basis for comparison," Tom said.

"Yes, but a situation like this is very awkward. Individuals have families; they have responsibilities. Some have sick parents. While some could just pick up and leave, others could not. They were forced to endure him, at least for awhile, and they did their best to treat him with the respect due his office. He would sense their discomfort and the situation would be that much worse. Gray Sullivan, on the other hand, would enjoy their discomfort, but Brienza was not a sadist. He was simply an inept, vain fool."

"Catholics speak of sins of omission and sins of commission," Tom said. "Brienza would have specialized in the former, Sullivan in the latter."

"Yes, exactly, and since a don must act and Brienza could not, he was dependent on Sullivan for all decision making and with those decisions came a host of attendant crimes. Structures had to be maintained and Brienza could not do it. He hardly even understood the organization and its enterprises. But when Sullivan erected structures or replaced those that had preceded them, his actions always seemed to bring additional damage. Change itself is always difficult and those who embrace it are generally those who are certain that they will benefit from it. When Sullivan brought change it was always accompanied by cruelty and heartbreak. Sometimes, of course, it would be accompanied by the spilling of blood, but at the least it would bring a sort of heartsick nausea. *Ripugnanza.*

"You must remember that their operations were always failing. They were not embracing new opportunities and looking toward better days. They were clutching at what was falling through their fingers and Sullivan's response was to grasp tighter and squeeze harder. And there were expectations … "

"The other families demanded their portions," Tom said. "If the pie expanded they wanted the same percentage. If the pie contracted they wanted the same number of dollars."

"Yes. They are not like quiet stockholders who will accept whatever they are told. It was very difficult … "

"It is always hard when you are asked to work more in return for less," Tom said. "But if you are told to work more in return for less, with threats hanging over you as well … "

"Yes, and it was very unfair. They were blessed for awhile, but then they destroyed that blessing. There was a man who had worked for Don Carlo. He was one of Don Carlo's captains, a very effective man. His name was Barone. Thomas Barone. They called him Tommy Barone or Tommy B. He was a magnificent earner. And he was very fair and very sparing in his use of violence. He offered services at a fair price and the services were of high quality. I spoke of those who were unable to leave … "

"Yes … "

"Tommy could not. His wife's mother was ill and could not be moved. It was a lingering illness. In fact, she lingered for nearly twenty years. Tommy promised Victor Brienza that he would be loyal to him and earn money for him, which he did. But that was not enough. When other operations declined or failed, Brienza demanded more of Tommy. Tommy explained—politely, and with all respect—that he could only do so much and that failing operations had to be closed or altered. He could not—singlehandedly--carry the entire organization.

"Brienza did not know what to do. He was intelligent enough, one supposes, to realize that once you tax an individual into poverty there is nothing left to tax, but where is the tipping point, as we now say? He turned to Sullivan for advice, but like the fool that he was, he assumed that Sullivan would actually try to help him, whereas Sullivan was more interested in punishing Barone than in helping his don or his organization. In fact he *hated* Barone. Many said he hated him because he so envied him. There was also some bad blood from the past. Sullivan had made some request of Barone (I am not certain of the details) and Barone had rebuffed him ... "

"So Sullivan wanted revenge," Tom said.

"Yes, and—as he always did—he wanted to exact something else. He wanted Barone humiliated. He wanted his reputation as a great earner ruined. When Barone was unable to make bricks without straw Sullivan would suggest, quietly, that the man was actually incompetent. He had names for him, names which he would only use with Brienza. Remember—he was at heart a coward."

"So what happened?" Tom asked.

"Sullivan persuaded Brienza that Barone was disloyal. He had resisted the confiscatory taxes that were to be imposed on him and Sullivan portrayed him as contemptuous of Brienza's authority. He 'pushed all of his buttons', Tom. He told Brienza that Barone did not respect him. He accused him of mocking him. He told him that it was Barone who had called Brienza *Marcel* and *the Model* ... "

How would Orsini know all this, Tom wondered. Either he was making it up to enhance his story or he had some source—some very *high* source—who had informed him. Tom made a mental note, but let the consigliere continue.

"You must remember, Tom, that Sullivan's position was always tenuous and that he was always anxious to preserve it in any way that he could. Barone was the one person within the organization who was capable of actually *running* it and if he was ever asked to do so, the first thing that he would do is eliminate Sullivan. While the men from the old days made comparisons between Don Carlo and Brienza, the new men made comparisons between Brienza's failure and Tommy's success. Sullivan was seen as a simple extension of Brienza. It was commonly said that no one could trace the line between the two and see where one ended and the other began. Barone was thus a bona fide threat to both. Sullivan realized that and convinced Brienza that Barone would have to be eliminated."

"Killed."

"Yes, but with malice, given Sullivan's jealousy. You should also know that Brienza had served as godfather to Barone's son, Andrea. He had made protestations about how close they were and how dearly he loved Barone and the members of his family. Later, Andrea died. It was very tragic. He was only six years old. A freak accident. Brienza attended the funeral. He had a black cashmere suit made especially for the occasion. He covered the casket (it was a small one—so sad) in roses and nearly acted as if he was the boy's father. Now he was prepared to *kill* the boy's father.

"I believe that the normal way to do this would be simple and straightforward—a single bullet to the brain. The other captains would be informed that he had been stealing from the family and, regrettably, that could not be accepted. He had been an excellent earner in his time, but, well, that time had unfortunately passed and now they would all move on.

"Sullivan urged otherwise. He said that they should make an example of Barone, particularly for the disloyalty and disrespect which he had shown his don. And so . . . he was beaten to death. Mercilessly."

"But a man who commanded such respect . . . who would be willing to do that?"

"There was a man," Giancarlo said, "a man who was willing to do anything … "

THIRTY-ONE

"The surprising thing, Tom, was that he was not some thickheaded, broad-shouldered enforcer. He was more of a ferret or weasel, perhaps a bit of both. He even had their look, though I must say he favored the weasel, with his weak chin. He was no taller than 5'8" and weighed no more than 140 pounds. You are probably wondering how a little man like that could beat a man like Tommy Barone to death … "

Tom nodded.

"He had accomplices. People who would do whatever he asked them to do. And if all that I heard about him was true, he probably stabbed Tommy first or shot him—anything to weaken him enough so that he could not strike back."

"You haven't mentioned his name, Giancarlo."

The consigliere paused and took a drink of the sweet dessert wine. "His name was Devito. James Devito, actually, but no one ever called him that. They called him Jimmy to his face; behind his back they called him 'J. C.' Not because he was Christian. Far from it. They called him 'J. C.' because he looked as if he had bought his clothes at *J. C. Penney's*. I have never seen anyone dress so badly in all of my long life. He bought shirts based on price rather than size. Whenever the store announced that they would hold a sale he would immediately reach for his wallet. It was the only time he would buy anything. Sometimes the collars on his shirts were so large that you could put four fingers between them and his neck. At other times they were so tight that he had difficulty turning his head. He paired them with cheap ties, cheap belts, and cheap shoes.

"When I first saw him I thought that he looked like a poor farmer who only wore a suit and tie on rare occasions. Perhaps, I thought, he inherited those clothes and could not afford better, but I was wrong. It was not that he was poor. He was simply cheap and he had no taste. He *did* have ambition however. It was the one thing that he possessed in abundance."

"Was he an . . . assassin, Giancarlo?" Tom asked.

"No, no. He was little more than an assistant, though he acted like a slave or a servant—the kind of bad servant one sees in Shakespeare, the minor character always ready to do the bidding of his master, no matter how evil. He was Muschina's man; I will tell you about him later."

"Muschina was ... ?"

"One of Brienza's captains, initially."

"Right. So Brienza sought Sullivan's help; Sullivan formally sought Muschina's help and Muschina directly sought Devito's ... "

"Yes, and they were all perfect for the task. Muschina would do anything to advance himself by serving Sullivan or Brienza and Devito would do anything to help himself by serving Muschina. The fact that Sullivan and Brienza had specifically suggested Devito's help and might reward his service handsomely provided even greater incentives for him.

"You see, he was not even what the journalists call a 'made man.' He was a petty criminal who aspired to become a member of the family. Muschina used him whenever it was convenient to do so."

"Was he ever invited to join the family?" Tom asked.

"I will tell you about that when the time is right," Giancarlo said. "Remember, I have to tell the complete story, with all of the details in order. I want you to see the pattern . . . the structure. It is all like a drama, Tom. It is like the *Divina Commedia*, or at least two-thirds of it. We began with paradise and then we experienced hell. Finally we will see ... "

"What, Giancarlo?" Tom asked.

"Justice," he answered.

"That is what we all seek," Tom said.

"Yes, that is why I knew you would enjoy the story, Tom. But that is enough for one night. If I talk until I am hoarse I will not be able to conduct my other business. I am a lawyer, remember. That would take away my livelihood."

"I understand. I want you to know that I *am* enjoying your story and I am enjoying your company as well."

"And I yours," Giancarlo said.

The moment Tom returned to his room he started up his laptop and began making notes. An hour later he called Chris Dietrich.

"He's really opening up, Chief."

"In what way, Tom?"

"He's talking about who ordered hits, about who was killed and about who actually did it."

"Are you writing this all down?"

"I'm putting it on my laptop, but I'm making some paper-and-pen notes as well. If I lose the electronic data I want to have a backup, something I can use to help me reconstruct the account."

"Has he said anything about Sullivan's death yet?"

"No. He's filling in all the background first."

"I wonder if he took the oath of silence. He must have. Why would he open up like this?"

"He's much more guarded when he talks about his direct associates, Chief, or when he talks about those he admired and respected. Right now he's talking about the Brienza regime."

"And he's not holding back."

"No. He holds most of them in contempt. *Hate* is not too strong a word. Before I forget, here's something that you should check. He has explicitly blamed the murder of a man named Tommy Barone on a man named James Devito."

"Just a second … " Dietrich said.

He returned in a little over a minute. "Barone's body was recovered.

He was strongly suspected of being connected with the mob, but he was never indicted or arrested."

"How did he die, Chief?"

"He was found in a ditch off the highway in the Mojave. He had been beaten to death. Nearly every bone in his legs, arms, and chest was broken. There were bloodied pieces of lead pipe found next to the body."

"Anything on Devito?"

"He was arrested for a series of crimes—burglary, rape, manslaughter, a few smaller things when he was younger. He actually did time for perjury."

"Is there a picture in the file?"

"Yes. Taken when he was in his late twenties."

"What does he look like?"

"Like a rat."

"How about a weasel?"

"Yeah, that would work," Dietrich said. "Does this square with what Orsini told you?"

"Yes, exactly."

"That's a good sign."

"What finally happened to him, Chief? Is there anything there in the record?

"No, it looks as if he simply disappeared."

THIRTY-TWO

The next day was hectic, with Gina informing Tom that the Signore had an unexpected meeting in Messina and would be unable to dine with him that evening. Tom took the opportunity to flesh out his notes and polish them, adding any details that he could pull up. He confined himself to his room and confined his diet to a succession of carafes of black coffee and an occasional dry roll. His narrative now stretched to nearly forty pages. He added sidebar comments concerning Giancarlo's statement that the story might best be seen as a three-act drama. At this point in their discussions most of the actual facts fell into the second act. The first section—the description of Carlo Monte—was long on idealization and short on detail.

In some ways that was to be expected. The consigliere was a young man at the time. The foundation of his story consisted of a collection of reminiscences from his elders, most of them, doubtless, wistful and rose-tinged. First and foremost, Don Carlo was a great man who died. The fact that it happens to all of us did not counterbalance the effects of its suddenness or excuse the fact that there had been no contingency plan in the event of its occurrence. Those who felt its effects most dearly considered it to be no less than a full-blown tragedy.

Among the people discussed by Giancarlo, Barone was particularly interesting—the key link between the family of Don Carlo and that of the vain individual who had succeeded him. Giancarlo told Barone's story at some length and in some detail. Surely there must have been others who stayed on, at least for awhile. And surely there must have been many other examples of friction and reprisal. Giancarlo had hinted at this in a series of generalizations, but none were tied to a specific name in the way that they were tied to Tommy Barone's.

Perhaps it was the drama that attracted Giancarlo to him. Tommy had been remarkably successful and his fall had been precipitous, his death ugly and violent. The treatment accorded him perfectly illuminated the personalities of Brienza and Sullivan and simultaneously depicted the mutually-reinforcing parallel behaviors of their second- and third-line counterparts, Muschina and Devito. It all seemed to fit together like the various pieces of a fictional tale—the kind of thing that would attract a storyteller like Giancarlo. But it was also true, at least as far as discrete elements of the story could be tested against the LBPD's official records.

At some points he thought of Giancarlo as an informant, at others as a scop or troubador, but not an informant in the sense of a source or stoolie (Giancarlo called such individuals *pentiti*: squealers or rats). He was rather the kind of *informant* on whom anthropologists rely—an individual from another culture, capable of elucidating and explaining the particularly fascinating details of their system of attitudes, behaviors and values to a curious outsider.

His motives remained shadowy, while his polished exterior and easy manner helped to block Tom's attempts to grasp them. Perhaps he was simply indulging himself in his role as *superstite*. It is, after all, a lonely position in which to find oneself. At the same time, the *survivor* is the sole conduit for a generation's worth of stories and it would be cruel to withhold them from a curious listener.

All in all there were many mysteries beyond the cause and occasion of Michael Sullivan's death and the sudden and inexplicable (or at least as yet unexplained) disappearance of the family within which he played the gray eminence. Why did his skeleton appear now? Was that planned or was it purely fortuitous or accidental? Why was it so well preserved, though truncated? Why did Giancarlo agree to speak with a detective? And why was he so forthcoming in some areas, less so in others?

He was a master storyteller and a convincing one. His laughter seemed as real as his occasional tears and his descriptions—particularly of those who had replaced his beloved Don Carlo—were polished and refined like smooth stones recovered from rushing water.

That afternoon Tom visited two villages: Forza d'Agrò and Savaca. Each was said to have been used for footage in *The Godfather*. Riding the local buses and hiring local drivers he hoped to gain a feel for the places that inspired real men but also served as backdrops for fictional stories. Perhaps he wanted to test the line that divides the two; perhaps he simply wanted to clear his mind and leave the tourists behind for a few hours. Gina had suggested he try some windsurfing or mountain biking but then checked herself, admitting that she was treating him like a tourist and apologizing with a bottle of rich wine made from grapes grown on Mt. Etna.

When he returned to his room that evening and found the bottle waiting for him—along with some bread, cheese, and fresh fruit—he wrote a note of thanks and returned to the text on his laptop.

His respite that afternoon had enriched his perspective. He was able to cast Giancarlo's story in a different, though not unrelated, light. Now the narrative had become a morality play involving the downfall of the proud and vain, the goddess Fortuna turning the wheel and, in the process, meting out justice. This could be a novel or a play, he thought. It could also be a fairy tale or a parable. Perhaps a little of each.

In the early evening he toured churches—the Duomo (the church of San Nicola) and then San Pancrazio, the patron saint of Taormina whose church sat on the ruins of a Greek temple. He bought a bottle of almond wine from Castelmola and returned to the ancient theater, looking out over the darkening bay and wondering what else he was to hear and learn.

His thoughts faded into a momentary reverie that was suddenly interrupted by the twitch of his cell phone. The screen illuminated but the local provider somehow disrupted his caller i.d. All he saw was a long succession of numbers.

"Hello," he said.

"Tom, it's Chris."

"Hi, Chief. It's good to hear your voice. What have you got?"

"Nothing big. I just heard from the M.E. He was talking to his anthropologist friend, Sally Cornell."

"Yes?"

"As you know, there was some speculation that Sullivan's body might have been wedged into a box or casket of some sort."

"Yes."

"The M.E. told me that she now has concrete evidence to that effect."

"How so?"

"She said that even though the cuts across the top of the feet were clean there was enough texture in the bone to pick up some of the surrounding material."

"And did she find wood there?"

"Yes. Walnut, as a matter of fact."

"Pretty fancy," Tom said. "If I was putting away somebody I didn't like I'd probably use a pine packing crate."

"Right," Dietrich said, "but we've been thinking about the body turning up in the water and have assumed that it had been in the water from the get-go. That may not be the most likely possibility."

"You're saying that there might have been a funeral and a formal burial."

"It's possible."

"So that the body was exhumed recently and then put in the water."

"Yes, or the casket was just slid off of a mausoleum shelf. Could have been, at least."

"Then whoever did it wanted us to find the body."

"Yes."

"But why now?"

"That's the key question, of course," Dietrich said. "Anyway, I wanted you to know what she had found."

"Thanks, Chief. I'll keep it in mind as Orsini tells his story."

"Right. Anyway, I'm glad I caught you. Hope I wasn't interrupting anything," Dietrich said.

"No, I was just sitting here staring into space and hoping for answers. At least I have another question now. That could help."

"I'll talk to you tomorrow," Dietrich said.

"Thanks, Chief," Tom said, his mind already racing to new possibilities.

THIRTY-THREE

"How was Messina?" Tom asked.

"Messina is always the same, Tom. Bustling. Exhilarating. It lifts my spirits but then it tires me and after a day or two I am anxious to return to Taormina."

They were dining at *La Botte*, a popular place for locals in the Piazza San Domenico. Decorated with ceramics and wooden wine barrels, the prices were moderate and the food plentiful. Very little English was being spoken. The waiters seemed to know most of the patrons and orders were sometimes abbreviated and accented with familiar gestures. Orsini had still not invited Tom to dine with him in his home and Tom had not been able to find his address in any of the local directories. Perhaps he simply valued his privacy. Or perhaps he was dissembling. Either way, he continued to appear to be forthcoming in his statements, though this evening he seemed a little tired in his appearance.

"I was looking forward to this, Tom," he said. "I am getting too old to be running up and down the coast of this beautiful island. I even took a nap this afternoon."

"So did I, Giancarlo."

"But you probably swam vigorously first," Orsini answered.

(He had. Had Gina so informed him?)

"Yes," Tom said. "How could I resist that beautiful pool?"

"They sell memberships to the locals," Orsini said. "Anyway, I think we should order some food and continue our discussion."

Orsini ordered grilled seabass with a white wine sauce; Tom chose gnocchi and some soup made with local vegetables.

"Tonight we leave room for the chocolate invention," Giancarlo said. "Now, I was telling you about the death of Tommy Barone and the manner in which Sullivan had turned to Muschina and Muschina to Devito … "

"Yes … " Tom said.

"Muschina's hope was to be elevated. Don't misunderstand . . . he was a willing tool in Sullivan's hands on any occasion, but eliminating a captain was a . . . *consequential* . . . step. He hoped that it would bring commensurate results. And he was correct. With Sullivan now functioning as underboss—to the chagrin of the Sicilians—Muschina was appointed consigliere. The other captains were appalled … "

"Because they sought the position?"

"No, because the appointment was so inexplicable. The ideal consigliere (mind you, I have some biases in this matter) should have some distance and objectivity. Much of the advice which a don seeks truly *is* of a legal nature and legal training is a significant *desideratum*. Muschina had no legal training whatsoever. And he had no legal instincts; the only instincts he seemed to possess were a desire for personal survival and an unending thirst for personal success.

"Worst of all, he was completely inarticulate. I am not saying that his speech was somewhat halting, nor that he required constant prompting, like Brienza. No, when he opened his mouth nothing came forth but nonsense. His words carried no conceivable meaning and those who listened to him thought that he was a (what would you say?) *non-native* speaker or someone who had been afflicted by a recent stroke. The street soldiers called him 'Billy Mush' or 'Mush Mouth'."

"But how could someone such as that command the respect of the other captains?" Tom asked.

"He couldn't, I'm afraid. But it made no difference. Sullivan had told them all that there was no need to deal with Muschina. If they had any concerns they should bring them directly to him. Muschina became a person with an empty title, both because of his incompetence and the fact that he had sold out to Sullivan in order to obtain it. That was probably a good thing, for he was, like Brienza, a complete fool. However, where Brienza had his vanity, Muschina exhibited a pomposity that was based on what he perceived to be his broad experience. You see, he had moved from position to position, never really accomplishing anything in any of them. An American management expert would have said that he had exhibited a pattern of *progressively-increasing responsibility.*"

"He ran quickly across the cracking ice," Tom said.

"Yes, precisely. I like that," Giancarlo said. "I warn you, I'll use it," he added, smiling and tipping the edge of his glass toward Tom. "Muschina would love to be approved by management experts. He read their books. I have seen such individuals before. They believe that there is actually some secret, some *porta segreta* that could be opened and would then lead to a room that would contain the key to all of the mysteries for success in life. You see, such men have no instincts, no insight, no judgment, little knowledge and no wisdom, and hence they believe that others are just like them; *they* have been successful because of some secret knowledge or awareness of some magic technique. They are pitiful. I am not sure if they are willfully stupid or simply imbeciles."

"If there really were a secret we would have bottled it long ago," Tom said.

Orsini laughed. "Yes, we have a similar expression," he said. "At any rate, to return to my story, the Brienza family had an Irishman for underboss and a gaping, inarticulate idiot for consigliere. Where Sullivan tried to remain inscrutable, Muschina projected no personality at all. Regrettably, he was quite ugly—with a prominent nose and acne-scarred cheeks. I try not to hold such things against a man, for he cannot really help them, but this man could have softened his appearance by . . . for example . . . wearing glasses. Instead, he wore contact lenses, presumably out of vanity, since they were very difficult to care for in those days. Where he might have appeared to be somewhat scholarly or at least serious he looked like some predatory bird."

"Wetting his beak?" Tom asked.

"That was certainly said," Giancarlo answered. "That was his constant purpose and he was equipped for it . . . at least in his physiognomy."

"But not if you have trouble finding the source of sustenance or knowing it when you see it."

"Right, Tom, and not if you can't describe your intentions or wishes with any degree of clarity."

"What happened to his tool—what was his name--Devito?" Tom asked.

"He remained in the shadows, taking on petty roles and assignments, always aspiring to something that he would never have. That is just as well. The Brienza family already had enough ruthless individuals capable of destroying their organization."

"And the other captains?"

"Yes, I will tell you of each of them in turn. It is sometimes difficult to keep them all straight, because there was so much turnover in their positions. With a fool like Brienza in charge, a monster like Sullivan at his beck and call, and a nonentity like Muschina wandering around beneath them, they often looked to what Muschina's management experts would have termed 'other opportunities'. That usually meant retirement, of course, unless there were protectors in New York or elsewhere who would shield them. The very worst of them was a man called 'the knight'."

THIRTY-FOUR

"I am assuming that the term was used ironically," Tom said.

"Your assumption is correct," Giancarlo said, smiling, and signaling the waiter to bring an additional bottle of wine.

"Actually, I misled you earlier," Giancarlo said. "I told you that these men characteristically had three names. The knight had four or five. His name was John Graffali, but he changed it to Giovanni Graffali—apparently reaching for a bit more authenticity, or at least that was what was assumed. He was often called 'Johnny G' or 'Johnny Short Iron'. The latter name came from the fact that he was an avid though inept golfer who bored people with endless discussions of his achievements in attempting to 'strengthen his short irons game'. You understand what that means … "

"Yes," Tom said. "But I'm guessing that they changed it to 'short iron' in reference to his compensating for some physical shortcoming."

"Precisely. And politely put. There was never any actual indication that his endowment was a small one. It was his behavior that led people to that conclusion. He was always seeking attention—whether with expensive haircuts, flamboyant clothes, or boasts with regard to his golf handicap."

"And why was he also called 'the knight'?" Tom asked.

"Ah yes, *the knight*. That will take a few minutes to explain … "

The waiter brought the fresh bottle that Giancarlo had ordered, gave him a clean tasting glass, uncorked the bottle with a flourish, splashed some wine in the glass, swirled it, and offered it to Giancarlo. He tasted it approvingly, the waiter bowed, poured a half measure into each of their glasses, and left. Giancarlo took a longer sip, said, "Very nice, I think," and continued with his story.

"Graffali was a bad man and I say that with full awareness of the group with which he was compared. He managed the portion of the organization that dealt with the sale of drugs. He brought in an enormous amount of money but—at the same time—created a great many problems. There was scandal after scandal—the addiction of the very young in particular. His overriding concern was for wealth and he paid little attention to the unofficial rules under which this business is generally conducted. Scandal is not good for business. Death is not good for business. Pain and suffering are not good for business. The human costs, however, were never of any concern to this man, who was, like Sullivan, absolutely ruthless.

"Needless to say, he posed enormous problems for his don and that don's underboss, since they themselves were addicted to the money that he generated but, simultaneously, embarrassed and hurt by the adverse publicity which he caused and the endless encounters with law enforcement which resulted from his lack of control and discretion. They wanted the money but none of the problems attached to it and he told them that that was simply impossible. 'Drugs are different from other operations,' he would say. 'You do not understand them as I do and you must give me greater latitude in which to operate if you wish to continue receiving the money which I make for you.'

"Brienza was befuddled, as always, though Sullivan tried—generally with little success—to rein Graffali in. This eventually led to the collapse of the organization. The drug operation represented the largest share of the family's revenues and those who shared in those revenues—those in Los Angeles, the Midwest, and New York—forced Brienza to maintain it. At the same time, those individuals refused to share in the downside costs that resulted from Graffali's handling of that operation. Those costs were Brienza's problem, not theirs. Thus, the other operations within the

Brienza family ended up subsidizing the drug operation which, because of its size, eventually brought down the entire house of cards."

"So was Graffali eliminated?"

"Not in the sense in which you are using the term, Tom. He actually was replaced. And then his successor was replaced. And *his* successor . . . and so on—all within very short periods of time. I do not know what eventually happened to Graffali himself. He simply disappeared. The assumption was that he was playing golf somewhere, working on his short irons game."

"And his nickname—'the knight'?"

"Oh yes. Graffali was wracked with guilt, or so it was assumed, and so he attempted to buy his way into heaven. That was what was said, at least. I would have said, 'buy his way out of hell', because I cannot imagine a man such as this in the celestial regions. I am also not so certain of the notion that he carried a heavy burden of guilt. It is very difficult to watch a man like that do what he did—as long as he did it—and assume that guilt played any role in his personal psychology. I could not read his mind, however. He was called 'the knight' because he purchased a membership in The Equestrian Order of the Holy Sepulchre of Jerusalem. He prided himself on it, though he never spoke of the costs required for membership. Not that all members of that organization are individuals such as Graffali, but money does play a role in admission to it. The Holy See specifies the requirement of 'passage money' as well as 'an annual oblation' but it is clearly true that some members are selected because of their personal holiness and spirituality. Many are doubtless leaders within the Church and people of great piety and devotion.

"Graffali was none of these, of course. Depending on your estimate of his character and personality he was either assuaging his guilt or simply seeking attention. I consider the latter a far stronger possibility. The knights, after all, are permitted to wear a grand set of robes with beautiful accessories and decorations. Graffali's rank was 'Commander, with Star,' a relatively recent designation, though not created exclusively for him.

"He was, of course, a *commander*, a commander of individuals who sold drugs on the streets and corrupted the morals and destroyed the lives of countless individuals. Upon investiture, the knights are presented with a beautiful scroll. I am told that Graffali's was encased in a golden frame and displayed prominently in his home. There were always two requirements in that home. You were compelled to listen to his wife sing (mind you, she sang far better than he pitched or putted) and you had to see his scroll, then, presumably, listen to his lengthy account of his receipt of that honor. If you were particularly unfortunate you might also be required to inspect his robes of office."

"I have heard of the organization," Tom said. "I believe that the local cardinal (in California) is a member."

"Quite likely," Giancarlo said. "There are thousands of members."

"But you yourself never enquired concerning membership," Tom said, teasing him gently.

"No," he answered, smiling. "Hypocrisy is something I try to avoid. Lawyers who serve as counsel to organizations such as those which we have been discussing should do all that they can to maintain their personal independence. Their credibility requires that. They should also cultivate personalities which are self-effacing. The lawyer is a representative and must be capable of representing honestly and fairly, without permitting his own personality to intrude and cloud the issues. That is what I have tried to do, at least."

"Let me ask you a technical question, Giancarlo."

"Certainly."

"Would a captain who represented a division of the operation that was particularly lucrative be permitted to keep a commensurate share of the revenue?"

"You mean—would a person who sold drugs be paid more than an individual who directed a numbers operation? (You see, Tom, I can be as direct as you wish me to be.)"

"Yes, exactly."

"That would depend on the don. An intelligent and effective don would estimate reasonable productivity and then reward exceptional productivity, so that all captains would be suitably motivated. My understanding is that Giovanni Graffali was handsomely compensated regardless of the productivity of his operation. Brienza was too great a fool to manage with any wisdom or insight and Sullivan doubtless considered Graffali to be a potential threat. After all, Graffali was generating income; Sullivan was a simple administrator. At any rate, he granted him a wide berth. He also probably assumed that Graffali would only serve for a brief period of time anyway, so why choose to work on a problem that would eventually solve itself?"

"But that was very shortsighted if his practices were bankrupting the organization."

"Indeed. I have never said that Sullivan was intelligent. He was simply devious. I believe that he felt that the money lost by Graffali's operation could always be found elsewhere. But then, sometimes individuals stood up to him and to Brienza, individuals such as Tommy Barone."

THIRTY-FIVE

"Increasingly, Barone appears to be the hero of this story—at least this phase of the story," Tom said.

"Yes, particularly when judged against those we've been discussing. I have not mentioned all of them. Brienza's accountant was a man named Mandello. Frank Mandello. A congenital liar, but essentially a nonentity. Sullivan brought him in because he knew that he could be easily controlled. When the lies prompted by Sullivan and Brienza were revealed, Mandello was quickly scapegoated. That eventuality had doubtless been anticipated at the outset."

"Was Mandello eliminated?"

"Reassigned," Giancarlo said, smiling. "Seriously. He *was* reassigned."

"And has he been seen since?" Tom asked.

"Not to my knowledge," Giancarlo said. "There was also a man named Rizzo. Michael Rizzo. He was responsible for the Brienza family's numbers operation. An honest man. He too grew tired of subsidizing Graffali's failures. Fortunately for him he was old enough to retire. Sullivan was anxious to see him go anyway. Rizzo was a person of integrity and Sullivan wished to renegotiate that captain's share of the operation. He recruited a man named Scarlatti, again a person who Sullivan could control.

"They were less successful in replacing Muschina. Brienza had pressed for the promotion of a street soldier, a man named Fratellino. The *little brother*. Jimmy Fratellino had been loyal to Brienza and Brienza believed that he could control him. Sullivan was skeptical, but bided his time. Muschina was angry because he knew that Fratellino would be far more successful than him in the captain's role and highlight his own inadequacies. Fratellino quickly realized the nature of the position in which he found himself and arranged a transfer to Kansas City. Brienza was angered by the ease with which he was able to leave, but Muschina was happy to see him go and assured Brienza that they could do better. He was pressing for his lickspittle, Devito, but Sullivan blocked that and they settled on a street soldier from Barone's crew. The cash flow from that division quickly diminished because of the man's lack of experience."

"How long was it before the entire operation imploded?" Tom asked.

"It was in difficult circumstances after four years, desperate circumstances after eight. Brienza remained in place for a little over ten years. They had utilized every option available to continue making payments to the external families. Eventually that became impossible."

"And who reached that conclusion?"

"New York. In prior years they had examined Brienza's books twice a year. Toward the end they were examining them monthly. The downward spiral was unmistakable and, they concluded, irreversible."

"Had there been significant impact from the efforts of law enforcement to curtail their operations?"

Giancarlo smiled. "No, Tom, not really. The overriding cause was incompetence. A very special form of incompetence. Brienza combined the worse traits imaginable. On the one hand, he was weak and indecisive. At the same time he was highly controlling. He could not make a decision, but he would not permit anyone else to do so."

"And so Sullivan made the decisions, but under the pretense that Brienza was really in charge."

"Exactly, Tom, though the real facts were transparently obvious. A man who asks an underling to run a meeting for him will always have a great deal of difficulty convincing those attending the meeting that he is actually in charge."

"And when the reckoning came . . . the members of the family simply disappeared?"

"Yes. Brienza, Sullivan, Muschina, and Graffali. Other positions were vacant at the time. Those who might have filled them were probably fortunate in not having done so."

"And Devito?"

"Oh yes, how could I forget him?"

"So you believe they were all eliminated, with prejudice."

"I know that they disappeared. I doubt that they left willingly."

"But your brother Dominic replaced Brienza, Giancarlo."

"Yes, but as I told you, Tom, I was a counselor, not a soldier. I was not close to those decisions. I was also experienced enough to realize that the making of such decisions might not always be part of a straightforward process. You are well aware that things must be done through channels; at the same time there are many possible back channels … "

"I don't understand … " Tom said.

"What I am saying is that a person cannot simply be removed without permission. There are protocols. At the same time, when one reaches a certain position and when events have reached a certain level of, shall we say, *disorder*, steps are taken that are outside of channels or, at least, *exceptional*. Dominic could not act without securing certain permissions. At the same time, Dominic might not have been the proximate cause of the actions."

"He could have been recruited for the task by one or more of the external families."

"Precisely."

"And it would have been to his advantage to have the facts of the case remain unclear. The external families would want to retain a due distance from the . . . *removals* . . . and your brother would want to be perceived as a strong leader capable of rescuing a failing operation and doing what needed to be done to make the changes … possible."

"Exactly. It was clear that he was not acting as a lone wolf. That would be impossible, given the weakness of the Orange County operation. *Very* hard work would be necessary to restore it to its earlier levels of success. And that work would be impossible without external support. Dominic *had* to have the blessings of the external families. At the same time, he had to have the strength to take on the task. Whether the initial idea was his or whether he was recruited for the role . . . that remains unclear."

"What had he been doing prior to taking over control of the O.C. operation?"

"He was in New York, Tom."

"But not working in the garment district."

"No, he was not doing that," Giancarlo said, smiling.

"And you were in New York as well?"

"Yes, in private legal practice."

"But with clients in Dominic's line of work?"

"Occasionally," he said.

"And you came with your brother immediately after his *reassignment* to Southern California?"

"Shortly thereafter," Giancarlo answered. "I can see that you have many questions, Tom. Perhaps we should have some coffee and then perhaps some grappa or limoncello."

"I am always at your disposal, Giancarlo. Every selection you have made so far has been perfect."

"But you are worried about my answers to your questions ... "

"You have been very generous so far, Giancarlo, with your time and with your account of events."

"Trust me, I will tell you what I can," the consigliere responded.

THIRTY-SIX

"I *would* like to talk more about Sullivan," Tom said. Giancarlo nodded approvingly, as if to say, 'go ahead, Tom.'

"When you spoke to your granddaughter she must have mentioned to you that we believe that we have found Sullivan's remains."

"Yes. And as you can well imagine, Tom, I could not resist making a call or two to old friends in California. They said that Sullivan's remains washed up on the beach in Laguna."

"Nearly *complete* remains, Giancarlo."

"With attached flesh?"

The question had a direct, naked sound to it. "No, the remains were skeletal, but they were nearly complete."

"That is quite amazing, given the length of time involved," Giancarlo said, "and the sea . . . the sea is very unforgiving. One might almost suspect … "

"Yes, Giancarlo?"

"One might almost suspect that the remains were placed in the sea shortly before you found them. I am a lawyer, not a scientist, but it would seem to be impossible that the remains would remain intact for that period of time."

"The only things missing were the lower jaw and the feet."

"One sees many skulls without a lower jaw," Giancarlo said. "Again, Tom, I am not a scientist. I am simply speaking as one who has read articles written for laymen in popular magazines."

"The missing feet are more interesting," Tom said.

"Were they severed cleanly or . . . *abruptly?*" Giancarlo asked.

"Cleanly."

"And I'm sure someone suggested that they might have been encased in cement … "

"The possibility was mentioned."

"But if the body sunk to the bottom of the sea it would have been exposed for many years and the skeleton would not have survived and remained intact."

"Right," Tom said.

"Could you tell me more about the manner in which they were severed?"

"We think that it might have been done with a Skilsaw," Tom said, watching Orsini's eyes for a reaction. There was none.

"There could be a very simple explanation for that," he responded.

"Yes?"

"Gray Sullivan was very tall, particularly for those times. Perhaps his feet were simply removed so that his body would fit more easily in a standard-size coffin."

"But if he were put in a coffin, how did he end up in the sea?"

"I can't answer that, Tom, but he must have been put somewhere for a time, since the body would have come apart if it had been put directly into the water."

"I have never heard of a case of a body being dismembered by an undertaker," Tom said.

"But certainly there are many cases in which undertakers must do restorative work."

"Yes, certainly."

"Their function is to make the person look like he or she did in life."

"Yes."

"So they are not averse to making . . . adjustments."

"No, but … "

"And what if the undertaker was, shall we say, unsympathetic?"

"What do you mean, Giancarlo?" Tom asked.

"Let's say that the person paying for his services was not a devoted member of the family … "

"The *family* family, not the organizational family."

"Yes. Let us say that the undertaker understood that the case was one in which delicate feelings need not be a concern … "

"A pure business transaction."

"Yes."

"Perhaps the most accessible casket available was a small one."

"Oversized caskets would be rare. They could be more difficult to obtain."

"And the purchaser might be most interested in timeliness," Tom said.

Giancarlo nodded affirmatively. "Undertakers sometimes provided shoes that appeared to be new—for appearance sake. These shoes would actually be quite inexpensive, because they would not require the glues and the stitching and the precise processes required for shoes that would undergo normal service."

"They could be slipped over the stumps, perhaps lightly glued in place."

"If the decedent had expensive shoes an unsympathetic undertaker might substitute the inexpensive models . . . or simply cover the ends of the legs with a satin blanket."

"Yes," Tom said.

"Tell me, Tom," Giancarlo said, "if you can . . . was there any evidence of trauma to the body?"

"No. No broken bones or evidence of gunshot wounds," Tom said.

"That is interesting, is it not?"

"Yes. Was anything ever said about Sullivan's suffering from a serious disease?"

"Not that I know of," Giancarlo said.

"It's very puzzling," Tom said.

Orsini looked into his eyes before speaking. "Yes, Tom, it is *very* puzzling, but there must be *some* explanation."

"I had hoped you could help me with that," Tom said.

"I was very distant from the actions which followed the removal of Victor Brienza, Tom. Remember, I was a young lawyer working in New York. When my brother was asked to move to California and take on the responsibility for that operation I was quite peripheral to the discussions. He asked me a question or two, but nothing *material* to your concerns. There was some talk, however … "

"Talk, Giancarlo?"

"Yes. Simple rumor. Nothing very specific. A word here or there. Something dropped accidentally … "

"Yes?"

"There was talk of a *coordinatore*."

"A coordinator."

"Yes," Giancarlo answered. "Consider, Tom. If a decision had been made to remove a large number of individuals, it could not be accomplished without a significant amount of planning."

"Person by person. In the most effective sequence. With proper provision made to insure that one would not learn of what happened to the others and hence be on his guard. With intelligence on each of the individuals, where they were likely to be at any moment . . . their habits and routines . . . their information networks . . . where they might be taken, without . . . incident."

"Yes," the consigliere said. "It would be very complex."

"And require a person of consummate skill," Tom said.

"And dedication," Giancarlo added.

THIRTY-SEVEN

"He's starting to open up, Chief. At least he seems to be."

"With regard to Sullivan?"

"Yes, and with regard to the others who disappeared. He itemized them for me, leaving one out. When I asked him about that person he acknowledged that he had disappeared as well. I don't know whether he was trying to mislead me or if he had simply forgotten."

"What did he say about Sullivan?"

"He keeps reiterating that he himself was in New York at the time—a young attorney in his late twenties. His brother got the call to take over the O.C. family (or had it appear that he had been so invited) and Giancarlo followed later. He said that his brother had a few questions for him at the time, but he continues to maintain that he was at the peripheries and largely ignorant of the manner in which the Brienza crew was removed."

"But he admits that they didn't just get lost at sea or something."

"Oh no. He believes that they were systematically eliminated. When we talked last night he added something new. Not that it's counter-intuitive, or anything, but he said that there were rumors to the effect that a specific individual coordinated the process."

"It would have to work that way in order to be effective."

"Right," Tom said, "they couldn't give any of them a chance to adjust or counterattack. They had to take them all out at once."

"How many individuals are we talking about?"

"Five. I'll put their names and functions in my email."

"That would require a large number of people. I mean . . . we're not talking Normandy Invasion-level logistics, but it's highly unlikely that the five would be in the same place at the same time. You'd probably need at least fifteen or twenty people to take them all down, because they weren't simply shot or stabbed and left to bleed out on the street. They actually disappeared. That means they were physically carried."

"And there may have been some serious cleaning up that needed to be done afterwards," Tom added.

"Right. There was some form of smash-and-grab and then the respective scenes were all cleared. Meticulously cleared, if the illusion of disappearance was to be sustained."

"There would also be serious security issues," Tom said. "If a single person tipped off Brienza the whole operation would fall apart. Each of the soldiers involved had to be absolutely trustworthy."

"And the slightest glitch would bring a postponement, so this must have been planned for weeks but executed over a fairly short period of time—at least to be maximally effective."

"Which it was," Tom said.

"If they kept the details from the incoming consigliere—who was also the don's brother—the security was exquisite. Assuming, of course, that Orsini is telling you the truth."

"And that may be a big assumption," Tom said. "I'm going to keep probing."

"We can at least check to see if his New York lawyer story is legit."

"Right, Chief. That would be very helpful."

"There'll be extensive files on his brother at least. I'll check with the NYPD. See what you can find out about Giancarlo's background and practice. He'll pick up on the fact that you're checking him out, but that's OK. If he prides himself on being straightforward with you, this will give him a chance to demonstrate again that his story is true."

"He knew all the details of Carlo Monte's education; I'll ask him about his own. If we can nail the alma mater we can find out where he's been for every waking moment since the time he walked off the graduation stage. Those alumni association and development operations have better records than the old KGB and the Stasi."

Dietrich laughed. "That's true. Good point."

"Anything new on the local front, Chief?"

"Not really. That anthropologist is still picking around. I think the M.E. has a thing for her."

"Really?"

"He keeps talking about her all the time. She hasn't come up with anything new, however--at least nothing that can be taken as definitive."

"Have there been any records of exhumations or any evidence of caskets being removed from mausoleums?"

"Good. I forgot to mention that. Hector's been working on it. No exhumations, except for some court-ordered things unrelated to this case. Some caskets have been moved around, but that's not really uncommon."

"I would think this would be very hard to track," Tom said. "All you need is for somebody to remove the remains from a casket and then leave the box in place. How long would that take—10 minutes? In the middle of the night?"

"Right. Hector's done some background checks on key individuals at all of the local facilities. If this was important enough to do well, they wouldn't just hire some minimum-wage gravedigger type to do the job. They'd need someone who could manage the security, the operation, and the coverup."

"I agree, Chief. I still can't figure out why they'd release the remains now. Neither can Giancarlo. At least he hasn't volunteered anything."

"That's the real mystery, Tom. And why did Sullivan surface and not the rest of them?"

"Right. There are a lot of reasons to believe that he was the major target in the original removal operation. They'd have to take out Brienza, of course, but Sullivan was the pivotal figure."

"The RD. The real don."

"Exactly."

"This is all very helpful, Tom. When do you meet with him again?"

"Tonight. We're eating at the *Vicolo Stretto*. Another week or so and we'll have eaten in every restaurant in northeastern Sicily."

"What time?"

"Around 8:30."

"That's practically my bedtime," Dietrich said.

"I know. I'm still not used to it, Chief."

"Check back with me as soon as you learn anything."

"Will do," Tom said and clicked off.

"So, Tom," Giancarlo said. "After you finish those shrimp you can start asking your questions. I want you to savor them. Don't hurry. We have plenty of time and I am in the mood to talk." He then signaled the waiter, who came over at once.

"*Si, Signore?*"

Giancarlo ordered in Italian. Tom heard the word *Gaja* and the word *Barolo*. The year was spoken too quickly for Tom to hear and comprehend it with his elementary grasp of Italian. One thing was clear: Giancarlo was going for the high-priced wine.

After he tasted it, approved it, and their glasses were filled, Giancarlo said, "Now, Tom. You may ask your first question. Any question. Feel free."

"Actually, I don't have a specific question on the case yet, Giancarlo. This is more a matter of personal curiosity … "

"Yes … ?"

"You spoke at length of Don Carlo's education, but you never spoke of your own. Did you attend Regis as well?"

"Oh no, my mother did not trust the Jesuits. Perhaps she thought they would try to convince me that I had a vocation to join them."

"You would make a very good Jesuit, Giancarlo."

"You may be right, Tom," he said, smiling. "But my mother . . . she wanted me to stay close to home. I attended the local Catholic schools in Brooklyn. My high school—St. Stephen's—no longer exists. It was combined with a girls' school and then relocated . . . many years ago. I attended college at NYU."

"And for law school?"

"Fordham. So you see, the Jesuits had me at last."

"I believe G. Gordon Liddy attended Fordham Law School," Tom said.

"No comment," Giancarlo said, smiling. "You see, I never expected to leave New York. It is sometimes very helpful to attend law school in the city where you hope to practice. I had an internship at a then very-prominent firm, for example."

"But you eventually went into private practice."

"Yes. I could not imagine myself in a building with dozens or even hundreds of other lawyers. I tried to carve out a niche for myself. I had studied the history of art at NYU; they are known for that. At Fordham I developed an interest in intellectual property law—very important in New York City. It also positions you to do agenting of various kinds . . . am I boring you to death, Tom?"

"No. This is fascinating."

"It is not what you thought I'd be doing as a lawyer."

"No, it's not."

"I did other things as well, but the subject still interests me—creating something out of nothing and then protecting it from the jackals that are always attracted by another person's success. That is the one thing that continued to be a part of my legal work … "

"Providing protection from jackals?"

"Yes, though it becomes a lonely occupation when those you have protected are all gone."

"You are the *superstite.*"

"So it is said," he answered. "Sadly, it is true."

"I would like to talk about that, Giancarlo, but before I forget I would like to hear your thoughts on another subject."

"You want to talk about the *coordinatore*."

"Yes," Tom said.

"A very important subject," Giancarlo answered, as he sipped his wine.

THIRTY-EIGHT

"I know you appreciate the fact that something like this would require a great deal of planning and coordination, Tom," Giancarlo said.

"Yes, of course," Tom answered. "There would have to be a central planner, someone who knew the schedules of all concerned."

"Down to the moment," Giancarlo added. "There were no cell phones then, of course, but communications would still need to be . . . what? . . . circumscribed."

"Each would have to be surprised simultaneously or at least nearly so."

"Precisely," Giancarlo said. "And remember one of the key rules of war ... "

"Go ahead, Giancarlo ... "

"You need three times more people if you are on offense than if you are on defense."

"This would involve at least fifteen people, probably more like thirty or forty."

"Yes, exactly."

"That is a large number of people to coordinate."

"And the coordination would only be a part of it," Giancarlo said. "The intelligence would be far more difficult."

"*Intelligence* in the military sense. Someone would have to acquire the information on the individual plans and locations of those who were to . . . disappear."

"Exactly."

"And that would have to be someone who was highly placed and also highly trusted," Tom said.

"Precisely," Giancarlo answered. "Remember—Dominic was in New York, as were the majority of the individuals who were to become his captains."

"And counselor," Tom added.

Giancarlo bowed and smiled.

"So the *coordinatore* was a member of Brienza's organization."

"Possibly," Giancarlo said, "but not *necessarily*."

"It would have to be someone close enough to the organization to be able to acquire the needed intelligence," Tom said.

"Yes. And that could be any number of people. Brienza was surrounded by individuals from outside the family. He had his own chef, for example, and he had a personal tailor. The chef was with him constantly and saw the others come and go. He was there when they dined . . . probably no more than fifteen or twenty feet away for much of the time."

"Servants become invisible," Tom said. "They are looked at as part of the furnishings."

"And no one would ever expect them to have the courage to betray not just their master but all of his key associates."

"It would be bad for business for one thing," Tom said.

Giancarlo smiled and said, "Unless that individual's actions led to other opportunities."

"But probably not immediately," Tom said. "There would be grieving relatives . . . surviving street soldiers . . . any number of individuals who might take revenge on him if his actions in any way indicated that he might have been the source of the betrayal."

"Yes, Tom, but remember—none of the individuals who . . . disappeared . . . commanded any personal respect and none, probably, commanded any particular loyalty."

"Did Dominic bring any of the surviving members of the Brienza family into his own organization?"

"Of course," Giancarlo said. "Those were the individuals who did the real work, the men who knew the streets . . . the men who had the contacts and the clients. The first thing that Dominic did was call them together and reassure them that he understood their feelings—on *all* of the things that had happened. He told them that the personalities and behaviors of Brienza and Sullivan, Graffali and Muschina—and particularly Devito— were all well-known. He told them that he knew what they had undergone and what demands had been placed upon them."

"And they would all have known that your brother could not assume this role without the consent of the external families."

"A group that had led to their troubles, to some degree."

"Yes," Tom said, "a group that might cut your brother some slack and, in the process, cut them some. Or tighten the screws further."

"Yes. You were made for this kind of work, Tom. You understand it perfectly."

"And there was no way for them to know whether your brother was to be their lifelong don or simply a transitional figure . . . the good cop to be replaced by a very bad one later."

"Exactly."

"They would take some comfort in his reaching out to them, but none were naïve men. They would know that this could all be a prelude to something quite different. Hence, they were well advised to be cooperative, to welcome him and to pledge him their loyalty."

"Which they did. And it was wise of them to do so, for it led to decades of success and prosperity."

"Though if he had been unsuccessful the external families could have withdrawn their support ... "

"Immediately ... " Giancarlo said. "So this was a significant moment. One thing, however, was absolutely certain ... "

"Brienza, Sullivan, Graffali, Muschina and Devito would not be coming back. There was no reason to hold out any hope or, for that matter, have any fears."

"Or leave any porch lights burning," Giancarlo said, smiling and sipping his wine. "This is superb, isn't it?"

"It's fabulous," Tom said.

"So if there was a betrayer in their midst, that person had betrayed those who weren't coming back and probably wouldn't be missed anyway."

"And the enemy of my enemy is my friend."

"Even if he happens to be an anonymous friend," Giancarlo said. "Almost like an angel."

"An angel of death," Tom added.

"In scripture the 'angel of the lord' is very busy," Giancarlo said. "Smiting Assyrians, smiting Egyptians . . . smiting everyone in the opposing camp."

"Yes," Tom said. "And it is best to attempt to insure that the angel of the lord not make any premature visits to your own home."

"Discretion is often more important than valor, especially misplaced valor," Giancarlo said.

"But how can we identify this person?" Tom asked.

Giancarlo took another sip of his wine, this time more pensively.

"You were in New York," Tom said.

"I was."

"And you could not have done this."

"No, Tom, I could not have done it."

"But you are the *superstite*."

"Yes, I am."

"So if we could identify this person there would be no arrest or prosecution."

"No, that would be impossible," Giancarlo said.

"So you will continue to help me ... "

"Of course I will. I told you that I would. But there may be a condition ... "

THIRTY-NINE

"A condition?"

"Yes. Consider one possibility. A purely fictional one. What if the *coordinatore* was Brienza's driver? To my knowledge there was *no* such person. The don would be driven by a street soldier or, in some cases, a captain, but let us say, for the sake of argument, that he had a driver. Let us further say that the driver had a son who became a famous surgeon and that he had a son who became the Mayor of Laguna Beach. As long as we are indulging our imaginations, let us make him the Mayor of Los Angeles. If we would discover that his grandfather had played a role such as that which we have been discussing—and that that role had been unknown for decades—it is very likely that his honor the Mayor would not like that fact revealed. There would be no prosecution in any case, so … "

"So if such a fact were determined, it could be used to close out the files, but there might be guarantees offered to the effect that the pertinent individual's identity would not be made public."

"You see, Tom, you are always one step ahead of me," Giancarlo said, smiling.

"And you understand, Giancarlo, that I would have to secure permission from my superior in order to make such an offer … "

"Of course . . . ah, here are our entrées." Giancarlo had persuaded Tom to try the grouper *involtini*. "Many do these *roulades*, but none quite as well as *Vicolo Stretto*. Economy of scale, Tom. They can only serve thirty at a time, so they serve them with perfection. How were those shrimp?"

"Excellent, Giancarlo."

"You were not brave enough for the raw fish . . . and you call yourself a native Californian."

"True. I'll try to exhibit more courage with the dessert."

"And you will need it, Tom. I know the chef here. With the things that *he* creates from chocolate he will have you sweating underneath your eyes."

"I suppose we'll have to ask them to make the espresso doubly strong."

"Here they need no such encouragement, Tom. If you tell them to make it stronger you'll feel your heart beating through your chest for at least four hours."

"Instead of the usual two."

"Yes, instead of two," Giancarlo said, smiling. "Now . . . the *coordinatore*."

He was refocusing on the subject. Tom wondered why he was anxious to do so. "Yes, Giancarlo, the *coordinatore* ... "

"As we have said, it could not be someone from the external families."

"Not even Los Angeles?"

"No, their presence would have been met with immediate suspicion."

"No one likes to see the tax collector," Tom said.

"Particularly when the tax collector is not providing services in return. Los Angeles was collecting for *protection*, not providing actual protective services."

"Extortion, in short."

"Yes," Giancarlo said. "As I said, it would have to be someone inside, someone who was knowledgeable, someone who was trusted."

"Perhaps several people?"

"I doubt that," Giancarlo said. "The problems with security multiply geometrically with the inclusion of every additional individual."

"But those problems would have to be faced," Tom said.

"In what sense, Tom?"

"The *coordinatore* would need access to the soldiers capable of conducting the operation."

"True … "

"And if there were fifteen or thirty or even more . . . the security risks would be astronomical. If one person betrayed them, traps would be set for all of the rest of them."

"Yes, but … "

"Wait," Tom said. "What the *coordinatore* would need is access to *external* soldiers, soldiers who would not be recognized immediately, soldiers who could come and go and prepare for the proper *disappearance* of the gang of five."

"The *gang of five* . . . I like that," Giancarlo said.

"The *coordinatore* would be a person who enjoyed both knowledge and trust within the Brienza family, but would be sufficiently known by one of the external families . . . I should think the more distant the better . . . let us say . . . a New York family . . . that he could both convince them that the gang of five had to be removed and also persuade them that he would be prepared to lead the operation."

"There would be little difficulty in convincing anyone that the gang of five had to be removed," Giancarlo said.

"The soldiers employed would have no loyalty to the Brienza family, but they would have supreme loyalty to their own don … "

"Yes, certainly … "

"Thus reducing the concerns with regard to security."

"Because they would have nothing to gain in warning the gang of five, since the eventual fate of those fools was already clear," Giancarlo said, savoring the last of his wine.

"And the price for betraying their own don and the other soldiers within their family would be very high."

"Indeed," Giancarlo said. "Then I have only one question."

"Yes?"

"Why do you need me to figure out these things, Tom? You are clearly an expert at this."

"Oh, I very much need you, Giancarlo," Tom said. "We may have traced a likely scenario, but we have no names … "

"True, but remember … "

"You were in New York."

Giancarlo bowed, but there was disappointment in his gesture of approval. "I will have to give much more thought to this," he said. "Meanwhile, we need that dessert and coffee."

The double espressos were followed by a flourless chocolate cake laced with liqueur.

"Tomorrow I must be in Catania," Giancarlo said, "and, unfortunately, I will return late. I propose that we return to your hotel's restaurant the following evening."

"They haven't disappointed me yet," Tom said.

"That will give me more time to think and you more time to swim . . . and, perhaps, contact your superior concerning our discussion … "

"I'll do that," Tom said. "Travel safely."

"I will try," Giancarlo said, "but the Italian drivers . . . they have no sense of fear."

"And I have no jurisdiction here," Tom said, each of them now smiling.

FORTY

Tom called Chris early the next morning. The air was still cool, though the sun would soon change that. He was sitting by the pool, with a towel around his shoulders and some rolls and coffee on an adjoining table.

"Progress?" Chris asked.

"I think so. We still don't have any names for the person Giancarlo calls the *coordinatore*—the coordinator of the actions that led to the disappearance of the five Brienza principals—but we're still working on it. At least I think we are."

"What do you mean?"

"Well, sometimes I think we're moving forward, sometimes just laterally. Giancarlo was in New York when all of this happened (or claims to have been), so that we're brainstorming together in trying to tease out possible candidates for the role."

"Pretty tricky," Chris said, "since the person would have to have the confidence of the Brienza family in order to know how to reach each of them more or less simultaneously as well as the confidence of whoever delivered the small army to take them out. It couldn't be a pure internal insurrection because sooner or later one of the people approached would go running to the people at the top and the whole house of cards would collapse."

"Exactly," Tom said. "And it *would* take a small army. A handful of people couldn't carry it off."

"There's another possibility," Chris said, "a more obvious one."

"What's that?" Tom asked.

"This could all be smoke," Chris said. "I mean . . . one of the top people from L.A., Vegas, the Midwest or East could ask for a sit-down with the Brienza family, lock the door, open fire, and call for the body wagon to meet him at the loading dock. Maybe just put some dynamite under the floor of the room or do a Goldfinger with some poison gas . . . a lot of ways you could slice it. Put some strychnine in the cannoli or anisette ... "

"Right. The 'coordinator' story is more convoluted and there are no clear answers, at least not yet. That makes me wonder if he's really playing it straight with me or purposely obfuscating. I know that he would want to protect the members of his brother's family. There hasn't been a single negative word about any of them. He presents them as a group of kindly business experts who stepped in to repair a dysfunctional organization and brought with them the second golden age of O.C. crime. Except that he'd say something like 'personal services'—looking after the gambling, medicinal, and sexual needs of their clients."

"It *is* true," Chris said, "that there *was* a notable difference in the levels of violence between the Brienza period and the Orsini period, violence, of course, not being good for business."

"Yes, and at the outset they at least projected a sanitary approach to the problem. The previous administration simply vanished. There were no grand examples made, no carefully-posed tableaux with lots of blood and missing limbs."

"That's true. And from what I can see, a number of the Brienza street soldiers came over to the Orsini side and made nice. At least that's what the record (such as it is) shows."

"Right. So I keep going along with the 'coordinator' story, hoping to make some progress. One thing that suggests that he's telling the truth is the fact that he's asked for a promise that if we identify this individual the LBPD will guarantee that his identity will be kept secret. We could clear our cases, or at least know the person who was principally responsible for their so-called *disappearance,* but we'd then have to seal the record in some way."

"Why does he want us to do that?"

"To protect the reputation of any innocent descendants."

"I see. I'll talk to the D.A. but I don't think that would be a problem. The key would be to keep the fact that the cases were cleared as quiet as possible. Otherwise the press's bowels would be in an uproar and they'd start taking steps to get the records unsealed. In the past they've been able to get into domestic relations court records and other places previously considered out of bounds, so anything is possible. Once the hue and cry is loud enough and the political juggernauts start to move it's hard to keep the seals in place."

"I understand."

"Speaking of the press, there's been an interesting development at this end. Yesterday I got a series of requests from a *Register* reporter for information on the Sullivan remains. The long and the short of it is that we had to release the information on the identity of those remains. The story ran and we had an immediate set of requests for death certificates."

"From who?"

"Mostly from the press—local, national, wire services, Drudge, and the other usual suspects. We also had a request from a local attorney named Drewes."

"Who was he representing?"

"He wouldn't say. He invoked attorney/client privilege."

"That's interesting, particularly in light of our belief that Giancarlo Orsini is the lone survivor."

"Right. You might run that past him, see if he has any ideas."

"I will. Is there any possibility that Drewes's firm may have actually represented Sullivan in the old days?"

"None that I can see. Muschina was Brienza's putative *consigliere,* but from all accounts he'd have trouble opening his fly in the dark, so they'd hardly tap him to actually be their counselor at law. He wasn't a lawyer anyway. So it could be possible that they had outside counsel, as it were, but it couldn't have been Drewes. His father is a history professor at UCLA and his mother is a veterinarian. No known aunts, uncles, or grandparents in legal practice . . . Drewes himself is a thirty-five year-old in private practice."

"Maybe a stalking horse … "

"Could be," Chris said.

"I'll ask Giancarlo."

"Watch his eyes when he answers."

"I will," Tom said, "but it's not likely to do any good. He's one very cool individual, even after a half-dozen drinks. Maybe even more so then … "

"By the way, Drewes's first name is Carl. Are you meeting tonight?"

"Tomorrow. He's off to Catania today."

"For a man his age he seems very active . . . *very* active."

"He claims that's what keeps him young."

"Let me know what he says."

"Will do, Chief."

"Oh yes, and Tom … "

"What, Chief?"

"Julie asked me if you'd do her a favor."

"Yes?"

"Would you bring her back one of those Italian bowls or crocks—the kind with all the bright yellow and blue colors? They cost a small fortune in the states, but she figured you'd be surrounded by them there."

"Sure, Chief," Tom said, clicking off. Everybody's succumbing, he thought. In all that sun and with all that wine it's hard to stay focused on the body count.

FORTY-ONE

"*Ciao*, Giancarlo," Tom said, as Orsini approached the table. He was carrying three bottles of wine.

"Greetings, Tom. My fee for my work in Catania," he said, placing the bottles on the corner of the table. "My friend there preferred to pay me in kind. From his very private cellar. Believe me, I came out well on this and you will be an unexpected beneficiary."

"I always trust you with the wine, Giancarlo."

"You are a wise man," Orsini answered. "Each of us has expertise and that expertise is best shared. How was your swim? I can see some tan in your face."

"Perfect. I had the pool to myself most of the time. Gina joined me for lunch."

"She is a wonderful young lady."

"Yes. I also had some time to read."

"Something morally uplifting, I trust."

"Indeed," Tom said. "I was reading about . . . *survivors*. On the internet, of course. I wouldn't leave *that* pool to go to the library. I discovered that there is a long tradition of songs being sung by survivors. The 'lay of the last survivor' is the phrase for the genre."

"Really?"

"Yes. The oldest such poem in English is in the Exeter Book—one of the major manuscripts of Old English."

"At Exeter Cathedral?"

"Yes. The poem in question has been called *The Wanderer*. It is narrated by a man who no longer has any kinsmen and, most important, no longer has a lord. There is no one to give him rings or other treasures, no one to give him approval, no one to host him in a warm mead hall. The wanderer is lost and bereft. He no longer *belongs*. We would probably say that he suffers from *alienation*. There are strong hints in the poem of an overarching religious dimension. The liege lord who is now gone is emblematic of the true Lord. Ultimately the poem is about the human condition itself; each of us is a lone survivor; each of us is, in an important sense, a *wanderer*."

"And does that poem remind you of me?" Giancarlo said.

"Surprisingly, it does not," Tom said.

"I have never lost my faith," Giancarlo said, "and I continually feel the presence of God."

"Yes," Tom said. "And the empty world of the poem … "

"Yes?"

"It is empty of friends, but it is also empty of enemies."

"The truly empty world," Giancarlo said, "is the world without justice. If one believes that justice exists, one can tolerate nearly anything else."

"Even emptiness," Tom said.

"Yes, especially emptiness," Giancarlo said. "What did Caesar's father-in-law say? *Fiat justitia, ruat coelum.*"

"Let justice be done, though the heavens fall."

"Yes. One might fairly say that it is an Italian belief," Giancarlo said, "perhaps even a core belief."

"Pascal said that he would not wish to live in a world without meaning," Tom said, "so you see—even the French agree with you."

Giancarlo smiled and then looked very seriously at Tom. "It is justice that lets us know that the world makes sense and that it is a place in which we can feel at home. Even an empty world can be a just one. It can be a world that was purged, a world that had been *tainted* and is no longer so. Justice trumps survival, Tom. That is what separates the true soldiers from the civilians. They believe that certain things are worth dying for."

"And worth killing for," Tom added.

"Absolutely," Giancarlo said. "But this is a very serious way to begin our dinner. And besides, Tom, you said that *I* do not remind you of the wanderer you described so beautifully."

"You are surrounded by friends and people who respect you, Giancarlo. They need you. They depend on you. It is rare to see someone as *comfortable* as you are in your world. And I do not imply by that that you are in any way lax or negligent. Far from it."

"I have spent the last decades that God has granted me building such a life," Giancarlo said. "The emotions of your poem . . . I have felt all of them, felt them very deeply. What you see before you," he added, smiling, "is a man who has truly *mellowed*."

"I told you I would always be honest with you, Giancarlo."

"Yes, and I with you."

"I am thinking that there may be another *superstite*."

"Another? Why do you say that, Tom?"

"Because whoever coordinated the disappearance of the five must have survived, at least for some time. Perhaps for a great deal of time … "

"Go on, Tom … "

"We now suddenly have Sullivan's remains and no sooner do we have them than a journalist is asking that they be identified. Hours after they are so identified other journalists are asking for copies of the death certificate. And the journalists are not alone; there is also a lawyer seeking a copy of the death certificate as well. The lawyer represents someone, Giancarlo."

"Then you honor me, Tom."

"Why is that, Giancarlo?"

"Because what you are saying is that it was not me who requested the document and it is not me who secured the services of this lawyer, assuming that he has been identified. You believe that I have been scrupulous in telling you the truth."

"I do, Giancarlo. It is fair to say, however, that withholding something is not the same as lying."

"We are back to our sins of omission and commission, Tom."

"We know that it was not you who requested the document, Giancarlo. The individual was a young man in private practice, a local man."

"Far too young to have represented Gray Sullivan."

"Yes."

"Though he could be representing me."

"Yes, he could."

"And no one else is likely to have suspected that the remains that washed up on your beach are those of Gray Sullivan except for me and the few individuals with whom you have discussed the case in California."

"There is always the possibility that someone within the LBPD mentioned it to a reporter," Tom said.

"Very true," Giancarlo said, "and I appreciate your considering that possibility."

Tom smiled and nodded toward him.

"Let us have some dinner," Giancarlo said, "and let us open this wine. I have more that I must tell you."

FORTY-TWO

"I must ask you something first, Tom," Giancarlo said. "Did you speak with your chief about the issue of confidentiality which we discussed?"

"I *did*, and he's pursuing it with the D.A. He doesn't think it will be a problem, but he can't guarantee that the journalists won't find a way—ultimately—to get the sealed records unsealed."

"But if only you and the Chief are aware of the full details of the investigation, that should help prevent leaks and—absent such leaks—it is far less likely that the curiosity of the journalists would be aroused."

"That's true, Giancarlo, and we would do all that we could to maintain that confidentiality."

"I understand," Giancarlo said. "The situation is always difficult. The discovery of Gray Sullivan's remains will whet their curiosity for awhile, but when that runs its course that interest will, hopefully, subside."

The waiter came and took their orders. Both had the fish specialty for their entrées and the soup specialty for starters. The wine steward approached the table and asked Giancarlo which wine he should open first.

"The Tignanello, I think," he answered.

"It should be very lovely," he said. "Particularly this vintage."

Giancarlo tasted it, nodded, and the wine steward poured a half measure into each man's glass. "It's quite good," Giancarlo said.

Tom tasted his, agreed, and then returned to the subject of the *coordinatore*. "Now, Giancarlo, we should talk about our previous subject."

"Yes, we must do that," he answered. "I believe that I may have misled you a little. I will not say that I lied, but I may have misled."

"In what way, Giancarlo?"

"At the time—as I told you—there was talk of a *coordinatore*. That is true, just as I said to you. However . . . consider the course of our more recent discussion … "

Tom scooted forward in his seat as Orsini continued.

"We agreed that it would have been most difficult (I think we can say, impossible) for a member of one of the external families to have played this role … "

"Yes."

"And it would not have been one of the five who actually disappeared … "

"No."

"It could have been one of the street soldiers (since the captains are all accounted for), but that too is somewhat doubtful … "

"Such a person would be taking on a great deal," Tom said.

"Yes."

"And putting himself between two sets of forces far more powerful than himself, each of which would have had no hesitation in making *him* disappear."

"Correct," Giancarlo said. "But what if a civilian were to express interest in playing this role?"

"A civilian?"

"Yes, Tom, a civilian."

"But how would such a person develop the access and the trust? . . . Wait a minute, Giancarlo. A civilian on the inside."

"Yes, Tom."

"A person who would be treated differently by the external families . . . not completely indemnified necessarily, but given more slack than a soldier would."

"Yes," Giancarlo said, sipping the deep red wine.

"Particularly if that civilian was a woman."

"Yes, Tom. In which case we would not be talking about a *coordinatore*; we would be talking about a *coordinatrice*."

"If these men could have angered other men they could surely have angered one of their women."

"Hell hath no fury, Tom."

"Was Brienza married?"

"No, he was not. He hired women to provide the adoration which no unpaid woman would have given him."

"Sullivan?"

"Not at that time. There were rumors that he had been married sometime in the past, but he gave his full attention to the feeding of his arrogance and the extension of his authority."

"Graffali?"

"He had a wife . . . a singer, remember . . . but she was never really in the picture. He believed that he was somehow on a higher plane than other men and she considered herself to be on a higher plane still. She was a pure civilian."

"Muschina?"

"He was married, but his wife lived in San Diego. She had a store there. There were rumors that Muschina had persuaded the family to pay for it, but . . . like Graffali's wife . . . she was barely in the picture."

"Devito?"

"She lived in Los Angeles, with their son. She was rarely seen."

"This is not very promising, Giancarlo. Except . . . wait . . . Did Tommy Barone leave a widow?"

"Yes, Tom, he left a widow."

"And Sullivan had Barone killed . . . brutally."

"He did."

"And Devito participated in it."

"Yes."

"And Brienza approved it."

"Yes."

"And Muschina stood to gain by it."

"Yes."

"And Graffali?"

"On another plane, remember."

"And was she capable of serving in this role—this role of coordinating their disappearance?"

"She was . . . by all accounts . . . a very formidable woman."

Tom took a deep drink of his wine, paused, and then spoke again. "You must tell me more, Giancarlo."

III

LA COORDINATRICE

FORTY-THREE

"Mind you, Tom, I did not say that she *did* serve in this particular capacity."

"Who else could it be, Giancarlo?"

"Only someone on the scene at that time could answer that question, Tom. As I said earlier, there is always the possibility that someone who served the family might have done it. Perhaps a client … "

"A client?"

"Yes, someone with a business relationship with the family."

"An unhappy customer?" Tom asked.

"It is certainly possible," Giancarlo answered. "Some would have supplied the family with goods; others would have consumed their goods and services. An important client—someone capable of seeking other suppliers—might have contacted one of the external families and conveyed his concerns regarding the goods or services he was receiving from the Brienza family."

"A secondary-market drug dealer, for example … "

Giancarlo nodded. "It is possible. I cannot say if it would be *likely* or not, but it is certainly possible."

"But as we surveyed the members of the principals' families, the only individual who actually stood out was the widow of Tommy Barone."

"Yes," Giancarlo said.

"What more can you tell me about her?" Tom asked.

"I can tell you that she was very competent, very intelligent and very beautiful."

"Then you met her."

"Oh yes. She was in her late thirties when I came to California at my brother's request."

"And you would have been ten years younger or so … "

"Ten years and change," Giancarlo said, smiling. "A remarkable woman. As remarkable as my Clara."

"Of course, you were married, Giancarlo."

"Yes, I was truly blessed. Unfortunately, she died far too early; my only consolation was that her life was so beautiful."

Tom paused before proceeding, allowing Giancarlo to do so as well.

"So the principals of the Brienza family were all gone, but Mrs. Barone remained."

"Yes … "

"Then she was the … "

"The *sopravvissuta,* Tom."

"There are several survivors here. As I told you, Giancarlo … "

"We were both tenacious," he said.

"What was her given name, Giancarlo?"

"Carlotta."

"And did she ever remarry?"

"No, like me she chose not to do that." He said it without hesitation.

"So you kept up with her, then."

"She stayed in southern California after her husband's death."

"And what was her role?" Tom asked.

"I'm not sure that I understand your question, Tom. She did not have any official role within the Orsini family. She commanded respect, just as her husband had commanded respect."

"But if she had been the *coordinatrice* … "

"Yes?"

"Wouldn't that have put her in some special position?"

"Privately, yes, but this was all done with great secrecy, Tom. The identity of the *coordinatore* or *coordinatrice* was never widely known.

I'm not sure that anyone in our family even knew. You see, as we have discussed, it is most likely that this individual would have worked directly with one of the external families."

"And your brother was then approached after the disappearance of the Brienza principals."

"Yes."

"And your brother was not a don at that time."

"No. He was second in command of one of the New York families."

"And he maintained close connections with that family after he was invited to southern California."

"Oh yes, of course."

"So it is likely that his New York family might have supplied the soldiers for the California . . . *operation*."

"It is most certainly *possible*. I cannot say with any degree of certainty that it was likely."

"And your brother never talked to you about it."

"He chose not to do so," Giancarlo said. "I have no way of knowing how much he actually knew, but remember . . . I was his counselor. He was protecting me."

"Giving you *deniability*."

"I would say that he was enabling me to keep an appropriate distance from details that I had no direct need to know. Keep in mind, Tom, that these events had all transpired at a time when we were thousands of miles away. And remember also, at that time it took a DC-3 nearly 18 hours to fly coast-to-coast westbound. That would include three refueling stops. Brooklyn was very far from Newport Beach in those days."

"That's a good point, Giancarlo. So please tell me more about Carlotta Barone."

Before he could answer, the waiter came, removed their entrée dishes and took their orders for coffee. As soon as he was out of earshot Giancarlo continued.

"She was raising her children when I arrived. I would see her occasionally . . . at weddings and funerals, sometimes at holiday dinners. She was very striking. She always dressed in white or light pastel colors, never in black. You know, of course, that some Italian widows dress in black for the rest of their lives. She would always say that she was the wife of Tommy Barone and that she would continue to dress in the manner that he most preferred."

"And she was still a very young woman."

"Yes, as I said she was in her late thirties, but what do they say now, Tom, that 'fifty is the new thirty'? Then it was not. Look at pictures of your grandparents. When they were in their thirties they looked as if they would be in their seventies now. That has all changed. When social security was originally created no one—statistically—would have been expected to live to collect it."

"Right."

"What I am saying is that you should not imagine her as a 'merry widow' surrounded by dancing men in tuxedos, but more as a grande dame who commanded respect for her personal . . . dignity. People would whisper, 'That is the widow of the distinguished captain, Tommy Barone.'"

"And she is no longer alive now," Tom said.

"Oh no. Regrettably, our generation did not enjoy the longevity of your generation, Tom. She lived a full life, exceeding expectations, but she is no longer with us. In that regard, I *am* the last survivor."

"And have any of her relatives survived?"

"Unfortunately, her two sons died decades ago and her daughter died in childbirth."

"And did any of them have children, Giancarlo?" Tom asked, dragging the answers from him.

"Neither of the sons married. One died very young and the other became a scientist. The one who died young was named Andrea; I mentioned him to you earlier—Brienza was his godfather. The other son, the scientist, was named Mario. He was quite distinguished . . . at the University of Bologna, actually."

"And the child that the daughter was carrying?"

"Her first and only child."

"Yes."

"She survives, Tom."

"And where is she, Giancarlo? I would like to speak with her."

"I think I should speak with her first before I tell you that, Tom. I am not trying to be coy or duplicitous. I am merely respecting her privacy."

FORTY-FOUR

"He's promised to get back to me the day after tomorrow, Chief," Tom said.

"I'll check on Carlotta Barone at this end," Dietrich said. "This is significant progress, I think."

"Yes, but I can't say that he's been as forthcoming as I might have expected."

"Perhaps the granddaughter is Orsini's client," Chris said. "He may want to have a sit-down with her before he advises her one way or the other. If she *does* agree to talk to you she'll probably want to set some parameters first. I certainly would."

"I agree, but remember that Giancarlo has been preparing the way . . . asking for assurances that the so-called *coordinator's* identity will be kept secret, etc. He knew where this was going, Chief. He's had fifty+ years to think about it and tease out each and every one of the separate details. And yet, he's forced me to talk him through each of the various possibilities, with him then easing out a bit of information at a time, but never all of it at once."

"You think he's trying to mislead you?"

"No, I think he's dragging his feet. Not that I expected a simple memo from him, summarizing all of the details. He said he wanted me to hear the story from the beginning so that I could see all of the events in context ... "

"He wants you to be sympathetic," Chris said. "He wants to turn a mob takeover story into a battle between the forces of evil and the forces of righteousness."

"I'm sure that's part of it, Chief."

"And from what you've told me he's done a pretty good job of it."

"He sees it as a case study," Tom answered. "His version is that the kind of dysfunctionality represented by the Brienza family can be found everywhere in society."

"And that's *true*," Chris said, "but telling it that way insures that reasonable, fair-minded people will be sympathetic, because nobody likes asswipes who are vain, controlling, indecisive, and fundamentally incompetent."

"And we hate even more the kind of opportunistic sleazebags who rush into the power vacuums created by such people."

"Precisely," Chris said.

"It's still all *true* though."

"Yes, but it's a truth that fits his purposes."

"And those purposes go beyond a desire to sit down every night over pasta and the catch-of-the-day and shoot the breeze with a curious detective with a long list of questions."

"Yes."

"No matter how enjoyable that experience might be."

"Thanks for the benefit of the doubt, Chief."

"I'm not exaggerating, Tom. I wish *I* was the one breaking bread with him. It sounds like he's wrapping a riveting story in the vacation of a lifetime."

"Maybe that's the point, Chief. Maybe *that's* the point."

"What, Tom?"

"He's extending the vacation, knowing that everyone would understand."

"I'm not following, Tom."

"You said you wish *you* were here, Chief. That's a natural reaction, just as natural as the thought that no one would want to see this story and the food and sunshine in which it's wrapped ever come to an end."

"Yes … ?"

"Meanwhile he's doing something behind the scenes."

"He's been buying time."

"Yes," Tom said. "He's been buying time."

"And that's why there have been these interruptions, the trips to Messina and Catania . . . the open days."

"Right, but why? What's he up to?"

"That's the question," Chris said.

"And how is this all related to the fact that Gray Sullivan's skeleton (or most of it) just washed up on the beach after being held in cold storage (or maybe warm storage) for sixty odd years?"

"Maybe the 'coordinator' is the key," Chris said.

"Possibly," Tom answered. "It *does* seem to be the case that the 'coordinator' is the end point of the story."

"Or at least the point at which Orsini wants the story to end," Chris said.

"Right, but there's also some logic to it. We want to know who killed the principals of the Brienza family. We're not likely to ever learn the names of all the Tonys and Guidos who aided in the process, but it would be nice to have a single, key name to draw a circle around and put on the bottom line on some police forms."

"Agreed. Go for it, Tom. And keep me posted. Where are you now?"

"I'm actually sitting by the hotel pool, finishing up my breakfast."

"Which consists of?"

"Just some very strong coffee, fresh fruit, and some rolls."

"Still warm from the oven?"

"No, they were, but now they're warm from the sun."

"But the butter's not melting, because it's in a little silver container lined with ice."

"And with a blue napkin wrapped around the sides for insulation."

"I hate to see that vacation end," Chris said, with a smile on his lips. "You're like my terrier, Sophie. I work and she lays in the sun in my name."

"I don't mind your thinking of me as your surrogate, Chief," Tom said. "Just remember--if I need to, I *will* bite."

"You'll bite who?" a disembodied voice asked, as Tom closed his cell phone.

FORTY-FIVE

She was standing just behind him, the curves of her outline silhouetted by the morning sun. When she walked around him he saw that she was wearing tailored wool slacks and a flowered, silk blouse, accented by a small scarf with a matching floral design.

"Good morning, Gina," he said.

"Good morning, Tom. Do you mind if I call you that?"

"Of course not. I'm practically a fixture at your hotel by now."

"And you have been enjoying your stay?"

"Very much."

"And your discussions with the Signore?"

"They have been very interesting."

"He is a good man, Tom. I know that his brother led an . . . *unconventional* life, but I am told that he was a fair man and not a cruel one. You must understand the local beliefs and traditions. It was originally understood that such men would protect the powerless. Sometimes that was true. Like any ideal there has been divergence, sometimes considerable divergence, but the ideal was at least pure. The Signore tries to embody that ideal. He does a great deal to help people. Very often he collects no fee."

"I haven't seen any reason to doubt that. He appears to me to be a true gentleman . . . regardless of any *unconventional* actions in the past."

"He is particularly protective of women," Gina said. "I am young enough and modern enough to realize that he sees women in an old-fashioned way, but I do not judge his attitudes because I know that his intentions are pure. If you walk around this city—not the places frequented by the tourists, but the places where the people live—you will always hear his name spoken with great love and respect."

"Perhaps there is a touch of penance involved in his pursuit of good works. What do you think?"

"Perhaps," Gina said. "I think that all of us have reason to do penance, but not all of us actually do so. There are people who do great evil, who cause great harm and inflict great pain, who simply take their behavior to be a normal part of life. That is what one does to survive, they would say, but there is no reason for the cruelty which they practice. They are simply bad people. Giancarlo is not a bad person."

"I agree," Tom said, "though I don't know him as well as you. What you have said strengthens my own impressions."

"There was an old woman in a local village," Gina said, "who was in a very difficult situation. Her husband had long been dead and she had been helped by her son, but her son died tragically in a terrible road accident. He was only 50 years old and suddenly she was all alone. She did not have enough money to buy food and she was about to lose her modest home. Giancarlo spoke to the bank and arranged for them to convert the equity in her home into an annuity so that she could keep body and soul together and continue to live in dignity. Whenever she sees him she kisses his hand. He brings her flowers and tells her how happy he is to see her so well. That is the kind of man he is, Tom. He helps others in countless ways—people with whom he has no personal or family relationship. He has helped *me* in many ways."

"He brings many customers to your hotel," Tom said, smiling.

"Yes, and patronizes our restaurant regularly," she added. "But he has done other things as well. I am very far from my home here and he is always a friend to me. Whenever we have problems he refers us to people who can be of help . . . craftsmen, financial consultants, even fishermen and farmers. Part of my success with the hotel is due to his support."

"How did you meet him?" Tom asked.

"I met him many years ago," Gina said. "My mother died giving birth to me and my father was desolate. Years later I learned that Giancarlo had helped my father and me in various ways, some personal, some having to do with the law."

"Where did you grow up, Gina?"

"In California.

"And did Giancarlo help you to be posted to Taormina once he had moved here?"

"He says that he put in a good word, but I suspect that he has been helping me in many ways for many years. Not with threats or anything of that sort. I have had to perform well or I assure you I would have been fired long ago. Still, he has been my advocate, helping me when my blood relatives were mostly gone."

"Mostly … ?"

"Yes, I do not have any brothers or sisters or parents alive, Tom."

"Grandparents?"

"No, not anymore."

"Your father was named Abruzzi?"

"Yes, he was from San Francisco. He was an installer of tile; he was highly skilled and much sought after. People spoke of him as an artist rather than as a craftsman."

"And your mother's maiden name?"

"You have a lot of questions this morning, Tom."

"I'm sorry. It's what I do. I don't want you to feel uncomfortable, Gina."

"I'm fine, Tom. I know that if I answer your question you will have many more for me."

"I won't make you uncomfortable, Gina."

"I know you won't, Tom. You have probably already guessed it anyway. My mother's maiden name was Barone."

FORTY-SIX

"Giancarlo warned you about the direction that our discussions have been taking ... "

"Yes, he did. He wanted to protect me, but he also said that he thought I could speak with you safely."

"Tell me about your grandmother, Gina."

"She was very . . . how would I put it? . . . very regal. At the same time she was very simple and straightforward. She was a person of great dignity. You were always aware of her as a strong physical presence. She dressed beautifully and wore simple jewelry and commanded great respect. At the same time whenever she spoke you felt as if you were with a person to whom you could tell anything, a person who would keep confidences and never betray your trust. She was the perfect grandmother. Of course, it is often said that children have a special bond with their grandparents. They share their parents in common, but see them from very different perspectives. The parents are the authority figures to the child, but to the grandparents they will always—to some degree—be children. This moderates their view of them and creates special linkages between them and the grandchildren. I always felt as if I could go to my grandmother with my questions and concerns, particularly in light of the fact that my mother was gone."

"And did she actually raise you?"

"Yes, to a degree. My father was there and some other friends and relatives, but she was a very strong force in my life."

"And she herself never remarried."

"No, she didn't. She was devoted to my grandfather. His pictures were everywhere, Tom; her house was like a shrine. Here, let me show you … "

She reached in her purse, removed her wallet, and showed him a picture. It appeared to have been reprinted though the image was very old—a man and a woman, standing arm in arm in a garden of flowers, each wearing formal jackets and hats. Each appeared to be tall and the connection between them was obvious. His hand was tight around her waist, the material from her suit gathered under his fingertips; she was looking at him lovingly rather than simply posing for the camera.

"Their tenth anniversary," Gina said.

"It is easy to see that they were very much in love," Tom said.

"Yes, isn't it?"

"I can only imagine how she must have been affected by his death," Tom said.

"And the nature of it," Gina said. "It was unspeakably brutal."

"She spoke to you of such things?" Tom asked.

"Yes, when I was older . . . when she thought I was ready to hear them. I was like you, Tom. I had many questions."

"I hope you'll share some of the answers with me," he said.

"Come to my office this evening," she said. "I will have some food for us and we will talk about the old days. Is seven o'clock good?"

"I'll be there," Tom said, "and I want you to know . . . I truly appreciate this."

"I know," she said. "It is not painful for me to discuss it, particularly not now."

"How so?" he asked.

"My grandmother is no longer with us," she said. "I feel it is now fair to discuss her life. It was a source of pride to her, as it is to me."

"Seven o'clock then. I look forward to it," Tom said.

She smiled, nodded, turned, and walked away into the shadows, toward the rear entrance to the hotel.

FORTY-SEVEN

Tom finished his breakfast, had a final cup of coffee, and then walked slowly back to his room, wondering now if his actions were being observed. The positioning of the pool, the presence of heavy winds, and his care in the use of his cell phone had mitigated any possibilities that he was being overheard through the use of high tech listening devices or simple parabolic microphones. Besides, he had never really said anything that would have surprised Giancarlo or Gina. Giancarlo in particular was aware of the fact that he was in communication with his Chief and would have anticipated precisely the sort of editorializing that had accompanied Tom's characterizations of Giancarlo's narrative. If anything, the openness of all of the processes had been their most salient characteristic.

But being heard is one thing, being observed another. The one thing that both Giancarlo and Gina were most likely to fear was unanticipated, precipitous action. Much of Tom's success was due to the fact that he had been honest and above board with each. Now—as he came closer and closer to an actual account of guilt—he needed to reassure them, by his actions, that nothing had changed; he was the same Tom as the quiet, fair individual who had been met by Gina days earlier at the Greek theatre.

Nevertheless, he needed to prepare for his meeting with her. When he returned to his room he shaved and showered, dressed casually, and found a comfortable chair in which to systematically study the notes of his conversations with Giancarlo. He needed to check names and facts and revisit the timeline which he was continually revising and editing. If Gina was as proud of her grandmother's life as she claimed, she might share it with Tom in all of its details. For his part, he needed to see the manner in which her story converged with the narrative that had been fashioned by Giancarlo.

At 1:30 he took a break and walked into town. Moving in and out of tourist shops and continually checking his surroundings he did not believe that he was being followed. If he *was* being followed, it was by a real professional. At 2:00 he stopped in a small trattoria for lunch, passing on wine, since he planned to review his notes again when he returned to his hotel room.

Gina had changed her clothes when they met for dinner. She was dressed in simple slacks and a cotton blouse. Tom had received a note from her earlier, telling him that he should dress comfortably and bring his appetite along with his questions.

Dinner consisted of a caprese salad, with fresh tomatoes, lightly-seasoned mozzarella, basil leaves, and a touch of olive oil and black pepper. The entrée was Florentine steak with a side of gnocchi in a light vodka sauce. Strong black coffee was followed by thin wedges of chocolate cake. "If you want more of anything, just let me know," she said.

"This will surely hold me," he said, as she refilled his wine glass. She was matching him, drink for drink.

As she finished her third glass she sat back in her chair and spoke. "My grandmother was a very beautiful woman, but also a very strong one. Everyone commented on her beauty, but many underestimated her strength. After my grandfather's death she was expected to mourn for a decent period and then remarry. She was still, after all, a young woman and she had a number of suitors anxious to court her. She made it clear that she was not interested in that and assumed the posture of one who would protect and burnish her husband's memory rather than cherish it but soon move beyond it.

"Sullivan was bothered by this. He had hoped that she would simply move away and his comments to that effect found their way back to her.

What he did not know was that she had inspected her husband's body in detail after his death. They had thought that she would not wish to do so, that the sight would simply be too upsetting. They believed that the undertaker would first make him presentable, cover him with makeup and fill his cheeks and nostrils with prosthetics. 'Put a rosary in his hand and a smile on his face,' Sullivan was reputed to have said, but my grandmother knew the undertaker and demanded to see her husband's body before the man began his work.

"His body had been destroyed, nearly every bone broken with kicks and clubs. They had been careful in avoiding his head and face until the end, perhaps because they did not want him to lose consciousness. This was a very cruel death, Tom, an appalling death."

"It went beyond simple efficiency," Tom said. "There must have been a great deal of anger … "

"And envy," Gina said. "He not only had the most beautiful wife; he was also the most effective captain. The rest of them looked like fools next to him and they knew it. They had lived with the comparisons for years. Some, of course, aspired to take over his place and they had bitterly resented his success and consequent longevity. I believe that if he had been allowed to retire quietly my grandmother would have understood. She knew what fools they were and to some degree he had come to be embarrassed to be a part of them, but when they killed him so mercilessly, she was not prepared to stand aside and tolerate it."

"So she contacted one of the external families … ?"

"She must have. She never informed me of the details, but the five individuals in the Brienza family could not have been removed without considerable help. You must understand, Tom, that my grandfather was well known throughout California and New York. He had fewer ties to the Midwest, though he knew people in the Kansas City organization. We're unlikely to ever know whose help she sought, but it is clear that she sought someone's and it is clear that they were forthcoming in their support."

"And effective in their actions," Tom added.

"Yes, very effective. There was something else that motivated her, Tom."

"Yes?"

"Gray Sullivan had made overtures to her."

"Overtures?"

"Yes. Sexual overtures. I would not say *romantic* overtures, for she believed that he had no interest in her in any serious way. He had removed her husband and now he wanted to also conquer her. He had made comments about her, comments that had been reported to her. Things were said about my grandfather . . . about his *appetites* and about the ways in which she must have been able to satisfy them. Now it was assumed that she was lonely and *needy*. Sullivan volunteered to do his part to 'be of service' to her. That was very surprising to many, since he was generally very circumspect in his words and actions. Sexual bravado was never expected from him. It was, of course, interpreted to be his way of further asserting his superiority over my grandfather, but it was still odd."

"And a great mistake."

"Yes, a very great mistake. There are many reasons for calling it a *family*, Tom. People talk. They gossip. There are secrets that are kept from the outside world, but within the family there are very few secrets. My grandmother knew of Sullivan's statements and she knew that he was prepared to act on them. After my grandfather's funeral she had seen him on one or two occasions. He said things, nothing too overt, nothing too offensive, but their implication was clear. Eventually he asked her to come see him. It was at night. The meeting did not concern business; he had said that he 'wanted to get to know her better.'"

"And did she have enough notice to . . . prepare a proper response?" Tom asked.

"Yes, she did, but she was not yet certain what precise form that response would take. She was prepared to respond in different ways, depending on the nature of his words and actions."

"Can you be more specific?" Tom asked.

"I can be *very* specific," she said, finishing her glass of wine, getting up, and walking to a cabinet on the far wall of her office. She opened a door, removed an object, and returned to the table. It was a large velvet box. She put it on the table, refilled Tom's glass and her own, took a sip of the wine, and then picked up the box. There was a thong on the front that fit over an ivory button. She slid the thong over the button and slowly opened the box, turning it toward Tom so that he could see the contents. There were a pair of ribbons on the inside of the box within the box which kept the lid from falling away and two compartments in the inner box's bottom. She allowed him to examine the contents. On the left was an ivory-handled straight razor and on the right was a wooden-handled ice pick.

FORTY-EIGHT

"You can go ahead and touch them, Tom," Gina said. "They've been cleaned and polished regularly for decades. There's no remaining evidence on them."

The straight razor's ivory handle carried an etched scrimshaw-like design: a rose laying atop a gleaming saber. The design was also imprinted on the blade itself. "Be careful," Gina said. "It's still very sharp. My grandmother liked to keep it that way."

The ice pick had a practical wooden handle. "Some are far more finished instruments," Gina said. "There was actually a psychiatrist at the time—a man named Freeman--who used them to perform transorbital lobotomies. From Washington, D.C., I think; my grandmother talked about him from time to time. He believed that mental illness was caused by overactive emotions. By cutting the brain he released it from its enslavement to them. He began by using electroshock therapy to render the patient unconscious. Then he took his instrument and inserted it above the patient's eyeball, just through the orbit of the eye and into the frontal lobes, moving the instrument back and forth. Then he repeated the procedure on the other side of the face. Some claimed that the results were very positive."

"Is that what your grandmother did to Sullivan?" Tom asked.

She paused before answering, smiling at him coyly. "No, not really. Besides, I'm getting a little ahead of myself," she said. "I promised to tell you the whole story. My grandmother agreed to meet with Sullivan, but knew that the putative purpose of the meeting—something to do with the payments she was receiving from the family—was little more than a pretense that he was using to persuade her to see him. Sullivan had bragged to others that he would enjoy her as her husband had and joked that Tommy Barone had 'willed her' to him.

"My grandmother dressed in red for the occasion. She told me that she did it in order to distract him. She said that he would think that she was dressing that way to give off positive signals of her availability to him. Actually, she was dressed in red so that any blood splatter would be less apparent if it found its way to her clothing. She was really very clever, you see. She was always able to *anticipate* things … "

"The *coordinatrice*," Tom said.

"Yes, exactly. Anyway, she went in to see him and he offered her a drink. Scotch, I think. Very old and very expensive. She accepted it and sat comfortably on a sofa that he had in his office. She really *did* feel comfortable, because she knew that the individuals in the outer office who might have come to Sullivan's aid would be quickly removed and she would be alone with Sullivan, with help—for *her*—just outside the door if it was needed.

"He poured himself a drink, but added more water to his than he had to her's. 'It was so obvious,' she said. 'The man had no imagination whatsoever. He had probably also feared that too much alcohol might make him impotent. Sullivan was like Brienza in that respect; neither could stand to be embarrassed in any way.' After awhile he offered her a second drink and then a third. She had lined her stomach with a glass of milk a few minutes before she entered his office and the adrenalin was racing through her system. 'The drinks had no effect on me at all,' she said, 'though I pretended that they had.'

"For a time she thought about simply slicing his throat," Gina said. "It's not a crime to ask, after all, and if he had treated her decently she might have dispatched him swiftly and efficiently. Instead he started to paw at her. There were no soft words or light kisses first . . . Not that she had expected anything romantic from a person such as that, but as she put it, he was more like an impatient shopper examining merchandise roughly and not putting it back in place afterwards. He'd grope her and pinch her and ask her how she liked it. Presumably he thought she'd admit to a taste for aggressive sex. 'I can do it harder if you like,' he said.

"At that point she decided that she would be harsher with him than she had originally planned. 'It was karma,' she said. That was the California side of her coming out. 'I tried not to see it as revenge or retribution. He was the sum total of his own deeds and those deeds would be concluded in a way consistent with their nature.'

"'Just a second,' she said to him. 'I need to get something.' He thought it had to do with birth control and he seemed very pleased and encouraged. She ran her hand over his face, taking its measure, and he undid his tie and unbuttoned his shirt. She slipped off her shoes—again, not wanting to splatter them with blood—though he thought that that was the first step in her disrobing. As he waited for her on the couch she walked over to the table and started going through her purse, glancing at him and smiling while she looked. That raised his expectations. She palmed the chosen instrument, shielding it from his view with her wrist and forearm. Then she walked slowly back to the couch.

"'Do you like the taste of women?' she asked.

"'I don't taste them; they taste me,' he said.

"She smiled, bent closer, leaned into him and then, suddenly, plunged the ice pick into the center of his eye. 'How do you like the taste of that?' she asked."

"I take it he didn't much care for it," Tom said.

"No, actually, he didn't. He began screaming uncontrollably and flailing at her with his right hand. She had removed the pick and was using it to protect herself from his hands. At the sound of his scream the office door had opened and her partners were standing there, ready to help her. She gestured to them to hold off. As Sullivan grabbed at her she raised the pick and when he tried to slap her brutally she watched its point penetrate his palm and come out on the other side of his hand.

He flailed with his other hand, but she wasn't bothered by the slaps and punches he tried to land … "

"So he bled out there … " Tom said.

"No, actually not. She wasn't really finished with him yet. She called the two men into the room and they wrapped him in a red blanket and carried him out. The red blanket was her idea. Always planning . . . After putting him in the back of a van one of them waited with him and the other returned to help her finish cleaning up his office. It was much simpler in those days, as you know, Tom. There weren't crime scene investigators with industrial-strength luminol and other chemicals. She had also been lucky. Most of the blood was on his shirt and slacks and tie. Her partners had wrapped him up quickly enough to prevent any major spills. There were some smears on the walls and on the furniture, but she cleaned those up quickly. Ten minutes later the room looked as if it had just been redecorated and she and her partner left and joined Sullivan and the other man in the van."

"And Sullivan was still alive."

"Yes, and apparently making a lot of unpleasant sounds and using some very bad language."

"It may have been the first time in his life he showed any evidence of possessing an actual personality," Tom said.

"That's exactly what my grandmother said. At one point she pulled back the blanket, exposing his face, and said, 'You haven't spoken that many words to me in my whole life.' He began to curse again and she covered his face with the blanket. Apparently the men with her were surprised by the violence which she exhibited and commented on the fact. 'I'm the wife of Tommy Barone,' she said. 'We don't do these things half-way.'"

"And you said she wasn't finished with him yet," Tom said.

"Oh no," Gina answered.

FORTY-NINE

"They drove to a construction site. She wasn't very specific with regard to the location, saying only that it was between Irvine and Anaheim. At that time it would have been considered a remote location—a new subdivision developed by a land speculator. She knew about it because the family was close to some of the craft unions. The men with her asked her why she wanted to go there and she said it had to do with something that Sullivan had said after she had stabbed him.

"They drove on, wondering, and she sat quietly next to Sullivan, still holding her ice pick. When they arrived she directed them to take him into the basement of a house under construction. The houses were built sequentially. At the end of the line was a set of vacant lots, then a space in which the hole for the foundation had been dug (these houses had basements—very rare today), then a lot with a standing foundation, a lot with a foundation and subfloor, a lot with a foundation and the wooden structure under roof, a lot with a house with windows and roof shingles, and so on. The various tradesmen moved from building to building, always working under tight deadlines. They took Sullivan to a building that was under roof, with the exterior doors and windows installed."

"To muffle the noise?" Tom asked.

"Yes," Gina said. "There was no one near them, but it was an extra precaution. With the basement poured there would also be a functioning floor drain … "

She said all of these things in a very clinical manner. There was urgency in her voice, but it was the urgency of a judge reading a sentence or a surgeon presenting a diagnosis and plan of action. From time to time she took a sip of wine, savoring it and not simply using it to keep her lips and mouth moist.

"There was water as well," she said, "and all of the electrical work had been roughed in. She began by questioning him. 'When you were striking at me and cursing at me,' she said, 'back in your office . . . you said something to me.' He just groaned at her. 'You said that you killed my husband and that you would also kill me. I have a question. Think about it carefully before you answer.' He turned his head away, trying to release himself from the blanket, which was wound tightly around his legs and arms. He was shuffling his feet, trying to gain some purchase from the cement floor. The men with her asked her if they should silence him or hold him and she said no. By now his eye socket was covered with dried, reddish-black blood and the blood from his hand had stained the blanket noticeably. She paid no attention to that, addressing him as if he was a witness on a stand.

"'You said you killed him,' she said. 'So you were actually *there* when it happened. You did more than simply order others to do it for you ... ' She waited for him to answer. His mouth had formed an ugly sneer and his remaining good eye was flashing with anger in the beams of the men's flashlights. 'Well?' she said. 'Were you there?'

"'I was there,' he said, his words halting but clear enough.

"'And what did you do to him, you cowardly bastard? Did you wait until he was nearly dead to come near him?'

"'He was barely able to breathe, but he continued to curse us,' Sullivan said. 'I'll stop that, I said. I kicked him in the stomach and he gulped for air. Then I kicked him again and the curses stopped.'

"'What a brave boy. After others had beaten him senseless you stepped in like the fearless leader you fancy yourself to be and you kicked him.'

"Sullivan was coughing and retching now. 'Ye-s-s,' he said. 'It was better than he d-d-deserved. As soon as I got home I cleaned m-m-y shoes to get his stink off of them.'

"'Did you now?' she asked. Then she whispered to one of the men with her, directing him to bring her something. He had to go to the next building, where the finish carpenter had been hanging doors and installing cabinets and molding. He returned in a few minutes, plugged the Skilsaw into an electric outlet over the stationary tubs, hit the switch and heard the whir of the motor. 'Bring it here,' she said. When he handed it to her she held it in front of Sullivan's good eye. 'You won't have to worry about cleaning your shoes now . . . or your feet,' she said."

"And then she cut off his feet at the ankles."

"Yes."

"*She* did it, not one of the men."

"Yes, *she* did it. The sound of the motor drowned out most of his screams. As he bled out she sat above him, staring at his eye and mouth. 'Welcome to Hell,' she said. 'Have a nice long stay.'"

Tom let her continue.

"The rest is anticlimactic, but my grandmother found it interesting. One of the tasks at construction sites was to clean up the grounds. It was an important task, though it was usually assigned to unskilled laborers. As soon as the exteriors were finished the sod layers would come in and install the lawn. Generally they'd do the front yard and part of the back, seeding the remainder. First the ground had to be carefully graded and later constantly watered. The general contractor was scrupulous about keeping the sites clear of trash, because potential buyers were inspecting the houses that were finished and he didn't want the accumulated junk—pieces of drywall tape or shingle ends, for example—to blow onto the freshly-sodded lots and spoil the effect. At that point everyone was focused on details—special house numbers, for example, or a high-end light at the front door—the kinds of things that caught buyers' eyes and helped sell the house. There were small fires going all the time—to consume the trash that would burn. The things that wouldn't burn—the end pieces of metal used for drywall corners, for example—were thrown down in the ground beside the foundation.

"It was rather odd. After the foundation had been poured it was tarred on the exterior and thoroughsealed on the inside. Sometimes the contractors would put on multiple coats of thoroughseal in the basement. The effect was very nice—almost as if the walls had been finished and painted. This was all done very carefully. No contractor wanted to be called back later to correct wet-basement problems. Anyway, after all of that care, they still used the space between the exterior basement wall and the surrounding earth as a garbage dump … "

"And that's where they put Sullivan's feet," Tom said.

"Yes. I should have told you. My grandmother first removed his shoes. They were expensive and she wanted to donate them to the St. Vincent de Paul Society. The feet went in with the construction garbage."

"I suppose that's appropriate in its way," Tom said. "We hear about people ending up in the poured walls of buildings in New York … "

"Yes. That's what my grandmother thought, except that she said that the walls would have been too good for Gray Sullivan. For him . . . the garbage pile."

"But she took much better care of the rest of the body," Tom said.

"Apparently so," Gina answered. "All that she ever told me was that they took 'what was left' to the undertaker."

"There would have been a specific undertaker, one who was under long-term contract."

"I don't know if it was quite like that," Gina said, "but I'm sure there was an individual who could be trusted to maintain confidences and do his work in a professional manner."

"Did she ever say where the body was buried or stored?"

"No, but it's clear that there was no funeral for either Sullivan or any of the rest of the key men in the Brienza organization. They simply disappeared."

"If your grandmother was a devout Catholic she would have insured that there would be no funeral masses," Tom said. "Let me rephrase that. If she was a devout Catholic seeking the purest form of vengeance, she would have done whatever she could to deny them the spiritual benefits of the Mass of the Dead."

"I hadn't thought of that," Gina said. "That may be one of the reasons why they all disappeared. An accident could have been fabricated, for example, but that's not what happened. One day they were all there and the next day they were all gone."

"Why celebrate their memory if the memories were all bad?" Tom asked.

"Good question," Gina answered.

"So your grandmother never explained what happened to the others."

"I didn't say that, Tom … "

FIFTY

"**B**ut she didn't share any of the specifics."

"No, but she said that their disappearance was the result of a carefully-orchestrated plan. She didn't comment on the details, but she said that they were all *removed*."

"That could mean many things," Tom said.

"Yes, but she did not say that they were killed, at least not right away. She said that their individual locations were all identified and that they were then removed from them."

"Not killed on the spot."

"She implied that they were not. Of course, she could have been protecting me from the details. They might have each been killed in a brutal fashion and their bodies then removed."

"Yes, but she didn't protect you from the details of Sullivan's death."

"That's true. Of course, his case was very special to her. She always singled him out whenever she discussed the Brienza family. She believed that he had a greater share of the responsibility for their actions because the rest were all fools. 'Selfish fools' she called them. I believe she considered their motives to be simplistic. They were ruled by vanity and greed and ambition, but generally in their crudest forms. Sullivan, she said, was the *mostro*--the monster. He was intelligent enough to be a positive force, but instead he systematically chose to make things worse. He saw through the rest of them, saw through their silliness and their triviality, but then he consistently exceeded them in evil and vileness."

"She must have believed that he had a responsibility to use his gifts to do better things."

"Exactly. My grandmother was an extremely *moral* person. She was capable of doing things which she herself saw as sinful, but she was always aware of what she had done and never attempted to minimize it or explain it away. Her actions were a source of great pain and concern to her because she saw what she considered to be the immorality in them."

"That is a point of Catholic doctrine," Tom said. "If she did not have true contrition for her actions, the priest could not give her absolution for them."

"Yes," Gina said. "Later in her life she would undertake pilgrimages; she visited the Vatican once and secured a plenary indulgence, but her heart was never at rest. That is why she dedicated herself to do good works. She said that if God could not forgive her for what she had done (something that she would have done again) then perhaps He could balance His judgment of her with His awareness of the good things that she had done to expiate her guilt."

"Could you tell me about those things, Gina?" Tom asked.

"Of course. She gave alms to the poor to an uncommon degree and she looked after the orphans and widows of many of her husband's associates. She was a very kindly person. Those who knew her described her with words such as *saintly*. They were not aware of what she had done, of course."

"But she shared that with you."

"Yes, she thought it was very important. It was part of my upbringing. At the same time, she was very conflicted over it, as I said. She tried to inculcate a sense of responsibility, even if that responsibility might involve behavior that most would consider extreme."

"She saw herself as defending her family. And she *was* doing that."

"Yes. I always thought of her as a mother defending her children. If they could kill her husband so ruthlessly they could kill anyone. Someone had to prevent them from doing so. I walked in on her once . . . she was watching a television program. It was a nature show. They were talking about the dangers of the wild and noted that you should never approach cubs, no matter how gentle and cute they appeared to be, because their mothers would defend them at any cost. She was nodding approvingly. I said something to her about it and she said that that was good advice. 'If the parent does not protect, who else would do so?' she said."

"How often did you see her, Gina?"

"I lived with her until I left for college. After that I saw her whenever I could. She has been the most important influence in my life."

"And Giancarlo . . . did he know her well?"

"Yes, but he did not see her as often as he might have liked. The Signore has many responsibilities, Tom. His brother depended on him heavily and many continue to do so."

"I've been thinking of him as a sort of stepfather to you . . . or stepgrandfather."

"He is more like an old family friend. The best family friend. The one who was invited for family dinners, for weddings and baptisms and funerals. Lately I have seen him more often."

"I am sure he is happy to have you in Taormina."

"Yes, he says I am a link to the past and that that is very precious to him."

"It's a pity he and your grandmother never had a more . . . personal relationship."

"They were very much alike, Tom. He lost his wife when she was relatively young and he has never attempted to find a second partner. They were very close, just like my grandmother and grandfather. I think that brought him closer to my grandmother—the fact that they shared the loss of one so beloved—but it was a source of respect and affection between them, not romantic love."

"Perhaps they each perceived that the other would always remain faithful to the lost spouse. Anything between them could only be on circumscribed terms."

"I think you're right. They were like the sole members of a small club. They understood each other very well because they understood each other's feelings. She praised the Signore to me constantly, but there was a certain formality when they were in each other's presence."

"Each probably felt that if they had spoken more directly it could lead to tears. They were each, in their way, *survivors* and each knew the burdens that that entailed."

"It is almost as if you knew them, Tom. That is exactly how they were with one another."

"My father and mother were extremely close," Tom said. "She predeceased my dad and he has never gotten over it. He doesn't express these feelings very often, but they're always close to the surface. She has never left his thoughts, not even for a moment."

"That's very beautiful," Gina said. "I think that's why my grandmother tried to look after those who had lost their loved ones. She understood the depths of their feelings. She was a wonderful person, Tom, but, as I said, she was a very strong person when her family was attacked."

"When she told you these things … " Tom said, "what was her demeanor?"

"She was always very loving," Gina said, "but also very serious. She wanted to impress on me how important it was to do what you believed you should do. 'Follow your conscience,' she said. 'Follow it absolutely.'"

"Wherever it leads?"

"Yes, wherever it leads."

"That's very Catholic, of course. She should have reminded herself that God would forgive her if her conscience commanded her to do something."

"That is what the priest told her."

"She told you about her confessions?"

"Yes, she did, and I told her that I hoped that what the priest said would give her some comfort. I told her to listen to him. I told her that he *knew* about such things. She would smile gratefully, but it was never enough. What troubled her was that her actions were so carefully premeditated."

"The priest probably also told her that she should guard against having a conscience that was too scrupulous."

"He did, Tom. That is another very Catholic notion, is it not?"

Tom nodded approvingly.

"But she kept them, Tom," Gina said, lifting up the box with the razor and ice pick. She kept them . . . and she polished them."

"She thought that there was always the possibility that she might need them again … " Tom said.

FIFTY-ONE

Before Gina could respond her phone rang. The ring tone was muted—the sort of tone that one might choose if there were constant calls in a business day. "Excuse me, Tom," she said.

Her single-word responses were delivered in a monotone: "Yes . . . yes . . . fine . . . yes."

"I'm sorry, Tom, I have to go," she said. "A mini-crisis, not a maxi-crisis, but I have to attend to it."

"I only had one other question," Tom said.

Gina walked back to the table, remained standing, picked up her wine glass and took a final sip. "Of course . . . what is it?"

"When did your grandmother pass away?"

"Two and a half months ago," she said.

"I didn't realize it was that recent," Tom said, trying to suppress any expression of surprise. "Please . . . accept my condolences."

"Thank you," she said. "I have to go now. I'll be in all day tomorrow if you want to talk some more."

Tom stood while she walked to the door.

"Don't worry about the dishes," Gina said. "Somebody will come in and clean up. Feel free to finish the wine or take a glass with you."

He took a glass back to his room, put it on the nightstand next to his bed, picked up his cell phone and went out to the pool.

"Sorry to bother you, Chief, but I knew that you'd want to hear what I just learned."

"No problem, Tom," Dietrich said. "I was just taking a break. What do you have?"

"Clear testimony that Carlotta Barone masterminded the take down of the Brienza family. She also took out Sullivan . . . with an ice pick to the eye and a defensive ice pick through his hand. The men with her wrapped him up in a red blanket and took him to a construction site where she proceeded to take off his feet with a Skilsaw."

"While he was still alive?"

"Uh-huh."

"Sounds like somebody he shouldn't have crossed."

"Right. He admitted that he was there when her husband was beaten to death and kicked him until he couldn't speak. That's why she relieved him of his feet."

"What goeth aroundeth cometh aroundeth," Chris said.

"Precisely. The body was taken to a sympathetic undertaker, but never seen again . . . until this month."

"What about the rest of the Brienza family?"

"No details, beyond the fact that she planned their disappearance. They may not have been killed immediately when they were taken. Her granddaughter didn't know. Carlotta simply said that they were *removed*."

"So the granddaughter has been your informant."

"Gina Abruzzi, the manager of the hotel where I've been staying."

"The hotel manager?"

"Yes, I was surprised too."

"She has to be connected to the Orsinis."

"Giancarlo is a kind of best family friend. At first I thought he might have been involved in some way with Carlotta, but Gina claims that there was no romantic connection, just a close friendship based on some commonalities. Apparently Giancarlo lost his wife when she was still very young. He and Carlotta formed a sort of mini-community of grief."

"And he advised her legally."

"Yes, almost surely. And Gina as well, I suspect. Her mother died in childbirth, so she was virtually raised by her grandmother. They've formed a triangle over the years."

"Interesting. So Giancarlo knew all of this but he let the granddaughter reveal it."

"Yes, I'm sure he knew about it, certainly in its general outlines. He may not have known all of the details. Gina was very forthcoming, by the way. I could practically hear the screams and see the blood splatter as she told me."

"A Skilsaw would make a real mess. The Barone woman must have had a strong stomach as well as a steady hand."

"Yes, and a cool demeanor. Before she sawed off Sullivan's feet she removed his shoes. She wanted to avoid any bloodstains on them because they were good shoes and she planned to donate them to the St. Vincent de Paul Society."

"That was thoughtful."

"She was a devout Catholic as well as a devout killer . . . and planner. Prior to her confronting Sullivan she had scoped out a deserted construction site just in case it turned out that she needed it. It met all of her specific requirements—it had a dark, empty basement . . . a water source . . . and a functioning floor drain. She was well prepared for their little tango at the slaughter house."

"Will her granddaughter tell you more?"

"I think she will. She's already told me something I hadn't expected."

"What's that, Tom?"

"Carlotta Barone died less than three months ago."

"There's no record of her in Orange County, no recent record at any rate. Not that we had expected any. I always figured that she had eventually moved back to New York. There are a lot of Barones there. Hell, there are a lot of Barones everywhere."

"So the next question is, why did we find Gray Sullivan's remains shortly after she passed? The two events have to be connected."

"Maybe she was holding onto him, just for old time's sake. When she went there was no reason to keep him around any longer."

"Like a trophy kill? I can tell you this, Chief--she also kept the ice pick that she used on him. She had it in a case, along with a straight razor. Gina inherited the package. She said that when her grandmother went in to confront Sullivan she carried both. If he had been decent and straightforward she was going to let him off easily . . . with a quick slice of the throat. Instead he got ugly . . . and so did she."

"Think about it, Tom. She's got old Gray down in her basement. Every now and then when she's thinking about the old days--thinking about all that he had done to her and her husband--she goes down and puts the ice pick in the empty eye socket. Moves it around a little. Slips it between the bones of his fingers . . . Maybe there were some regular trips, some special anniversaries … "

"It's possible, Chief. I'll tell you this much . . . if I ever get married . . . and if anybody messes with me in a serious way . . . this is the type of woman I'd want to settle the accounts later."

"Talk about 'Stand by Your Man' . . . and like the guy on cable says, 'Measure twice and cut once.' What's your next step, Tom?"

"I'm going to meet with Gina again tomorrow and see if there are any last details that she's willing to share. Then I'm coming home. We've got to figure out the connection between her death and the discovery of Sullivan's remains."

"I'll do what I can in the meantime," Chris said. "So far all we have is a long shopping list of Barones—from sea to shining sea. Is it possible that she could have had a principal residence in Sicily?"

"I don't think so, because Gina said that she hadn't been able to see her as often as she would have liked to. My guess is that her grandmother stayed in the U.S. I'll check anyway. If Gina won't say, Giancarlo might, although I very much doubt that they've been operating independently. Carlotta was a great orchestrator, a great planner and coordinator. It probably runs in the family . . . make that families . . . the Barones *and* the Orsinis."

FIFTY-TWO

Tom rose at 6:00 and left a note for Gina, telling her that he'd be at the pool between 6:30 and 9:00 and available as well for lunch or dinner. As he swam laps, clearing his head and building an appetite, a waiter approached in a starched white jacket, black slacks, white shirt and black tie. He was carrying a large silver tray, which he placed on the table next to Tom's chaise longue. Tom swam over to the side of the pool and the man bowed to him, saying "Compliments of the Manager, Signore." There was a note card on the tray. It read:

Good morning, Tom. Have a nice swim. I have a lunch meeting already. Dinner at 7:30? Just let my office know. Have a pleasant day.

Gina

The tray contained a selection of cheeses and meats, including Parma ham, some freshly-baked rolls, butter in chilled containers, freshly-squeezed orange juice, and a carafe of coffee. As he sampled the choices he thought about the dinner meeting and the questions he might ask. Then, as he began to feel the morning sun drying his neck and shoulders and legs he thought about the still-bizarre circumstances in which he found himself—sitting in a paradisal setting, working a set of cases that were decades old and investigating actions that had occurred thousands of miles away. His principal informants were two individuals with no obvious reason to talk to him, informants who might even be characterized as enablers, since they continued to buy him dinner and breakfast and make themselves available to him as promptly as one might ask.

Why were they doing this? What did they have to gain? They certainly had a great deal to lose. Giancarlo Orsini was the consigliere of the head of a crime family. The more he revealed the greater the likelihood that someone would eventually be able to demonstrate his complicity in criminal actions, particularly the sort for which there were no statutes of limitations. Gina Abruzzi explained, in detail, her grandmother's central involvement in at least one major homicide case, possibly in four others as well. This woman, Carlotta Barone, was not just some individual from the distant past, but rather the person to whom Gina was closest in her life, the person who had actually raised her.

Cui bono? It was certainly to *Tom Deaton's* benefit. Clearing one or more major cases with no tools at his disposal but his wits and a willingness to try something that no one else would expect to bring results would bring plaudits and, possibly, promotion. *Chris Dietrich* would benefit. He had been willing to bet on the longest of long shots and he had smoothed the way for Tom, then supported him each step along the way. The *press* could eventually benefit. Even if the most salacious details were suppressed, the story was still a five-star winner. Sex, violence, love, revenge, justice, and the mob. Pick any two. No, take all six.

But how would the *superstite* benefit? Or the *sopravvissuta*? Their memories were precious to them, but why would they share those memories--memories of guilt and violence. Oh, there was pride as well, and justice . . . perhaps even heroism. And no one would be shedding any tears for the victims. They got precisely what they deserved.

Would Giancarlo and Gina tell these stories simply because of their desire to demonstrate the occasional workings of **Justice**? It was certainly a feel-good story, so long as you weren't troubled by the blood splatter from a Skilsaw and the thought of the sensations generated by an ice pick as it penetrates soft tissue. But great crimes, like all great actions, call for equal and opposite reactions. The stories were inherently interesting and compelling. But . . . what if they were . . . *what if they were* . . . complete fabrications? It was the one possibility that Tom had not yet considered. Perhaps they were straightfaced lies, lies that would substitute for real truths, the truths that Giancarlo and Gina were anxious to suppress at any costs.

Perhaps that is why he was filled with food and wine, why he was brought free breakfasts poolside. They were each playing an exquisite con and following every rule in the guidebook—earning his trust, earning his confidence, perhaps even earning his affection.

Look in the dictionary under *sucker* or *fool* and see the smiling face of Tom Deaton. And—right behind him, with his hand on Tom's shoulder, the face of Chris Dietrich. But Chris isn't smiling. His lips have turned down and his eyes have narrowed. He's just realized that he's been had.

The only winners are the members of the press. They still have their story, but it isn't the story that will lead to plaudits and a promotion. It's the story that will lead to scandal, to public embarrassment, to investigations and, eventually, to resignations.

Tom hadn't considered this possibility because it was too painful to do so. Was it the *likeliest* of possibilities as well as the most unpleasant? One thing was clear. If they were consciously misleading him there was no reason to proceed further in questioning them. If he was already in a deep hole there was no reason to turn it into a bottomless pit.

He decided on what must be his best course. He would ask Gina a few remaining questions, then proceed with his investigation back in the O.C. If he discovered that he had been lied to he could always return to Sicily. Chris would be as anxious as he would be to clear the record. He would open doors with the local authorities and they would all work the case under their auspices. It wouldn't be easy. It might not even be realistic to expect that the locals would implicate their own people— their own wealthy and powerful people—to help solve a set of cases from the distant past thousands of miles away. They could only try. In the meantime he would make his plans for his return and prepare for his meeting with Gina.

FIFTY-THREE

"It's a slow night for us," she said, handing him a menu. "The kitchen can prepare anything you like. Don't be shy, Tom."

He ordered the fish of the day, some pasta in cream sauce, and a light salad. She had the same. "And bring us the nice white Burgundy," she said to the waiter, "the Puligny-Montrachet. Not too cold."

The waiter bowed and left. She turned to him and saw something in his eyes. "What's the matter, Tom?"

"Why do you ask that, Gina?"

"Your eyes … "

"Are they red from the pool?"

"No, it's not that. You seem troubled, upset."

"I'm fine," he said.

"Tom, you must know that I make my living offering personal services to people. You're angry with me in some way."

"No, I'm not angry. I just had a feeling today and I haven't been able to sort it out."

"So tell me."

"Why don't we just enjoy our dinner?"

"I don't know about you, but I don't generally enjoy dinner when I'm sitting with someone who's angry at me."

"All right," he said. "I'll tell you. I've been wondering why you and Giancarlo have been so forthcoming with me. I don't see how any of this can be of benefit to you."

"You can't?"

"No."

"So you think we're both liars."

"I didn't say that."

"You certainly implied it."

"I'm sorry. You asked."

"It is of *great benefit* to us, Tom. In the first place, you have promised to keep the details of what we've told you as quiet as possible. Have you not?"

"I have."

"And you've sought the support of your superior in this regard."

"Yes, I have."

"And he's agreed. To the degree possible."

"Yes, he has."

"Do you not also see that we take pride in what our people have accomplished?"

"Yes, but you can have that pride without sharing the details with someone in law enforcement."

"We could, of course, but would you believe the story if you were not given the details? What if Giancarlo had told you that the Brienza family was bad and the Orsini family was good, that through some fortunate, but unknown occurrence the Brienza principals had all disappeared? What if I had told you that no one knows what happened to Gray Sullivan, but that there had always been some suspicion that a relative or friend of one of his victims had coordinated a grand act of revenge, an act that resulted in justice, but an act whose details belong to the mists of history? That would all be true, Tom, but would you have believed it?"

"Why is it important that I believe it, Gina?"

"Because you are the individual chosen by your department to pursue the case. Unless you are an inept fool you will pursue it until you reach a conclusion. If you can reach that conclusion—the *correct* conclusion—with our help, then you are far more likely to cooperate with us in keeping the details as private as possible. You are also less likely to pursue false leads that will only lead to our embarrassment (and, potentially, your own). Why do you think we have gotten to know you, Tom? Why do you think Giancarlo and I have talked at such length and under such . . . personal . . . circumstances? We wanted to get to know you, Tom. We needed to take your measure. What if you had been the sort of individual who approached this in an atmosphere of suspicion and doubt? What if you had been the type of individual who was incapable of believing that a person like Giancarlo could be an educated and caring man, a man who has done much good? If you had lumbered in, brandishing warrants and making threats, do you think we would have opened up to you? These conversations have been truthful, Tom. They have been . . . *authentic.*"

"Let's assume that they have been."

"Yes, let's do that, Tom," Gina said. There was impatience in her voice.

"Now *you're* angry," he said.

"I'm just a little disappointed," she said, "but it's good that this has come out. It was fair of you to have some doubts. I would only remind you of one thing, Tom."

"What's that, Gina?"

"You approached us. We did not approach you."

He thought about that, holding his expression.

The wine steward entered with their wine, went through the uncorking and tasting ritual, and left. "Try it," she said. "We can both use something to smooth out the edges."

"It's delicious," Tom said.

"I'm glad you like it," she said. "Now, are there any other doubts or concerns that you would like to raise?"

"No, let's enjoy dinner."

"And our discussion," Gina added. "Let's also enjoy that."

"Yes," Tom said.

"Now before you start to ask questions, I want to tell you something," Gina said.

FIFTY-FOUR

"In her will, my grandmother directed that funds be given to a foundation that she had established, a foundation designed to support widows, particularly military widows. She deeded her home to the foundation and created an endowment to support the operation. Because of the proximity of her estate to Camp Pendleton, it will be of particular help to local people, but it is not restricted to them. Widows will get psychological and financial counseling, no-interest bridge loans and scholarships for their children."

"That's very kind," Tom said, "and also very expensive."

"Yes, with a 5% payout on the endowment the foundation will need every penny of the money she's left them. The rest of the growth on the investment is put back into the principal so that the endowment will keep pace with inflation."

"How much is in the endowment?" Tom asked.

"Eight and a half million dollars," Gina said. "It's not much considering the total need, but it's still very generous, I think."

"And did she talk to you about this before she did it?" Tom asked.

Gina paused for a second and sipped her wine.

"If I'm getting too personal, just say so," Tom said. "I realize that you've just lost your grandmother and now I'm sitting here asking you a lot of difficult questions."

"No, it's fine, Tom," Gina said. "I understand what you're saying. The money that goes into the foundation does not go to the heirs, or, in her case, the heir. There will probably be some things left over for me;

I'm the residuary legatee. But to answer your question . . . yes, we talked about it in general terms. I supported her decision completely. For me it's a point of pride that she would want to help so many people, nearly all of them strangers. Her generosity contrasts with the greed of the people who killed her husband. Besides, I have my whole life ahead of me and plenty of opportunities to make money. It's not that important to me, anyway. As a manager of distinguished properties I already live as the rich do, at least when they're on holiday."

Tom nodded in agreement. "Where is your grandmother's home?" he asked.

"In the hills beyond San Clemente. The property was actually a winery. When the Spanish Franciscans came there they had grand agricultural plans. And who could blame them? In that climate the planting of orange groves and vineyards seemed to be a natural idea. As you know, however, the orange groves did much better than the vineyards. There are few areas below the central coast which are actually appropriate for viticulture. They learned this lesson by hard experience, but sometimes the remnants of their early efforts remain. My grandmother had a small orchard, but no active vines. There were some antique grape presses and other devices in an outbuilding on the property, but she gave them to someone in the wine industry association for one of their museum displays. If my grandmother had tried to grow grapes the end result would not, unfortunately, taste like this," Gina said, lifting her glass and sipping her wine.

"That's a pity," Tom said, "but few wines taste as good as this."

"You're looking at me as if you have another question," Gina asked, "one that you're hesitant to ask."

"Yes, I do," Tom said.

"Well, don't be shy, Tom."

"It won't come as a surprise to you that we've been trying to find information concerning your grandmother," Tom said. "There are no Barones listed in Orange County, at least none in any way related to your grandmother."

"No, she didn't use her married name. It drew too much attention, particularly just after her husband died and the principals in the Brienza family disappeared. She was bothered repeatedly by the local press, so she went away for a time and when she returned she used her maiden name for all legal documents. You wouldn't have found a phone listing, of course."

"And her maiden name was … "

"Monte," Gina said.

"Monte, as in Carlo Monte?"

"Don Carlo was her uncle," Gina said.

"So there really was a nice . . . roundedness . . . to all of this," Tom said.

"She would have said *karma*," Gina said. "As I mentioned to you, there was a California side to her as well as a New York side."

"Did you attend her funeral?" Tom asked.

"Yes, it was a very lovely service. She was buried in her wedding dress. It still fit her."

He sipped his wine.

"You're wondering why I didn't tell you, aren't you?"

"It crossed my mind," he said.

"I can see that it would be of interest, but I didn't see it as being of great relevance," she said. "The actions in which you are principally interested transpired some fifty years ago."

"Yes," Tom said, "and I don't mean to pry . . . except with regard to the cases. There I'm afraid I do mean to pry."

"I understand," Gina said, smiling.

"Can you tell me the name of your grandmother's lawyer?"

"I can, but I'll have to check on it," she said. "Just a second." She got up, put her napkin on her chair, and walked back to her desk. She opened the side drawer and flipped through a rack of hanging files. After several seconds she pulled out a set of papers lined with blue legal cap.

"This is her will," she said. "It's very straightforward. You're welcome to take a look, if you'd like. The attorney is in Los Angeles. His name is Carelli, Vincent Carelli."

Tom flipped through the pages of the will. It was, as Gina said, very straightforward and—given the money and property involved— very brief: pay her existing debts, transfer funds in her accounts to the foundation, and transfer any residuum to her 'beloved granddaughter'. The one item that was not straightforward occasioned his next question.

"Although you would be the principal heir and descendant, she did not make you executrix," Tom said. "The executor is . . . Giancarlo Orsini."

FIFTY-FIVE

"That was my idea," Gina said. "Giancarlo is an attorney; I am not. I wanted to insure that her wishes were carried out. There is no one I trust more to be able to guarantee that that would happen than the Signore."

"I understand," Tom said.

"And of course the Signore waived any executor's fees."

"And with you here rather than there, it is very helpful to have an attorney who can practice in both locations."

"Yes."

"Let me ask you another question, Gina."

"Go ahead, Tom."

"Have you ever heard of a man named Drewes?"

"Drewes?"

"Carl Drewes. He's an attorney in Orange County."

"I don't recognize the name, but the Signore might have used him as a representative there."

"He requested a death certificate for Sullivan—right after the identification of the remains had been made."

"Are you sure he was not a journalist, Tom? Those jackals always assemble quickly under such circumstances."

"No, they were there as well. Drewes is a lawyer. At any rate, he was not your grandmother's lawyer."

"Not that I know of. Sometimes people have different lawyers for different purposes, but my grandmother died before Gray Sullivan's remains were found, so it is unlikely that he would have acted on her behalf, or, more properly, on behalf of her estate. You might want to talk to Carelli."

"We spoke to Drewes and he refused to reveal his client's identity."

"Perhaps he was working on his own, looking for business in some way or other. They frequently conceal their actions by invoking attorney-client privilege."

"Yes, that's true," Tom said.

"What else can I tell you?" Gina asked. "We have covered a lot of business this evening, have we not?"

"Yes, we have," Tom said, "so much so that I'll be able to go back to the states soon."

"How soon is soon?"

"The day after tomorrow."

"So you are free all day tomorrow?"

"Yes."

"Then I have an idea. Will you put yourself in my hands?"

"I've been doing that right along and it's always worked," Tom said.

"Good. Be ready at 9:00. I'll clear my desk and inbox first thing in the morning and then we'll leave."

"When will we get back?"

"By late afternoon. Will that work?"

"Yes."

"And I'll have a car ready to take you to Catania the day after."

"Perfect," Tom said. "Thanks."

He was up at 6:00, on the phone to Chris Dietrich. He filled him in on the newest developments and Chris promised to do some preliminary checking on the official records concerning Carlotta Barone, née Monte, her property in San Clemente and her lawyer in L.A., Vincent Carelli.

"Drewes could be working for Orsini," Tom said.

"Yes, that's the most likely possibility. If Carelli was already involved with the Barone estate and Orsini is the executor the two of them would have been in contact. He may have turned to Drewes because he wanted to keep Carelli out of it."

"Right."

"What's your return route look like, Tom?"

"Catania to Rome, Rome to Gatwick, Gatwick to New York, New York to John Wayne, via Phoenix."

"So you get in here sometime next month."

"Just about. That's all right. I have a lot of notes to review and a lot of fresh information to digest along the way."

"Stay hydrated and avoid alcohol," Chris said, with skepticism in his voice.

"Right, Chief," Tom said, in a military tone.

"Do you need someone to pick you up?"

"My dad's going to do that. Thanks though, Chief."

"Get in, get a hot shower and a little rest and then we'll go to work," Dietrich said.

"Will do."

When Tom came down to the lobby Gina was waiting for him. She was wearing loose-fitting shorts, a polo shirt and white tennis shoes. "Ready for our adventure?" she asked.

"Absolutely," he said.

"I'm glad to see that you brought your sunglasses," she said. "You'll need them." They were hanging from the center of his V-neck shirt.

Her's were in the car, a white Mercedes convertible, which was idling just outside the front door of the hotel. Five minutes later they were making their way down to the A18. The sun was blinding and the bay could have passed for the Côte d'Azur. When Gina turned north, Tom asked, "So, are we going to Messina?"

"We're stopping there," she said, teasing him.

At Messina she parked her convertible at the marina and led him to a boat moored there. A 48' motor yacht, it was named the

Giorni Migliori

"The Better Days," Tom said.

"You're learning your Italian well," Gina said.

"That's the name of *my* boat," Tom said.

"Truly?"

"Yes. If I was a skeptical person I'd think that you changed the name just to make me feel more comfortable."

"And put you off your guard?"

"Perhaps," Tom said.

"But you *are* a skeptical person," Gina said.

"And I know that you know that, so … "

"So it must be a coincidence," she said.

"Perhaps," he said, smiling.

"The boat is being rented from the owner. It was selected because of the name."

"Then you and Giancarlo did a background check on me—a detailed background check."

"Wouldn't you do the same, Tom?"

"Of course," he said. "But it's *obvious* that it couldn't be a coincidence."

"Then in order to make you feel at home we had to reveal that we checked on you."

"That would mean that my comfort was more important to you than the secrecy of your actions."

"Yes, Detective Deaton, or it could all simply be a coincidence, as I said. In which case, the lesson is that we all hope for better days. We are like you."

"You enjoy this second guessing, don't you, Gina?"

"With a clever partner," she said, smiling.

They pulled away from the slip and headed through the harbor. "There's bottled water in the refrigerator," she said. "Some stronger things too."

He brought her a bottle of water as well. As they left the harbor the air was noticeably cooler, though the sun was still blindingly bright. She headed north.

"Are we going through the strait?" he asked.

"Yes," she answered. "That was my surprise. No one should come to northeastern Sicily and miss the opportunity."

"I hope I'm safer than Odysseus," Tom said.

"*He* survived," Gina said. "There's no reason for *you* to worry."

"After losing six of his men."

"What was he to do, Tom? He could choose the monster or the whirlpool but he couldn't simply sail in between."

"Right. Hopefully we'll have better luck. When I was in college my lit teacher said that some people now think that Scylla and Charybdis were in Greece, not Italy."

"Lies, all lies," Gina said, smiling. "It's pure envy, of course. That, and a desire to attract tourists to their country rather than ours."

"So, Gina . . . in bringing me here . . . what are you saying . . . that I will soon be facing a difficult choice and that it will require some sacrifice, no matter what I eventually choose to do?"

"Of course not," she said. "We'll have lunch at Scylla. They are famous for their seafood. I have a friend there who has a small restaurant. Her name is Paola. After she feeds us you will learn the true lesson that I wish to inculcate."

"Which is … ?"

"That if you put yourself in my hands you will always be safe."

"I already know that," he said, smiling.

"I am serious, Tom. I have told you many things. Your head is filled with information and your heart is filled with questions. You have learned more than you thought you would learn and some of your most important questions have been answered. There are some things that I cannot answer. You may learn the answers yourself. You may learn things that I myself do not know. Whatever you learn, there are certain things that you must believe … "

"Yes … ?" he said, noticing that she was holding the wheel tightly, the white on her knuckles visible, even with his sunglasses on.

"You should take notes," she said, smiling.

"I have an excellent memory when it comes to anything that *you* say," he answered.

"Good. First point: whatever actions were committed that technically qualified as *crimes* were just."

"OK … "

"Second point. The cases in which you are interested occurred many years ago and the participants have all passed away."

"You're sure of that?"

"You're speaking of the other Brienza principals . . . I can't say that I have seen their bodies—alive or dead—but I think it's safe to say that there is no reason to keep the house light on for them. Besides, if they did not die as a result of my grandmother's actions there is no crime."

"Kidnapping perhaps."

"But if they were released they were removed for their own protection. At any rate, they have not filed any charges."

"What is the third point?"

"The third point is that you have promised to maintain secrecy with regard to these actions, to the degree possible."

"Yes, I have. Is there a fourth point?"

"The fourth point is that neither I nor the Signore have done anything *illegal* or *immoral*."

"But you are both *fattening*," Tom said, "or at least being in your presence is."

"Guilty as charged," Gina said, "but you are an unindicted co-conspirator."

"I certainly hope so," Tom said.

Lunch was *Pesce spada*, a swordfish steak cooked in an orange sauce, with some gnocchi and *Cassata*, a sponge cake with ricotta, nuts, marsala, chocolate, marzipan and candied fruit. The wine was a sweet *Moscato*. The coffee was black and strong.

"You chose well," Tom said, "as always."

Before returning, they sat in the shade outside the restaurant, enjoying more coffee and letting their lunch digest before testing the strength of their stomachs against the waters of the Messina strait.

Once aboard the boat and underway Tom returned to the issue of Gina's four points. "Just one question," he said. "Why did you feel the need to add the point concerning your and Giancarlo's innocence? Did you think I believed that you were guilty of something?"

"No, Tom, I didn't," she answered, "but as you continue to investigate—as I know you will—you may encounter information which raises questions. I have no idea what you might encounter or what you might find odd or out of the ordinary. All I am saying is that I know the Signore and I know his character. I also know what I myself have done and what I have not done. Whatever you learn . . . you should begin with the assumption that we are innocent. After all, it is the American way, is it not?"

"Yes, it is," Tom said, "and in this case I have the added benefit of knowing each of you." (Perhaps that was one of the reasons you agreed to talk with me, he thought.)

"If you trust us now, continue to do so," she said. "That is all that I am asking."

FIFTY-SIX

As she pulled in in front of the hotel a doorman came out to open her door. "Unfortunately, I can't dine with you tonight, Tom," Gina said, "I have to work, but I'd like to drive you to the airport tomorrow."

"That would be very nice," he said. "Thanks."

"What time?"

"Early, I'm afraid. Could we leave at 5:30?"

"Of course," she said.

As they drove off the next morning, the sky was a light gray, the smoke issuing from Etna adding an ominous note. She saw that he was looking at it. "It does that all the time," she said. "Don't worry about it. We get flank eruptions nearly every year but they don't have much impact. We have learned to live with it and we cherish what it does for the local soil. If there is a true problem, there is no mistaking it. When the people are truly frightened they yell '*Scassau a muntagna!*' which roughly means 'The mountain has broken'. Fortunately, it looks completely intact this morning." Tom smiled and nodded at her.

Ten minutes later Gina asked him about his itinerary. He described it and she offered a few words of consolation. "It's the only drawback to living in Taormina," she said. "There are many other compensations, of course, but it's hard to get here and it's hard to get out again. You were lucky. You had a nice long visit. The next time you come you should make it even longer. I'll take you on a tour of the entire island. You saw the pictures on the postcard—the island as a woman with three great legs . . . I'll make sure that you see each knee, each ankle, and each foot. You've only seen a part, though we believe that it's the best part."

"I'd like that," Tom said. "You're the perfect guide."

"Thank you, Tom. You know, I think you will come back."

"Why?"

"Because you'll miss us."

"Not because I'll have more questions?"

"I have confidence in you, Tom. You'll find the answers that you seek."

"The answers that you don't have or the answers that you haven't volunteered?" he asked.

"*All* of the answers," she said.

"I appreciate your candor," he said.

"I have never misled you, Tom."

"Giancarlo and I talked about the difference between sins of omission and sins of commission."

"I can't say that I am *sinless*," Gina answered, "but I told you that I am innocent of any crime. So is the Signore."

"That will always be my starting assumption," he said.

"That's all that I asked," she said. "Trust me. When all of your questions are answered you will be satisfied and you will come back to us because you wish to see us and talk to us in normal, human fashion. No investigations, just a visit with friends. You will let some time elapse. It would not be prudent of you to develop a reputation as a friend of a prominent consigliere and you are a prudent man, Tom. However, after awhile, after the journalists have gone back to chasing the celebrities and your department has moved on to other concerns . . . after Gray Sullivan is buried, permanently, and after you have had the time to develop a perspective that is only possible *through* the passage of time . . . you will return to Taormina."

"You should come to San Clemente," Tom said. "You should visit your grandmother's gift to the widows. Oh, but of course you have already."

"Yes, I *have* seen it, Tom. It is quite historic. I have seen it change. It was in a state of decay when my grandfather and grandmother bought it. All her life she worked to bring it back. Now it will be shared with others, with people in pain who will benefit from its beauty. My grandfather and grandmother are buried there. Did you know that?"

"No, you hadn't mentioned it," he said.

"I think that is part of the reason why she gave it to the foundation," Gina said. "If the property was sold she would have had to provide for the relocation of her husband's remains. 'He was always very happy there,' she said, and she did not want to disturb him. Instead she has joined him. It is in a lovely setting. It is very spiritual and the marble for their burial vaults is from Italy—the very best."

"I'll visit the site and say a prayer or two," he said.

"I was there recently, remember. Stand in front of the mausoleum. Look directly at the names carved in the stone. That is where I stood. Perhaps you will feel my presence as well as their's."

"I'll visit it as soon as I can," he said, "and report back to you when I return."

"I would appreciate that," she said.

The airport was already bustling with activity, with tourists and wealthy locals, catching early flights. Gina popped the trunk and Tom removed his luggage. She got out of the car, walked over to the curb, and kissed him goodbye.

"Travel safely, Tom. Thank you for coming to us and for talking to us."

"Thank you for your hospitality," he answered. "It was a pleasure . . . a great pleasure."

"Now," she said, "no tears and no sad words. You go do your job and then come back to see us."

"I will," he said.

"I know you will," she said. "I know you, Tom."

IV

IL CAMPANILE

FIFTY-SEVEN

Tom made the connections for each of his flights, but each was full or nearly so and it was hard for him to sleep. On the transatlantic leg of his trip he had a full lunch with decaf coffee and two mini-bottles of brandy and was finally able to close his eyes. His dreams were clearly analogous to his recent experience. In the first he was conducting a lengthy interrogation of a garrulous suspect who spoke endlessly but told him nothing. In the dream Tom was working from a list of prepared questions—something he would never actually do—while the suspect used each of the questions as a starting point for an irrelevant, rambling account of something totally unrelated.

The questions were pre-written on a child's school tablet, but the handwriting was not Tom's. He had a single pencil stub with a small point and no eraser. This was a subject of concern to him, but as the suspect spoke there was nothing for him to write down. He rephrased the questions and directed the suspect to answer them but the individual would smile politely, say "Of course," or "Certainly," and then go off on another tangent.

He awoke from the frustration dream, repositioned himself in his seat, and then began to dream again. The second dream was also analogous to his experience with Giancarlo and Gina. This time the dream was violent. Filled with ice picks and knives and hammers, it consisted of the systematic stabbing and bludgeoning of shadowy individuals, whose faces were unclear but whose blood flowed profusely. The individuals administering the punishment were dressed in judges' robes, but their faces were as blank as those of their victims. Tom himself was a bystander in the dream, aware of his presence in a corner of the room where the individuals were being attacked.

"Well," he thought, as he awoke, "at least I don't need a board-certified analyst to help me interpret those." He checked his watch and realized that he had only been asleep for a little over an hour. He sat back in his seat, closed his eyes, and tried—with limited success—to rest.

The flight attendants served what they termed *afternoon tea* an hour and a half before landing at Kennedy. It consisted of scones with raisins (the British would have probably said *sultanas*), clotted cream, strawberry jam, and a side portion of grapes and sliced oranges. Everything was miniaturized. This time Tom asked for regular coffee and passed on anything containing alcohol.

He cleared customs in New York, went to the gate for his flight to Phoenix, which continued to John Wayne, and called Chris Dietrich to assure him that he had made his connections.

"That's good, Tom. Are you able to sleep on a daytime transatlantic flight?"

"More or less," Tom said, but not for more than an hour or two. I spent a lot of time going over my notes and getting them in order."

"I've got a new document at this end," Chris said. "Nothing earth-shaking, but it's a point of departure at least. Presumably it's just like the one you saw."

"The will?" Tom asked.

"Yes."

"Who prepared it?"

"Vincent Carelli. You had mentioned his name earlier."

"In Los Angeles."

"Century City, actually," Chris said.

"Any major details?"

"Just what you had already told me. She left her home to the County. Nice-sized place. Down behind San Clemente. It's to be used to help military widows, women who are down on their luck. Nice gesture. We haven't gotten the paperwork on her foundation yet. I figured you'd want to be involved with that. As you had said earlier, she left the bulk of her estate to her pre-existing foundation and the foundation will now administer the facility in San Clemente. There are provisions for an endowment—as we discussed. Just doing some seat-of-the-pants figures it doesn't look as if they'll be awash in money at first, particularly with the maintenance costs of a place like that, but the endowment will grow over time and her gift will end up doing some good."

"Is Gina mentioned explicitly in the will?"

"Yes, as residuary legatee, but it's not clear what would be left over."

"Her grandmother's already given her some of her items. Her ice pick and straight razor, for example … "

"Yes," Chris answered. "Merry Christmas and handle with care."

"Presumably there were other things," Tom said. "I'll talk to the attorney. I assume that whatever's not explicitly given to the foundation is Gina's, unless some other heir is mentioned."

"Right. All of her grandmother's personal stuff, for example."

"And Orsini is the executor."

"Yes, just as the Abruzzi woman said. I'm not sure there's much for him to do, however, since the house, land, and contents are deeded to the foundation and nothing else is enumerated. You'll have to check with the attorney on the executor's compensation."

"He's waived executor's fees," Tom said.

"Oh, OK. I wasn't sure what happened when virtually everything is given to a single recipient—in this case, the foundation—and when the bequest is philanthropic. Under the circumstances I doubt that she would have wanted a hefty piece of the bequest to go back to the executor."

"Right. It looks like a very special case. The will is extremely simple, even though there's a lot of money involved."

"Yes," Chris said, "but as we've said all along—there isn't going to be a long list of recipients, since they're basically all dead. Except for the granddaughter the only one still around from those days is Orsini. If he's not left anything we can forget about his descendants."

"And he doesn't need any money, as far as I can tell," Tom said, "and he's made his decision to settle in Sicily rather than in the O.C."

"Right."

"Have you had a chance to check out the place in San Clemente, Chief?"

"As a matter of fact I was down there this morning. It looks different than it did in the old Franciscans' time, now that there are multimillion dollar estates around it, but it sits on a nice piece of land. A developer would salivate at the thought of pulling down the original structure and throwing up a few dozen McMansions. Very, very pricey real estate. The original building is a little bit faded-glory, but it appears to be in reasonably good condition: no major external defects. It could use a good landscaping. There's a lot of dust and scrub around the edges. With a little spruce-up it'll be a little short of palatial, but it's still a very nice place and the size of the land on which it sits is exceptional."

"Acres?"

"Oh yes. Probably three or four."

"I'm anxious to see the inside," Tom said.

"That's what I figured," Chris said. "It's your case, so I didn't push. And time doesn't appear to be of the essence. Given the time when the Brienza family disappeared, this is more archaeology than a current criminal investigation."

"Maybe," Tom said.

"Why do you say *maybe,* Tom?"

"Because Gray Sullivan's body just turned up a few weeks ago. It was being held for a reason."

"Yes, unless this is all happenstance."

"With this much money involved and this much blood, I wouldn't bet on happenstance, Chief."

FIFTY-EIGHT

Tom hadn't been to Phoenix in years and he was struck by the growth in and around the airport. He saw the saguaros as the plane was in its descent and thought of the very different flora that had surrounded him in Sicily. The layover was an hour and fifteen minutes, but they had flown into strong headwinds and the flight landed twenty-five minutes later than scheduled. He stayed on the plane, but stretched his legs after the aisle was cleared by the passengers completing their flight there.

The leg to John Wayne was on time and uneventful. This time Tom watched for fan palms instead of saguaros. His father picked him up at John Wayne.

"How about some dinner, Tom?"

"Sounds good, Dad."

"Do you have to have Italian now or do you want anything but?"

"Whatever you'd like, Dad."

"You know me, Tom. If I can't have your mother's lasagna and sausage I revert to steak and potatoes."

"I can do that," Tom said. "Steak and potatoes sounds great. It's really good to see you. How are you feeling?"

"Sound as a dollar. Let me rephrase that. Sound as a gold coin."

They went to a place in Laguna because Wayne knew that his son would want to get home promptly and have a long hot shower and the chance to sleep horizontally instead of vertically. The restaurant was part of a local chain, but it was a step up from fast food. They talked about Tom's flights and about his time in Sicily. He gave his dad the general outline of the case and his view of the questions that remained.

"Sounds to me as if the key thing is the release of Sullivan's remains," Wayne said.

"I agree," Tom said. "There's something else there as well."

"What's that?"

"Organization. First, you have to assume that the remains were in some secure location. I'm thinking something semi-permanent like a mausoleum interment with a phony name above the casket. This was a big deal and the remains were released for a reason. It's not as if somebody was driving around with the body in the trunk of their car for fifty years and then waited for the opportune moment, drove out on a pier or over a bridge, popped the trunk and tossed the skeleton into the water. This would require careful planning and some heavy lifting—literally."

"It could have been kept in a warehouse or something," Wayne said, "but then you'd have to keep tabs on it for fifty years. Warehouses turn over; people walk through them … "

"Yes," Tom said. "The best place would be to hide it in plain sight, in a place where there was ongoing maintenance, a place that you could book for the long haul."

"A cemetery."

"Right," Tom answered, "but probably not in the ground. If you were planning on eventually removing the remains you'd have to be able to do it quickly and at some time when there would be no one around to observe your actions. Those actions would also have to go undetected— no empty holes or freshly-turned earth. If we're talking about sliding out a coffin, maybe getting up on a ladder first, removing the contents—very carefully—and then putting everything back neatly, taking the contents out to sea and releasing them in the right place and at the right time . . . we're talking *organization*; we're talking several people; we're talking access to equipment and the need to maintain absolute secrecy. This isn't a matter of hiring a couple of derelicts and giving them each a $50 bill. This is a professional job and the employer is somebody either in the mob or very close to it."

"The secrecy is key," Wayne said.

"And the ability to contact and employ the sort of people who know how to maintain it," Tom added. "You can't look in the Yellow Pages under *Skeletal Remains—Confidential Disposal.*"

"Orsini would know such people," Wayne said.

"So would the Century City lawyer if that's his usual clientele."

"It'll be interesting to see what he's like."

"Yes," Tom said. "He's going to be my first stop."

FIFTY-NINE

Vincent Carelli's office was located in a small building overshadowed by Fox Plaza. It was nicely, but not grandly, furnished. The sign on the door indicated that Carelli had two associates, each of whom shared his surname. His children or his son and daughter-in-law?

He was younger than Tom expected. Somehow he thought that Carelli would be closer in age to Giancarlo, but he appeared to be in his mid fifties. The support staff consisted of a receptionist and legal secretary, all of their names ending in vowels.

"Welcome to Little Italy, Detective Deaton," Carelli said. He was fit, with dark, closely-cut wavy black hair and gray-blue eyes. He was wearing a white shirt and burgundy tie. No cufflinks, no gaudy rings. "Would you like some coffee? I'm going to have some."

"That would be very nice," Tom said.

The lawyer made a call to his receptionist, Sylvia.

"No anisette," Carelli added, smiling. "Too early in the day . . . even if you *have* been spoiled by Signore Orsini."

"He ruined me for life," Tom said.

"He spoke to me briefly about your visit. As you doubtless know, he is the executor for the Monte estate. I should perhaps say the Barone estate, but Carlotta has always been Carlotta Monte to me."

"How long did you represent her, Mr. Carelli?"

"About twenty years. Prior to that Mr. Orsini handled whatever legal needs she had that required attention. When he moved to Sicily she told him that she wanted an Italian attorney. I was fortunate enough to be selected. Most of my practice concerns non-profits. She had been thinking about establishing her institute for widows and I helped her establish the foundation."

"I suppose it's quite complex, with all of the tax implications," Tom said.

"Yes. You can deduct certain portions of gifts in certain years; once you've established a charitable foundation you have to give a certain amount of money away each year . . . it's not higher mathematics or anything that complex, but you must be careful to follow the regulations, even when your sole purpose is to do good."

"And that's your legal specialty."

"Yes. I do some work for the archdiocese and some for Catholic Relief Services. I'm on retainer to Loyola Marymount. My son and his wife just graduated from Loyola law school; they've joined me here."

"And they're interested in work with non-profits as well?"

"*She* is; Tony has aspirations to be a litigator, but for now he's focusing on tax work."

"A surer thing," Tom said.

"Always. It's how I started. This country is run by lawyers, Detective Deaton, and the tax code they've created is just under 80,000 pages in length. I sometimes think that their goal was to create more lawyers rather than more revenue."

"Though they disagree internally about interpretations of the code they wrote … "

"Hence more lawyers … " Carelli said, smiling. "It's not exactly the work that Perry Mason would do, but then, Perry Mason lives in fiction. I live in Westwood. I do not have the Drake detective agency; I have a mortgage."

Tom smiled, as the receptionist, Silvia Carovillano, brought in their coffee. "If you'd like it a little stronger, just say so," Carelli said. Tom sipped it. "It's perfect," he said.

"Well, Detective, what can I tell you about Mrs. Monte?"

"She was obviously a very generous lady."

"Yes. As you doubtless know, she had been hurt very deeply when she lost her beloved husband. She had an intense appreciation of the pain experienced by widows. She also had a deep sense of the fears that they have. Part of the purpose of her institute is to help these women get through the difficult transitions in their lives, transitions that they had not prepared for because they had not anticipated the necessity for them. You see, the services which her institute will provide are targeted at the needs of young widows, not elderly women who were able to prepare for their husbands' deaths and who had established a financial base which was largely unaffected by those deaths."

"I gather that she also provided some scholarship support for their children."

"Yes. You see, for several years now she has made contributions to scholarship endowments at Loyola High School and at Loyola Marymount University. The funds accumulate year by year, with all of the growth returned to principal. Now that her institute is up and running the widows' children will have access to the scholarship resources."

"Do you mind my asking how much is in the endowments?"

"Approximately $900,000 in the High School endowment and twice that in the University endowment. Most institutions pay out around 5% annually and return the rest of the growth to principal, to keep pace with inflation."

"So . . . around $100,000 a year to help students at the University."

"Yes, and if there are no eligible students in a given year the money is returned to principal. As you know, Detective, it does not take long to spend $100,000 at a University these days."

"But every bit of it counts," Tom said.

"Precisely," Carelli said. "Mrs. Monte knew that she could not do everything, but she wanted to do something, and I believe that she most certainly has."

"She must have been very careful with her own money over the years," Tom said, "in order to be able to do something like this."

"Yes. She was by no means cheap, but she was always very cautious. The shock of a sudden loss does that to you; it reminds you of the great uncertainties of life. She made an exception for her granddaughter, however, whom she loved very much and loved to spoil. You have met her, I gather."

"Yes, I have, and I believe that she returned her grandmother's love. She's an accomplished woman; I didn't see any signs that her grandmother's affection spoiled her in any of the wrong ways. She's sweet and polite and she works very hard. I believe that she commands the respect of those who work for her, but that she also enjoys their loyalty and affection."

"I have only seen her once—at her grandmother's funeral—but I was also very impressed with her."

"And she is the residuary legatee … "

"Yes, she is. There are still some personal items turning up. When we locate them we send them to Ms. Abruzzi. We recently found some golf clubs and an antique tea set. Anything that we would not use at the Foundation goes to Ms. Abruzzi. Its principal value is sentimental, of course."

"How did Mrs. Barone support herself, Mr. Carelli?"

"She had an annuity, Detective Deaton. She also had some social security income and some miscellaneous income."

"*Miscellaneous* income?"

"Yes. There are some avocado trees on her property. A restaurant in Newport Beach paid her a regular fee to harvest them. Her husband also left a large boat behind when he died. She entered into a partnership with a man who took tourists to Catalina. That was many years ago, but the company is still in business. The original boat is gone, but she still has a share in the operation. Those funds—along with the avocado income—will become part of the Institute's revenue."

"Do you happen to remember the name of the boat tour operation?"

"Yes. *Pacific Cruises.*"

"Thanks very much," Tom said. "You've been very helpful."

"Thank you, Detective. Please convey my best wishes to Ms. Abruzzi when you talk to her."

"I will," Tom said. "I definitely will."

SIXTY

"Hi, Dad, it's Tom."

"I can barely hear you; where are you?"

"On the 405, on my cell."

"How's the traffic?"

"Normal . . . awful."

"What do you need, Tom?"

"Information on an outfit called *Pacific Cruises*."

"Bill Hennessey's company. I've known him for years. Very corporate. Everything by the book. Large vessels . . . steady business. They run two ships. When one leaves Newport Beach the other leaves Avalon. Wave at each other when they pass. They're a little pricey, but very dependable."

"Has Hennessey's family always owned the operation?"

"Bill's father bought it from another guy. Only had one boat then. More of a mom and pop operation. Italian, I think. Bill's father built up the business and Bill took it over when the old man retired."

"Is he likely to be at the harbor this afternoon?"

"Yes, he's always there--at the ticket kiosk. He's got a little setup in the back—an office, a TV and coffee maker . . . He doesn't usually work the window for the day trippers; he handles the special requests—parties, dinner cruises, burials at sea."

"You mean scattering ashes."

"Right. They don't dump coffins overboard."

"How about dumping sketetal remains?"

"You think Hennessey may be involved in the Sullivan case?"

"Carlotta Barone partnered with the original owner of the cruise service. She continued to receive a piece of their income when the company was sold to Hennessey."

"That would be convenient," Wayne said, "but I don't think it would be very likely."

"Why's that, Dad?"

"Bill's strictly straight arrow. Very no nonsense. Has to be . . . too much liability. With all the drunks and the druggies you have to maintain tight discipline."

"You mean among the patrons, not the crew."

"Right. They get out in the sun, figure somebody else is in charge and responsible for everything and they let themselves go. Bill's vessels hold sixty passengers each. All you need is one person to take a swing at another or start fooling around with the equipment and you're two steps away from a full blown disaster. Bill's people are all solid citizens. A lot of them are retired Navy petty officers . . . used to maintaining order. They enjoy it."

"And you can't imagine Hennessey being involved in anything shady."

"No, he makes too much money being legit. Fishermen . . . sometimes their nets are full, sometimes they aren't. Either way they incur the same expenses. Cruise guys . . . they're golden. Once they're established, at least. You'll see ads and discount coupons for *Pacific Cruises* in every hotel magazine in southern California. They've got the reputation and they work very hard to protect it."

"I'm going to check him out, so I can report to the Chief," Tom said, "but what you've told me is very helpful."

"Sure. Sorry that he's probably not your guy. At least I don't think he would be. This would be a big deal—dumping the bones of a major O.C. gangster. You'd need absolute secrecy. I don't know why they tossed Sullivan into the Pacific, but they did it for a reason, probably an important reason. They wouldn't want any slip-ups."

"Maybe Hennessey was threatened. She knew he was reliable. He could have done it out of fear rather than greed."

"Threatened by an old lady in her nineties?"

"She had friends, Dad."

"Right. Anyway, she's dead now. Talk to Bill. Use my name if you think it could help."

Hennessey looked more like a regional manager than a boat captain. His shirt was starched and pressed and he wore expensive slacks, leather shoes and a silk tie. He greeted Tom formally, asked him if he'd like coffee, and then ushered him into the small office behind the ticket window.

"What can I do for you, Detective? You're Wayne's son, aren't you?"

"Yes, sir," Tom answered. "He speaks highly of you."

"Best harbor master we ever had," Hennessey responded. "Old school guy. His word as good as a million dollar insurance policy. So, what can I do for you?"

"You were in business with Carlotta Monte."

"Inherited the relationship," Hennessey said. "My father, Walter Hennessey, bought the original boat and company name from a guy named Cammarata, Phil Cammarata. Phil had started his business with the help of Mrs. Monte. She had a quarter interest in the operation. My father was essentially buying the company name; he had to replace the ship right away. Eventually he added a second. He approached Mrs. Monte and offered to buy her out. They talked awhile and she told him that she was a widow and had come to depend on the income from *Pacific*. He made her a second offer, said he'd guarantee her the same income she had received from Phil, but inflate it each year by the CPI. They shook on the deal and that was that."

"And she never tried to renegotiate?"

"I've never met the lady, Detective. When they struck the deal it went on the books and became part of the ongoing operation . . . it's all handled by our accountant. A guy in Irvine. His name's Carl Stringer.

You can check with him; he may have had some contact with her or her accountant, but I kind of doubt it."

"Why's that, Mr. Hennessey?"

"Well, it's more like a stock thing. You buy a little Procter and Gamble . . . every three months you get a dividend check. You don't expect a call or an offer to have lunch from the company president. Only here, the income's guaranteed and so is the rate of increase, so there's nothing to discuss. The only other difference here is that her income check went out every month rather than every quarter. Actually, it was directly deposited. Machines talking to machines. Carl explained it to me when I took over from Dad."

"How long ago was that, Mr. Hennessey?"

"Fourteen years ago."

"So it was strictly a matter of electronic transactions … "

"Like I said, machines talking to machines. The money's real, of course, but the human relationships are, well, a thing of the past. If there's ever a problem of any kind, Carl lets me know. Until recently he hadn't mentioned her name in years. We sent her a calendar at Christmas time, treated her as we would treat a major investor, but the money's a tiny part of the operation now. She helped Phil get started and Phil did a good job, so we're all in her debt, but that was decades ago. There's no personal relationship anymore."

"And you know that she died recently."

"I heard that, but our deal still stands. The money just goes into her estate. She's got a foundation or something. Carl mentioned it to me. Sounds like she wanted to do some good. Probably was a very nice lady. I'm sorry I never got to sit down with her . . . talk about Phil and the old days … "

"Let me ask you something else, Mr. Hennessey."

"Sure … "

"Do your ships ever go out at night?"

"We do twilight dinners sometimes, but those are specially chartered. There are no runs to Catalina after dark."

"And when the ships are in port, they're secured."

"Like a bank vault, Detective. Why do you ask?"

"Did you see the story about the skeletal remains found in Laguna a couple of weeks ago?"

"Michael Sullivan?"

"Yes."

"Actually, I did."

"We have reason to believe that there were contacts between Mrs. Monte and Mr. Sullivan."

"Back in the day?"

"Right."

"And you're wondering if we might have been involved in the burial . . . or . . . what would you call it--the jettisoning?"

"Yes."

"We do do burials, but we just scatter ashes, Detective. We don't slide boxes into the ocean with flags draped over the top of them. I see where you're coming from, though. It's a fair question."

Tom waited for him to continue.

"It wouldn't be a big deal for us. I guess I can imagine somebody wanting a sea burial like that. It's a little grisly, but it wouldn't be the first skeleton found in the ocean. The thing is . . . there's no big money in that, unless you have a catered party or something in connection with it. Anyway, any requests for something like that would have to have come through me."

"And none did."

"No. If it was something that somebody wanted done on the q.t.— something shady . . . "

"Yes?"

"Well, they'd do much better with a single guy. Somebody with a small motor yacht, for example—something big enough to maneuver around here but small enough that it wouldn't draw any attention. Our ships require a crew of five. Anything that happens . . . especially something shifty . . . well . . . people would notice. A single guy in a boat . . . he could go out any time, wait for high tide, wrap the remains in some floating kelp, look around, see who's within his lines of sight, and slip the whole package over the side. No muss, no fuss. That's how I'd do it. Using *Pacific* . . . it'd be like taking a body on a tour bus rather than putting it in the trunk of a car."

"I understand, Mr. Hennessey."

"If I hear anything I'll let you know, Detective, but somehow I doubt that I will. I'm not trying to dodge or anything. I'm just saying that if something serious was going on here . . . something mob-related . . . they'd know how to keep it quiet."

SIXTY-ONE

Carl Stringer's office was in a strip mall, a block from Jamboree, next to a State Farm office to the north and a cell phone dealer to the south. The front door was equipped with an electrolock and a speaker. Tom announced himself and was buzzed in. The receptionist had already left for the day and Stringer was gathering up his papers, putting them in an aged leather briefcase, with two belt straps. He was wearing a light-weight tan suit and brown plaid tie. He appeared to be in his mid-fifties, with lined facial features, probably from a serious nicotine addiction or early exposure to the Orange County sun, maybe both. There was a 12-cup coffee urn in the corner of his office and a large ceramic cup on his desk that looked as if it was in need of a good scouring.

"Sorry, I should have called," Tom said.

"No problem, Detective," Stringer said. "I got a call from Bill Hennessey a couple minutes ago. He said you might come by. It's just as easy to meet with you now as make you come back tomorrow."

"I appreciate that," Tom said. "Then you know why I'm here."

"To talk about Mrs. Monte. I only met her once, years ago, and I only saw her for a minute or two. She seemed very nice. She offered me iced tea. Or maybe it was lemonade. Either way, she was nice. She referred me to her accountant, a guy named Lucatti--Mike Lucatti. Mike used to do the books for the fishermen at Newport, back when there were a lot of them there. He died a couple years ago."

"Do you know who replaced him as her accountant?" Tom asked.

"No, sorry, but then I wouldn't . . . I mean, once we set up her payment plan there was nothing left for me to do. She gave me a voided check and I arranged to have her money wired every month, straight into her checking account. Once a year we'd recompute the payout based on the CPI. I'd send her a note and tell her what the new amount would be. It stayed the same then for the next twelve months. No rocket science here, Detective."

"Can you tell me how much she received?"

"Sure, no problem, just take me a moment." He turned on his computer and waited for it to start up. "This will only take a second," he said. "I finally broke down and got a fast machine and a fast connection."

They waited for about twenty seconds as the screen illuminated. Stringer logged in, typing what appeared to be a very long password. "Gotta be careful," he said, "there's a lot of sensitive information here. OK, here we go," he said, accessing the *Pacific Cruises* file. "Mrs. Monte's estate receives $2,784.31 each month. Weird number; that's from all the CPI adjustments. Nice little piece of change, as long as you don't have to live on it. Back in the early days of *Pacific* she was getting a larger share of their actual income, but now it's much less . . . not quite budget dust, but still a relatively small piece. A little more than she'd get from Social Security though. Think of it as a nice little top-off."

"Right," Tom said. It was slightly less than half of what he cleared every month.

"Anything else I can help you with, Detective?"

"It would save me some time if you'd give me her bank and checking account number information."

"Sure," Stringer said. He turned on his copying machine and went to his file cabinet. He needed a larger model; each drawer was crammed with files. "I never throw anything away," he said. "Here, just a second … " He removed a set of files and put them on top of the cabinet, then went through the files at the back of the drawer, removing one of them. He opened it and took out the voided check. "Still got it," he said. He made Tom a copy. "There you go," he said, "easier for you this way than writing down all the numbers."

"Thanks a lot," Tom said. "I appreciate your help."

"Not a problem," Stringer said. "I understand that Mrs. Monte's foundation is set up to help widows, especially military widows. That's a good cause. We're happy to do our bit … "

If he was in an emergency situation he would have gone directly to a judge's house to secure his warrant, but the bank would have been closed for the day anyway, so Tom returned to the LBPD office to prepare the paperwork for the request.

Chris Dietrich was gone when he got there. He had been in court in the early afternoon and in Rancho Santa Fe on a case thereafter. The office was quiet. The desk sergeant was taking routine calls and gestured hello to Tom as he entered. Tom put the ceramic bowl he had bought for Julie Li on her desk, finished his paperwork, called his Dad, thanked him again for his help, and drove to the grocery for some soup, bread, ham, cheese and a fresh gallon of milk.

He spent the night on his boat at the Dana Point Harbor marina, first cleaning out his galley refrigerator and then making a quick dinner. He turned on his TV, noting that the news hadn't seemed to change since he left for Sicily. The politicians were still insulting one another and the budget squeezes had all gotten a little tighter. The weather was good, as long as you weren't in Oklahoma City, Dallas-Fort Worth, or Denver and the stock market was edging up again. The commercials hadn't changed and neither had the drug-addled starlets.

He opened up his bed, brushed his teeth, wedged himself into his mini-shower, washed, and toweled off. He had planned to read, but the movement of the water relaxed him and he fell asleep a minute or two after his head fell against the pillow.

SIXTY-TWO

He awoke at 6:00 and got ready for his day, arriving at the office at 7:15. Chris arrived at 7:30 and they talked for a few minutes over coffee.

"Try Judge Wallace," Chris said. "He's an early riser and he won't give you any trouble."

The judge was pruning his roses when Tom arrived. He was still dressed in his bathrobe and slippers, though he was shielded from the street by a wooden fence that protected his garden from wildlife and his house from thieves. "The yellow ones always seem to do better than the red," he said. "What have you got for me, Detective?"

Tom explained the case and handed him the paperwork.

"Following the money, huh?" the Judge said.

"Yes, sir," Tom said. "I'm still looking for connections between the death of Mrs. Barone and the recent discovery of Michael Sullivan's remains."

"Ancient history," the judge said, "but no statute of limitations on murder."

"Yes, sir," Tom said.

"And little likelihood that Sullivan died from natural causes, not with the missing feet."

"You heard about that, sir?"

"Yes," he answered. "Hard to keep something that juicy under wraps."

"Yes, sir," Tom said, as Judge Wallace signed off on the warrant. "Thank you, sir."

"Go get 'em, son," Wallace said.

The receptionist at the Newport Beach Wells Fargo branch on Corporate Plaza Drive referred Tom to the branch manager, a woman named Caroline Lindsay. She was on the phone when Tom approached her glass-enclosed office and he waited outside for her to finish. As soon as she hung up she invited him into her office and asked how she could be of help. He told her that he would like to see the bank records for Carlotta Monte Barone and handed her the warrant.

"Certainly," she said. "We were all sorry to learn of Mrs. Monte's death. Just have a seat, Detective, and I'll see what we have here." She scooted her chair and turned to the monitor and keyboard at the side of her desk.

"I have her checking account number, if that would help," Tom said.

"Thanks, but I've got her file," she said. "It's alphabetical, very simple. Now, let's see . . . she had a small savings account of $27,000. That money was transferred to her foundation, as was the money in her checking account. Let me see . . . there was $14,000 in that account at the time of her death. There's no record of her having had a safe deposit box and she had no loans with Wells Fargo."

"How about a money market account?" Tom asked.

"No, sorry," she said. "And no credit card either. She apparently had a very simple financial life."

Tom was still absorbing the notion that a $27,000 savings account was considered small, and reminded himself that he was in Newport Beach, not Newport, Kentucky.

"Could you pull up the records on her checking account?" Tom asked. "I know that she was receiving income from an investment in *Pacific Cruises.* Were there other direct deposits in that account?"

"Just a sec," Ms. Lindsay said. He could hear the computer clicking quietly. "She received a Social Security payment each month—a little over $1,700. She must have had a job when she was younger . . . or it could be from her husband's account. There's another regular deposit as well . . . a transfer from another bank."

"And what was that amount?" Tom asked.

"A little over $108,000."

"Over what period of time, Ms. Lindsay?"

"Each month, Detective."

SIXTY-THREE

"Can you pull up the records from her checking account, Ms. Lindsay?"

"Of course. Any particular month and year?"

"How about the last couple of months before her death?"

"Sure . . . let's see . . . there are very few actual checks. Here's one for groceries . . . and one to a wine store . . . most of the transactions are automatic debits—for her utilities, her mailed medications, her insurance premiums, her cell, landline and internet services . . . a regular transfer to her foundation . . . and transfers to other bank accounts."

"*Her* bank accounts?"

"I can't tell just from the numbers, Detective. None of them are to Wells Fargo accounts. I can offer a guess … "

"Yes?"

"Mrs. Monte had a large house and she was quite old. My guess is that these are salary transfers. The amounts would be monthly segments of annual salaries in the thirty to seventy thousand dollar range. One might be for her private nurse, one for her cook, one for her maid, one for her driver, a couple for her landscapers, etc. I'll print them out for you, so that you can check."

"Thanks very much. I appreciate that," Tom said. He scooted closer but the angle was such that he couldn't get a clear view of her computer screen. "How much was she transferring into her foundation account each month?"

"A little over $50,000."

"Could you go back several months . . . say a year or so . . . and see if the pattern is pretty much the same?"

"Sure . . . OK . . . here it is . . . the transfer *in* is a little less than $108,000, but just a *little* less."

"It's inflating," Tom said.

"Probably," Ms. Lindsay replied. "The transfers to individuals are a little smaller, but the pattern is the same. Raises, in the most recent records, would be my guess. The cable service is cheaper then; they're always raising that, of course. There's also a check for the installation of a water softener. It's to a plumber, but there's a notation on the bottom of the check that specifies that she had a softener installed. No wine this month, but from the size of the later check she either bought by the case or bought very high-end items. Otherwise, it looks pretty much like the more recent months."

Tom thanked her again and returned to the office to prepare the warrant paperwork so that he could check the other accounts. Judge Wallace was unavailable this time, so he went to Judge Hensley. When he checked the last of the accounts later that afternoon he saw that Caroline Lindsay had been right. The transfers were to individuals, most with Hispanic surnames. The banks were in the hinterlands. Orange County offers plenty of work, but little affordable housing.

The one account that he was unable to check was the most interesting of all—the account from which the $108,000 issued each month. The bank was in Los Angeles and it was too late to pay them a visit.

The next morning he drove first to the office, had a cup of coffee with Chris Dietrich, briefed him on the progress of his investigation, and told him that he'd be out of the office for much of the rest of the day. "The bank's in Pasadena, Chief. I'll be a while."

"It's always a crap shoot," Dietrich said, "but I'd probably take the 605. Don't try to take the 210 in rush hour, unless you just want to sit there and watch the smog move toward the edges of the San Gabriels."

"I agree, Chief," Tom said.

"This could be very interesting," Dietrich said. "I'd like to have a sugar daddy dropping 100K or so into my checking account every month. Hell, I'd settle for one who only came calling once a year."

"Right," Tom said. "The interesting thing is that I've been proceeding on the assumption that everybody else from those days is long dead. Of course, it could be an annuity or something like that."

"A very *good* annuity," Chris said.

The bank was downtown, near the city hall. An old bank in a spiffy new building. Tom was referred to the manager, a man named Holloway. He looked the part—a gray suit, muted maroon tie, lightly-polished wingtips and the onset of male-pattern baldness. "Robert Holloway," the man said. "How can I be of service?" He wore a simple wedding ring, but no other jewelry or accessories.

Tom introduced himself, handed him the warrant, and told him he'd like to see the file on the account.

"Let's go into my office; we'll be more comfortable there," Holloway said. He offered Tom a cup of coffee, wrote down the account number on a post-it note, and left, saying "I'll be a few minutes."

Two minutes later a young woman brought Tom the cup of coffee, with a saucer and a napkin with the bank's logo. "You did say black, didn't you, sir?" she asked.

"Yes, this is fine. Thanks," Tom said.

"If you change your mind, my name is Laura. Extension 2715. Just let me know; I can get you whatever you need."

"Thanks again," Tom said, smiling at her as she turned and walked back to her work station.

Holloway returned nearly ten minutes later. "Sorry about the delay," he said. "This is an old file and I had to go down to the basement and then find the rolling ladder."

The folder was brown with age but it didn't appear to have been handled very often. "I'll get you copies of whatever you need," Holloway said, "but let's just have a look first … "

SIXTY-FOUR

"The account is for a company," Holloway said, "though I can't say I recognize the name. Of course, it's very easy to incorporate and that simple legal action offers a number of advantages, not the least of which is anonymity. The name here is the *SPF Corporation*. The account was established nearly sixty years ago. Deposits were made for several months and then, suddenly, they stopped … "

"Does it specify how funds were to be disbursed?"

"Yes, it does," Holloway said. He paused for a second as he flipped through some loose sheets of paper. "Just wanted to make sure," he said.

"Yes?"

"The funds could be accessed by two individuals . . . a Michael Sullivan . . . and a Carlotta Barone, née Monte. Barone was to receive 1% of the income from the corpus, payable monthly. Sullivan could withdraw money from the account, but Barone could not, unless Sullivan co-signed. Presumably they were the chief officers in the corporation, but Sullivan had the principal control of the account."

"Could you check the pattern of the disbursements over the years?"

"Yes, but I'll have to do that on the computer," Holloway said, putting the file on the desk and turning to his computer. The screensaver was a splash of red and white flowers. Holloway tapped one of the keys and then checked the post-it note for the account number. As the flowers disappeared the bank home page and a prompt box came up; Holloway entered the number, typed in some codes, and waited.

"Here we are," he said. There have been regular disbursements to

Mrs. Barone. Actually, she's been using her maiden name for quite some time. I don't see any disbursements to Mr. Sullivan. Let me go back a ways ... "

Three minutes later Holloway made some additional keystrokes. "The older records were added later. They're in a separate file . . . OK . . . here we are . . . no, still no disbursements to Mr. Sullivan. Let me check the current status on the account, because there were no recent disbursements to either one of them . . . hm-m-m, oh yes ... "

"What's that, Mr. Holloway?"

"The account was just closed. The paperwork is with the bank's lawyers. You'll doubtless want to see that. I'll give you their names ... "

"Does it say how much was left in the corpus when the account was closed, Mr. Holloway?"

"I can certainly find out. Just a sec . . . OK . . . yes . . . just prior to its being closed the account contained a little over one hundred and thirty million dollars." He held his expression as he told Tom the amount.

The lawyers were *Crandall, Bridges, and West*. The *SPF Corporation* case was handled by the senior partner, William Crandall. Holloway contacted his office and Crandall invited Tom to join him for lunch at the Jonathan Club. "The one at the beach, if that's OK," Crandall said.

Crandall, Bridges, and West were in Century City and it was an easier run for him to Santa Monica than to downtown. They met at 12:30. Crandall was waiting for Tom when he arrived. He was dressed like Holloway, but three or four steps up in quality. The lightweight wool suit was obviously tailored for him personally and the tie was unlike anything Tom had ever seen in nature--a step beyond muted Armani, but a few steps short of gawdy Tino Cosma. Instead of a pocket square there was an unadorned silk handkerchief. Tom wondered if Crandall got his hair cut every day. Maybe he had a special barber for every strand. He was holding a file in his left hand; Tom figured that he had been studying it intently for the last half hour or so.

His manner was more down to earth than his aristocratic appearance. "I'm Bill Crandall," he said, extending his hand.

"Tom Deaton," Tom responded. "Thanks for meeting with me on short notice."

"Thanks for driving so far to meet me here," Crandall replied. "I'm happy to help in any way that I can. Actually, I've been expecting you."

"You have?"

"Yes. Mrs. Monte-Barone's executor said that I should expect a call from you."

"Really?"

"Yes. He said that you were very able. Should we sit down and order lunch?"

Crandall wrote down his order for a Club sandwich and iced tea. "The Club they serve downtown is the best on the planet, at least as far as I've been able to tell," Crandall said. "The one here is a very close second."

"Then I'll have one too," Tom said.

"I think you'll be pleased," Crandall said, handing the written order to the waiter.

"Now," he said. "Where should I start? My father wrote the original agreement for Michael Sullivan. The *SPF* acronym stands for *Sullivan, Private Fund*. At least he was polite enough not to say *slush*. We represent the bank, of course, and my father counseled Mr. Sullivan that we would not hesitate to bring an action on behalf of the bank if the deposits and disbursements in any way compromised the bank's integrity. He pled the usual, of course, that he was involved in a host of legitimate businesses and that the moneys deposited would be part of his share of the profits from those businesses.

"In his way he was something of a social climber and he aspired to respectability. My father always believed that he liked the arrangement with the bank and liked even more his brief association with *Crandall and Bridges*, as the firm was called in those days.

"As you know, the organization of which he was a part had no straightforward retirement plan. My father believed that each person at the top of the organization took on responsibility for the survivors of specific members of the organization."

"Sullivan killed Barone, so he bore responsibility for Mrs. Barone," Tom said.

"Yes. There was also something personal there as well. At least my father believed that there was. Sullivan instructed the bank—through my father—to take special care of Mrs. Barone (she began using her maiden name—Monte--to reduce any possible publicity)."

"And were there any other designated beneficiaries of his largesse?"

"No. Sullivan made significant deposits when the account was established and then a few thereafter. Mrs. Barone's was the only other name on the account. She was to receive 1% of the income each year and Sullivan left a provision that she could draw some of the principal so long as Sullivan co-signed. The 1% was to meet regular expenses and the other provision was there to cover emergencies or unanticipated, significant needs. Sullivan, of course, could draw down some or all of the principal whenever he so chose, but that never happened. For years Mrs. Monte-Barone has received 1% of the interest income and the rest has been returned to principal. Let me clarify that. If the account was paying 5% interest, she received 1% or *20% of the interest income*, with the other 4% returned to principal. If it was paying 4% she still received 1%, but then it was *25% of the interest*, with 3% returned to principal."

"I see," Tom said, "and Sullivan disappeared before he could take any of the income *or* principal."

"Yes, along with the other members of the Brienza organization. This was all shortly after the establishment of the account."

"How soon after?" Tom asked.

"Less than five months," Crandall responded.

Tom held his expression and let Crandall continue.

"Anyway, flash forward 50+ years. Mrs. Monte-Barone dies and

Michael Sullivan's remains are recovered. A short time thereafter I received a call from the executor of Mrs. Monte-Barone's estate … "

"Mr. Orsini."

"Yes. He presented me with three death certificates, one for Michael Sullivan, one for Mrs. Monte-Barone and one for a man named John Devito."

"Devito?"

"Yes. There was a Devito in the Brienza organization. He and his wife had a son named John. Mr. Orsini assured me that DNA tests would show that the father of this son was actually Michael Sullivan."

"Why do you think he told you that?"

"Because Michael Sullivan had not married and John Devito—the putative son of James Devito, but actually the son of Michael Sullivan-- had never married. That exhausted the number of individuals who might file a claim against the *SPF Corp* account."

"So that the sole survivor with a plausible claim for the assets of the *SPF Corporation* assets was … "

"The residuary legatee of Mrs. Monte-Barone's estate."

"And you advised the bank to release the funds to her."

"Yes, there were no other survivors and we had Mr. Sullivan's request that the bank look after Mrs. Monte-Barone. My father always believed that he was in love with her or at least deeply infatuated with her. Given the terms of the agreement and the absence of any other claimants— combined with Sullivan's strong feelings for Mrs. Monte-Barone—the fairest and most defensible settlement was to respect Mrs. Monte-Barone's feelings."

"Which is to say, the terms of her will," Tom added.

"Yes, exactly."

"So the funds were released … "

"Yes. We put a notice in the Court Register, asking that any persons believing themselves to be the heirs of John Devito come forward. No one did. And those claims might have been tenuous anyway, since the only names on the account were Sullivan and Barone. Still, as Mr. Orsini noted, there might have been a claim from the illegitimate son's heirs, if there had been any."

"Actually he wasn't legally illegitimate, if you pardon the seeming contradiction."

"No, technically not."

The waiter brought the club sandwiches, which were garnished beautifully and served on bone china with the club's logo. "I think you're going to like that," Crandall said.

"So there you have it," Crandall said, as the waiter brought coffee.

"Do you know where the funds are now?" Tom asked.

"They were actually wired to another bank."

"An American bank?"

"Oh yes," Crandall said, opening up the file and retrieving a small envelope with Tom's name written on the outside. "Here's the account number and the bank's address . . . I thought I'd save you the trouble of running around. The good news is that the bank is actually in Orange County. The rest of the file is your's also. Enjoy. It makes for interesting reading."

SIXTY-FIVE

"That's very, very helpful," Tom said. "Thanks very much."

"You're welcome. Interesting case, isn't it?"

"Yes, it is. What did you think of Mr. Orsini? He made a special trip to see you?"

"We face-timed, actually. Very professional. I knew of his relationship with his brother's organization, of course, but I have to say that I was impressed with the way in which he had prepared himself for the discussion. All of the documentary evidence was in order and he had put together a full brief on why the funds should become part of Mrs. Monte-Barone's estate."

The Friday afternoon traffic on the 405 was hellish, but Tom was exhilarated, his head spinning with ideas. He called Chris Dietrich on his cell. Chris was in a meeting with one of his lieutenants, but called Tom back fifteen minutes later.

"What have you got?" he asked.

"Quite a bit," Tom said. "It looks as if Sullivan was hitting on other married women besides Carlotta Barone."

"Yes?"

"Orsini talked to the lawyer for the Pasadena bank which was looking after Sullivan's slush fund—a cool 130 mil, by the way—and told him that Sullivan fathered a child by James Devito's wife. It was a boy and he's dead now. Orsini gave the lawyer the death certificate, along with a copy of the death certificate for Sullivan and Mrs. Monte-Barone. The lawyer said that individual members of the Brienza family were responsible for the widows of the people they killed … "

"He would have learned that from Orsini … "

"Possibly. He said he learned it from his father, who established Sullivan's original account. Anyway, Sullivan had his own private fund and Carlotta Barone received 1% of the interest. Let me rephrase that. If the account paid 5% she received 20% of that; if it paid 4% she received 25%--a full 1 percent."

"One percent of 130 million is huge."

"Right, but it wasn't 130 million from the get-go. The account was set up so that Carlotta automatically received her piece, but she couldn't dip into the principal without Sullivan co-signing. Over the years everything above and beyond her piece has been folded back into the principal and the payout has escalated."

"So Sullivan set it up and then suddenly disappeared."

"Exactly. He never got to make a withdrawal. I figure that he set it up as part of his plan to cozy up to Carlotta Barone. He said, 'Look at what I'm doing for you; now think about what you can do for me … '"

"And instead of slipping into something comfortable she slipped her hand into her little case, took out the ice pick and put it in his eye."

"Exactly."

"But only after she was clear on the fact that the agreement was airtight and the payments were flowing."

"No doubt."

"Was the Devito boy on the account also?"

"No, and neither, of course, was Devito's widow, since Devito and Sullivan disappeared around the same time. Sullivan may have made some other provision for him, maybe a cash payment or annuity of some sort."

"But Orsini figured that he could have filed some claim against Sullivan's slush fund."

"Yes, but not when he was dead, and he had never married."

"So that cleared the way for Carlotta's estate to make a run at the full corpus."

"Yes, a successful run. Gina Abruzzi is now a multimillionaire. At first it looked as if she was going to get the letters and figurines and personal bric-a-brac that didn't go to the foundation. Now it's pretty clear that she and Giancarlo had their eyes on a far bigger prize."

"Are you thinking what I'm thinking?"

"What's that, Chief?"

"Why they were so anxious to talk to you at such length … "

"Yes. It was all a major distraction, so that they could buy the necessary time to dot all the legal i's and cross all the legal t's. They wanted to keep me occupied so that I wasn't futzing around with the lawyers and bankers in California."

"Of course, in fairness, we have to say that they kept their part of the bargain. They gave you the back story and they fingered the person responsible for Sullivan's untimely demise. That's what we wanted."

"Yes. And while there are some rather large items that they left out, there is no example yet of anything that constitutes an actual lie."

"So what are Ms. Abruzzi's plans for her newfound wealth?"

"I hoped to find that out first thing tomorrow morning. I've got the bank and the account number to which the funds were wired."

"Nearby?"

"Pacific Western at Dana Point."

"Right on the PCH? I'm less than ten minutes away. Give me the account number. If the manager balks I'll tell him that I'll be back in the morning with a warrant and that I'll want copies of all the documents. All I need now is a general sense of the disbursements."

"All he can say is no, Chief."

"Give me the number. I'll call you back in a few minutes."

He called back in 25. "Guess what," Dietrich said, "the money's staying in the O.C."

"Really?"

"Yes. The principal's intact and nearly all of the interest is to be transferred to the Barone Foundation."

"And the remaining portion of the interest is returned to principal?"

"Yes," Dietrich said.

"To build a hedge against inflation."

"That's what I would figure."

"There have to be tax implications driving this," Tom said.

"I would think so," Dietrich said. "The only other alternative is that we're dealing with *two* saints--Cosa Nostra saints."

SIXTY-SIX

Maybe sainthood was too much of a stretch. How about simple self-interest, Tom thought. Better to play straight with the police rather than lie, cheat and steal and as far as Tom could see the two of them had more or less done so. If he wasn't fully on their side he wasn't, at least, working directly against them. And Gina was set for life, legally. If the full corpus was indeed in her hands she could stop transferring the interest to the Barone Foundation at any time and enjoy a very large pay day. Giancarlo may have executed some sort of agreement with the IRS and its California counterpart to keep the taxman at bay until they could implement Plan B, in which, for example, Gina Abruzzi might become a senior officer in the Barone Foundation with a hefty salary and generous vacation package. Even without the full corpus, she could muddle through on an extra mil a year. Maybe she'd set up a new office for the Foundation—something modern, maybe overlooking the harbor at Newport Beach, complete with a 65-foot Foundation launch to tool around in and contemplate new ways to do good.

In the meantime Tom decided to pay a visit to Carl Drewes. With a little luck he might arrive before Drewes left for the day. In the meantime, he called the office and asked them to text message Drewes's home address, just in case he needed it.

As it turned out, he didn't. He arrived at Drewes's office a minute before 5:00. The secretary/receptionist was just headed out the door, but Drewes was in his office, eating an ice cream cone. Tom introduced himself and Drewes shook his hand and offered him a seat.

"Sorry to be eating in front of you," Drewes said. "I'm addicted to these things. Sometimes I skip lunch and have one of these instead. Coconut—that's my favorite. I also like real Strawberry—the kind where you can actually taste the berries. Funny, it doesn't spoil my appetite for dinner … "

"My weakness is Piña Colada," Tom said. "The ice cream, that is, not the drink."

"Yeah, you really taste the pineapple in the ice cream," Drewes said. "Well, Detective, what brings you to my humble legal abode?"

"Just a question or two, Mr. Drewes."

"Of course."

"We recently discovered the remains of a man named Michael Sullivan … "

"Yes, I know," Drewes said.

"And you requested a copy of the death certificate."

"Actually, two. The client needed an original and I got an extra one for my files—just in case he decided he needed another one later. Save me a trip."

"Because he needed to submit the original and all he'd keep is a photocopy."

"Right."

"Would you be comfortable telling me the name of your client?"

"The LBPD already asked me, Detective, and I invoked attorney/client privilege."

"I know that, Mr. Drewes, but I thought that you might reconsider."

"Normally I wouldn't, Detective; it's a matter of general practice, but in this case I can make an exception."

"Why is that, Mr. Drewes?"

"Because the client told me you'd probably be dropping in and he asked me to say hello to you and wish you well in your investigation."

Tom smiled. "I think I know who we're speaking about then."

"A friend of Mr. Orsini's has a daughter who once studied with my father at UCLA. He teaches Italian history. The daughter teaches at UCSD now."

"And Mr. Orsini somehow found out that your father had a son who is a young lawyer in the O.C."

"Actually, I gave the daughter a little legal help when she bought her condo. It's a small world, Detective, and Mr. Orsini seems to know most of the people in it, at least most of the people who have anything to do with Italy."

"What is your father's specialty?" Tom asked.

"The Renaissance in general, but more specifically the machinations of the Renaissance popes," Drewes answered. "At least that's how he would describe it. You know what?"

"What's that?" Tom asked.

"I think Mr. Orsini could have given them a run for their money."

Tom spent the night on his boat. Dinner was a microwaved package of macaroni and cheese and most of a pint of Piña Colada ice cream. In the morning he called Chris Dietrich and asked him if he was going to come into the office.

"Anything pressing?" Chris asked.

"No, I was just going to chat with you about yesterday. I talked to Carl Drewes—the young attorney who picked up one of the Sullivan death certificates … "

"Yes. He wouldn't tell us who he was representing."

"He told me yesterday."

"Orsini?"

"Yes. He said he wouldn't ordinarily violate the attorney/client privilege, but in this case he'd make an exception. Orsini told him that I'd probably be stopping by and he wanted Drewes to say hi and wish me well on the investigation."

Dietrich laughed. "OK, then," he said, "pick one—he's either a genuinely nice man or he's jerking your chain."

"Maybe a little of both. He knows I haven't stopped snooping around or at least he suspects that I haven't. That means he figures there are a few outstanding items that are still gnawing at me."

"It's almost too good to be true—the Mafia angels and all that stuff—so you'd have a natural curiosity and a healthy sense of skepticism anyway," Dietrich said, "even if most of the major questions on the case had already been answered."

"Right," Tom said. "It's funny. I feel as if I've made a deal with the devil but, in retrospect, it may have been a pretty good deal. I bought a used car but it's still running well and I haven't found any major defects. Still . . . it seems like too much of a long shot, even if he was the honest consigliere, the fixer who always stayed within the law."

"It still doesn't look as if he's violated any laws, Tom. Carlotta Barone did apparently and she had to have had some help from a lot of street soldiers, but *they've* all gone off to their eternal rewards."

"True," Tom said.

"So what are you going to do?"

"Is that a rhetorical question, Chief?"

"Maybe."

"I thought maybe I'd get a cup of coffee and drive down to San Clemente—check out Tommy Barone's house and see what his wife and granddaughter are doing with it."

"I've got a mountain of paper and a soccer game to attend," Dietrich said. "My niece's. Give me a call if you see anything that looks interesting."

"Will do, Chief. There's something else … "

"What's that, Tom?"

"Both Orsini and Gina Abruzzi told me that I'd be coming back to see them sometime."

"Yes … ?"

"I wonder why they said that."

SIXTY-SEVEN

The basic architectural design was simple and unadorned, more like a vast farmhouse than a Tuscan villa. When he thought about it, however, he realized that many of the original California missions were simple in both style and execution. The priests were clerics first, not architects, and it was easier to create blank walls with an occasional window than structures resplendent with great sheets of glass offering views of the shimmering waters in the distance.

The ocean you always have with you, presumably, particularly in the days when there were no neighbors purchasing tear-downs and eking out every square foot of living space that a tiny parcel of ground would yield. The soil and the weather were far more important than the human comforts which are now taken for granted.

The grounds were impressive. A sloping hill behind the main structure insured that no one would build there, thus providing maximum insulation and privacy for the minimum investment of acreage. Though not in complete disarray the avocado orchard and few citrus plantings would benefit from the influx of new capital from the *SPF Corporation*. Various landscaping projects had been undertaken over the years, including the planting of ivy, some pachysandra, and sprays of bougainvillea. The colors of the plantings contrasted nicely with the earth tones of the main structure's walls and trim and the relatively few windows were highlighted by boxes of seasonal flowers that functioned like eye-liner on a plain-faced model.

Mrs. Barone's assistant, a woman named Lydia Melendez, showed

Tom the building's interior. The many functional rooms and open work spaces that had characterized the original structure were all gone, as the building had been reconfigured to accommodate modern needs and tastes. The interior walls and support pillars carried the appearance of authenticity, but they were clearly not part of the original design. Similarly, the electrical fixtures and plumbing installations were later additions as well. Sometimes they appeared to be integral to their surroundings, sometimes they were clearly overlays. Need and convenience had trumped architectural authenticity or purity.

"This was Mrs. Barone's favorite room," Lydia said. It was a library at the southeast end of the first floor. The casework occupied one corner; the rest of the room contained couches and wing chairs, with occasional tables and area carpets. "She would take her coffee here in the morning and her tea here in the afternoon," her assistant said. "The books were all Mrs. Barone's. Her husband was not a great reader. 'He was a doer,' she would say. Her favorite writer was Lampedusa. She has here over fifty editions of *Il Gattopardo*. Some are quite valuable. Lately she had been reading Andrea Camilleri. Her favorite was *The Terra-Cotta Dog*. 'It was lighter reading,' she said, but she enjoyed it very much. By the way, the picture on the west wall, there, is her husband, Tommy. I would never feel comfortable calling him that, but she always did."

The hallway connecting the rooms on the first level was relatively narrow, but it was brightly lit. The living room was more functional than decorative. "This is where people sat before and after dinner," Lydia said. "The couches were arranged so that they could drink their wine or cocktails and relax. Later they had their coffee and cordials here. Mrs. Barone insisted that the furniture be comfortable. 'This is a home, not a museum,' she would say. 'I want my guests to feel as if they are in their own homes, a place where they can lean back and enjoy themselves.' There is no family room, Detective Deaton. The living room *is* the family room and the library was Mrs. Barone's personal space. The dining room is just here . . . follow me.

"You see, it is somewhat narrow, but the table will easily accommodate twelve guests. The sideboard there was actually used. Food would sometimes be brought in from the kitchen and placed there; Mrs. Barone would then supervise its distribution. She liked large plates and bowls. 'This is not a restaurant,' she would say. 'It is a home.' There were always great plates of antipasti. She loved peppers and she loved meats and cheeses. They were always organized very imaginatively, like works of art. There was always a pasta bowl. Mrs. Barone would grate the reggiano personally before serving it. The desserts were hidden until they were ready to be served. She wanted them to be surprises, not distractions. She loved cakes and bowls of fresh fruits. For years there was a large espresso machine on the end of the sideboard, but it needed to be replaced just as Mrs. Barone became ill. She thought that the Foundation would want something simpler."

"When will the building be fully converted, Mrs. Melendez?" Tom asked.

"That will depend on Ms. Abruzzi," Lydia said. "I know that she wants to maintain the essential elements of Mrs. Barone's home. She does not want it to appear antiseptic or institutional. While the Foundation is to help the beneficiaries of Mrs. Barone's philanthropy, her home is to be a memorial to her as well. 'It should evoke her presence,' Ms. Abruzzi said. She was not able to spend as much time here as she would have liked, but she treasures her memories of those times. In my opinion, Detective Deaton … "

"Yes … ?"

"I believe that she wants to preserve it for herself as well as for her grandmother. This is the seat of her memories of their time together. It is very precious to Ms. Abruzzi. Shall we look at the upstairs? That is the kitchen there on your right. It is large and functional, designed for the serious preparation of food."

Tom looked in as they walked toward the steps to the second floor. There were no marble countertops or hypertrophied stainless steel appliances, but large work surfaces, pantries, and storage facilities. Funny, he thought to himself, the kitchen is now so important for sellers and buyers, though no one really cooks anymore, not, at least, in the way that his mother or, apparently, Mrs. Barone did.

"The upstairs will be remodeled, Detective Deaton," Lydia said. "It is now designed for a family—a large master bedroom, several guest bedrooms, and two bathrooms. You did not see the bathroom on the first floor, by the way. It was across from the library—a small half-bath only. When the upstairs is remodeled there will be more bedrooms, but they will be smaller and each will have its own bathroom. This was Mrs. Barone and her husband's room … "

It was huge, perhaps 25'x25', and the bed sat on a wooden platform, one step above the floor level. It was antique and canopied—like something out of a villa in Fiesole or, perhaps, Taormina. The thick, dark drapes added further weight to the room. It was a place to which one might be summoned rather than invited.

The other bedrooms were larger than those in contemporary homes, though the bathrooms were somewhat smaller, the tilework dating them. The fixtures were elegant, most of them marble or crystal. Mrs. Melendez was standing at the end of the hall, waiting for him near the steps. "You saw the grounds when you drove in," she said. "Let me show you the bell tower."

As they walked outside Tom noticed a brass plaque, designating the estate as part of the historical registry. Mrs. Melendez was a few steps ahead of him, pointing at the tower. "Some people think of it as a quaint decoration, perhaps even as a folly of sorts, but it still marks the canonical hours. In the early days the bells were activated by a system of ropes and pullies. One of the workmen would be assigned the task of ringing them. Now it is all done by computer. The neighbors seem to like it; there have been no complaints."

The tower was simple enough, rising three stories higher than the main structure. The surprise came when they went inside. The walls were painted and decorated with religious statuary in recessed alcoves. At the center of the room, several feet above floor level, there were two fully-exposed sarcophagi. Each was marble, with a connecting canopy above them, Tommy to the west, Carlotta to the east. "This is their mausoleum. It is very spiritual, is it not?" Lydia asked.

"Yes, it is," Tom responded. "Partly it's the exposed area above, suggesting the ascent to heaven. It's very church-like. I can almost smell the incense."

"There is a small holy water font on the wall next to the entryway. You probably did not see it when you entered. Most do not notice it. The paintings above the statuary were actually done by an Italian artist. You can see his name over in the corner there, beneath the image of the angels." Tom looked; the name was Matteo Caligheri.

"So Mrs. Barone was recently interred here … "

"Yes, though the structure had been created many years earlier. It was ready for her. She took great comfort in that. She said that the sounds in the *campanile* were very holy and that they would enable her to sleep in peace for all eternity."

"I heard the bells when I drove in," Tom said.

"Some think it is a little overdone, but I think it is very beautiful," Lydia said. "I also think that the canopy between their tombs is very lovely and very romantic. She was devoted to him and he to her."

"I can see that," Tom said, his head filled with thoughts and images. I wonder where Gina plans to spend her eternity, he thought to himself.

SIXTY-EIGHT

"I just have one other question," Tom said.

"Yes?"

"Where will the administrative offices of the Foundation be?"

"I'm not sure," Lydia said. "Ms. Abruzzi talked about renting some office space nearby—nothing extensive—a few hundred square feet. The principal on-site administrator will have a small work space in the corner of the library. Ms. Abruzzi said that her grandmother would have wanted the bulk of the income from the endowment to support the Foundation's operations rather than its administration."

"I understand," Tom said. "Again, thank you very much for showing me around the grounds and buildings. I appreciate your taking the time to do so."

"I hope you learned what you needed to learn, Detective Deaton."

"Yes, I did," he said, shading the truth.

As soon as he got in his car Tom got on his cell and called Chris. He described the grounds and main building, but spent most of the time describing the bell tower mausoleum.

"It sounds very medieval," Chris said. "Stone tombs in the middle of a church . . . that sort of thing. I guess if they had been English there would have been brasses for tourists to rub."

"Right," Tom said. "There isn't a particularly military feel to it, though. It's very romantic in its way, especially with the canopy thing that connects the two burial vaults."

"I've seen structures like that in cemeteries," Chris said. "I think it's the next new thing. On the other hand—having your own bell tower and your own statues and holy water font . . . that sounds like the real deal."

"It's not gawdy," Tom said, "but it certainly grabs your attention when you walk in. I sort of thought of it as being like a presidential museum."

"What do you mean?" Chris asked.

"You know, Chief . . . when you visit a presidential library . . . that sort of thing . . . the president and the first lady are usually buried there in the garden. It's a little strange at first, because you don't expect a museum to also be a cemetery. On the other hand, it seems natural—*different* and very *special*—because the final things you want to see are their graves. If they weren't buried there you'd feel as if the place somehow wasn't *special* to them. *Oh yeah, check out the museum and all, but don't expect us to be there too.*"

"I see what you mean," Chris said. "It's the end of the tour."

"Yes, and it's *their* place. *Really*. They're not leaving."

"And it actually looks as if the Foundation operation is on the level."

"Yes, even down to the fact that Gina doesn't want to spend any more money on administration than she has to."

"We've got to be missing something," Chris said.

"I know what you're saying, Chief," Tom answered. "Every step of the way I've had the same feeling . . . it's all too good to be true. At the same time, I haven't felt as if I've had the wool pulled over my eyes. I've gotten *most* of the real story and no sense that I've been told lies or been subjected to misdirection."

"Right. I still think that they needed to do some fast legal maneuvering, maybe some fast financial maneuvering as well, and the fact that you were in Sicily rather than in Orange County may have worked to their advantage. At the same time, they weren't just stringing you along. They i.d.'d Sullivan's murderer (maybe I should say *murderess*) and tagged her as the person who organized the removal of all of Sullivan's playmates."

"And they honestly acknowledged that I didn't have each and every answer," Tom said, "because they've sent their best wishes for my success in the continuing investigation. They know that I don't have enough to simply close the books and lock up the file cabinet."

"That's true," Dietrich said, pausing before continuing. "It's been an interesting case—unlike anything I've ever seen," he said.

"I'm going to try to clear my head a little," Tom said. "With the weekend here there are a lot of things I can't really do anyway. I want to get out on the boat for a few hours, visit with my dad, maybe drive back to the Barone house again, get a good night's sleep and then go through all of my notes one more time. I don't know if anything will jump out at me or not, but I feel that I'm too close at this point. I need some distance and some perspective."

"It's hard to let go of it when you've been given signals that it's not over," Chris said.

"That's right, Chief, and that's a very important point. Why would they suggest that I'm not finished? It's in their best interest to see me simply walk away."

"Maybe they really like you and really did want to strike a deal with you. Maybe they've been straight with you all along. I know it feels like a long shot, but . . . well . . . this whole case has been something of a long shot from the beginning."

"Right, Chief. It does seem too good to be true, but who knows? They had other options … "

"What do you mean, Tom?"

"Well, when I got to Taormina they could have given me a nice case of food poisoning and sent me to bed for awhile. Anything too serious would have drawn attention, but there were intermediate things that they could have done—things serious enough to sideline me while they went about their business. There was no necessity for them to host me for long dinners and even longer conversations. And there was no ultimate need to give up Carlotta Barone, particularly when Gina was so close to her."

"*Really* close," Chris said. "A hundred and thirty million close."

"Right."

"Follow your instincts, Tom. Rest up and then get back to it all on Monday. The victims are all dead anyway and so are the perps."

SIXTY-NINE

The Pacific lived up to its name that afternoon, as Tom made his way up the coast to Newport Beach. His father asked him about his schedule and they agreed on an early dinner.

"We didn't get to talk as much as I would have liked the other night," Wayne said.

"I'm not fresh off the plane this time," Tom said. "What do you feel like?"

"Let's do steaks again, this time something a little more special."

"They do steaks in Italy," Tom said, "but you're always afraid you're going to hear a pained breath when you cut into them."

"Important to get back on your regular feed," Wayne said. "Are you still a little jet-lagged?"

"No, it's not bad flying west; it's flying east that gets you."

"But you had a nice cushy bed and a big swimming pool to help let you down easy when you arrived there … "

"Yes, I sort of miss them," Tom said, "though I'm glad to be back."

"Well, things haven't changed too much while you were gone. House prices probably only went up another twenty percent or so and taxes another twenty-five. Have you talked to Sarah since you got back?"

"Actually, I haven't," Tom said. "I'll give her a call." Wayne remained his ex-girlfriend's staunchest advocate. Since he lost his wife he'd probably been hoping that Tom might settle down and have some of the joy that he himself had experienced. He couldn't accept the fact that her feelings for Tom had cooled, not to the point of chill, but far short of passion or romantic love.

"I think she's got a new job," Tom said, as Wayne smiled, feeling that there was still some level of communication between them.

"Well, as you know, Son, I've always liked her."

"I've always liked her too, Dad. What have *you* been up to the last couple of days?"

"Same old, same old," Wayne answered. "Nothing bad and nothing really to write home about. Mostly I've been working on the boat. Nothing too arduous. Just stretching my arms and legs a little. By the way, I checked on yours while you were away. Everything was OK."

"Thanks, I appreciate that," Tom said.

"So, is your case closed yet?"

"Not quite. I want to run through my notes again . . . see if I've overlooked anything. In the meantime I'm just trying to clear my head."

"Nothing better for that than some steak, potatoes, and a little red wine," Wayne said. "You can sleep at the harbor tonight and go back down the coast tomorrow."

"Sounds good," Tom said. "You convinced me."

The next day he was back at his desk, poring over his notes and timeline, studying details and hoping to find something crucial that he had somehow continued to overlook. After three hours he stopped, slid his chair back from his desk, and made a fresh pot of coffee. After the third cup the acid in his stomach and throat dissuaded him from pouring a fourth.

It's here, he thought to himself; it has to be. He worked another hour and a half, but still came up empty. He walked over to the coffee maker and thought about that fourth cup, but the acrid smell crowded out his appetite for the caffeine. He turned off the warmer, pitched the filter and grounds into the trash container, and waited for the urn to cool. If systematic work didn't help, he'd try busy work instead.

Eventually he cleaned up the entire kitchenette in an effort to clear his head. Then he went to the drink machine, bought a bottle of water, and returned to his desk. He stared at the 4"-high pile of papers and decided he wasn't ready for another slog through it. Instead he got on the internet and extended his break.

After a few minutes surfing Sicilian sites he checked the website for the National Register of Historic Places. He was impressed that the Barone estate had been listed there and decided to see how many other Orange County sites had been so selected. The list was far longer than he had expected. Each was dated. When he got to the Barone estate he saw the date and his eyes widened. The designation had been approved within the last month.

Why then? Particularly when the property had been in the family for over fifty years and Carlotta had had every opportunity to submit the proposal and lobby for its approval. He checked the FAQ page that was linked from the home page. The designation process took months. Not years, but months, depending on the speed with which the state board studied the request and forwarded its recommendation to the national board. This could not have been done in a matter of days or even in a matter of weeks. Carlotta Barone had to have made the proposal while she was still alive, perhaps at the onset of her last illness.

Again, he asked himself, why then? Why the sudden urgency? Was this an instance of personal vanity? If so, why did she wait so long to indulge it? Or was it done on the advice of counsel? And again, why? And which counsel—Carelli? Orsini?

Surely it was a point of pride. This was the home purchased by her beloved husband and it was fitting that the world would see it as an estate of historical consequence. Also, as Lydia Melendez had pointed out, the Foundation and the house were living tributes to Carlotta and to her work. Why not put that tribute in a wider and deeper context?

All of the answers made sense but none of them really satisfied him. Carlotta Barone was nothing if not deliberate. She planned and she calculated. Her decisions were rooted in rationality and hard reality. If she did this, she did it for a reason, and since it would not have been simple to do, the reason for doing it would have had to have been an important one.

Tom clicked out of the Register site and went into Ask.com. He knew that that search engine did not really answer questions; it simply responded to keywords, but he had a question and he asked it there: *Why would you want to designate your property as part of the National Register?*

He got a flurry of hits, most of them answering frequently-asked questions about the Register. On the third page of hits, however, he found a reference to a film script and a few lines of dialogue:

James
I think we should have our home listed on
the Historical Register.

Elaine
Why would you want to do that?
Then nothing could ever be changed.

SEVENTY

She did not want anything moved or altered. This was the site where her husband was buried and soon she would be buried beside him. Years from now, when the Foundation was awash in money and the founders' names were fading into the distant past, some one might be tempted to sell the property—which would be worth tens of millions, perhaps hundreds of millions of dollars—and relocate their burial vaults to some forgotten cemetery somewhere. This was a way to prevent that.

Then he thought better of it. The answer was plausible, of course, but was it complete? Was there something else that she wanted to preserve, or, perhaps, something else that she wanted to remain undisturbed? Were there other secrets protected by that estate? Graves, for example?

At first light on Monday morning he and a team of junior officers were combing the grounds with devices designed to provide images of buried objects. They found rusting farm implements and even the remains of old pottery, some of them of potential historical significance. He made a mental note to check in with the ME's anthropologist friend, Sally Cornell. They found an old well, but without any human remains, and what appeared to be a wine cellar connected with the original structure, but long walled-off and sealed. He entered it from a crawl space below the main structure, but there was nothing remaining there but some old racking for the barrels and bottles and an occasional shard of pottery.

He found a cave-like alcove that contained some now-crumbled statuary, but nothing more, and the skeletal remains of a large animal, perhaps an ox. By now the afternoon sun was hot and the coastal winds had subsided. He told the men on his team to take a break and he went into the main house to get some water. At first he had thought about splashing some water from the font in the bell tower on his forehead, but thought that using holy water in that manner might be somehow sacrilegious.

This gave him a chance to check out the small bathroom on the structure's first floor which he had skipped on his earlier tour. There were no clues or answers there, but a nice pedestal sink, scented soap, cold water and some soft towels. Refreshed, he accepted Lydia Melendez's offer of a large bottle of chilled spring water. Drinking it in sips he walked back outside, past various sites that they had unearthed that day and then returned to their previous condition.

He walked into the bell tower, enjoying the cool stone and the shade. He sat down on the platform supporting Carlotta's burial vault and enjoyed the rest of his water.

As he sat there he saw some lights flickering on an electric panel on the far wall and heard the bells above him begin to ring. He had just studied the canonical hours. The bells would be signaling the time for the midafternoon prayer: None. It was too late for the midday prayer: Sext, or the evening prayer: Vespers.

He had feared that the sounds might be so loud as to bring discomfort, but they were actually quite lovely. There was a certain amount of insulation achieved by the architectural detailing in the tower, so that the sounds were principally directed into what was once the coast and countryside. Inside the tower itself there was a mellowness to the sounds, as if they were coming from afar.

I should probably stop thinking about acoustics and say a prayer, Tom thought. It's the one thing I haven't yet tried. He put down his bottle, closed his eyes, and covered his face with his hands, just as the nuns had taught him to do after receiving Holy Communion. "This will help you avoid distractions," they would say, "and make it easier for you to pray." When he opened his eyes, rubbed, and refocused them, he saw it.

SEVENTY-ONE

It appeared to be a simple floor drain, but there was no water source in the bell tower and hence no sanitary sewer, no septic system, and no need for a functioning or even decorative floor drain. If water was spilled on the floor or blew in through an open door it could simply be swept or squeegeed out that door. Tom got down on his hands and knees and looked down the drain. He could see some narrow pipework, but nothing else. He put his ear against the metalwork and thought he could hear the movement of air, though it could have been the ocean-sound-from-a-seashell effect that comes when the ambient sound is modified and magnified by the shell.

He hurried out to his car and got his flashlight, returning to the space between the Barone burial vaults, and shining the beam down the pipe. He could see a drop of at least two or three feet and then a turn in the pipe. He returned to his car again and looked for some curved object to drop down the pipe and assess the depth of the space beneath him. He found some washers and some old shotgun shells. Removing the plastic casing of one of the shells over a kleenex he let the primer cap, wad and powder charge fall into the tissue, and slipped a small handful of the shot into his pocket. He would have preferred something larger, like a golf ball—something that would make an audible sound as it fell--but the grill work over the piping was too tight to accommodate one. He settled instead for the shot and returned to the mausoleum level of the tower.

He closed the door behind him and checked his watch, in case the bells sounded on the half or quarter hour. When it was as quiet as it was likely to be he stretched out on the floor, put his ear against the grillwork, and dropped one of the pieces of shot. He heard it drop against the turn in the pipe and then heard it roll for a second or two. He thought he heard a second drop, but after that he heard nothing. He tried a second one, with the same result, and finally a third . . . again, to no effect. Then he returned to his car and drove to the closest hardware store.

He found some round, glass lamp finials. They were smaller than golf balls and several models had recessed threading to accommodate the screw on top of the detachable lamp harp. He bought several sizes and drove back to the Barone estate.

After two unsuccessful attempts he tried a third and thought that he could hear the glass ball drop several times and eventually hit a remote floor. He tried again with a slightly larger ball and this time he was sure that he heard the ball strike the floor and shatter. However, without precise measurements of the length of the piping and the angles at the turns he could not estimate the distance from the opening in the floor to the end point at which the ball shattered.

He drove back to the hardware store, purchased a yardstick, and then drove to a sporting goods store where he purchased a large, round, lead sinker and a roll of high test line. He returned to the estate, tied a small knot on the bottom of the line, inserted the line in the sinker and then squeezed the sinker tightly against the line with a pair of pliers that he had in the utility toolbox in his trunk. He did this as evenly as he could, to retain the object's round shape. Then he put the yardstick on the floor, dropped the sinker into the pipework and played out the line until it went slack. The distance was nearly twenty-five feet. He then retrieved the line. The sinker caught in the pipework several times and he had to play out the line and then retrieve it quickly, working around the various angles.

He then returned all of his materials to the trunk of his car, fearing that Lydia Melendez or some workman might walk in on him and see what he was doing. When he began to return to the bell tower Lydia met him in the field between the driveway and the structure.

"Detective Deaton . . . can I help you in some way?"

"No, I'm fine," he said. "Thank you for asking. I am fascinated by the tower and the burial vaults. I thought I might have a tape recorder in my car so that I could record the notes played by the bells, but unfortunately my recorder must be back in the office. I was able to take a picture or two, however. You see, my grandparents are buried in an outdoor mausoleum with a connecting arch linking their vaults . . . this is back in Kentucky . . . I got the pictures to show to my father. The Barone vaults are far more extensive, of course, but I thought he might be interested in them … "

"The music was chosen by Mrs. Barone," Lydia said. "Actually, the bits of music are parts of songs that she particularly loved. Her favorite was *Con Te Partirò*. The most famous recording is probably by Andrea Bocelli and Sarah Brightman. The lyric means … "

"I will go with you," Tom said, regretting saying it the moment the words escaped from his lips, since he had said nothing to Lydia about his trip to Sicily and his attempts to grasp elementary Italian.

"They changed it," Lydia said, "to *Time to Say Goodbye*."

"I know I've heard it," Tom said. "It's lovely. That's really very, very sweet," he added.

"I never knew her husband, of course," Lydia said, "but I heard Mrs. Barone talk about him so often that I sometimes feel as if I did know him. Would you like another bottle of water, Detective Deaton? It is still very warm out and you might find it refreshing."

"Thanks very much. I would," Tom said. "Then I want to go back to the tower for a few minutes and just sit and rest and listen to the bells."

"They will strike on the hour," she said, "so you have a few minutes in which to enjoy your water."

As soon as he returned he took a large drink, closed the door behind him, and began his search for an access point to the space beneath the burial vaults. He checked the floors and the walls; there was no break in the stone. He slipped outside and checked for a point of ingress and egress, but there was none. Then he decided to climb the steps to the top of the tower and see what might await him there.

SEVENTY-TWO

He was imagining the kind of steps he had seen in films such as *Vertigo* or its comic counterpart, *High Anxiety*, but he realized immediately that the tower had been opened to convey the feeling of a cathedral spire rather than spoil the atmosphere of the Barone mausoleum by positioning it in purely functional space. The entrance to the access point was a small door at the rear of the tower. The recessed handle turned at his touch and he stooped under the top of the door in order to enter the space.

There were no steps, just a steel ladder attached to the side of the wall. Every fifteen rungs there was a small niche and seat rest carved out of the opposite wall, so that the climber could lean back and pause awhile before continuing the climb. Beside the ladder was a continuous piece of steel casing that enclosed the wiring for the computer controls. The mechanisms were at the top of the tower, but the control panel was in the wall on the entry level of the building, thus reducing the need for a technician to make the climb to the top in claustrophobic space in order to make routine adjustments.

Between the entry point and the belfry there were no exit points that might have provided access to the space beneath the burial vaults. He probed what appeared to be loose stones with the blade of a large screwdriver, but nothing gave way. When he reached the top of the tower—after a climb that took nearly ten minutes—he stepped onto the platform, studied the strike mechanism, and, again, looked for an access point to the space below. There was none.

When he returned to the mausoleum level he turned off the tower access light, closed the door, and began to inspect the stone flooring. He looked at the edges and the mortar joints and searched for any evidence that he could find that suggested that the floor had been patched in some way. Again, there was none.

He walked outside, carrying his water bottle and acting as if he was simply enjoying the beginning of sunset. The tower appeared to be sitting on a rise that gave it architectural prominence, but it was entirely possible that the ground had originally been level and that earth had been trucked in and then graded –covering the lower level and making the remaining portion of the tower appear to have been constructed on a small hilltop. The full stone floor at the current entry level was then installed to both conceal the lower area and provide a base that would support the burial vaults and the connecting canopy that linked them.

There may have been a wooden floor there earlier, along with a set of open steps leading to the belfry. Below that wooden floor was the room below, accessible by another set of steps. Now the lower space was subterranean and the stone flooring—perhaps fifty years old—sealed it off forever.

As he took the last sip of his water and screwed the cap back on the bottle he thought about his options. In the first place, it might be difficult to secure a warrant, particularly one involving the destruction of a portion of antique flooring that might require tens of thousands of dollars to repair and replace. If the end result was the discovery of a room filled with dust, trash and the remains of the objects that Tom had dropped into it, the LBPD would be embarrassed and the judge would be manifestly disappointed.

An alternative would be to excavate. Once the earth surrounding the lower level had been removed, a window or two might be exposed that would enable them to observe whatever remained in the lower level. That too would be expensive and, potentially, ultimately embarrassing. The judge would be likely to dither over the requirements of the National

Register of Historic Places. So long as the current conditions were fully restored, however, they would almost surely be able to secure the various permissions, but the process would be cumbersome and—worst of all—it would risk attracting the attention of the local press.

He checked the space again, making sure that the light switches were all flipped, the doors were all closed, and the condensation ring from his water bottle was wiped dry. He carried his plastic bottle to the rear of the main structure, depositing it in the recycling bin next to the trash dumpsters. He could have taken it with him, but he wanted the extra few minutes to gather his thoughts and consider what he would need in order to answer his questions.

As soon as he got in his car he called Chris Dietrich, told him what he had discovered, and described the equipment that he thought would be required to explore the subterranean space. Twenty minutes later he and Chris were sitting in Chris's office.

"Coffee, Tom?" Chris asked. "Or maybe something cold?"

"I'm fine, Chief. The woman at the Barone estate kept hydrating me on a regular basis. She was very helpful."

"Good," Chris said. He was drinking something unspecified from his coffee mug. There were condensation drops on the outside.

"I've been thinking about what you told me," Chris said. "While you were en route here I talked to one of the bomb squad guys. Basically you need a light and you need a camera. You also need something with smooth, floating wheels—wheels that will find their way around corners and not get caught up or hung up in the process. The bomb squad has robots with cameras and mechanical hands and all kinds of good things. The light wouldn't present any big problems. The tricky thing will be the wheels. Tricky but not impossible. The bomb tech also thought that he could fabricate something that would enable us to direct the camera once it's in place. The light would be mounted just above the camera lens, for maximum illumination. The wiring for the light and the camera will be super thin and attached to the line that will be used to lower the assembly through the pipework and into the space below."

"I know they have all kinds of things like that that they use in modern surgery," Tom said, "but unfortunately this device has to be larger. The space that we're exploring could be as large as twenty thousand cubic feet, maybe even larger. It's not like we'd be looking at a narrow corner of somebody's spleen."

"Right," Chris said. "From the way you described it we *will* have to remove the grillwork at the top, but that shouldn't be a big deal. I'll get the warrant and explain to the judge that this is the most minimally-invasive technique we could find."

"Great," Tom said, "and reassure him that the burial vaults will not be disturbed in any way. We've found something inexplicable and we need to have our questions answered in the simplest, most efficient way."

"Right," Chris said. "There's simply no reason for them to have left that grillwork in place if they were going to the trouble of sealing off the whole area. They were either depositing something there or listening for something. We could find S.P.E.C.T.R.E. headquarters down there . . . or, of course, a roomful of dirt and dead spiders. The only way is to take a look."

"How soon will it take the bomb techs to fabricate the device, Chief?" Tom asked.

"Maybe a day, possibly less," Chris said. "I put an **Expedite** slip on the request form."

SEVENTY-THREE

"I've tried to make it as user-friendly as possible," the sergeant said. His name was Bill Hansen. He was dressed in a white lab coat and was wearing glasses with magnifying lenses of various strengths. He had thin hands with carefully-manicured nails that contrasted with his chiseled features, thick black hair and overall fitness. At one time he had actually been a cornerback for the San Diego Chargers, one of the rare NFL players to have a degree in engineering. Tom noticed the scars that criss-crossed his fingers but also noted that he held them perfectly still, particularly when he was pointing at elements of the device that he had fabricated.

"I've got a mockup version on the table behind you," he said. "You can work with the joystick here in the lab for awhile and get a feel for it. The camera will move horizontally and vertically with the movement of the stick and the toggle switch beside it will enable you to move in and out for close-ups and distance shots. Push forward to go in, back to come back. The images will appear on the laptop screen. The button on the top of the joystick functions as a digital camera. Whenever you have an image on the screen that you want to keep, just hit that button. We can then return to the lab and print out any hard copies that we need. Go ahead and try it."

"Will the images be in color?" Tom asked.

"Of course," Bill said. "Nothing but the best for you guys. You want some coffee while you're practicing?"

"Yes, thanks," Tom said.

"How about you, Chief?" Hansen asked.

"Yes, thanks Bill," Chris responded.

"It won't take long to get used to, Tom," Hansen said. The tricky thing will be getting it through the pipework. At first I thought about motorizing it, but I decided instead to just go with gravity. I think it'll be OK, from the way you described the space."

"It works like a bandit, Bill," Tom said.

"Yeah, it's cool, isn't it? Actually, Chief, I'm glad you requested it. I think we can make use of it in other ways in the future."

"Good," Chris said. "What do you think, Tom? Are you ready to take it into the field?"

"I'm ready as soon as Bill's ready," Tom said.

Tom visited first with Lydia Melendez, telling her that he had some colleagues who wanted to see the burial vaults. "We may be awhile," he said. "One of them wants to take some pictures. If you could give us some privacy, we'd very much appreciate it."

"There's no one scheduled to come today except for the landscapers," she said. "There's plenty to do around the main building. They'll arrive in about an hour and I'll tell them to begin there. I'll check with you before I allow any of them to come near the *campanile*."

"That's great," Tom said, jotting his cell number on a slip of paper from the top of the kitchen pad. "Just call me on this number. You don't have to walk all the way over there."

"Of course," she said.

"Good grief," Bill said, as he entered the tower. "This looks like a corner of a cathedral. If they were going for a big effect they certainly achieved it. This is almost basilica-level as far as the surfaces and architectural details go."

"The access point is on the floor, just between the vaults," Tom said.

"I hope there's something down there worth seeing. I'll feel bad if you've gone to all this trouble for no good reason."

"Like I said," Bill answered, "it was worth putting the device together, if for no other reason than we can use it in the future. I can think of a half dozen applications for it right off the top of my head."

"It's worth a shot," Chris said. "I've been thinking about what you said, Tom, and I see what you mean about the way in which the tower is sited. Somebody's made some changes here and the changes were not inexpensive. I don't think the outside surface was original, but neither was the surface on the main building. Still, they predate the interior of the tower. This floor is old, but it was done by very professional masons or tilers. The remodeled elements of the tower probably also affect the acoustics. The paintings are professional and the statuary is not some off-the-shelf stuff from a religious goods store. This was thought through very carefully. If they changed the floor but retained that grillwork and pipework they did it for a reason."

"Thanks, Chief. I appreciate the vote of confidence," Tom said.

"Tom, will you give me a hand?" Bill asked.

He had already silently removed the grillwork. "The end prongs extended into the mortar," he said. "All I had to do was pinch it a little and it popped out. I can probably get it back in without leaving any noticeable marks."

Tom noticed the padded pliers which he set beside the grillwork. "It looks easier without that in the way, doesn't it?" Bill asked. "The angle of the pipework is pretty steep, but I still think I'll be able to negotiate it."

"What can I do?" Chris asked.

"If you could hold the spool," Bill said, "I can play out the wire a little at a time. Let's give it a check first." Bill booted up the laptop and attached the extension wire at the base of the spool to the computer. Then he turned on the light and the camera and told Tom to go ahead and try the joystick.

"It's working," Chris said, as he looked at the image on the computer screen.

"This is left . . . this is right . . . in . . . and out ... " Tom said.

"Working like a champ," Chris said.

Tom aimed the camera at the entry point in the floor and said, "Smile," hitting the button at the top of the joystick.

"The image froze on the screen and there was a slight click," Chris said.

"Picture number one," Bill said. "Let's go ahead and get the rest of them now."

SEVENTY-FOUR

The first angle in the pipework was tricky, but after that the device rolled down the inclined plane with relative ease. A few seconds later, Bill asked Chris if he felt the tension on the line increase.

"Maybe just a little," Chris answered.

"Harder to tell when you're holding the spool," Bill said. "I think it's hanging free. Let's try it. He leaned back toward Tom, checking on the settings and the image on the computer screen. Light on . . . camera on . . . whoa . . . big space."

"It's almost like looking down from the top of the bell tower," Tom said.

"Yes, though it's probably not really that far," Bill said. "Let's get a little closer."

By now Tom was sitting intently, working the joystick each time that Bill moved the device closer to the bottom of the room.

"The room is remarkably clean," Tom said. "I was afraid it would be the tower rubbish dump. Wait a sec . . . there's an object on the floor." He used the trigger button to come in closer. "You'll have to lower it a little bit more, Bill."

"OK," Bill said, "how's this?"

"A little more."

"OK … "

"That's good," Tom said, moving in closer. "Oh my God," he suddenly said.

"What is it?" Bill asked.

"It's a straight razor," Chris said, leaning over Tom's shoulder to look at the screen.

Tom took the picture, then panned slowly to the left. "Check it out, Chief," he said.

"What is it?" Bill asked, this time more insistently.

"What's left of a human hand," Chris said.

They were there for more than two hours, taking hundreds of pictures from multiple angles and from varying distances. They also took pictures of the bare areas of the floor and pictures of the walls.

"Before we go," Bill said, "I want to check the laptop and make sure that we've got all of the images."

Tom stood up and made room for Bill to scoot back. Chris moved out of his way, holding on to the spool tightly.

"We've got them," Bill said, a few moments later.

The device was a little more difficult to retrieve than it had been to insert. When Bill freed it from the opening in the floor, he patted it on its top and said, "Good work. We'll do this again sometime."

He then picked up the grillwork and the padded pliers, checked the prongs and the entry points in the mortar and reinserted the grillwork in its place. Except for a few specks of loosened mortar it fit precisely.

Twenty five minutes later they were back at the station, drinking black coffee and staring at one another. "I want to go back to Taormina," Tom said. "I have to go back. I need to tell them."

"They may already know some of it," Chris said. "They were just waiting to see if you'd discover it all."

"Yes," Tom said, "but I need to look into their eyes and see their reactions when I tell them."

"Do you plan to ask them who released Sullivan's remains?"

"I'm not sure that it really matters," Tom said. "So long as he was missing, the payments to Carlotta Barone continued. They only needed definitive confirmation of his death after she died. Giancarlo could have directed someone to do it. My own guess is that Carlotta had planned for this just as she had planned for everything else. There was probably a contract of some sort, to be honored immediately after her death."

"In some ways Sullivan is the least of it," Dietrich said. "It's her story after all; none of them were ever a match for her; now those who cared about her deeply will have to hear the rest of her story."

"And live with it," Tom said.

SEVENTY-FIVE

He called Orsini first and told him that he needed to meet with him. "I am at your disposal, Tom. Remember . . . I told you that you would return and see me again."

"Will you be in Taormina, Giancarlo?"

"No, unfortunately. Both Gina and I leave tomorrow for Tuscany. She is examining a property for her company and she has asked me to accompany her. As you know, the architectural laws in Tuscany are severe in the extreme. The property in question is beautifully sited and historically significant, but it will require a great deal of exterior work. We will be there for at least five days. She will talk to engineers and contractors while I talk to lawyers and judges. We would be delighted to meet with you, Tom, and hear what you have learned."

"I think I should talk with you first, Giancarlo."

"Is it so dark that you think Gina might be disturbed by it?"

"It is . . . very unsettling, Giancarlo."

"She would understand your doing that, Tom. She is not so modern as you might expect. You could tell me and then I could tell her, softening it, perhaps. I would not want to put you in a position where you were forced to conceal or to dissemble. But, as always, you should say whatever you feel that you should. Gina is an adult and I am sure that she would want to know everything. Sometimes when we learn the real truth, however, we begin to change our minds . . . but that is not for me to decide. I am only the counselor. My role is to help and I am happy to help both you and Gina."

"Where will you be, Giancarlo?"

"In Florence. Actually—just above, in Fiesole. The hotel property she is examining is just below the center of the village. We can easily arrange for a hotel for you. I was there several years ago and stayed in one in the village proper. The view of the Duomo was spectacular. I could sit there for hours, watching the light change. I am not sure that a place of such beauty is the proper location for discussing that which is unpleasant, but I would hope that it might help to soften things . . . and I would look forward to seeing you there if you would be able to join us."

"I will join you there, Giancarlo."

"Wonderful."

"Can I ask you a question?"

"You know that you can, Tom."

"When you told me that I would return and speak with you again . . . Gina said the same thing, by the way . . . "

"Yes . . . ?"

"Did you know what I would find?"

"I knew that there were questions still unanswered, Tom, and I believed that if anyone could answer them it would be you."

"And Gina?"

"I cannot speak for Gina," he said. "She knows, of course, that there are unanswered questions. Perhaps she was simply being kind . . . *and* speaking from the heart. She wanted to see you again and hoped . . . even wanted to believe . . . that you would feel the same and that you would return."

"It is hard not to want to return to Taormina, Giancarlo," Tom said, lightening the moment.

"And hard not to want to see your friends," Giancarlo added, "even those who are recent friends . . . even those you would not expect to become your friends . . . those you may still not be sure are your friends . . . "

"You never lied to me, Giancarlo."

"No, I did not, Tom, but at the time I did not tell you everything.

Of course, philosophically, how *can* one tell everything? But I will not subject you to casuistry. That which I did tell you was true. I know that you have learned other things since your return to California; in fact, I know that you have learned things of which I myself was not aware. What I want to say is . . . that I look forward to seeing you again and that I hope that you see that I was always trying to aid you in your quest."

"You mean my *investigation*."

"Yes, but I think it is that and more. We must see life as more than just a succession of decisions related to a job of work."

"Carlotta Barone certainly did," Tom said.

Fiesole was more accessible than Taormina, but not by much. Tom first flew to London and then to Pisa. The station for the train to Florence was at the Pisa airport. Giancarlo offered to send a car for him. "You will see the same countryside," he said, "but you will be much more comfortable. You will also be able to drive directly to Fiesole rather than securing a car at the station in Florence. Florence is not as serene as it looks from the villas of Fiesole. I want your first impression to be a comforting one."

Tom thanked him. While the driver spoke in halting English he was attentive and efficient. The small Mercedes was indeed more comfortable than the train—filled with students—was likely to be. Before leaving the city the driver took him to see the leaning tower. "At the request of the Signore," he said. "You should not miss it. It will take a few minutes only."

The driver parked at the edge of the open shops near the tower. Nearly all sold replicas of the tower in every size and shape imaginable, in brass, in bronze, in wax and in plastic. They also sold artwork of various kinds and wool shawls. "Best value," the driver said of the shawls. "In Rome . . . five times as much as here."

The drive to Florence was uneventful, the landscape nondescript. It was not ugly but neither was it memorable. When they got to the outskirts of Florence and drove up the hill to Fiesole, everything changed.

SEVENTY-SIX

Giancarlo had reserved a room for him at the Aurora, a small hotel with a magnificent view of the Arno Valley and its jewel, Florence. The light was bright, with cloudless skies and the slightest hint of haze encircling the city like a light halo. The duomo was postcard perfect, dominating the skyline in the shimmering sun.

The desk clerk at the Aurora was working in English, French, and German, as well as Italian, and even muddling through in Japanese. He asked Tom for his passport and told him that he would return it to him in approximately thirty minutes. Tom went up to his room in the rear of the hotel to wash, shave, and change his clothes. It was modest, with antique furniture and a well-functioning shower, but with a view that could only be described as breathtaking. There was a small porch beyond the main window, but while it featured some bright flowers in terracotta pots he doubted that it would support his weight.

When he went back to the lobby a half hour later the clerk handed him his passport and asked him if the room was satisfactory. Tom said yes and the clerk told him to give him a call if he had any questions or required any services. "There are three acceptable restaurants nearby," he said, "and the one in the hotel is quite good."

Tom thanked him and walked out the door and into the village. He saw two of the restaurants immediately. Diners were finishing their lunches and sipping wine and chilled mineral water at their outside tables. He was not to meet with Giancarlo for hours and decided to stretch his legs after his flights and the drive to Fiesole.

He had actually made a checklist of places he wished to see, though as he began to walk down the hill toward the Medici Villa and the Villa San Girolamo he realized that the walls would restrict his views of the properties. When he arrived there a few minutes later he realized that the steepness of the hill would give him more exercise than he had anticipated. He at least felt the presence of the walled Medici Villa and its position above the Valley. San Girolamo—across the street--was easier. At various times a nunnery and a rest home, it had served as one of the settings for *The English Patient*.

Walking, or, more properly, climbing back up the hill to the village, he went to the Roman amphitheatre and found a shaded stone seat. He looked down at the remains and thought about what he had discovered in the basement of the Barone *campanile*. The photographs were in his luggage but he didn't need to look at them to refresh his memory. The images were burned there forever.

As the shadows began to lengthen he realized that he had been sitting at the amphitheatre for nearly an hour, his eyes opening and closing in the warmth of the late afternoon sun. He was struck by the fact that there were so few tourists. They were probably all buying gold jewelry on the Ponte Vecchio or standing in line to enter the Uffizi. He saw a few people, but they appeared to be very scholarly, checking their guide books and making notes as they visited the various sites within the complex.

When they did speak they spoke very quietly, the words lost in the winds which blew through the trees that partly encircled the amphitheatre. There were Etruscan antiquities as well and great churches in Fiesole, but Tom passed on them as well as the local museum. He returned to his room, set his travel alarm for 6:30, and took a two-hour nap. He neither dreamed nor fidgeted fitfully and when he awoke he opened the shutters of his window and looked out over the Valley.

The light was nearly purple now and the city looked like a vast, miniaturized movie set, drawing his eyes the way a candle draws insects from the shadows. He set out his clothes for dinner and retrieved the accordion folder of photographs from his luggage. He had arranged each of them carefully, planning to show them after dinner, when the wine had taken its effect and the food was settled on their stomachs.

SEVENTY-SEVEN

His phone rang at 7:50. "Good evening, Tom," the voice said. "I hope that you had a pleasant flight and that your room is acceptable. It is not as grand as that in Taormina, but the view should be very nice."

"The view is exquisite, Giancarlo," Tom said. "Are you downstairs?"

"Yes, but take your time. I will wait for you here."

"I'll be right down," Tom said.

Giancarlo embraced him when he came down the steps. "You have brought your file, I see."

"Photographs," Tom said.

"*After* dinner, I assume," Giancarlo said.

"I think that's best."

"The restaurant is just across the square. It is a simple trattoria but the food is fresh and they have a small private room for us. Not with your view, I'm afraid, but I think it will serve our purposes."

"How is Gina?" Tom asked.

"Fine, though a little apprehensive, as you might imagine," Giancarlo said.

"I understand," Tom answered. "Is it the Aurora that her company is considering?"

"No, actually, the former Villa San Girolamo."

"I was there today," Tom said. "I had a few hours open and I decided to take a walk there."

"There are many trade-offs," Giancarlo said. "If she takes it upscale the parking is totally inadequate. But then there are the history and literary associations . . . particularly for the British and the Americans … "

"I noticed the fact that the principal structure was positioned on a very steep hill."

"You always notice such things, Tom. That is why you are an excellent detective. The entire facility could, one morning, find itself on the property of the adjoining owner, one level below. In the meantime, the structures that would be required to reinforce it, safely, would require permissions that the local authorities are unlikely to provide. You can always take the risk of building them anyway and then seek forgiveness later . . . we are a Catholic country after all."

"But the *magnitude*, Giancarlo. This is not like changing a chimney or installing a small dormer."

"Precisely, Tom. That is her problem."

"Nice address, though."

"Indeed," Giancarlo said. "That is why we are here. And seeing you is an added benefit. I told you that you would return."

"Yes, you did," Tom answered.

"To complete the loop," Giancarlo said. "And that is very important, but the next time you come you should come for your vacation or holiday. No investigations, no business, just old friends getting together to enjoy each other's company in a beautiful setting."

"I would like that," Tom said.

"So would I; so would Gina, I believe. Ah . . . here is our restaurant. The owner's name is Mario; he will make us very comfortable."

It was obvious that Giancarlo had planned the evening carefully, for the owner met them at the door and showed them to a quiet room on the second floor. There was already chilled mineral water, with lemon slices, on the table and a bottle of expensive wine from Montepulciano.

Tom tasted it, at Giancarlo's insistence, and he said that it was lovely. "It's very soft and velvety and the taste is subtle and rich," he said.

"I knew that you would like it, Tom," he said, "but I can see that your thoughts are elsewhere. Something is troubling you. You want to ask me something."

"Yes, I do," Tom answered.

"Don't hesitate. You know that I will tell you whatever I can."

"Whatever you *can* or whatever you *know*, Giancarlo?"

"Fair point," Orsini answered. "Try me."

"You were very forthcoming with me in Taormina," Tom said. "We spoke for hours, for days. You wanted assurances that we would keep the results of our investigations as . . . subdued . . . as possible … "

"Yes … "

"Weren't you also buying time, so that you could settle the financial affairs of Mrs. Barone and insure that her estate would receive the remaining funds in Sullivan's private account?"

"Yes, I was," he said immediately, "and I do not believe that that has proven to be a bad thing. Those funds will continue to support Carlotta's Foundation—a noble purpose. In the meantime you have been able to close the Sullivan case, which was your announced purpose from the start."

"True," Tom said, "though Sullivan's money was, in all likelihood, acquired from criminal activities and the state might have wished to place some claims upon it."

"Granted," Giancarlo said, "but it is very unlikely that they would make any better use of it than the Foundation—a moral point, if not a legal one—and it would be very difficult, probably impossible, for them to identify the source of those funds at this late hour."

"True," Tom said, "but they would still have wanted to make their claim, something they might yet do."

Giancarlo nodded.

"Was there anything else, Giancarlo? Was there any other reason for delaying me?"

"There *was*, Tom. There *was* something else."

"Listing the property as part of the historical registry?"

"Yes, though that process had begun prior to our meeting."

"But once the proposal had been submitted you were concerned that it be approved. You wanted to avoid any potential complications. A police investigation would have posed a major complication."

"Exactly, Tom. The proposal was very important, more important than the money. Carlotta insisted on it. As sick as she was, she summoned all of her strength and impressed on me the fact that I *had* to do this for her. You must realize that she did not ask a lot of me. We were always much more friends than we were attorney and client. When she told me that this *must* be done I knew that I could not allow anything to stand in the way of the process."

"Including my investigation."

"Especially your investigation, Tom," Giancarlo said, smiling, "but I did not break the law."

"No, you did not."

"But what *did* I do, Tom? That is what you know and I do not. I knew at the time that she was pursuing this matter for a reason—for her a very important reason, but a reason she did not share with me."

"Did not or would not?"

"Both. When I pursued the issue, ever so gently, she cut me off instantly and refused to discuss it. You know why, Tom. It is you who has the advantage here; you know her reason and I can only hope that you will share it with me."

"I suspect that she did not share it with you because she feared that you would share it with Gina," Tom said, "and she wanted to preserve the relationship that the two of them had built. If Gina looked at her grandmother in a different way that relationship would be jeopardized . . . or destroyed . . . forever."

"Ah, here is the waiter," Giancarlo said, "try your soup. It is best when it is hot."

"It's delicious," Tom said.

"The local ingredients ... " Giancarlo said. "They always make the difference. That is the secret to Italian cuisine. You see, the French take poor ingredients and make them great. The Italians take great ingredients and allow them to be themselves."

"They do not stand in the way," Tom said.

"Precisely," Giancarlo said.

"Nor do they hold them back until they lose their freshness."

"No," Giancarlo said. "We are talking about chefs now, not lawyers."

Tom smiled, and after a few moments elapsed, he spoke again. "You must understand, Giancarlo—I do not want to ruin Gina's relationship with her grandmother either, but the facts are strong and the truth for which they serve as a foundation is . . . not easy to contemplate."

"I would not expect it to be," Giancarlo said, "but I would expect it to be . . . fitting."

"Perhaps it is," Tom said, as the waiter removed their soup cups, refilled their glasses, and brought the pasta course.

"The cavatelli you do not see so often in America," Giancarlo said. "The sauce may contain rabbit. I hope that that is all right."

"I'm sure it will be excellent," Tom said.

"If you can deal with Carlotta's work you can deal with Mario's," Giancarlo said, then instantly thought better of it. "Excuse me. I should not have said that."

"It was true, nonetheless," Tom said.

"You must see that when one loves that deeply one can also hate that deeply."

"I would not characterize it as *hate*," Tom said. "It was what she would have seen as *fitting* and it was not done in a moment of sudden passion. She had contemplated it at length."

"The veal is next," Giancarlo said. "It is like a veal marsala, but not like the veal marsala that is made in American restaurants. The local mushrooms make the difference, along with the quality of the wine that Mario will use."

"And the artichokes will be fresh," Tom said.

"Yes, if he uses them they will be. You have become a connoisseur, Tom."

"Strong coffee," Giancarlo said to the waiter.

"Certainly," he answered.

"I think you should first show me what you have brought and then we will have some grappa . . . or if that is not to your taste, something else."

"I think that's a good idea," Tom said, reaching for the cardboard folder that was leaning against the table leg.

SEVENTY-EIGHT

"The estate's designation as part of the historical registry insured that it could not be changed in any significant way," Tom said. "It was her desire that the exterior of the structures never be altered. The reason is simple. The *campanile* appears to stand on a hill. It does not. The surrounding earth was reshaped to alter the tower's appearance. The first floor—actually the equivalent of several floors—is now under ground."

"There is space beneath the burial chamber," Giancarlo said.

"Yes, considerable space," Tom said, removing the photographs from the envelope.

"The remains of four individuals rest there," he said, handing Giancarlo the first picture.

"That one is Devito," Giancarlo said, "the little one."

"So we assume," Tom said.

"Do you have any close-up shots of any of them, Tom?"

"Yes, of all of them," he said, handing Giancarlo four 8x10 pictures.

"That is Graffali," he said, pointing. "His hands are twisted by arthritis. It frustrated his desire to continue playing his beloved golf. His enemies were pleased at the time. Small, petty pleasures ...

"And that is Muschina. I would know those teeth anywhere. Crude, horse-like teeth. Some said that that was the reason he was unable to speak well. He always looked like a peasant. At least the acne scars are gone, with the flesh that was pitted by them ...

"Then this one must be Brienza. Even without the hair or eyes he looks stupid."

"Look at this," Tom said, showing him another picture.

"What is that?" Giancarlo asked. "It appears to be a window."

"It *is* a window," Tom said, "but it is hard to see with the earth pressed against it. It is approximately twenty feet from the floor. And it is fully intact … "

"They could have escaped by standing on each other's shoulders," Giancarlo said. They could have removed the glass and then tunneled through the dirt … "

"Yes, but they would have had to trust one another first," Tom said. "Those remaining below would have had to believe that the person who was permitted to escape would return with help and save them."

"But they could not trust one another, even with their lives at stake," Giancarlo said. "That comes as no surprise," he said, "no surprise whatsoever."

"Look here, Giancarlo," Tom said, handing him another set of photographs. The first was of the floor.

"It is stained," he said.

"Yes," Tom said, "and look at this one."

It was a closeup of the arm of Devito. "The bone looks as if it was cut and scraped," Giancarlo said.

"Look at the next picture," Tom said. The object was resting next to Brienza's hand.

"A razor. They killed . . . and . . . cannibalized . . . one another."

"Yes, and it appears that Brienza survived them all, though one cannot be certain," Tom said. His body is resting against the wall, not spread out on the floor."

"The stains on the floor … " Giancarlo said.

"Yes?"

"The blood is everywhere. They fought over the razor. They did not choose an order of death and offer themselves for sacrifice. They simply tore each other apart. I can see them . . . afraid to rest or sleep . . . always on guard . . . worried that the strong would pair off and attack the weak . . . Then there is the slaughter . . . and a moment of satiety . . . but only a moment … "

"Yes, with Brienza perhaps hanging back and letting the others destroy themselves first."

"*That* would be fitting," Giancarlo said.

"In the Andes plane crash … " Tom said, "when the athletes survived by consuming one another's flesh … "

"Yes … ?"

"They cut very delicate slivers and shared them as if they were Holy Communion. It was a spiritual process, a *sacred* process. This, on the other hand … "

"This was the action of brutes, of monsters," Giancarlo said.

"That is only the beginning," Tom said.

SEVENTY-NINE

"There was no clothing in the room," Tom said. "If there had been some it would have survived. They might have eaten shoe leather but they would not have eaten wool or cotton."

"She put them there naked."

"Yes."

"It is also a statement," Giancarlo said. "It speaks to their nature."

"Yes," Tom said, "and it told them what she thought of them, what she *knew* of them."

"I don't believe that Gina should see these pictures," Giancarlo said.

"There is more," Tom said. "Above them, in the floor, was a system of pipework … "

"I remember seeing a floor drain between the burial vaults," Giancarlo said. "I didn't give it any thought at the time."

"The pipework was angled so that they could not see anyone above who might be listening to them."

"Perhaps it is more recent … "

"Probably not," Tom said. "It's lead."

"They may have been placed there, the pipework installed, the floor completed and sealed … "

"Yes?"

"And then she slid the razor down to them."

"Possibly," Tom said.

"Was there light in the chamber?"

"Yes, a single bulb, next to the pipework in the center of the ceiling."

"Perhaps she drizzled water down . . . to torment them."

"Possibly," Tom said. "Scottish lairds would sometimes capture their enemies, feed them salted meat and then deny them water. She might have given them a drop or two, just enough to dissolve in the dust before they could reach it."

Giancarlo stared at him, resisting the sudden impulse to reach for his glass of chilled water, beaded with condensation.

"She wanted to hear their screams," Tom said.

"But the sounds were indirect," Giancarlo said, "They would have been muted and distorted. She may have been thinking of that torture device . . . oh, what was it called?"

"The brazen bull," Tom said, "the execution device that was fabricated for the Greek tyrant, who then put its maker inside and roasted him alive. The pipework turned his screams into the sounds of an enraged bull."

"Yes. And the smoke from the roasting was treated with incense so that the tyrant and his guests would be pleased rather than disgusted with the smells that arose from it."

"Only a theory in this case," Tom said, "but the overall intention is clear. She wanted to hear their screams. More important, she wanted her husband to somehow hear them."

"And now each of them can hear the screams of the ghosts of their enemies for all eternity."

"Yes," Tom said. "It explains the reason for her intention that the structure not be changed in any way."

"I helped see to that," Giancarlo said. "I am happy that I did not have to listen to their screams as well."

"It confirms several things, Giancarlo," Tom said. "Carlotta Barone *did* know how to plan. She *did* know how to *execute* a plan and she *did* know how to take revenge on her enemies. Forever."

"Yes, Tom. And if what she told Gina about Sullivan was correct, she was probably involved in all of the details of these deaths as well. She was there. She spoke to them. She confronted them. She would want them to know who was responsible for their deaths."

"And," Tom added, "she would want them to think about the consequences of their actions. Perhaps she did not give them the razor for days or even weeks. They may have been told about Sullivan's fate so that they might then think about all that they had done and contemplate what their own might be."

"Fascinating, is it not?" Giancarlo said. "A woman of such love, of such fidelity, and of such compassion. They all coexisted very easily with the most exquisite cruelty."

"To each, as they deserved," Tom said. "She was born for Greek drama, not for street crime in a working class neighborhood."

"True," Giancarlo said, reaching for his water and taking a deep drink. A few moments later the waiter approached and said, "*Dolce*, gentlemen? There is very nice *zuppa inglese*."

"Not for me," Tom said.

"Nor me," Giancarlo added. "Tom . . . some brandy or cognac?"

"Yes, certainly," Tom answered.

"I have a very nice Armagnac," the waiter said, "ten years old."

Giancarlo looked at Tom, Tom nodded, and Giancarlo said, "We'll have that."

When the waiter left, Giancarlo said, "It keeps you thin, Tom, and it also keeps your heart healthy. It lengthens your life."

"We should speak more of life, Giancarlo," Tom said. "There has already been more than enough talk of death."

"Under the circumstances, Carlotta would have considered death more delicious than the Armagnac," Giancarlo responded. "But, as we say in America, to each his own. I have always preferred life."

"But not for your *enemies* … "

"I am a lawyer, Tom. For me, the term is more *fluid*."

"But you are also Sicilian, Giancarlo," Tom said.

"That is true, Tom, but my time in California softened me."

They both smiled at that, as the waiter brought their Armagnac.

"We should enjoy ourselves for a moment," Tom said. "Then we must speak of Gina."

EIGHTY

"She is with the estate agent representing San Girolamo," Giancarlo said. "They are feeding her, hoping no doubt that she will pay more attention to the wine than the retaining wall beneath the villa."

"She won't forget that," Tom said.

"No, she won't," Giancarlo said. "I will have breakfast with her in the morning. I will tell her the facts that you have uncovered, but I will not dwell on the details. I know that she will want to speak with you anyway. Perhaps if you could be available tomorrow evening … "

"I will," Tom said. "In fact, tell her that I'm looking forward to seeing her again."

When Gina entered the restaurant at the Aurora Tom barely recognized her. She was wearing a black suit with a single strand of small white pearls; she looked as if she was in mourning for the world. Her eyes were red and her hair was slightly tousled. When he kissed her on the cheek he felt the remains of a tear there.

"How are you, Tom?" she asked. "How was your flight?" The words were half-hearted and formulaic. She was trying to keep her lip from quivering.

"I'm fine, Gina. How are you?"

"I'm not so good," she said.

"Then you talked to Giancarlo … "

"Yes. We spoke this morning. He told me what you had learned. He tried to be as gentle as he could. He withheld things and when he spoke he spoke in euphemisms. I questioned him and, eventually, extracted the truth from him. I know that he has my best interests at heart. He is trying to protect my grandmother's memory, but Tom, it is so horrible … "

"Yes, it is."

"And I do not blame you, Tom. It is your job to investigate such things. You cannot stop just because you see how ugly things are becoming. You must follow them to their conclusions."

"Yes," Tom said, "but sometimes the entire story is better than the individual details … "

"And sometimes it is worse," she said. "Taking vengeance against the man responsible for the death of her husband . . . that I can understand, even when the methods are extreme . . . but this . . . this was extended torture."

"They had other options," Tom said.

"Yes, Giancarlo explained that, but my grandmother was not a fool. She knew them. She knew them well. She knew what they would do and what they would not do. She created the conditions for them to . . . to be themselves."

"But she did not create them," Tom said. "They themselves made all of the choices which brought them to that point. Even if you believe the conclusions to be inevitable, they still had other choices."

"In extreme situations people show who they truly are," Gina said. "She was putting rabid dogs in a cage … "

"I think she may have seen it somewhat differently."

"How? What do you mean, Tom?"

"Let's get something to eat, Gina. Then I'll tell you what I think."

"I'm not really very hungry, Tom," she said.

"We can have something simple," he said, "just some bread and some wine and some soup."

"All right," she said.

She left half of her soup, but ate two pieces of bread, with some olive oil, and drank two glasses of wine.

"I don't like to see you sad," Tom said, "and it makes me feel worse to think that I have caused you to be that way."

"I am happy to see you," she said, "even if I don't appear to be. I know that you have a different role to play than that of the Signore, but I also know that you have my best interests at heart as well."

"I do," Tom said. "By the way, I think it's wonderful that you'll be continuing the work of your grandmother's Foundation."

"Money is not really important to me," she said. "I am already blessed. I knew that that would be my grandmother's wish and I would never do anything that would contradict her wishes."

"The endowment will last forever," Tom said, "literally, *forever*, and the modest payout will insure that the support of the Foundation will keep pace with inflation. I don't mean to sound like a gifts officer, Gina, but I think you should look at this as your grandmother would . . . *all* of it."

"I understand … "

"When she took her vengeance it was very severe, but in the larger scheme of things it happened very quickly. It is the larger scheme in which she was always interested. You saw the mausoleum, Gina. She wants it to last forever as well. To her it's part of a single image, sometimes beautiful, sometimes brutal, but something that must be seen and understood as part of a totality. She's taken a bell tower and turned it into a church--a Catholic church, with everything but the incense.

"She has the frescoes and she has the statuary, the vaulted ceiling and the Holy Water font. She took apart the insides of the structure and rebuilt it to make her point. A church represents the history of Christianity, Gina. The focal point is the altar on which the sacrifice occurs. Every time the mass is said the sacrifice is reenacted and the story retold. The story is about salvation and about the ascent to heaven and the freedom from the hell below. Every church is sited at the center of human history, because to Catholics--indeed, to all Christians--this is the central fact of human history. It *is* hell below her, in her church, but that is the point. *That* is the point that she wants us all to take away with us. She and her husband are free now from that hell below them and they are free forever."

Gina took a sip of her wine and looked at him. "You believe that?" she asked.

"Yes, I do," he said. "I believe that that is what she saw and I believe that that is what she wants us to see. It is what she wants *you* to see."

"It is no less grim, Tom."

"Hell *is* grim, Gina, but she knew that you could accept the truth of that."

"What do you mean, Tom?"

"All she needed to do was fill the space with cement, Gina. First she would have removed the grillwork and the pipework, then poured the cement through the opening and, later, filled in the gap in the flooring with matching stone. Their remains would never have been discovered."

"Giancarlo said that she wanted to hear the cries from their spirits."

"Perhaps," Tom said. "Perhaps that was a gift to her husband, a bit of reassurance of the level of her fidelity."

"Some would just send roses," Gina said.

"Not your grandmother," Tom said.

"And what will you do now, Tom, now that you know this?"

"We've cleared the cases," he said, "and we'll do our best to keep the press away."

"And will you fill in the floor in the mausoleum?"

"That might be perceived as evidence tampering," he said. "Besides, it is not our property. The property belongs to the Foundation."

"So that is for me to decide. And would I be tampering with evidence if I did so?"

"I can tell you what your grandmother would say," Tom said.

"What is that?"

"She would tell you that it is a Catholic principle that you guard against having a conscience that is too scrupulous. We have pictures already, Gina—all that we would need. Our evidence is filed and sealed. There is no reason to tempt the curious with a floor drain in a building without water."

"And you won't be troubled if I do that?"

"I'll be troubled if you come to California and don't see me," he said.

"Don't worry," she said. "I'd never do that."

Later that night his phone rang. He looked at the time on his travel alarm. It was 1:30. "I'm terribly sorry," the voice said, "but I had to speak with you."

It was Giancarlo.

"Whatever you said, Tom . . . it helped very much," he said.

"I told her the truth, Giancarlo."

"I know that you did, Tom, but I wanted to thank you. She is mature beyond her years but this was very much to absorb. Very much."

"I was happy to do it," Tom said.

"Thank you again," Giancarlo said. "If you ever need a Sicilian lawyer, call me. Call me anyway, Tom."

"I will," Tom said. "Take care of her."

"You should not worry; I will."

EIGHTY-ONE

"I can't say that I'm conflicted," Tom said. "I'm simply not sure what finally happened, and why."

"You wanted to complete the loop," Wayne said. "You learned things and you wanted the people closest to the case to know what you knew, to learn what you learned . . . even though it was painful for all of you. It was the *right* thing to do. People deserve to know the truth. You're confused because you still have trouble believing that they could actually have wanted to help you."

"Perhaps they didn't know as much as I thought they did."

"And they were depending on you to tell them," Wayne said.

"Perhaps."

"You're young, Tom. You're still learning about things like love and violence . . . and revenge. You're like Gina in that regard. You're still absorbing what you've learned. It's like a powerful book or a terrible part of human history . . . it takes days to digest it and . . . accept it."

"What do you think about Carlotta, Dad? What do you think about what she did?"

"Well, Tom, I'd like to think that she was like your mother."

"Like my mother?"

"Not that your mother would have gone to those extremes, but that she would have done everything she could to protect the person she most loved and, failing that, do whatever it took to somehow make things right afterwards. This is a love story, Tom."

"With razors and ice picks."

"Yes, with razors and ice picks. Your problem, Tom, is that you have to become more accustomed to cultural differences."

Tom smiled. "Maybe you're right," he said.

"Of course, I'm right," Wayne said, smiling. "I'm always right . . . at least when it comes to things like the love between a man and a woman."

"Different people express it in different ways," Tom said.

"Yes, and not all have the opportunities and resources to express it as strongly as they might choose."

"I want to believe that Giancarlo Orsini *was* primarily a lawyer and not a simple criminal," Tom said.

"What you're saying is that you don't want to believe that he used you."

"No, I don't," Tom said.

"He depended on you, Son," Wayne said. "He depended on you to keep the lid on this . . . to solve your crime and close your cases without spreading it all over the newspapers and tabloid TV. He's probably more worried about being used by you than you by him."

"Maybe," Tom said.

"And the cases *were* closed."

"Yes, they were," Tom said.

"And it would be impossible—at this distance—to tell how much of Sullivan's money was legitimately earned and how much of it was not."

"True."

"And the money *is* going toward a good cause."

"Yes."

"You know what, Tom . . . "

"What's that, Dad?"

"You're a police officer. You don't live in a simple world. Years ago, the fishermen here . . . they'd go out in the morning and come back when their holds were filled . . . sometimes they'd go out and come back with nothing. They'd worry about the fish and they'd worry about the seas; they'd worry about putting food on their family table . . . they'd worry about a lot of things, but their world was relatively simple. It wasn't easy and it wasn't always predictable, but it was—in the greater scheme of things—simple. Your world isn't. Sometimes you have to arrest men and women who are fundamentally good. Sometimes you see bad people escape. *Most* of the time you probably see bad people escape and even the bad people have some good in them and sometimes they might actually have gotten caught when their intentions were pure and their motives good. Obeying the law is sometimes a lot easier than enforcing it, son. And sometimes . . . when you do enforce it . . . you might question your own reasons for doing so. What I'm saying is . . . you can't worry about it, or at least not worry about it so much that it keeps you from doing your job."

"I haven't talked to the Chief yet," Tom said. "I'll do that tomorrow. He'll want to know what they said and he'll want to know why I felt the need to talk to them."

"At considerable departmental expense," Wayne added.

"Yes. He won't say that, but it will have crossed his mind."

"What do you think you'll tell him?"

"I'll tell him that, fundamentally, they were my informants and that I never even had to pay them . . . that I wanted to see their reactions to what I had to tell them . . . to try to assess if there was anything more there, anything that I had missed. I'll tell him that I feel good now, that we can put this behind us without any doubts or regrets."

"Even though you may still have some."

"Right."

"You always do, son. And he knows that."

"Right," Tom said.

"Now what you need to do is literally put this behind you and get on with your life, not just your professional life, but your personal life as well."

EPILOGUE

Three weeks later Tom was in San Clemente meeting with the Chief of Police Services, Lieutenant Carl Odem, on another case. Law enforcement support is provided there by the Orange County Sheriff's Department. The case was a routine one, involving stolen property. Stolen in San Clemente, the merchandise was offered for sale in Laguna—nothing dramatic like an original artwork, just some construction materials and expensive tools.

They completed the paperwork and finalized the arrangements for the return of the lumber, the copper pipe, the appliances and the wrenches. "Always a pleasure," Carl said. "The good people of San Clemente appreciate the cooperation of their friends to the north. Or should I say the north/northwest?"

"No problem, Lieutenant. We live to serve."

Before returning home he drove by the Barone estate. It was late in the afternoon and the shadows were lengthening across the hills. Lydia was just getting in her car to leave when he arrived.

"Detective Deaton, it is good to see you again," she said. "Did you come to see the improvements?"

"Actually I was in the neighborhood and thought I'd just come by and say hello," he said.

"You *must* see the improvements to the *campanile*," she said. "And wait, just a second … "

She went into the main structure and came out with a cardboard box. "Ms. Abruzzi sent it," she said. "She emailed me and told me that she was sending you something and that I should give it to you the next time you stopped by."

"Thanks," Tom said.

"You have her phone number and her email address."

"Yes, I do."

"I'm sure it will be something nice," she said. "Anyway, I must go now. The guard will not lock the *campanile* for another hour. Feel free to see it."

As she drove away he put the box on the passenger seat in his unmarked and walked over to the bell tower. There was a new stone pathway installed, so that visitors could walk from the main structure to the tower without walking in the dust. He opened the door. A sensor clicked and the semidarkness was replaced by a warm glow. There was a small grouping of statues on the wall opposite the burial vaults—the Holy Family, complete with a rack of vigil lights which could be lit without charge. Several still flickered and the smell of the melted wax filled the space.

The flooring had been replaced with Carrera marble and the result was stunning. The grillwork was gone and the glow from the marble added a new sense of solemnity to the space.

"Now it is truly a church," a voice said.

Tom turned and saw an elderly man in dusty work clothes.

"Is this your work?" Tom asked.

"Yes," the man said. "You see . . . I worked with Miss Abruzzi's father. Years ago. She is the head of the Foundation now. A very nice young woman. She asked me to do this. Her father was a kind man. He was my employer but he was also my friend. As I did this work I thought of him . . . and of the old days. It was very special for me. When we finished . . . I believe he would have approved."

"It is very beautiful," Tom said.

"Thank you. Please go ahead and light a candle before you go. I always do."

"I will," Tom said.

When he got back to his car he opened the box. Inside was an expensive bottle of wine and a small note card.

> ### *Sorry I couldn't share this with you, Tom. I had much to deal with and was not the best hostess. Next time we will smile again.*
>
> ## *Gina*

When he returned home he put the bottle in the cupboard, on its side, and noticed the flashing light of his answering machine. He hit the button and heard a woman's voice: "Tom, it's Sarah. I hope you're all right. I haven't heard from you in awhile and I was wondering if you'd like to have dinner sometime. I know that you're very busy. Call me when you have a chance."

ACKNOWLEDGEMENTS

Many thanks to my friends Sam Stout and Lee Lyman for help with the details of forensic anthropology and for introducing me to the work of their colleague, Marcella Sorg. Thanks also to my friend Carol Lazzaro Weis for the gift of a novel by Andrea Camilleri which helped plant the seed for a novel with Sicilian scenes. Many years ago Mike Collins took me to the Villa San Girolamo. Since then he has helped me in other, innumerable ways with this book. Special thanks go to Brady Deaton and Brian Foster for providing me the research leave to finish this and other projects. Most of all, I want to express my appreciation to my wife Judith, who has both the strength and the generosity of Carlotta Barone and the wisdom to use both in the proper proportions at the appropriate times.